S0-ASE-222

Beautiful Dreamer

BEAUTIFUL DREAMER

JOAN NAPER

ALLIUM PRESS OF CHICAGO

Allium Press of Chicago
www.alliumpress.com

This is a work of fiction. Descriptions and portrayals of real
people, events, organizations, or establishments are intended
to provide background for the story and are used fictitiously.
Other characters and situations are drawn from the author's
imagination and are not intended to be real.

© 2009 by Joan Naper
All rights reserved

Revised edition by Allium Press, 2010
Originally published via Booksurge, 2009

Book and cover design by E. C. Victorson

Cover image: from author's private collection
Cover background: detail of Rookery Building façade
Title page image: women shoppers in front of
Marshall Field's, Chicago, circa 1905; DN-0002553;
Courtesy of Chicago History Museum

ISBN: 978-0-9840676-4-0

To Tom Lavin,
for helping me find and follow my bliss

ONE

Christmas Day, 1899

Christmas morning, Kitty pulled back the plaid curtain and rubbed her hand against the kitchen window to clear a spot to view the steady fall of snow. All was white: the sky, the streets, even the cottages across the street could hardly be seen, covered as they were in deep, fluffy snow that erased all the dirt, soot, and smoke that usually spoiled the view. She shivered in the steamy heat of the kitchen that misted the window again immediately after she had cleared it. The air was filled with the scent of roast turkey, potatoes and cabbage, cooking in preparation for the Christmas dinner she and her mother would serve at two. She wondered if the snow would prevent her aunt and uncle from joining the rest of the family for Christmas.

The warm kitchen was quiet except for the bubble of the saucepan on the stove and occasional crackling from the oven. Her father and the boys must still be asleep upstairs, it was never this quiet when the boys were up and about. Her mother, sitting in her own world in a corner of the parlor, was folding napkins as carefully as if they were to be offered to nobility, not her own boisterous family members. Kitty's sister Margaret, who lived down the street with baby Sean and husband Kevin O'Connor, would arrive just before the meal was served, as usual, so Margaret could sit at the table like a guest and not be running in and out of the kitchen with her face red from the heat and her hair all falling down with the hustling. That role fell to Kitty, the dutiful younger daughter, not yet married with a husband and child of her own. Kitty picked up her cup of tea from the table and sat down in front of the open hearth, placing her slippered feet on the fireguard in her favorite position. She stared at the flames, wondering if she were destined to be an old maid, living in her parents' house forever, taking care of them in their old age, being aunt to Margaret's children and any children her brothers might have, should they ever get off their arses and actually marry the neighborhood girls they pretended not to see while they watched them so wishfully. Or maybe she would marry one of the neighborhood boys and settle down to live near her parents, as Margaret had. She picked up the poker from beside the fireplace and stabbed at the logs, creating a rising shower of sparks.

Kitty's reverie was broken by her mother's return into the kitchen, her face reddened with the heat of the house. The two of them worked together pulling plates and cutlery out of the cabinets and piling them in their arms and aprons to bring them into the parlor. The parlor itself wore a festive air, with boughs of ivy draped across the mantelpiece and pinned up around the doorways. A thick bunch of mistletoe wrapped with red ribbon hung from the central gas fixture in the middle of the parlor ceiling. Their voices must have awakened Mr. Coakley, because he came down the narrow stairway in his stocking feet, looping a suspender over one shoulder.

Michael Coakley stretched and yawned and then beamed at his wife and daughter. "Christmas Day it 'tis, my dears and here you are slaving away to make a feast for the rest of us. And just where are those lazy layabouts, not yet out of their warm beds?" He turned and called up the stairs: "Michael, Patrick, John, William, Daniel. Up and about, you lazy lumps. It's a merry Christmas we're planning to have, with you or without you. So move your sorry carcasses down here straightaway."

Silence above, and then the slap of bare feet on the wooden floorboards, dresser drawers pulled out, a shout or two, and then one by one the boys appeared, tumbling down the stairs. Such a rousing call from their father was not to be ignored, even though all five of them were adults, in age anyway, ranging from Michael, the oldest boy, at twenty-eight, to Daniel, the youngest at twenty-two. Margaret, aged thirty, and Kitty at age twenty were the engine and the caboose, Mr. Coakley liked to say, the oldest and the youngest with the train of boys in between. To those who didn't know them, the five Coakley boys were variations on the same Irish theme: freckled, red-haired and willing to fight. But Kitty had lived her whole life with them, and couldn't imagine how someone could mistake one for another.

Daniel, the brother she was closest to, was quiet and thoughtful, sneaky too, sometimes. She thought he was the best-looking of them all, his occasional freckles more like beauty marks on his smooth, warm-looking skin.

William, next up in age, was the scholar, the only one she might see with his nose in a book, even though, like the others, he had barely finished at the parish high school and used his back more than his brain in the work he did.

John was the smallest of the five and the one with the most freckles and the least hair. He had a temper and a smart mouth, and would fight a man twice his size.

Long and lanky Patrick lacked the temper, but was always willing to help John take on any man who bothered him.

Michael, usually called Mick or Mickey to differentiate him from his father, was the biggest of the brothers and had the worst temper of them all. His little sister Kitty, though, had learned early on just how to get his attention and he had adored her since she was born, which annoyed their older sister Margaret. Kitty sometimes thought his love for her had been born out of his need to put his big sister Margaret in her place, but she never complained about his obvious devotion.

The five brothers all worked the warmer months on the ore boats that sailed the Great Lakes. It paid well and didn't require any education or connections, like so many jobs in the city did.

Daniel came over and hugged his mother. "Merry Christmas, Ma. It smells like a feast in here." The other boys followed his example, mumbling and running their fingers through the red curly hair they all sported, and then flopping down on the sofa in front of the parlor fire. Other than Daniel, whose cheeks blazed as if reflecting the flames, the boys looked much the worse for wear, as Mr. Coakley asked, "And what time was it that you boys tumbled in? The crack of dawn?"

"Is that what cracked?" John muttered. Mick dug his elbow into John's side.

Mr. Coakley looked stern and said, "I asked you what time you came in."

Daniel replied, "We were all there at the five o'clock Mass this morning. All five of us."

"Bah, the drunkard's Mass," Mr. Coakley said. "And I suppose you can remember the sermon?"

Daniel looked at the others before he answered his father. "It was the birth of Jesus, of course it was. And what else would you expect on Christmas morning?" His four brothers nodded seriously, as if to say they supported Daniel's interpretation.

Mickey rubbed his face with his hand and said to his sister, "We could have used your lovely voice last night, little Kitty. Who knows how much more money we could have pulled in if our caroling had actually pleased the crowd."

"And here I thought we were making even more money with the gentry paying us to go away," said John.

"So it was out caroling, you boys were?" Mrs. Coakley asked, a worried look on her face. "With all that snow coming down so fiercely?"

John said proudly, "We made a pot of money last night. Might have been the snow that made our voices sound reasonable."

"And we warmed up from time to time in a comfortable place," Patrick added.

Mr. Coakley said, "I hope it wasn't the bars you were frequenting last night on Christmas Eve." He had taken the pledge as a youth back in County Cork, after his own father had fallen off a roof he was patching because he was drunk, and died in the yard in front of him. He hadn't had an alcoholic drink since then, more than thirty years before.

"A lad has to come in out of the snow," said John.

Mrs. Coakley asked the boys to move the chairs into the parlor and set up the table where they would eat. The boys, joking and pushing one another, put together a large table from four sawhorses and a long wide board that were kept in the shed out back. When it was covered with Mrs. Coakley's best Irish linen tablecloth that she had stayed up late to iron, the makeshift table could hardly be distinguished from ready made. Except, as Kitty found when she came to set the plates upon it, it wobbled dangerously when she knocked against it.

After setting the table, Kitty retreated to the small room behind the kitchen that was her very own, and pulled out the red dress she had worn at Midnight Mass the night before. She loved wearing it—the bright red showed off her dark hair and the glow of her blue eyes and red lips against her white skin. She checked herself in the mirror that rested on top of her dresser, lifting her hair up to see how that would look and then letting it fall. Why bother putting it up if I'll be in the kitchen all afternoon? she thought. And besides, it's just family. She roughly tugged her hair back and tied a red ribbon around her head to keep it off her face.

"Katherine," her mother called from the kitchen. "Come help me with the potatoes."

When her mother called her Katherine, Kitty knew there was no stalling or arguing. She gave the mirror one last look, bit her lips to redden them even more, and joined her mother in the kitchen. She pulled an apron from the drying rack beside the fireplace and tied it around her red dress. Then she and her mother together drained the heavy pots that held the cabbage and the potatoes that they would mix together for colcannon, the family favorite.

"And we mustn't forget the trinkets," said Mrs. Coakley, opening a drawer in the kitchen sideboard and pulling out a small cloth bag. She poured them out on the table: a small gold ring, a silver dime, a thimble, and a button.

"Oh, Mama, really, that silly superstition," Kitty said. "And besides, I thought we did that at Halloween."

"Shush, girl. Remember the boys were off on the boats in Lake Superior then and we didn't have a proper colcannon. What's it to you, miss, if you don't believe in it anyway?"

Kitty shook her head and turned away. How could she admit to her mother that she feared getting the tiny thimble that would predict spinsterhood for her? Or even the gold ring, which foretold marriage within the year, what with no beaux lining up for her at the front door. She didn't want the others to laugh at her. Besides, nothing she ever said had ever deflected her mother's behavior, once she had gotten it into her head to do something.

"Come along, Kitty. It's a harmless thing, it is," her mother said, her nimble fingers dusting off each token. "And we can make sure you don't get one at all, at all, if that's what you want."

"That's all right, Mama," Kitty said. "I'd prefer to find nothing in my colcannon. Except my fork, of course."

"Of course. Now why don't you go and light the candles for the Baby Jesus? 'Tis probably as dark as it will be getting, with all that snow falling down."

"Actually, the snow seems to have stopped itself, I do believe," Mr. Coakley called in from the parlor, where he had stationed himself near the window to watch the weather. "Is that the sun itself that's coming out?"

Kitty rushed to her father's side to peer out the front window. The snow had stopped falling and the way the sun hit the heaps of snow made them glow as if a magic spell had been cast upon them. "You'd never see snow like this in County Cork," Mr. Coakley said. "No, not ever. Just a mean cold rain, that's all we'd get for Christmas."

"Ah well, then," Kitty said. "You know they always say that the streets of America are paved with gold."

Her father laughed. "We'll be sending the boys out to shovel soon. Perhaps for them the gold will be forthcoming. Once they put their strong backs into it."

Kitty lit the white candles she and her mother had set in the windows to light the Baby Jesus on His way. And just as she was blowing out the taper, she could hear the kitchen door opening and Margaret, Kevin, and Sean O'Connor trooping in, boisterous and happy. Kitty's parents immediately began to fuss and coo over their only grandson.

Margaret entered the parlor, fluffing out her hair, and leaned over to give her sister a kiss. "Happy Christmas, our Kitty. And what a pretty dress! Is that the same one you wore last Christmas?"

Kitty laughed. Margaret was so predictable—she never offered a compliment that wasn't wrapped around a little dig. "No, it's new for this Christmas, it is. And didn't you see me wearing it—singing at Father Egan's Mass at midnight?" she asked, knowing full well that Margaret and her family had not appeared, even though she had said they would try.

"Well, that explains the bit of incense I smelled when I came into the room," Margaret said, hanging her long dark blue cloak on the stand next to the front door. She ran her hand over the cloak, smoothing it. "And did you see the fine wool cloak my Kevin bought me for Christmas, Kitty? He bought it at Marshall Field's, he did, although it cost a packet." Kevin O'Connor had started as a junior bank clerk when he was not yet twenty and had risen slowly to more authority in the fifteen years since. Kitty believed that money was all he and Margaret ever talked about, so keen he seemed on it and what it could buy. Kevin gave Kitty an affectionate kiss on the cheek when he entered the parlor. And he was by far the best-dressed man in the room, in his sleek black suit, white shirt and bright red tie, no contest with Kitty's brothers who appeared one by one, wearing collarless shirts with no ties and corduroy trousers. Only Mr. Coakley himself sported a dark green tie, but he remained in his shirtsleeves, his red suspenders adding a note of holiday cheer to his outfit.

Mrs. Coakley entered the parlor, removing her apron and folding it carefully. "All right, my dears, I do believe we're ready to serve. Kitty, come into the kitchen and help me now. And Margaret . . ."

"That's all right, Mama. I must see to our Sean," Margaret said, seated already in the chair to the right of the head of the table, her three-year-old son wriggling on her lap.

Mrs. Coakley hesitated, then shrugged her shoulders and accompanied Kitty into the kitchen.

"But what about Aunt Mabel and Uncle Patrick?" Kitty asked anxiously. "Shouldn't we wait for them before we serve?"

"No sense in waiting for them when the food is hot," Mrs. Coakley said. "Mabel said not to wait, anyways, she was concerned that they might not be able to make it on time, so she said not to delay our dinner. Implying of course that civilized people have their Christmas dinner much later in the day, God save them, and don't sit down at the table until the sun goes down. Hmmph. Them with servants don't give a care about what time the servants are finished for the day. When you're doing it all yourself, of course, that's a different matter. Not that your Aunt Mabel would understand that."

Kitty didn't quite understand it herself. Why did her mother get up so early to start cooking on Christmas Day, when she'd been out so late at Midnight Mass? And stayed up even later to iron the tablecloth? Why not sleep in and take it easy on Christmas morning, and save the big meal for late in the day, when everyone was awake and hungry? But her mother had always done it this way, as her own mother probably had done back in Ireland, and there was no changing her mind now.

Kitty was disappointed. Without Mabel and Patrick the meal would be no more than a family dinner, not a festive occasion. With the same squabbling between the brothers, their rude table manners and half-hearted rebukes from their parents, and Margaret's posturing about their rising status and wealth. It always seemed that her aunt and uncle—especially her aunt—added a touch of civility when they joined the wild pig-in-the-parlor Coakleys. Kitty sometimes wished that she were an only child, the only child of Aunt Mabel and Uncle Patrick. Their lace-curtain life would be much more pleasant, or at least much quieter. And she wouldn't have the Coakley reputation to live down.

Finally, they were all seated at the table, with Mr. Coakley at its head, carving the roast turkey, the hungry eyes of all upon him. As soon as he put down the carving knife, Mrs. Coakley called out, "Grace now, before we serve." And she made the sign of the cross and bowed her head. "Thank you, Lord, for that which we are about to receive. And bless all of us gathered here, as well as those who are not able to join us."

Kitty thought she saw a satisfied smile quickly cross her mother's lips as she spoke the last sentence, or she could have just been imagining it.

Just as everyone chimed in, "Amen," and made the sign of the cross to end the prayer, the front door opened and in came Aunt Mabel and Uncle Patrick, blown in on a rushing gust of cold air. "Merry Christmas, everyone," Aunt Mabel said, her arms filled with gifts, wearing an amazing hat structured of velvet and feathers firmly tethered to her pompadour.

"Happy Christmas to all of yez," said Uncle Patrick, tall, broad and big-shouldered, his face as red as a roast ham, looking like the policeman he was, even dressed in his Sunday best.

"Sit, sit," said Mr. Coakley, rising to take their heavy wraps. "Here, Kitty, lay these across the bed in your room."

When all were settled at the table, with Aunt Mabel next to Kitty on the side nearest to the kitchen, and her husband next to her, Mr. Coakley began piling slices of turkey on the plates stacked next to him. He passed these to his wife on his left, who spooned out great steaming piles of colcannon. Kitty watched her mother portioning the fried potato and cabbage dish, looking for telltale signs of the fortune-telling trinkets, but could see no indication, either in the lumps of potatoes or in her mother's eyes, of what was hidden inside.

While the plates were passed around, Mr. Coakley asked his brother about the world outside—how much snow had fallen and whether he thought it would paralyze Chicago in the days to come. Uncle Patrick regaled them with stories of how the snowfall had affected the citizenry he had seen that morning, with overturned carriages, bones broken in falls, and small boys pelting their neighbors with snowballs. He had them all laughing so that when Kitty put a forkful of colcannon in her mouth and bit down on something, she didn't immediately recognize what it was, thinking instead that somehow one of her teeth had fallen out. Then she realized what it was and looked accusingly at her mother, whose rapt attention was fixed on the face of her grandson across the table.

Then Daniel whooped, "I've got the dime, I've got the dime. It's the life of wealth for me!" His brothers cheered and slapped him on the back. Of all the five brothers, Daniel was the most likely to hold onto his money. The others said he'd pinch a penny until it squealed like a pig being butchered in the Chicago stockyards.

"So you'll be the one we'll be borrowing from," said John.

"Just you try and get it, brother," said Daniel. "You don't get wealthy by giving it away."

"What's this in my mouth?" said Mickey, spitting it out onto the table. "It's that blasted ring."

"Now, Mickey, watch your language at the table," his mother chided.

She might have also mentioned how rude it was to spit out food, especially at the table, Kitty thought, wiping her mouth with her napkin in such a way as to move the trinket from her mouth to her hand.

"Somebody call Peggy O'Neill," cried John. "She'd best be planning the wedding."

Mickey grinned and rubbed his face with his hand. "Aw, get off my back about the girl. She'd never be looking at the likes of me."

"Time you made an honest woman of her, Mick," said Patrick. "And haven't you been after her since you walked up the aisle behind her at your first holy communion?"

Mickey blushed, but said no more.

With all the attention focused on Mickey, Kitty opened her hand underneath the table and examined the trinket she had found in her mouth—the thimble, sure sign of spinsterhood. She clenched it in her fist, wondering if she could just drop it on the floor or into her shoe and pretend she never received it, when she heard her aunt's soft voice.

"Here, give it to me," Aunt Mabel whispered, placing her hand on Kitty's beneath the table. Kitty gladly relinquished the thimble and sat back while her aunt cried out, "The thimble, the thimble. So it's to be spinsterhood for me." She held up the thimble for all to see.

Her husband put his arm around her and kissed her. "I do believe I saved you from that," he said.

"Yes, but there's no shame to it," Mabel said, patting his big red hand contentedly. "A woman doesn't have to be married to have a good life."

Kitty happened to glance at her mother's face when Mabel made this proclamation. Mrs. Coakley curled her lip in contempt, whether for Mabel or for what she said, Kitty wasn't sure.

Then little Sean cried out, "The b'on, the b'on," and pulled from his mouth the small round button that signified a life of bachelorhood ahead. Everyone laughed and applauded the small boy, congratulating him on his good fortune.

"Perhaps by the time he's thirty, he'll have changed his mind," his grandfather said knowingly.

"Or maybe he'll be a priest," said his grandmother, her eyes shining. "A man of the cloth in our very own family." Groans came from the boys, but no one claimed a different future for the youngest member of the family, especially not Margaret, who had taken Sean onto her lap, cuddling him. She seemed to be taken with the idea herself.

"So Margaret, you ready to send your boy off to the service of the Lord?" asked Mickey.

"It's a bit early, isn't it?" said Margaret, brushing Sean's hair softly and kissing his head. "He's only three years old."

John, sitting next to Kitty at the far end of the table, turned halfway to her and whispered, "I saw you get that trinket, Kitty. What's the matter, too proud are you? So you let Aunt Mabel take the rap for you, didn't you? Hiding behind her skirts again?"

"What's it to you, Johnny?" Kitty answered. "It's a stupid tradition anyhow." And she turned her attention back to her plate.

"Feel how hot these potatoes are, Kitty," John said, looming over her. He put his freckled hand with its broken nails over the steaming mound of colcannon on her plate.

Fork in hand as if she were about to stab him, Kitty said, "As if I'm about to fall for that one, John Coakley."

John's hand darted out and grabbed Kitty's free hand, turning it so it landed in the pile of potatoes. She struggled in his grasp as he smashed her hand in the food to cover it fully with the mixture of cabbage and potatoes.

Her lips pressed firmly together, Kitty wriggled and wrenched her hand from her brother's grip, collecting a handful of potatoes as she did. "Let's see what you think about the temperature of these potatoes, boyo," she said, swiping the steaming white mass across John's face.

John pulled back, gasping at his little sister's audacity.

"Miss Katherine Coakley," said her mother from the other end of the table. "You apologize to your brother right now, you little minx. Such behavior. And on Christmas Day, the birthday of our Baby Jesus himself. You can just clean up the mess you've made, miss."

"I will not," said Kitty, standing up and stamping her foot. "Johnny started it." She turned, pushing against the table, which began to tip to one side and slide off the sawhorses. Sean's glass of milk spilled into his lap and onto his mother's skirt. Margaret dabbed at it with a linen napkin. Mickey and Uncle Patrick jumped up and seized the board beneath the tablecloth, steadying it to quiet the rattling of the dishes. Mr. Coakley stood, his mouth open to scold his children as Kitty ran past him through the steamy kitchen and out the back door into the snow.

Although it was just mid-afternoon, it was dark outside and the air was still. The gas lamps hadn't yet been lit, and snow clouds crowded the sky, their dark undersides promising more snow to come. There was no traffic on Adams Street, an unusual sight, its thin coverlet of snow still white and fresh and inviting, unstained as yet by the encroachment of manure and mud. Kitty walked down the block to the corner of Desplaines and sat on the cold stone steps of St. Patrick's, looking east. The lyrics of one of the carols she had sung the night before came into her head, "How still we see thee lie."

So unlike the little town of Bethlehem, Chicago's downtown lay spread before her, encircled by the iron band of the Loop, the rails of the elevated train. Although much stiller than usual because of the holiday, the tiny trains ran, shorter and slower than on a weekday, and the ever-present roar of traffic muffled by the west wind still rang out. Kitty breathed in the clean air that had overcome the usual miasma of smoke and coal dust, blowing it away from the city and over the lake. She tasted its purity on her lips and inhaled its energy, so different from the close and chaotic atmosphere inside the house. It gave the scene a clarity that it usually lacked, sharpening the cityscape that appeared on the horizon just a mile or so away across the railroad tracks and the river and block after block of falling-down houses.

Kitty remembered how her brother Mickey, who had worked on some of the skyscrapers as they began to pierce the sky, taught her their names: the Fisher Building and the Monadnock, as mountainous as the New Hampshire peak for which it was named, over on Dearborn. The Women's Temple, once the tallest building in Chicago, and the Reliance Building, its white terra cotta and broad glass windows pink with the reflection of the setting sun behind her, across from each other on State Street. She felt the city's energy and hope flowing through her own veins. She stared straight ahead of her, breathing in deeply several times, before she turned, head held high, to face what awaited her back home.

TWO

As she sat in front of the small mirror propped on her dresser, deciding whether to wear her hair up or down for the Young Hibernians' New Year's Eve party in the church basement, Kitty thought she should decide whether she should set her sights upon Brian as a potential husband or see what other possibilities she could find in the neighborhood. Maybe she was gravitating toward Brian because he was so easy, so comfortable. Had she ever looked beyond Brian to see who else might be out there for her? She had her dreams of singing on the stage, dreams that she hoped might take her out of the neighborhood into a larger, more glamorous world. But two years of pursuing that dream had only come up with a few opportunities, other than the choir at St. Patrick's. She had worked her way up from being a waitress at the Grand Pacific Hotel to singing at the occasional dinners they held, but the pay and the limited exposure weren't enough to fuel her dreams. She had been paid barely enough to cover her singing lessons with Madame Nettlehorst, lessons that she had begun in high school, but not enough to call it a career. Without a regular income or a man to marry, she had no way to become independent of her parents and move out of the confines of the small cottage she had grown up in.

Kitty stood at the bottom of the stairs to the church basement, still wrapped in her warm woolen cloak, with her parents on one side of her, her Aunt Mabel and Uncle Patrick on the other side, surveying the crowd that filled the low-ceilinged social hall beneath the church. At this early hour of eight o'clock, the party was made up of families, with all ages represented, from the tiniest baby wrapped in a shawl to old bearded grandfathers sitting in the chairs that lined the wall, tapping their toes in time to the fiddler's tunes from old Ireland. In the center of the floor, a haphazard Irish reel was being danced, with schoolgirls swinging on the arms of their fathers and uncles. On one side of the hall, knots of women whispered among themselves; on another, boys the ages of her brothers, she just couldn't call them men, clustered around the crystal punchbowl, set out on a red tablecloth next to biscuits and cheese. A fog of smoke covered the room, especially where the boys had gathered, smoking their cigarettes cupped in their hands as if to protect them from a non-existent wind.

Despite her reluctance to attend the party with her family, Kitty couldn't help her toe from tapping to the familiar rhythms of the fiddle music. She turned to her father, who said, "Give your cloak to your mother, dear, and run along and join the dancers."

Kitty slipped out of the cloak and ran to join the line of women. She smiled at Mr. McCarthy, the man across from her, a friendly neighbor who had once brought her brother John home, falling-down drunk, after another Young Hibernians bash. She dipped down in a curtsey, hooked her arm into her partner's, and twirled around, hairpins flying from what had earlier been her carefully arranged pompadour. Linking arms with one partner after the next, Kitty found herself joining in the laughter that permeated the bunch, their foreheads glistening as they danced through the growing crowd.

Finally, the fiddler took a bow to the cheering throng, and Jackie Fitzsimmons, the tenor who sang at weddings and funerals, took the stage. Kitty threaded her way to the punch bowl, where she saw her parents standing talking to Father Egan. She gratefully gulped a glass of punch that her mother handed her and stood next to the priest.

"Ah, Kitty," he said, patting her on the shoulder. "Didn't I see you out there dancing to beat the band? And here are your dear parents and aren't I just telling them how much our little choir depends upon you. And won't you be favoring us with a tune later on?"

"But of course, Father," Kitty said, catching her breath after the cold drink. "Perhaps later, though. I've seen so many people here that I haven't had a chance to catch up with. When I'm in the choir loft I see them in the church, but they're never around after."

"But at least they are there in the church," Father Egan said, chuckling. "And aren't I wondering tonight at all these faces I never see upstairs in the church proper."

"It's the services at the Clan na Gael camp they're attending instead," said Mr. Coakley, in a low voice. "You can't expect them to serve two masters."

Now, now, Michael," the priest said, clapping him on his back. "Ours is not to question our countrymen when it comes to politics."

"Yes, but, isn't our country now America? And aren't we all Americans, not bogtrotters no more?" Michael Coakley said, frowning slightly.

"Well, well, let's not worry about that tonight," said the priest. "And isn't Fitzsimmons singing a lovely song about a miss as beautiful as your young daughter here. And with the same name." And the priest pushed Michael Coakley over toward Kitty, who curtsied and took her father's arm, to dance to the tune of *Kathleen Mavourneen*.

"Father Egan is right," said Michael Coakley, looking down at his daughter's fresh face as they danced slowly at the side of the crowd. "You are one of the prettiest girls here."

Kitty blushed. It wasn't like her father to compliment her so lavishly; in fact, with all her brothers about all the time, he hardly ever spoke to her at all, except as one of the group. She was just about to compliment him back, when a hand reached out from behind her and tapped her father on his shoulder.

"I'll be cutting in on you and this lovely lass, Da," said Daniel. Kitty hadn't realized that Dan had outgrown his tall father and nearly towered above him.

"Aha, so that's your game, son. And here I thought you might be touching me up for some cash to pay for your drinks. I'll have to give her up to you, I suppose. I'm not getting any younger, am I, and aren't

16

I feeling this dancing in my knees. Time to sit down and talk to your mother." And Michael set off through the crowd, leaving his daughter in the arms of her youngest brother.

Kitty had to crane her neck to see her brother's face, which was red and shining with perspiration. "So, little sister, are you having a good time?" he asked, twirling her into the middle of the crowd. When he spoke, she could smell the whiskey on his breath.

"Fair to middling. Dancing with my father and my brother is something I could be doing in the parlor at home," she said, softening her words with a smile up at her brother. "And how are you doing, Daniel? Aren't there any lovely ladies here for you so you don't have to dance with your own sister?"

"I'm just checking out the territory," he said. "Of course, we all know you're the prettiest, so I'm having a difficult time finding any lass to compare to you."

"Oh, just have another drink or two, and you'll find that the girls get better looking," Kitty said, looking around the crowd. "I wish that would happen as well to the gentlemen here."

"What did you say?" Daniel asked, lifting his hand from her shoulder and cupping his ear. "It's so blasted loud in this room that I can't hear a word you're saying."

Kitty just smiled and said no more—her sarcastic tone was how she often spoke to her brothers. Noisy room or not, she never felt she got through to them. Talking, actually discussing things, was not really possible with them, they were more inclined to teasing or, more often, to action. She tried to match the erratic rhythms of her brother's dancing and was more than relieved when she saw a hand rest on Daniel's shoulder and found herself being passed over to Brian Kelleher. Brian never said much, even when drinking, as he obviously had been before he cut in on Daniel, so Kitty just moved in tune to the music, which now had been augmented by a tin whistle and the fiddler back again. It was comfortable dancing with Brian, who danced well, and because she didn't have to worry about what she had to say to him, she could think about what songs she would sing later on. When the music stopped, he spoke to her so softly that she couldn't hear a word he said.

"Say it again, Brian. I can't hear you." Kitty blew upward to cool her blazing face, and the draft pushed her hair out of her eyes.

"I was just asking, Miss Kitty, if I could walk you home after the party," Brian said, leaning over and whispering in her ear.

"Oh, thanks, Brian, that won't be necessary," Kitty said, briskly. "I've come here with my parents, don't you know, and I'm sure they will be wanting to leave quite soon. They're not much for staying out late, you know." She still felt uncomfortable about the kiss she had given him after Midnight Mass. She wasn't sure if she should encourage him any further.

Brian stared at her for a moment as if he were going to say something more, and then walked away through the crowd. Kitty shrugged her shoulders and looked around to find her parents and her aunt and uncle. She had said she was going to make an early night of it, hadn't she? And her parents were expecting her to return home with them. Maybe it was time to seek them out.

She hardly had taken a step in the direction of the punch bowl when another of her brother's friends, Andy O'Malley, came up to claim her for a dance. After that, Kitty did dance the night away, as her aunt had predicted earlier, laughingly passed from one of her brothers' friends to the next, young men who didn't have much to say, but who danced and sang and laughed with her.

At one point, Father Egan came up to her as she was dancing with the wild and handsome Danny Flood, and motioned her to the sidelines where they could talk.

"Are you having too much fun to sing a little song for us?" he asked urgently. "We're going to have to stop the refreshments soon, it's getting on toward midnight and we have to stop serving so you youngsters can take communion in the morning. I thought perhaps you could send us all out into the New Year with a sweet song in our hearts."

"I'd be happy to, Father," Kitty said. She hadn't been aware that it was getting so late—she'd barely had a minute to take a breath between dances. "Just let me freshen up a bit and I'll be with you in a moment's time."

She rushed to the room at the back of the hall that had been designated the ladies' toilette and pushed her way to the small mirror that was propped against the wall.

"If it isn't the Protestant Miss Kitty Coakley," a tall red-haired girl said through the hairpins in her mouth as she pinned up her long curly tresses.

Kitty spun around and looked her accuser in the face. "Oh it's you, Miss Brigid O'Toole. And what would you be calling me a Protestant for, Bridie, when you know that I sing in the choir in this very church here, every single Sunday of the year? And on Christmas as well. Just who do you think you're calling a Protestant?" Kitty had known the O'Toole girl from the neighborhood for quite a while—her older sister Mary had been in her class at the parish school.

"Ah, Bridie's just jealous that her beau Brian's been making eyes at you all night," said a young woman who was hugely pregnant and was sitting on the room's only chair with her shoes off. "She was hoping he'd be giving her a ring at Christmas, too, and she didn't get one. Pay no mind to her."

"Well, aren't you just too good for us here," Bridie persisted, now smoothing powder over the freckles that dotted her cheeks. "Going to that Protestant school, you were, instead of our own parish high school?"

"Lake View High School? Protestant?" Kitty asked. "That just shows us what you know, missy. Lake View is a public school, a school for everyone in Chicago, no matter where they come from or what religion they practice. You don't have to be a Protestant to go there."

"So why did you go there, Miss Kitty?" asked Brigid, standing with her two hands on her hips. "Wasn't St. Patrick's good enough for you? Or was it just for the likes of us?"

Kitty just stared at Brigid, biting her tongue to keep herself from making fun of her powder-caked face and falling-down hair. Brigid's sister Mary was said to have been carrying her first child, her first of four, so far, when she quickly married her classmate Marty Burns before they finished their second year of high school. But Kitty knew that anything she said in anger would travel quickly across the neighborhood and come back to her parents soon enough. And that they would chide her for being uncharitable, when she had so much, and the O'Tooles so little.

So she consoled herself with just smiling at Brigid and saying, "I must be off. Father Egan has been asking me to sing now, hasn't he." And when she got up on the little stage, she made sure that she smiled warmly at Brian Kelleher, who stood in the front row watching her. And she decided that she would accept his offer to walk her home. She'd show that Bridie O'Toole.

When the party ended, Kitty was standing talking to her brother John, sprawled by himself near the pile of coats. Brian was hovering nearby, so she beckoned him over to help pull John upright. John was in no shape to walk home by himself, so she and Brian escorted him home. Brian supported one of John's arms on his shoulder, and Kitty did the same, while John barely noticed the struggle it took to keep him moving forward, rather than down. His legs threatened to collapse like concertinas and land him in the snowdrifts that lined the cleared walk, and all the while he never stopped talking. The threesome moved slowly, with both Brian and Kitty laughing continuously at John's antics. John was an affable drunk, much given to telling Brian and even his sister, how much he loved them. His legs, however, weren't nearly as strong as his sentiments, and they tended to collapse beneath him or point him in a direction opposite to the one in which he intended to move. It wasn't a long walk from the church to the Coakley cottage, but it took more than half an hour what with transporting John in his condition. Behind her laughter, Kitty was pleased that Brian was accompanying them. It made up in part for the sting she had felt when Bridget O'Toole had called her a Protestant.

When Brian and Kitty managed to get John to the Coakleys' door without mishap, they could only stand there and continue laughing at the ordeal they'd been through. They were on the doorstep, dusting snow off John, when Brian said abruptly, "So Kitty, you'll come with me to the Hibernians' party at Coughlin's next week, will ya?"

Kitty looked up at Brian's sparkling blue eyes and smiling face, ruddy with cold. She smiled coyly at him, feeling her dimples stretch like the bubbles in bread dough. "Of course, I will, Brian. Haven't I been waiting all evening for you to ask me?" And before Brian could say another word, she turned the doorknob and, pushing John in ahead of herself, she entered the cottage.

The entrance hall was dark, but her father's voice came down the stairs like the voice of God, "Is that you, Kitty girl?"

"Yes, Da . . . with John. More or less." She stepped over his recumbent body, asleep already in a pile on the floor and removed her boots, put on her house slippers, and hung her cloak on the hook, brushing it gently to remove the snow sprinkled on it like sugar on a bowl of cherries. The new cloak was soft and warm. She smiled at the thought of the cloak, her brothers' gift, and made her way into her bedroom, removing the pins that held up her hair. The New Year's party had been much more fun than she had thought it would be.

As she gave her hair its requisite one hundred brush strokes, Kitty thought about Brian. She knew she should be careful—Brian wasn't her brother. Did she really want to build a fire under him? Where would that take her? Like her brothers, Brian wasn't ambitious and he still hadn't settled down to a regular job, although he did help his father out in his lumberyard. And, she suspected that like her brother John, he spent too much of his time drinking with the Young Hibernians. Although he had been there at Midnight Mass, not out drinking with her brothers. All her life she had treated Brian just like another brother. Would she like what might happen if she started treating him differently? But Brian was fun, Brian was comfortable, like her worn-down house slippers. She looked down at the beaten-up slippers and wiggled her toes. She would never wear them in front of anyone other than family, but they always reminded her that she had come home. Comfort was a good thing, especially on a cold winter's night.

THREE

I t was the day of New Year's Eve and the milky sun barely lit the sky, suffusing its meager light like an oil slick on the surface of a puddle. Lake, land and sky all shared the cold pewter shade of a Chicago January. Henry and his college friend Milton trudged from the isolated train platform through the desolate landscape of Jackson Park, the cold wind off the lake blowing icy bits of sand and snow into their eyes and pushing them away from their destination, the building that had reigned as the Palace of Fine Arts, six years before at the World's Columbian Exposition. A building that had once drawn more than twenty million people from all over the world, now stood alone in the blowing snow on this south side prairie.

"Whose idea was it to come out here, anyway?" asked Milton, ducking his head against the wind, his words causing a cloud of steam to emerge from his mouth, the only warmth near them, quickly blown away by the wind.

"We don't have to stay long," Henry said, tears in his eyes from the harshness of the wind. His mustache had already grown an icy fence across it, as if to freeze his mouth from talking. "I just thought it would be a good idea to sketch the caryatids on the building to prepare our hands for the drawings we'll be expected to do in Europe."

"Egad, Henry. Don't you think our hands will be much warmer on the Acropolis? I dare not remove my gloves to clutch my charcoal pencil in this weather." Milton tried to flex his gloved hand, but the cold and the bulkiness of his glove rendered it unmovable.

"We'll find a place that's sheltered from the wind," Henry said. "Once we're out of the wind, it won't be as cold. And we'll be able to work, at least for a little while. If we're going out to draw the wonders of the world's architecture, I'd like to have some examples of our own in my portfolio. If only to show that we're not still the wild, untamed west."

"Couldn't you have thought of this in September or October?" Milton asked.

The two young men found a stand of trees that blocked the worst of the wind, and pierced the frozen ground with the shooting sticks that had been slung over their shoulders. Perched on these precarious supports, they balanced their drawing boards on their knees. The wail of the wind accompanied their intent labor as they sketched the female figures that formed the pillars on the wall of the former Palace of Fine Arts.

"Why couldn't we just take a photograph? Then we'd have what we need and we could get out of this forsaken place," Milton muttered, pulling a silver flask from his pocket and gulping from it before he offered it to Henry.

Henry held the cold flask in his hand before he answered his friend. "I did think about it," he said seriously. "A photograph, if we had enough light—and I don't think there is enough natural light today— would render the contrasts of dark and light. I don't think, though, it would give us the depth that a charcoal drawing would. And besides— you know this, Milton—once you draw something, you learn it in a way that you could never accomplish with photography. With your pencil, you take it apart and see it not the way it looks in one dimension, but how it was put together. And as future architects, we are the ones who will be putting things together, or describing with our pens how buildings should look once they *are* put together." He took a deep pull from the flask, wondering how something so cold could burn all the way down his throat and somehow warm him from within.

The two continued their drawing in silence, passing the flask back and forth between them. The female figures took shape on their papers, the classical caryatids on whose heads were balanced the pedimented porches, the entablatures of the Greek revival architecture that had been created to resemble those of the Erechtheion on the

23

Acropolis of Athens, Greece. The young men shared their understanding of how the White City, as the Exposition had been called, had been erected to celebrate the four hundredth anniversary of Columbus's discovery of America, commemorating the event with the architecture of the ancient world, not the new. This particular building was designed by Charles Atwood, and it alone remained on the site, destined to be turned into a museum to house artifacts of natural history, the shards and beads and bones of settlements long past. One of their professors at the University had condemned the idea that the architectural styles of the past should be the blueprints of the buildings of this new era, a radical stance, but one that Henry secretly admired. His own dream, never expressed aloud, but kept in his own mind and heart, was to create a new formulation of architecture, one that suited its setting, not the stylebook. But he knew, however he would make that happen, he first had to know intimately the styles of the past, because whatever he thought of them, they formed the foundation of any new growth in the way buildings would be constructed.

Milton took the flask and turned it upside down. It was empty; nothing flowed from it. "See here, Mr. Thomas," he said to his friend. "No more fuel for the flames. I believe it is time to pack up our pictures and put this snowy waste behind us."

Henry pulled his watch from his pocket, rubbed a leather-gloved finger over its face, and consulted it. "Right you are, Mr. Sprague. The 2:10 will be stopping at the station in about half an hour. It will take us a while to make the trek, so I suggest we leave soon."

Their hot breath putting out billows of steam like the boats on the river, the two trudged through the snow toward the Illinois Central train station at 57th Street. They trekked through bald patches where the snow had been blown away, and then tripped as their steps brought them knee deep into drifts of snow speckled with sand from the beaches behind them. The flimsy snow fences, that lined the beach to protect it, did little more than delineate where the ice on the rim of the lake met the ice on the shore. With the wind at his back, Henry could raise his head and admire how this stark snowy landscape resembled a pen and ink drawing that he ached to copy into his notebook. In their skeletal precision, the bare trees suggested to him strength, the strong underpinnings that would support their later adornments of leaves and greenery. He tried to keep his voice level as he exchanged pleasantries with his friend, not wishing to betray the passion he felt in his heart for capturing the promise of creating new things. He marveled inwardly that through putting his pen to paper he could begin a process that would culminate in structures as intricate and as lasting as these very trees, as complex and fascinating as the human body.

The excitement of the profession which Henry was working toward effervesced in his brain the way the sparkling wine had fizzed in the Bavarian crystal glasses with which his family had toasted the New Year the night before. It had been a warm, homey gathering, just his family, including Vati and Auntie Lou, as well as Milton, his visiting university friend. They all sat in the front parlor, toasting one another. There had been much well-wishing of his father and the coming culmination of his project to turn around the Chicago River, forcing nature to submit to the needs and desires of the growing population of the burgeoning city. Henry and Milton's upcoming journeys, first downstate to Champaign, then across the Atlantic to Paris and beyond, were chronicled and toasted. Henry thought of how the success he looked forward to as his goal would rival his father's—he would be turning matter into massive monuments, buildings that would put Chicago on the map, not for what it possessed, but for what it could be.

He thought of sharing these thoughts with Milton, a fellow student of architecture, but he realized that this was the romantic reverie of a dreamer, not of a serious student. Perhaps he should begin keeping a journal on his tour—he could illustrate it with drawings, perhaps even share it someday with his family or, when success came to him, publish it. Instead of confiding his dreams, when the two had reached the comparative shelter of the little station, looking out to the west at the newly built gothic buildings of the University of Chicago, Henry asked his friend if he had attended the great exposition, six years before.

Milton came from a prosperous merchant family in Milwaukee, and he recalled taking the train with them to visit the White City on Wisconsin Day, when thousands had piled in from across the northern border of the state. The two exchanged reminiscences of their visit— or in Henry's case many visits, because his father had been as entranced with the fair as Henry had been. He told Milton about the camel that he and Auntie Lou had ridden—his sister, Eleanor, had been too afraid—led through the imaginary streets of Cairo by men wearing turbans, just over there on the Midway, not two hundred feet from where they were sprawled at the station. The motion of the camel had been so different from that of a horse, swaying side to side rather than proceeding straight ahead. Both the young men had ridden on the Ferris Wheel, so high above the ground that they had been able to see the tall buildings being erected during that time at Chicago's center, seven miles north of the fairground. For both of them, vision had been one of the deciding factors in their choice of education and profession. Henry told of how he had taken photographs from the very top of the wheel as he hung suspended in air, and promised he would show them to his friend when they returned to the university later that week. The train roared into the station, spewing black soot over the gray drifts of snow that lined the tracks. The two climbed aboard, seeking shelter in the warm and smoky passenger car.

"Just in time," said Milton. "I kept thinking of the Donner Party in the Sierra Nevada Mountains, wondering if we would ever see civilization again and whether I might have to eat you if all else failed."

Henry laughed. "I had no worry of surviving. Let's get off the train downtown and find something more appetizing to eat. And then perhaps we can have a look at the Reliance Building, Mr. Atwood's latest creation on State Street." The two sat back and exchanged stories of the buildings they saw and admired on the uneventful ride north to the central station.

Back on Kennesaw Terrace, the parlor where the family gathered for tea seemed stuffier than usual, after the cold, clear air of Jackson Park and the curiously quiet downtown area. Henry could smell his mother's fragrant eau de cologne wafting from her and the heavy aroma of his father's pipe tobacco. Winter's late afternoon darkness had settled upon the room. Henry sat back and tried to imagine how the familiar gathering would appear to his friend, although Milton, scion of Germans who had inhabited Milwaukee for several generations, probably experienced a home life much like his own. Henry watched his mother pouring tea and chatting to Milton. She seemed quiet and even elegant, dressed as she was in a pale blue velvet day dress, her hair carefully coiffed and covered with her favorite snood of pearls and net. But Henry could see the face-down novel on the arm of the sofa, and knew she would much rather be sitting reading it on her own in front of the fireplace. He had often suspected that his mother's frequent sick headaches, and other illusive illnesses, were her way to assure the solitude she preferred.

His father, on the other hand, enjoyed company. He had peppered Milton with questions about his family, his studies and his own ambitions ever since Milton had arrived three days earlier. Milton didn't seem to mind the attention—he answered respectfully and properly—but Henry could see that Milton was uncomfortable by the way he kept sticking a finger into his shirt collar as if to stretch it. Milton was habituated to soft-collared, tieless shirts and a favorite tennis sweater back at the university. And he preferred to talk about sports or sporting matches, like horse races and prize fights, rather than the loftier subjects Henry's father had introduced. He would be leaving on the train the next day. Henry could tell that Milton would be happy to return home, although he knew he had enjoyed his time in Chicago.

"I say, Father," Henry said. "I took Milton to see the Reliance Building on State Street, you know. I wanted to show him that Mr. Atwood could design buildings in his own style, in a Chicago style, without relying on classical Greece for inspiration."

Milton shot a grateful look to Henry. "Yes, it was most impressive. That white terra cotta . . . and all those windows. It's certainly like no other that I've ever seen. It's difficult to imagine, though, keeping all those windows clean. Especially in a city like Chicago."

"They say that white terra cotta washes clean as a dinner plate," Eleanor interjected. She was the one who had alerted her brother to the uniqueness of the building that held one of the stores she and her mother visited on their frequent shopping trips to the Loop.

"It would have to wash clean, what with Chicago's soot and grime," said Mrs. Thomas. "Why, we have to remove our curtains to be washed at least once a week during the summer months, when the windows are open. In the winter, though, the dirt comes from inside." She lifted her hand, palm upward, toward the fireplace.

"Let me tell you a story about that building, Mr. Sprague," said Henry Thomas, Senior, leaning back in his chair and tapping his pipe on the fireplace fender. "It is a true Chicago story, I tell you." And he launched into the tale of how when work was to begin on the new building in 1890, there was an old bank building on the site, and the leases had not yet expired on its upper floors. The First National Bank, which had occupied the basement and first floor, was moving out. What the builders did was support the upper stories on giant jackscrews so that the original ground floor could be demolished and the foundation for the new building would be built. Meanwhile, the tenants on the upper floors had to use temporary stairs to reach their offices, but it didn't seem to cut into their business at all. It wasn't until all of the leases had expired in 1894 that the upper portion of the old building could be razed and the rest of the new building, thirteen new floors, could be built. "You see what I mean, boys," said Mr. Thomas, complacently puffing at his pipe. "Now that's Chicago ingenuity."

"But what your story fails to tell, Father, is how innovative the finished building is," said Henry. "The windows are extremely large and are set nearly flush with the walls. That lets in a massive amount of light, even on a day like today. And the whole frame of the building is a steel skeleton, which supports the window walls and the floors. All on a spread foundation of steel beams and rails."

Mr. Thomas looked at his son as if to say, It's my story and you shouldn't be interfering with it. But he merely said, "Yes, and it comes as no surprise, I'm sure, that the new building was completely leased the day it opened, and has not had a single vacancy since then. Chicago is booming, boys, and don't you forget it—despite what they say about a so-called depression over the past few years. You might want to consider moving here yourself, Mr. Sprague, rather than going back to Milwaukee once you finish your studies. Chicago is a boom town—it's growing faster than any place on earth."

Milton looked suitably impressed and helped himself to one of the delicate sugar cookies left on the silver tray.

Mrs. Thomas watched his face as he ate the cookie, and said, pointedly, "Our Eleanor made those cookies today, Mr. Sprague. Aren't they delicious?"

Eleanor grimaced at her mother. "From Auntie Lou's recipe. It's too bad she had to leave this morning to go out to Palatine. But we're lucky to have *you* here, Vati, to stay for the holiday." She patted her grandfather's hand, momentarily waking him from the reverie in which he seemed to be isolated.

"Yah, yah. The first day of the new year. A whole year ahead for me without *mein* Augusta." He shook his head.

"The last year of the century," said Henry. "Just 364 more days to go, and we'll begin the twentieth century. Who knows what it will bring?" Henry hoped his optimism would influence his grandfather, who seemed mired in the past, living not in the present, but in the years he had spent with his devoted wife, Augusta, running their truck farm on the near north side. "We passed the old home site on Cass Street this afternoon," he said to his grandfather. "I showed Milton where they're building a big new hotel there."

"Do you know how much they got for that site?" asked Mr. Thomas. "I saw it in the *Examiner* just a few weeks ago. The developers were asking for more than $1,000 per quarter acre and they received bids for even more than the asking price. Why we ever let that real estate leave our hands, I'll never know. Think of what it's worth now. Hard to imagine."

"Yah, yah. It's easy to say that now, my son," said Vati, rousing from his ennui. "But remember what your mother and I had to do with all that land and no one to help us farm it. You and your brother, you had no desire to work the land. And your mother and I, well, we were getting old, there was so little that we could do. And now your sister and I have the store."

"I understand, Father, sometimes it's necessary to leave things behind and go forward," said Mr. Thomas. "If only Herman and I had had the money then, we could have kept it. But, you see, we just couldn't raise the capital then. Nor could we now, not for what they've been asking for it."

Henry looked at his grandfather and tried to remember the strong, weathered man he had been when Henry was a child. Their plot of land on the Indian Trail Road had been green and bushy, with rows and rows of bean plants and celery plants, and hummocks of potatoes, and dozens of other vegetables. He remembered as a small boy, removing beetles from the bean plants, his grandfather giving him a penny for each twenty he pulled and placed in a bottle. But as his father had explained to him at the time, with the railroads bringing in produce from the large farms around the state and through the Midwest, small plots like his grandfather's had so much competition, they couldn't afford to go on. He vaguely remembered when his grandparents sold the farm, and celebrated how much they had received, which they could use to buy the little grocery store on Illinois Street, down near the river. But he knew his grandmother, most of all, had missed the farm. He thought about her, tiny and gnarled, her hands so callused that it would be like holding on to a football when she'd take his hand and run it over the fruits and vegetables in the baskets at the front of the store, explaining to him how to select a melon or a squash that was ripe and tasty. Even though she had lived in Chicago since she was a very young child, and had talked with the Indians—as his grandfather liked to remind them—she never lost that guttural, German accent. Perhaps that was why his own father still said things like *Gott* and *Yah, Yah*. She, Augusta Thurman, had been a Chicagoan when his grandfather came to the city in the 1840s, living in the German section north of the river.

"Isn't it about time for you young gentlemen to get dressed for dinner?" asked Mrs. Thomas, as Maggie came in to take the tea tray. "I've asked to have dinner a bit early tonight, as you boys are going to the Turner Hall concert."

"And Eleanor, too," said Henry. "Father said we could have the carriage, so we should leave here about seven. The concert begins at seven-thirty."

"And it's Wagner, my favorite," said Eleanor, clasping her hands in front of her. "They're playing *Parsifal*, which I have never heard in concert form. Only pieces picked out on the piano."

"Wagner, hmmph," said Mr. Thomas. "That modern music, I wonder how you can listen to it. Give me the old masters, Beethoven and Bach and Brahms, any day of the week."

"Remember they were modern once too," said Henry, patting his father on the back as he headed for the stairs. "The old must give way to the new."

"Balderdash," said his father, setting down his empty teacup. "There's no reason to try to improve upon perfection."

⤌

After the concert, her eyes flashing with emotion, Eleanor begged her brother not to drive them home just yet. "I feel so, so stirred," she said. "I feel as though the world is so much bigger a place than what I live in. I feel . . . oh, Henry, I can't describe how I feel."

Henry, who was helping his sister into the carriage as she spoke, nodded his head. "It does seem a crime to go home right now," he said. "But where can we go? It's late, and I would imagine most of the cafés are closed."

"Just not back to Jackson Park," Milton muttered from the back of the carriage. "I still haven't thawed out from our escapade this afternoon."

"Well, there's a thought," Henry said. "The lakefront. The wind has changed, it's not blowing over the lake now, but across the prairies. So it's a good deal warmer near the water than it was this afternoon. And I daresay, with the clouds clearing away, we might be able to see a few stars."

Henry clucked to the horses and turned the carriage down Fullerton toward the lake. The darkness felt soft and comforting despite the cold, bundled as he was in his heavy overcoat, wool hat, and muffler, as well a carriage blanket over his legs and feet. There was no traffic and the cold air seemed to amplify the regular rhythm of the horses' hooves on the pavement. The occasional street lamp burned brightly but shed no more light than a match lit in the darkness. No one spoke, each was wrapped in the introspection the music had created.

It was a short drive to the lake, and Henry pulled up the carriage in the shelter of a shuttered boathouse. The three of them piled out of the carriage and stood on the embankment overlooking the lake. The few streetlamps scattered at the edge of the park barely pierced the darkness. They could hardly see the lake although Henry believed he could feel it, a seething presence locked within a wall of ice, amassing its power to finally break free and dash its waves against the shore.

"Look at the stars," breathed Eleanor, who wore a carriage robe over her head like an enormous shawl to protect her from the cold. "How they do twinkle like diamonds in the sky."

"An array like that would set you back a few bucks at the jewelry shop," said Milton, ducking down behind Henry to light a cigarette.

Henry said nothing. The bright stars against the dark velvet sky, the cold air, and the hidden immensity of the body of water before him, as large in its prospect as any ocean, made him feel as if his heart would burst. He thought about how much there was in the universe to explore, how fortunate he was to be teetering on the brink of so much—a new century, an ocean to cross, new frontiers to conquer and new problems to solve. He was exhilarated and energized, he wanted to open his arms and throw himself into this immensity that lay before him. But instead he said as he stared out across the frozen waters, "I suppose we should be going. The parents will be wondering where we are."

FOUR

T hey had traveled out to the Main Channel in the darkness of a cold winter morning, but the sun promised brightness despite the bitter wind. Just a small crowd of well-bundled men clapping their arms around themselves to stay warm at the side of a massive ditch. Henry wished that he had brought his camera to photograph the occasion. There should have been great crowds of people throwing their hats in the air, a military band playing the proud marches of John Philip Sousa, and throngs of newspapermen with cameras. But no, huddled together, next to a bonfire some enterprising soul had built, were the trustees of the Sanitary District board, his father and a handful of other men who were about to see the culmination of their life work—the piercing of the small divide near Kedzie and 35th that would turn the waters of the Chicago River into the great canal that had been engineered to reverse the flow of the Chicago River away from Lake Michigan.

This final linkage was to be done in secrecy, Henry's father had whispered to him as he roused him from his warm bed well before dawn that cold January morning, the second day of the new year, 1900. Politics had once again muscled its way into the process. The burghers of the town of St. Louis, jealous as always of Chicago's elevated status as premier city of the Midwest, claimed that the reversal of the Chicago River would flush enormous amounts of the city's sewage downstream to the banks of their fair city. And they threatened an injunction to stop this menace to the health of the Mississippi Valley. Late the night before, the decision had been made at a hastily called meeting of the board of trustees—let the waters flow, deal with the consequences later, if at all.

During the cold ride that morning bundled in blankets in the carriage next to his father, Henry thought about the role this massive engineering feat had played in his own life and the life of his family. He could remember the summer of 1885, when the Chicago drinking water was considered so foul and unsafe to drink that he and his sister Eleanor, then ages eight and ten, had been sent off to Palatine, northwest of the city, to stay with their cousins, and instructed to drink only well water. His father had brought home great vats of that well water, which tasted faintly like rotten eggs, to serve the needs of the rest of the household. The year after that, Father joined the Drainage and Water Supply Commission to work on ways to purify Chicago's water. And the summer of 1893, the year of the World's Columbian Exposition, that brought the world to Chicago—how proud his father had been to claim that not a single one of the twenty-one million people who visited the fair had been harmed by the quality of the city's drinking water.

The World's Columbian Exposition—the memory of that great event brought the blood to Henry's cold cheeks and set a fire burning throughout his body. For the source of Henry's bursting pride that morning was that he had been chosen to serve as a drafting engineer in the architectural office of the mastermind of that exposition, the city's foremost architect, Daniel Burnham, when he finished college that June. His father had been right—his experience during his college summers at the various sites of the canal and sluice works had given his career a sounder foundation than mere years of education. On that December morning when he entered the Rookery Building office of D. H. Burnham and Company and spoke to the managing architect, Ernest R. Graham, he had been able to show his drawings of mechanical devices that had already been put to work, rather than the fairy castles of a university portfolio. Mr. Graham had been interested in the dams and sluice gates of the Chicago River project—what Chicagoan wasn't?—and had kept him far beyond the allotted hour, asking him questions about how the various parts of the system worked and what made them work. So when Henry left the office, it was a dark December evening already, although his appointment had been set for just after lunch. And in the darkness of LaSalle Street, punctuated only by the flare of the gaslights, Henry realized that his career as one of Chicago's builders would begin when he returned from his spring semester studying art and architecture in Europe.

Now, returning his thoughts to the scene before him, Henry watched as the nine trustees brandished their shiny new shovels on the bank of the canal. They stood at the west fork of the south branch of the river, where the water was to be directed into a wooden chute from a river channel into the canal itself. Only a small ridge of dirt separated the channel from the canal. But try as hard as they might the nine trustees were unable to move much of the frozen earth. As they wiped their brows with large handkerchiefs, the trustees huddled and came to a decision. This was a job not for a man, but for a machine. They summoned a dredge that had been standing idle a ways up the riverbank. The small crowd stood and watched as the steam-powered machine moved through the piled-up dirt like a mythical beast devouring its prey. Two hours of mechanical chomping and the ridge disappeared. And the water from the Chicago River came rushing down the chute with a great gush of foam into the canal.

Henry ripped off his hat and waved it in the air. The cheer that blasted from his own throat mixed with that of the others, raising a roar so loud one would have thought a Mississippi steamboat was sounding its horn. The men milled around clapping one another on the shoulder, and shaking gloved and frozen hands. "Well done, well done," they congratulated each other.

Henry's top-hatted father came up behind him and patted him on the shoulder. Henry turned and saw how red his father's ears and face had become in the cold. "Time to go now, son," his father said. "Now that the work is all done, it's time for the politicians to take all the credit."

On the long carriage ride home, Henry Senior spoke harshly about the role the politicians had played in the creation of the canal and the reversal of the river, obstructing the process and demanding much more than their due. It was not just the officials in St. Louis and downstate who fought the project from the time it had been first proposed, but the Chicago politicians, too, who stood in the way of progress making sure there would be something in it for themselves.

"Mark my words," said Henry Senior to his son as they rode across the frozen prairie back toward the huddled houses on the outskirts of the city. "Those who have done the work will never get the credit for what we have accomplished here. And that's why, as you attend to your own career, always keep this in mind—believe in what you do, even if no one else does. And acknowledge to yourself your own accomplishments—because the world won't give you any respect, unless you respect yourself."

FIVE

B y the time Saturday night rolled around, Kitty was ready to go out once again. Bitter cold had set in, making it dangerous to go outside unless one had to. Her brothers lay around all day, unable to work outdoors digging the canal south of the city or shipping out on boats in Lake Michigan. The smoke from the hearth and the gas lamps hung in the air like a dark fog. Kitty could feel it bite her eyes and lungs and she swore she could taste the pungent air. It stained her white apron and she would smell it strongly when she brushed her hair. She and her mother spent more time in the kitchen, preparing meals to feed the boys' bored and hungry mouths. Laundry was more difficult, too, with water pipes freezing and needing to be warmed by small fires beneath. And no one would dream of hanging out clothes to dry in this weather. Not only would the clothes freeze immediately, so would whoever was foolhardy enough to go outside to pin them to the line. So their small kitchen was made smaller by the spider's web of clotheslines they strung to hang out the laundry. The wet clothes made the kitchen more humid yet, and Kitty found herself wiping her dripping face more often and fanning herself with her apron. "Whew," she said to her mother one afternoon when they were tripping over one another while trying to peel and add potatoes to a bubbling stew. "It feels like August in here, but then I look out the window and it's like the North Pole."

"Be glad you're warm enough, Kitty," her mother said. "There's plenty that would wish for a bit of this heat today. And a bit of this beautiful stew." She made a quick sign of the cross and mumbled a prayer for those poor unfortunates.

Kitty thought about the men and women she used to see settled down near the river beneath the bridges. Huddled around a small fire, draped in blankets, the expressions on their faces as cold as the frigid air. How would they ever survive a night like tonight? She too said a prayer for the poor, a prayer to her patron saint, Saint Catherine of Siena, who, although she had lived in warm, sunny Italy, had brought food and help to the starving poor in her own country. Or so said the story in the *Lives of the Saints* book that her parents had given her many years ago for her first holy communion, which she had read over and over again since then.

So Kitty was dressed and ready when Brian came to the door Saturday night. She couldn't wait to get out of the cottage, which had seemed to shrink more and more each day that the wind howled outside. The weather had warmed up a bit, she could tell by the sounds of the snow sliding off the roof in mini-avalanches when the sun shone on it and by the impressively long icicles that formed on the eaves like the sharp teeth of immense ogres. She flew to the door when Brian knocked, and brought him into the living room. She breathed in the crisp, clean cold emanating from his jacket and laughed when he pulled off his stocking hat and his blond hair crackled with static electricity. Brian greeted Mr. Coakley and the boys, who had dragged a piece of machinery into the living room and seemed to be taking it apart.

"And are you coming as well, Daniel?" Kitty asked, tying a plaid scarf around her neck.

"Not me . . . not tonight," Daniel said. "Them Hibernians are too wild for me."

Mr. Coakley looked at his son and laughed. "Too wild" was something that had most often been said about the Coakley boys, not by them.

"Let's go, then," Brian said, looking at Kitty and smiling. He had smoothed down his dark blond hair and loosened the blue wool neck scarf that had covered his mouth. His blue eyes gleamed and she noticed how white his teeth were. He looked so clean and healthy, like a man in an advertisement for a tonic, she thought. Well, he'd be a tonic, getting her outside this tiny house tonight. "Let's go," she echoed.

As they left the house, Brian said that he had checked that morning and been assured that the electric cars would be running that night. The cold had shut down the electricity earlier in the week, and the few people who ventured out in the cold had had to travel by foot or carriage, but the rising temperatures had helped to bring back the electric power that moved the cars. A car came quickly, and they jumped in and headed toward the empty seats in the back. Evidently, Kitty wasn't the only one who had felt like an animal let out of its cage, because the atmosphere on the car was one of energy and delight. Kitty and Brian sat after Brian had greeted several friends hanging from the car's straps. He said, "Everyone's ready for a night out."

"It'll be a hot time in the old town tonight," Kitty said, quoting a favorite song made popular after Chicago's great fire of 1871.

"So it will," Brian said, catching Kitty's eyes with his own and smiling.

The scene at Coughlin's wasn't that different from her own living room, Kitty thought as they walked into the bar, although the sawdust on the floor and the jar of pickled eggs on the bar were touches not found at home. Clumps of Irish men in shirtsleeves and suspenders, pints in their hands, stood around tables arguing in loud voices about this and that. The same fug of gas and smoke filled the air that Kitty had escaped from at home, although with more of an aroma of the brewery about it. Everyone seemed to know Brian, greeting him as he and Kitty walked though the bar to the back room where, judging from the sound, the party was in full swing. Kitty thought she recognized a few familiar faces of men from the parish.

As soon as Brian opened the door to the back room, Kitty could feel the message from her feet that now was the time to dance. They piled their coats on one of tables already heaped high and headed straight to the dance floor. Dancing with Brian was easy and familiar, and Kitty threw back her head and laughed with pure joy. The music didn't stop and neither did they, romping around the floor with abandon, not speaking except with a sparkle in their eyes and the smiles on their faces.

Finally, gasping, with her hand on her chest as if to slow her heartbeat, Kitty stopped at the side of the dance floor and said, "I must have a drink before I can dance another step."

"You've got it," said Brian, disappearing into the crowd.

Kitty looked around her with some curiosity. Although everyone looked like someone she might know, she didn't recognize as many of them as she thought she would. The men seemed older and tougher than those who had attended the New Year's party at St. Pat's, and there weren't as many women, and no children at all. Of course, you wouldn't be as likely to bring your children to a saloon as you would a church basement. The music had slowed, and most of the couples had left the dance floor, probably heading for the bar as Brian was.

Brian appeared next to her, holding a glass of orange soda for her and a pint of something for himself. "Let's see if we can find a seat."

Way off in a corner, beneath a window, piled high with coats, was a small table with one chair. Borrowing an empty chair from another table, and stacking the coats atop another pile, Brian fashioned for them a cozy little nook apart from most of the others. No sooner had they sat down, though, did they hear shouting and, with a loud "Take that!" a young man came sliding toward them on his back, his hand over his mouth.

"Looks like a fight," Brian said. "We'd best be careful."

Another, bigger man came running after the first and threw himself upon him, slamming his fist over and over into his prey's face. Kitty was so close to them that she could see the blood gushing from his mouth. She gasped and put her hands over her own mouth, and couldn't move another muscle. A group of men formed around the fighters, blocking them from Kitty's view.

"We'd best get out of here," Brian said, grabbing her arm. "Come, under here." And he pulled her along behind him as he burrowed beneath the table where the coats had been piled over and under. Silently, Kitty followed him on her hands and knees as he wriggled on his stomach behind the table and toward the door. She could just see the light from the door when in an instant the lights went out and a great scream went up from the crowd.

"Either the electricity's gone out or this place is being raided," Brian said in a whisper. "We'd best stay where we are for a bit, until things get sorted out."

It was warm in their little nest on the floor near the radiator, and under a table, and Kitty could smell the doggy odor of wet wool, as well as cigarette smoke and sweat, from the jackets that surrounded and hid them. She snuggled in next to Brian, her head on his shoulder, close enough to inhale his clean outdoorsy scent, like sawdust, she thought, like her father's scent when he came in from chopping wood. She was happy to be sitting there, with Brian's arm around her shoulder, feeling safe from the fighting they could hear just yards away. The fight seemed to have intensified, with more of the crowd joining in, and others cheering them on. The participants didn't seem as angry as they had at first, and the lookers-on sounded elated at being witnesses to the battle.

"Let's just slip out now," Brian whispered, looking down at her face. "You're not afraid, are you?"

Kitty looked up at him and smiled. "Afraid? Not me. It's just a hot time in the old town tonight." She felt her own body getting warmer as she leaned in against Brian. She wondered if snuggling like this could be an occasion of sin. She didn't think she was having impure thoughts, which of course would be sinful, just cozy ones. She couldn't speak for Brian, nor could she read the expression on his face in that position. She felt very safe.

"Let's get out of here," Brian said, standing up and grabbing their coats and Kitty's hand. The two of them raced out the door, pushing through the throng from the bar, which had swelled with those who had come in to watch the fight in the flickering light from the fireplace.

They ran down the steps, struggling into their coats and into the cold air outside. Kitty breathed out a great sigh and was happy to see the cloud her breath made. The cold air was refreshing, as it had been stuffy beneath all those coats. Running first, and then slowing to a walk, they continued hand in hand under the gas streetlights of Dearborn Street. "Let's get a bite to eat then," Brian said, and they entered the first diner they came across, a small hole-in-the-wall with the strong smell of grease. "You don't mind this place?" he asked nervously.

"Why do you ask?" Kitty said. "I've been eating in places like this all my life."

He looked intently at her. "I just don't think of you in a place like this," he said. "You belong in a much finer place. With linen napkins. Real silverware. Candles and fine stuff."

"Oh Brian, you know my home, my family. You've eaten at my dinner table, for pity's sake. Why do you act as if I'm lowering myself to eat in a place like this?" For all her words, Kitty was flattered by Brian's statement. She didn't want to spend her life eating in greasy places like this, where you could see the previous diner's spills and splots on the tablecloth and the marks of his lips on the water glass. Yet they were safe and warm, out of the wind and away from the fighting crowds at Coughlin's. You couldn't expect to be dining off fine china everywhere you went.

"I just think you're better than that, Kitty. And I know I'm not good enough for you." Brian looked down at the table.

"Bosh," Kitty said. "You're like one of my very own brothers. And who would be saying they're not good enough for their family? That's a good way to get your head conked in from your ma or your da." She remembered too late that his mother's death was still a deep and recent wound for Brian.

"Still . . ."

"Still what, Brian? I won't have you talking like that. You're a fine fellow. You're a great dancer. And I won't have you putting yourself down." Kitty stamped her foot on the pine floor to punctuate her words. Brian looked amused, the food arrived, and they applied themselves to what was placed before them.

As they walked home through the dark and quiet streets with pools of light around the lampposts, no longer holding hands, neither of them said much. Kitty kept quiet because she was tired and content, while Brian concentrated on making their way through piles of snow and manure and other dangers underfoot.

When they approached the door to the Coakley cottage, Kitty looked up at Brian and said, "I had a wonderful time, Brian."

Brian looked down at her and smiled. "I had a wonderful time, Miss Kitty." His mouth brushed gently against hers, and he turned and left.

Kitty slowly opened the door, kicked off her boots and jammed her feet into her slippers. As she was hanging up her cloak, her father's voice came down the stairs. "That you, Kitty?"

"Aye, 'tis me, Da. I'm home for the night." She removed the pins from her hair, changed into her nightgown, brushed her hair, and thought of Brian. If somehow she could make him more forward-looking and ambitious, maybe, just maybe he could be the one.

SIX

K itty sat in the waitress's cloakroom at the Grand Pacific Hotel, preparing for her singing appearance at the private dinner. Since this was still the Christmas season, she figured her choice of songs could include such traditional carols as *O Holy Night*, and *Joy to the World*, songs she had sung at St. Patrick's two weeks before. Consider them Protestant hymns, she told herself, as she quieted down the wild Irish rose in her cheeks with the rice powder her Aunt Mabel had procured for her at Marshall Field's grand store. Protestant was the look she must nurture in this elite establishment. Demure and Protestant, unlike the highly rouged colleens who sang at the more notorious spots along South State and Dearborn streets.

Kitty was happy for her job. It might not pay as much as those places of ill repute, but the tips were often good, and, best of all, she could hold her head up high, unlike the girls she had known from the parish school, who no longer showed up at Sunday Mass, God have mercy on their souls.

"Two minutes," Tommy said, poking his head between the curtains of the cloakroom.

Kitty ducked down to look again in the mirror, making sure the pins holding her hair over the mesh rats that supported her brunette pompadour were secure, dusting a few stray crumbs of the rice powder from the shoulders of her crisp white blouse, straightening the red tartan bowtie around her neck, and biting her lips to redden them. She stood and brushed off her black bombazine skirt, shined the tip of each patent leather boot on the back of the black stocking of the other leg, and prepared for her entrance. In her three years at the Grand Pacific, she had worked her way up from waitress to singing waitress, to solo performer at banquets like tonight. Even still, she felt the familiar agitation of butterflies in her stomach as the lights of the banquet room dimmed, and the gaslights brightened along the edge of the stage. A group of civic leaders who ran the Sanitary District were dining tonight. All she knew about them was what Tommy had told her, that they were in charge of the city department that removed the dirty, and supplied the clean, water to the city of Chicago.

Kitty bit her lips one more time and faced her audience of men in dark suits with bright white shirts and here and there a flash of color in a tie or handkerchief, as befitting the season. As she often did to quell any hint of stage fright, she imagined them as a field of cud-munching cows, staring at her with the calm contentment and lack of understanding of farm animals. Sometimes it was only such ridiculous scenes that would bring her through such an evening of polite applause and attention divided between brimming plates and glasses and the familiar songs she would sing.

She opened with *Joy to the World*, her favorite, keeping her eyes focused on a point above the heads of the men. For *O Holy Night*, she lowered her gaze to their faces, those who weren't addressing only their plates, to invite them with her song to share in the spirit of Christmas. So it was with a start that she found the eyes of someone she knew, openly and wholeheartedly watching her through the variegated light of the gas lamps. Taught not to dwell on any one member of her audience, Kitty swept her eyes from one wing of the giant U of the cloth-covered tables to the other. Henry Thomas! He had been in her class at Lake View High School just a few years ago. What was he doing now with these older, self-congratulating men? When she swept her gaze back, she examined his companions. The silver-haired gentleman with the broad, white mustache, wasn't that Henry's father? Henry the First, she remembered hearing Henry—who was, after all, Henry Thomas, Junior—refer to him, as if referring to a king. That's right, Henry the First was one of the men who had engineered the feat still in the works that had all Chicago boasting—turning the flow of Chicago's river backwards, so that sewage no longer flowed into Lake Michigan, the city's drinking water supply. One of the modern wonders of the world, the newspapers had proclaimed, just one more proof of Chicago's superiority over such competitors as St. Louis, the city to which Chicago would be sending its sewage, according to local wags.

Now, *Adeste Fideles*, as she called it, and Kitty fluttered her eyelids, singing the Latin hymn in English to these Protestants. This was her finale tonight—*O Come All Ye Faithful*. She sang out each syllable in the name of Bethlehem, as crystalline as if she were tapping the wineglasses that sat on the table in front of these gentlemen. She curtsied to their surprisingly hearty applause, and, as a thank you, burst into *God Rest Ye Merry Gentlemen*, while they stood and continued their applause.

Kitty curtsied again, and left the stage, wondering if Henry Junior had recognized her as well. As she changed her shoes and threw on her cloak, she hoped he might come and stand by the alley door to greet her as she left the hotel. Others had, for 'stage door Johnnies' were a familiar, and secretly desired, part of her working life. "Such men want one thing and one thing only," her mother had warned her. Which was why she always sent Kitty's brother Daniel to escort her home.

That night Brian waited with Daniel at the stage door as she rushed out into the cold and dark alley. The sight of these two large Irishmen would discourage any admirer, although no such man lurked around the door when they left. But that didn't stop Kitty from daydreaming about leaving on the arm of a worldly-wise silk-hatted man as they trudged though the sooty snow to the streetcar.

Both the young men had worked hard that day, so they had little to say as the streetcar took them through the dark to their West Side home. Although after departing the streetcar, when Kitty and Daniel turned right to go up their street, Brian lifted his hand and said in his low voice, "I hope to see you soon, Kitty, then."

Kitty clasped his hand, looked into his eyes, and said, "Until then, Brian."

It was after midnight when Kitty went to bed that night, but she didn't fall asleep right away. She punched her pillow and wriggled under the covers. She was tired, why couldn't she sleep? Maybe it was too warm in her bedroom—positioned as it was behind the kitchen, it retained all the heat generated from cooking. Perhaps she should open her window. But that would necessitate getting out of bed.

Should she continue to encourage Brian? Seeing Henry Thomas in the audience tonight and recalling the crescendo of applause she had received from that very staid audience made her realize that perhaps she should consider men beyond her own neighborhood. What was her hurry, was it just that dratted thimble in the colcannon? Was she really of an age to worry about spinsterhood? Twenty-one next year and Brian would be twenty-three, like Daniel. Young for an Irish man to think about getting married, but not for an Irish girl. Was there anyone else out there for her?

Her mother had married at eighteen, and then seven children came, one every year-and-a-half or so. What kind of life was that? All that laundry and washing up, and cooking three meals to put on the table every day of the year. No wonder she was looking so old and worn out, like her dresses that she had washed too many times. Even Margaret, with her one child, was looking old these days. And it wasn't just that she was worn out, she hardly lifted a finger compared to their own mother. And what had her mother to look forward to? Grandchildren—she did seem to be happy to see Sean. And she would love to see Kitty's children one day too, she had said that. Grandchildren and what else? Death, when it comes. At least she was sure that there's something after life, an easier existence in the kingdom of heaven. But was it worth the hardscrabble life she'd had on earth?

Her mother would call that blasphemy, questioning God's plan. And Kitty supposed she would agree. Faith wasn't a question with her, for she could as little imagine life without her faith as she could imagine life without music. It wasn't a question, it was an answer, an answer to what made her life meaningful. Life without music would be like life without breathing, she supposed. She sighed, wishing she could be confident that she would earn a good living from her singing. But she knew that her chances of that were one in a million. She had heard the tales backstage—for every Jenny Lind or Nellie Melba, there were hundreds of young women who gave up and went home, or who fell into life on the streets and the wages of sin. What kind of wages did sin pay? she wondered. Ah well, she'd never know. She couldn't be that kind of girl if she tried.

Even Madame Nettlehorst had never encouraged her to try out for the opera or the stage—New York or Paris or Vienna. She'd need to know so much more than she knew now, languages like Italian and French, and arias and all that. And she knew that her parents would never let her go off by herself to perform on the stage. Why, look how they were still sending Daniel to escort her home from the hotel at night.

Yes, and hadn't she been expecting to see Henry Thomas at the stage door that very night? Stranger things had happened. They had been friends in high school. He was the valedictorian of their class while she played the music for their commencement. That was almost four years ago, wasn't it? At Lake View High School, they were equals, of a sort. Of course, she never told anyone there that she didn't actually live in Lake View, she just used her aunt and uncle's address to allow her to attend the school. Even Father Egan had said that Lake View High School could offer her a much better music program than St. Patrick's. She never had to admit that she was really from the Cabbage Patch, where the Irish lived and bred. You wouldn't expect a genteel and well-dressed gentleman like Henry Thomas to come out of the Cabbage Patch—or even to come into it.

Look at her aunt, after all. She had been a spinster—almost until she was thirty. Ancient. And she had a career, that's how she and Uncle Patrick could afford to live in a townhouse in Lake View. And they had no children. Aunt Mabel could take the streetcar downtown to Marshall Field's every day, all dressed up she'd be and spending her days with quality ladies who also were dressed in the latest fashions.

49

Maybe she should plan on that, maybe Aunt Mabel could get her a job at Marshall Field's, and she too could dress up every day and rub elbows with the elite. She might meet a wealthy, marriageable man doing that, she might. She should speak to her aunt. Perhaps tomorrow, she'd visit Aunt Mabel at the townhouse on Magnolia, and ask her about a possible position at Marshall Field's. A place where she could see what opportunities might await her—opportunities of the marriageable kind.

That settled, Kitty fell sound asleep. She spent a restless night, dreaming that she had to protect a vast vegetable garden from hundreds of persistent rabbits trying to hop into it. It was her job to protect the carrots and lettuce and cabbages growing there from the onslaught of the rabbits. When she awoke, she was shivering, and all her warm bedclothes were tossed in a jumble on the floor.

SEVEN

T wo weeks of crowing headlines and long-winded oratory had passed, bombast that hardly registered with Henry as he dealt with his own thoughts of his future—first traveling through Europe and then returning to work in the offices of D. H. Burnham and Company. He didn't even mind the task of accompanying his mother to every store in Chicago to purchase a suitable wardrobe for that future. He had parted company from his mother that morning, as she hurried to a luncheon at a friend's house, and set off himself to take a look at the renewed river. As he approached the crossing at Monroe Street, he noticed a crowd of men and women lining the bridge. Had someone fallen—or jumped—in? He rushed to join the throng of people who were yelling wildly and pointing to the river below. Henry pushed through the crowd to the railing of the bridge. He knew that no one could survive for long in the icy river, but he was prepared to lend his help or even his warm overcoat if need be. But he stopped in his tracks as he saw below him what seemed to be a miracle taking place.

The sluggish brown river, more like a sewer than a force of nature, was clearing, its water turning blue. It even was moving with a current that it had never shown before, sending slabs of ice not downriver to Lake Michigan, but upriver and out of the city. The flow that had begun out on the frozen prairie had caught up the many miles of channel to the river and sucked down through the narrow straw of the Chicago River the clear blue waters of Lake Michigan. The process was complete. The Chicago River had been made to run uphill, no longer polluting the source of the city's water supply, but flushing the waste from the city to dilute and disappear through miles and miles of moving water.

Henry looked around at the admiring and jubilant faces of the people sharing with him the perspective of the bridge. Few of them would understand or care about the many years and money and men it had taken to bring about this awesome sight. But all would benefit from the clean water and the reduced threat of disease it promised. He wondered how long it would take for the miracle to become an everyday sight, hardly noticed in the fast pace of city life. And if the Chicago River could run clear and free, why couldn't his future?

As one of the fortunate few who braved the cold and bore witness to the final dredging of the main canal, Henry was invited to celebrate at a festive dinner at the Grand Pacific Hotel. He arrived early in the darkness of the winter afternoon, and sat in the ornate lobby, watching the hordes of visitors arrive at the immense hotel, so large it covered nearly an entire square city block. It was a city within the city, and the lobby was an elegant stopping place to watch the buzz of activity. Carriages unloaded under the glass dome of a forecourt as grand as a royal palace's, many travelers arriving from the nearby Rock Island Railway depot. On the floors above were more than five hundred guest rooms, wired with electric annunciators, bells to call for service such as those found in the finest private residences. Electric elevators carried passengers like a vertical railroad to all floors. A mixture of the modern and the elegant, Henry thought, as he watched warmly clad people enter and gape at the heavy gold draperies, glowing electric lights, thick oriental carpets, tropical plants and gold-framed oil paintings that decorated the lobby. Necks craned when the photographers' bright lights flashed, for the hotel was known to cater to the rich and famous, and everyone wanted to see who they were.

Henry's father strode in, removing his gloves, and looking like one of the rich and famous himself in his top hat. Henry stood and joined him, and his father introduced him to his companion, Lyman Gage, with whom he had worked on a number of Commercial Club of Chicago committees.

"Are you ready for a feast, young man?" the genial Mr. Gage asked. "Mr. John Drake, Jr., who runs this hotel, makes sure that no one leaves with an empty stomach."

"I've heard tales of his father's wild game dinners," Henry said, wanting the civic leader to know that he was no newcomer to the delights of the table that Chicago offered. "It's a shame that they were discontinued."

"Yes, in his eulogy just a few years ago, John Drake, Senior, was accused of decimating the buffalo herds of the Great Plains," chuckled Mr. Gage. "As if anyone could ever make a dent in those numbers."

The men walked down a long corridor and entered an unmarked door. Inside, a tuxedoed maitre d' took them into a large dining room containing a U-shaped table draped in thick white damask and bearing cutlery of the heaviest silver. Henry sat down between his father and Mr. Gage and took in his surroundings. The table faced a small stage surrounded by gaslights not yet lit and covered with a deep purple velvet curtain, tasseled in gold braid. Around the dark mahogany-paneled walls were draped evergreen garlands studded with gold and silver fruits and nuts. The scent of pine trees overlaid the stronger scent of years of cigars smoked in the room. Henry inhaled a deep breath—it was the smell of power, the smell of money.

Soon they were joined by the other Sanitary District trustees. Henry recognized faces he had last seen that frigid morning two weeks before, faces that had been red with cold, now rosy from the wines and spirits being poured liberally around the table. The food was served by white-gloved waiters, who moved without a sound, dispensing liberal amounts of clam chowder, then cold oysters and clams on crushed ice, and then broiled brook trout in a bath of seasoned butter. With each course came a new wine, the glasses exchanged to suit the white and the red. Boiled quail came next, presented on a platter with potatoes and carrots. Then beefsteaks and more wine. And now Henry noticed guests fidgeting in their seats, opening first their vests, then, surreptitiously, the top button of their trousers' waistbands, making room for more delicacies of the table. Someone at the end of their leg of the table began to snore as loudly as a steam engine.

As the tables were cleared and brushed for crumbs, throats opened and the speeches began, claiming Chicago's superiority in creating the eighth wonder of the world, the river that ran backward. Jokes were made about sending the city's sewage down to St. Louis. Heartfelt thanks were given for the lives that would be saved because of the purity of the water. And champagne glasses were held high to toast the era of pure water that had just begun.

Henry soon grew tired of the constant flow of food, drink and rhetoric. He couldn't see that much difference between this group of prosperous businessmen and the men in his college eating club, once drink was taken in large amounts. Similar pride and puffery, the same self-congratulations and hyperbole, the ingesting of superhuman amounts of food and drink that would lead to gastric distress that night and the next day. He tried to keep from such overindulgence himself, not wanting to dull his own senses and his ability to do well what he set out to do. Still, he chided himself, he shouldn't forget that these men had worked for long years, defying political infighting and disputes over the project's routes and engineers, and the never-ending battles over costs to accomplish what others had said was impossible. They deserved their celebrations.

Waiters entered with immense silver platters of sweets, and others followed with silver pots of coffee, and Henry sat up, hoping that this signaled that an end to all this Lucullan feasting was in sight. He then heard, above the hubbub of the crowd, the notes of a piano playing, and the maître d' appeared on the stage, announcing the evening's songstress, Miss Katherine Coakley. Where have I heard that name before? Henry wondered, and then sat back, grateful for the diversion of music.

A young woman appeared on stage, modestly attired in white shirtwaist and long black skirt, with touches of red around her neck and waist. Henry sat up very straight and gazed at her. She was beautiful, her clear white skin accentuated by rosy lips and cheeks and haloed in a froth of glossy black hair. The sound of her singing rang out as clear and sweet as the chiming of a silver bell. He knew that voice, and he recognized the singer as well. It was Kitty Coakley, he was sure, and the last time he had seen and heard her had been at their graduation from Lake View High School, nearly four years before. He couldn't say that she hadn't changed at all, it wasn't a physical change as much as it was an intensification, a deepening of her beauty, like that of a rosebud into a rose. The sounds of his dining companions diminished as the voice rang out, and Henry was transfixed.

Miss Coakley seemed overwhelmed by the thunderous applause her Christmas songs elicited, and tried to leave the stage, but the applause and even cheers of the diners brought her back to the stage for a rousing finale of *God Rest Ye Merry Gentlemen.* There was more loud applause and a few who even yelled "Brava!," to which she modestly curtsied and left the stage.

Henry sat back down again and stared at the untouched crystal glass of champagne on the table in front of him. Kitty Coakley. How he had admired her musical gifts in high school, singing and playing the piano at many a school assembly, including their own graduation ceremony. What a wonderful voice. What had ever happened to her after graduation? So many of his class, including some of the girls, had reappeared on the university campus, and he'd seen many others at dances and parties during university vacations. But Kitty Coakley had disappeared. Yet here she was tonight. Could she have been working here all that time? Wouldn't he have run across her here or somewhere else in the city? Chicago was a large city by any standard, but his friends and classmates seemed to create a small community where it was not unusual to run into each other many times a month. How could he have missed her? He debated with himself over leaving the dinner and meeting the lovely lady by the stage door, should there be one, but he looked over at his father and knew that Henry the First would demand that his son drive the carriage home. Not that his father was drunk, that was not his style at all. But he had reached that stage where he had begun speaking the German of his childhood, and Henry Junior knew that his father soon would fall gently asleep. It was time to get him home. But he had just enough time, he strategized, to make a stop in the florist shop he had noticed in the lobby. Why not take the opportunity to let Miss Coakley know that she had been seen and appreciated?

EIGHT

Boarding the streetcar to go up to her aunt and uncle's home put Kitty in a much better mood. Aunt Mabel and Uncle Patrick were lace-curtain Irish, a term Kitty's mother would mutter in derision. But for Kitty, lace curtain was a wonderful way to live, especially in contrast to the small cottage shared with her noisy brothers. Or Margaret's rat's nest of a house, where, thankfully, she hadn't had to linger. Sean was napping, and her mother and Margaret sat gossiping over the kitchen table, so Kitty didn't feel she had to stay. It felt good to get away from that stuffy little house and breathe the cold air outside.

The graystone townhouse on North Magnolia Avenue where Aunt Mabel and Uncle Patrick lived had a front room with a wide bay window, and the intricate white lace curtains that graced it left patterns of the cold winter sunshine on the hardwood floors. Aunt Mabel herself wore luxurious silk blouses with lace collars and cuffs of the most brilliant whiteness. And in the guest bedroom in the back, behind the parlor, which Kitty considered hers, the bed clothing was adorned with white eyelet ruffles. When she was attending the high school, she stayed with Aunt Mabel and Uncle Patrick several nights a week because of the distance from home. The room had seemed like heaven to her. As had the meals. It will be like going to boarding school, Aunt Mabel had said. But even Kitty knew that the meals at any boarding school, no matter how exclusive, could never surpass the cooking of Aunt Mabel's live-in cook and housekeeper, Elsa, whose solid stews and delicate pastries delighted the eye as well as their stomachs.

Aunt Mabel was conferring with Elsa in the kitchen when Kitty walked in. The kitchen was warm, but shadowy, ensconced as it was below the level of the sidewalk. Once this lowest floor of the house had been on the same level as the street and sidewalk, Uncle Patrick had explained to Kitty. But the city, such as it was in those days, had raised the street grade to be able to lift them above the level of swampland on which Chicago had been built. Which explained why the older houses on the block had front staircases that arched up to a first floor and also led down to a lower floor, tucked beneath the street. Kitty had always found it charming to come in the lower door, as if she were entering a magic castle in a fairy tale.

Both Aunt Mabel and Elsa made a fuss over Kitty when she came in, brushing the snow off her shoulders and taking her coat and scarf. A pair of her very own house slippers sat warming by the fire in preparation for her arrival. Elsa brought these to Kitty and knelt to place them on her feet after she removed her dripping boots.

"Wait until you see what I have for you," Aunt Mabel said to Kitty, her eyes brimming with joy.

"Another present? But Christmas was two weeks ago," Kitty said, her hand resting on Elsa's shoulder.

"It's a lovely gift all right, but not from me. Come upstairs with me and I'll show you where I put them in the parlor."

"Them? Lots of presents?" Kitty asked, her face alight with surprise. She followed her aunt up the narrow stairs and, when they emerged in the hall, caught her breath. There, proudly displayed in a silver vase on the sideboard in the parlor, was a wealth of red roses. The intensity of their color shimmered in the pale light that fell through the lace curtains. Kitty felt herself drawn to them and ran her fingers over the velvety surface of a single bloom. "So beautiful," she said. "And in the middle of winter. Did Uncle Patrick give you these?"

"No, Kitty dear, they're your surprise. They arrived for you this morning. Do you have any idea who might have sent them?"

Kitty could hardly speak, she was so overcome with the scent, the beauty and the obvious expense of the roses. "Who might have sent them?" she repeated after her aunt.

"Whoever it was chose a good florist. A very good florist downtown, some of my customers use him," Aunt Mabel said. "I put them in this vase, of course. And you can tell the florist knows what he's doing because, look, there isn't a full dozen flowers, but eleven."

"How could it be a good florist if he didn't give a full dozen?" Kitty found her tongue to ask.

"Silly," Aunt Mabel said, patting Kitty's shoulder. "One should always send eleven roses rather than an even dozen. Because that implies that the woman to whom they are sent is the loveliest of all and completes the full dozen."

Kitty sighed, staring at the flowers. What a romantic notion. "Yes, but . . . ," she started.

"Oh, silly me," Aunt Mabel said, removing a small envelope from the pocket of her full tartan skirt. "You probably want to see from which one of your many admirers your flowers come." She handed the envelope to Kitty with a smile, for they both knew that while many young men had admired Kitty over the years, few had had the courage to approach her. Or at least that's what Aunt Mabel had always opined, when she and Kitty would have their teatime conversations about such matters.

Kitty held the envelope reverently. "Miss Katherine Coakley," it read in a careful, distinctive hand, and beneath her name, the Magnolia Avenue address. When she pulled the cardboard rectangle from the envelope and examined it, she let out her breath, which she was not aware she had been holding. "It is him, and that is why they were sent here."

"Him?" Her aunt held herself back from taking the card from Kitty's hand. "What possible him would be sending you roses?"

"Henry Thomas. Henry Thomas, Junior, that is. I thought he was in the audience the night I sang at the hotel. And I was right, I was right, I was right." Kitty danced around the room.

"And who, may I ask, is Henry Thomas?" her aunt asked, amused at her niece's display. "I gather he is someone you know."

59

Kitty dropped down breathless onto the padded piano seat. "Henry Thomas—Junior—is a fellow I attended high school with. Oh, don't you remember, Aunt Mabel, the one who gave the valedictory address at my graduation. Remember—you said how smart he was— not just intelligent, you said, but well dressed? Well, he was there the other night at the Grand Pacific Hotel. I thought I had caught his eye, but I wasn't sure and of course it's not really proper to be too familiar with one's audience, and then I thought he might be waiting for me as I left, and then he wasn't, and then, oh . . ."

Aunt Mabel held out her hand for the card. "Miss Coakley," it read. "As a former classmate (Class of '96), would you be so kind as to allow me the pleasure of taking you to dinner on the night of Sunday, 14 January 1900? Please reply, at your convenience, to the following address." And there was an address on Kennesaw Terrace, followed by his carefully symmetrical signature: "Henry J. Thomas, Junior," under which he had drawn a bold, black line.

"Kennesaw Terrace," Aunt Mabel said. "A very good address. A small, quiet street, but lots of large homes on big lots. Just a few blocks east of here, near the lake. But why did he send the flowers to you here, Kitty, rather than to your home address?"

"Don't you see, Aunt Mabel . . . ," Kitty said as she rummaged through the sheet music stored in the piano bench. "He must have used the school directory . . . the high school listing." And she and her aunt laughed that the ruse they had used to ensure her a good high school education had been so completely accepted.

After playing *Beautiful Dreamer*, the solo she had played at her Lake View High School graduation, and discussing at length with her aunt what she might possibly wear on Sunday night and where he might possibly take her to dinner, Kitty retreated to the little room kept just for her to compose a reply. Her aunt gave her the formal stationery with the engraved Magnolia Avenue address to write on.

Kitty sat down at the little white and gold desk and pulled out a piece of scrap paper from the drawer. She would have to write out a rough response first, before she put pen to the beautiful paper her aunt

had given her. She wanted Henry's impression of her writing to be of a
gentle lady, not some madcap Irish girl who couldn't string more than
two or three words together. What might he have thought of her,
singing at the hotel? She hoped that he didn't get the impression she
was an easy type of girl he could have his way with. She paused for a
moment, resting her cheek on her hand, and looked out the window
on the snowy scene below. Hmm, what would she wear? She did have
that beautiful lace blouse her aunt had just given her for Christmas, but
then she had been wearing a white blouse when he saw her the other
night. She didn't want to suggest that she had only one set of clothes.
She had first noticed him in high school because of how beautifully he
dressed. Suits of the finest woolens, and bright silk ties that looked as
if they had come from the finest markets of Araby. Wherever that was.
Yes, she had to make a good impression on him. Which meant he
would have to pick her up here, at Aunt Mabel's, and not at home.

Kitty went into the parlor, where her aunt sat, going over her own
correspondence. "Aunt Mabel," she said with a frown on her face.
"What if Mother won't let me go? You know she absolutely hates it
when I go out in the evening, especially with someone she hasn't met."

"Kitty, dear, you're a grown woman, nearly twenty-one," her aunt
said. "It's time you learned to do what you want to do, not just what
others expect of you. How do you expect to make your way in this
modern world if you're still tied to your mother's apron strings?"

She would have to take another tack, Kitty thought. What she
wanted was for her aunt to invite her to stay over the night she went
out with Henry. How could she make that happen?

"Besides, Kitty dear," her aunt continued. "Who says you have to
tell your mother where and with whom you're dining Sunday night?
Let's just say you're staying here. After all, isn't this where your adoring
young swain will expect to pick you up and deliver you? And if you
must give your mother an explanation . . ." She looked down at the pile
of handwritten invoices on her graceful secretary desk. "Let's just say
that I need you to help with my year-end accounts. That's it. And, by
the way, dear, I could use some help. Do you think you could give me

a few hours, if not on Sunday itself—of course not, you'll be getting ready to go out—but perhaps on Monday morning? And then you can tell me all about your dinner with Mr. Thomas."

Kitty breathed a sigh of relief. Aunt Mabel understood her in ways that her mother could not begin to understand. Kitty had always looked up to her aunt. If there was anyone who practiced what she preached, it was her Aunt Mabel. Born to a family of ne'er-do-well immigrants from Northern Ireland, Mabel Kennelley had found her own way out of the tenements of Bridgeport, apprenticing herself when she was still in her early teens to a hardened German milliner in the garment district near Maxwell Street on the city's south side. At a time when young working women were rarely able to support themselves without turning to prostitution, she worked until her fingers bled to achieve respectable status as a milliner. And when, at the old maidish age of thirty, she married the ruddy Irish cop who walked the beat outside her tiny shop, she did not forsake the career she had chosen and remain at home as matron and housekeeper, as others in her family had assumed she would. In fact, she built up her craft and her clientele until Marshall Field himself had invited her, just a few years before, to reopen her shop in his magnificent emporium on State Street. Her comparative freedom and prosperity caused a great deal of jealousy among her sisters—and her sister-in-law, Kitty's mother—who lived at much lower levels of status in the south and west divisions of the city, and who accused Mabel of aspiring too far above her station. Aspirations that Kitty herself shared.

NINE

S unday finally arrived. Kitty had counted the hours, the time moving excruciatingly slowly at home with her parents and all her brothers, who weren't working and had plenty of time to antagonize their little sister. She felt like an escaped prisoner when, after Mass and breakfast on Sunday, she carried her bag to the streetcar and rode uptown to her Aunt Mabel's. The sun was shining, and the streetcar splashed through the puddles of dirty melting snow left by the warm-up. From the streetcar, she had a short brisk walk to Magnolia Avenue. Kitty stopped on the pavement in front of the townhouse and looked up at the bay window shining above. She couldn't see through the lace curtains that covered the window, but she imagined her aunt and uncle relaxing in the dining room after their own late Sunday breakfast. She entered the townhouse at the lower door, slipping into her slippers at the threshold to avoid tracking mud onto the sparkling wooden floors. She sighed. Wouldn't it be nice to live in a peaceful home like this, unlike her own home where you had to stumble over at least five pairs of heavy, muddy work boots to reach the kitchen?

She joined her aunt and uncle, who were lingering over their meal in the dining room, and they sat and drank tea and talked for hours. Uncle Patrick always had funny stories to tell about the city's police and the characters they met in the streets and in the barrooms. And Aunt Mabel would chime in with anecdotes about the customers she dealt with at Marshall Field's. When Kitty went downstairs to her own room to change, she was still laughing about one of her uncle's stories about the politician Hinky Dink Kenna. Then she became serious and sat down in front of the mirrored vanity table and contemplated her long, dark hair. Up or down? she pondered. Which hairstyle would make her look most like she wanted to look, a sophisticated woman who dined alone in a restaurant with a young man almost any day of the week? And who was that young man? How had he changed from the quiet, well-dressed classmate who excelled in mathematics and science in high school? She had a picture of him in her mind from high school. How would he resemble that young man four years later? Had the university changed him? Had he become a man about town, squiring heiresses and college girls to clubs and parties? And what did he expect of her? Did he expect her to be "easy," having found her singing in a hotel restaurant? Or stupid, because she hadn't gone on to university? What compelled him to send her the roses?

Absorbed in her thoughts, Kitty vaguely heard the doorbell ring, and footsteps crossing the floor above. A few minutes later, her aunt's cultured voice called down the stairwell. "Kitty, dear, Henry has arrived."

Kitty wet her lips and gave herself a final once-over in the mirror. She wore her bright red Christmas dress, her black hair up in a pompadour supported in back by a wide red ribbon spread out like a giant butterfly. Her white skin was heightened by bright patches of natural color on each cheek. She breathed deeply to calm herself the way she would before going on stage to greet an audience. She walked slowly up the stairs, and stood framed in the doorway of the parlor, where Henry was sitting on the dark horsehair sofa. He jumped up from the sofa when she arrived, looking as nervous as she herself felt. His mustache had become blonder and bushier since high school, she noticed, while his forehead had enlarged as his dark blond hair receded. His shirt collar was stiff and sparkling white, his silken tie a rainbow of bright colors. He wore a proper dark suit that made him look older, more businesslike.

"Good evening, Henry," Kitty said, her eyes sparkling. "I take it you've met my aunt."

"Yes, indeed," Henry said. "And admired your lovely home."

"This is my uncle, Patrick Coakley," Kitty continued, as Patrick appeared behind her aunt in the hallway, looking huge and threatening in his off-duty corduroy trousers and shirtsleeves.

"Pleased to meet you, sir," Henry said, meeting his eyes and stretching out his hand. Kitty was pleased to see that Henry, although much thinner, was at least as tall as her uncle, which made him seem more grown up.

"Take good care of our Kitty," Patrick said. "We'll expect her back no later than half past nine. She's precious cargo, you see."

"Uncle Patrick!" Kitty said, her color heightening. "Half past nine!"

"Don't worry, sir," Henry said gravely. "I'll protect her as if she were my own."

Kitty felt as if her face matched the burgundy cloak her aunt draped over her shoulders.

She placed her hand on Henry's outstretched arm and walked with him to the door, which he opened with his free hand.

"Good night, Mr. and Mrs. Coakley," he said.

"Good night, Aunt Mabel and Uncle Patrick. We'll see you later."

Henry told Kitty that they had a reservation for dinner at Henrici's on Randolph and, he apologized, they'd have to take the Clark Street car, as he wasn't able to borrow his parents' carriage for the evening.

"That's quite all right," Kitty said, her breath forming a little cloud in the cold night air. "I take the cars all the time. I find they're quite reliable." She hadn't expected a carriage, no one she knew had one, they all rode the electric cars.

The clanging tram, filled with merry partygoers, appeared almost as soon as they stepped onto the corner. Henry helped Kitty up into the car and dug into his overcoat pocket for the coins to put into the fare box.

The conductor saluted him. "Many thanks, guv'nor."

The two sat down next to each other on the slippery straw-upholstered seat. "So, Henry, did you have a lovely Christmas? I did, and this beautiful cloak was a gift from my five brothers, isn't it just gorgeous?" She held out the cloak by its corners as if she were about to take flight. Kitty remembered that Henry had never been the talkative sort in high school, so she figured she would have to do much of the talking. She hoped that he didn't consider her a chatterbox, but she didn't fancy just sitting there, saying nothing. She had composed in her mind a list of appropriate topics to talk about and they all seemed to come to her mind at once.

"Of course, that was my aunt and uncle's flat. On Magnolia? I don't live there now, you see, I just stayed there when I went to the high school. I live with my parents and brothers in the western section, St. Patrick's parish, that is. But I'm staying with them, my aunt and uncle, for a few days. We thought it would be easier, you see, and, of course, my aunt would like my help in preparing her receipts for the end of the year." Kitty then launched into a long description of her aunt's millinery business and her association with the great man himself, Marshall Field, that took them all the way to the corner of Clark and Randolph Street, their stop for Henrici's. She hardly stopped talking until Henry waved his hand in front of her to get her to disembark from the streetcar.

The cold and the muddy aftermath of the December snows vanished as they stepped inside Henrici's restaurant. Kitty recognized the music the orchestra was playing as a Strauss waltz, and was surprised that no one was dancing. She would have liked to dance, she loved to waltz. The ornate tin ceiling and the black and white tiled floor amplified the sounds of the music and people talking with the overall effect of a high level of gaiety. The plump maitre d' in his black tailcoat brought the couple to a white damask-covered table in a far corner of the crowded restaurant. "Away from the draft of the door," he said as he seated them, handing them both large parchment menus.

The elegance of the surroundings quieted Kitty's tongue for a while as she looked around at the other customers and what they were wearing. She then glanced at the menu and found to her dismay that it was written in old-style German. She looked across the table at Henry, who had hardly spoken a word, and said, "I'm afraid I don't know what any of these dishes are at all. I can't read this writing."

Henry seemed surprised that she would have difficulty with the menu. "I didn't realize this was written in German," he said. "My family eats here often, and we hardly ever even look at the menu."

"Oh then, what would you recommend?" Kitty asked, relieved.

"Definitely the Wiener schnitzel," Henry said. "It's even better than our cook's."

Kitty was embarrassed to say that she still didn't know what that was, having never tasted it, and, hoping that it wasn't something inedible like tripe or brains, said, "Then that's what I would like, if you please. And why don't you order the rest of the meal?"

She watched Henry discussing the menu with the waiter in German and tasting the wine he poured, and she felt as if she had been transported to an entirely different place. This couldn't be taking place in the Chicago she knew. "You speak German very well," she said.

"My grandparents still speak German at home—or did, when my grandmother was alive," he said. "My grandmother—she died last year—came here as a baby. She was one of Chicago's earliest settlers. She always used to say that she came to Chicago when the Indians were still here, that she talked to the Indians."

"Did she speak German to them?" Kitty asked, giggling. The bubbles from the white wine tickled her nose.

Henry looked at her solemnly. "You know, I never thought to ask," he said, brushing his mustache lightly with his forefinger.

There was a lull in the conversation while Kitty tried to recall the list she had made up of topics. Finally, she returned to a question Henry hadn't had a chance to answer on the streetcar. "So, how was your Christmas?"

"Quite nice. Although at dinner, I had a bit of a run-in with a somewhat savage chap who was singing Christmas carols outside our window," Henry said, picking up his knife and fork. "Can you believe he actually knocked me down?"

Kitty expressed concern that such a thing could actually happen, thinking angrily about her brothers, and quickly changed the topic. "I remember you were going off to the university downstate when you graduated from Lake View. Are you still attending classes there?"

"Yes, I finished for the semester just before Christmas. Next semester, I will be traveling to Europe to study in Paris, at l'École des Beaux-Arts," he said, pronouncing the French words with a flourish. "Many famous architects got their start there."

"So it's an architect you're planning to be?" Kitty asked. It was as if she had turned on a faucet that had been shut off for a long time, because Henry came out with a torrent of words about his studies and his dreams of architecture. He described his courses at the University of Illinois, his plans for travel in the next six months, and even the buildings he planned to build in Chicago when he had finished his studies. Kitty had only to nod her head or say, "Oh really?" and Henry talked on and on. She found that she was imagining the big enormous buildings he was describing and herself at his side as he was gaining awards and acclamations throughout the world. Time moved faster than it ever had before. Just after the waiter had taken their order for coffee *mit schlag*, which Kitty was relieved to find was hot coffee heaped with foamy whipped cream, Henry pulled his watch from his waistcoat pocket, and they both were startled to see that it was already ten past nine.

"I will be getting you home rather late." Henry said to Kitty. "Will your parents—I mean your aunt and uncle—be worried?"

"I hope not," Kitty said, licking her finger and pressing it against the pastry crumbs on the tablecloth before her. "But let's not worry, I'm sure they will understand." She might have felt like a child when they left her aunt and uncle's, but after this sumptuous dinner and the way the other patrons of the restaurant, as well as Henry, had been eying her all evening, she felt more sophisticated and grown-up than she ever had before.

While Kitty's aunt and uncle may have understood Kitty's late arrival home, they made it clear that they didn't approve. Uncle Patrick's bulk filled the doorway when the couple arrived at the Magnolia Avenue residence, and his stern, cop-like stare would have frightened off any miscreant. But again Henry stood straight and met Patrick's eyes, shook his hand, doffed his hat, and conveying his thanks to Kitty for a wonderful evening, disappeared into the shadows of the quiet, gas-lit street.

"Really, Uncle Patrick," Kitty said as she followed him up the stairs, removing her hand-knit scarf as she climbed. "I'm not a child anymore, you know."

"'Tis true, you're not a child anymore, my darling, but 'tis also true that you're staying under my roof, and that you'll be following the rules set down in my household."

Aunt Mabel, standing at the top of the stairs, wearing a mauve dressing gown and hugging herself against the chill, echoed her husband's sentiments. "We were worried, Kitty dear," she said. "What if something had happened to you—and with a young man we don't even know at all. What would we have told your parents?"

The buoyant mood Kitty had floated along in the whole evening melted like candy floss in the rain with these remarks, and she mutely handed her cloak to her aunt and started down the hallway to her room. But halfway there, her spirits brightened—hadn't Henry said something about seeing her again before he left for Europe? And hadn't she been out on the town with a refined and sophisticated gentleman? She returned to the hall to kiss her aunt and uncle goodnight. "I'm sorry I worried you," she said, up on her tiptoes to kiss her uncle's cheek. "We just lost track of the time."

"That's all right, dear," her aunt said, smoothing the tendrils of hair that had escaped like ivy across Kitty's forehead. "I hope you'll tell me all about it in the morning. Now, scoot, it's late, to bed you must go."

❧

Kitty sat on the edge of her bed and wiggled her toes to bring back the warmth into them after her walk through the melting slush. She had worn her good boots, which weren't nearly as warm as those for everyday. She removed the hairpins one by one from her drooping coiffure, holding them in her teeth so she wouldn't drop them into the snowy drifts of her down-comfortered bed, and thought about Henry as she slowly brushed her hair. Henry. She had always liked Henry, even when they were classmates at Lake View High School. He was different from the other young men she knew, serious, even studious. Committed to achieving something in the future. Committed to making something of himself. Committed to building a Chicago even bigger and better than the city she had grown up with. Even the careful way he held his wineglass, she decided, showed that he was a much finer sort. As she pulled her nightgown over her flowing hair, she wondered if he had liked her. She was sure that she'd lie awake for hours debating this point, but in truth, her eyes closed and she sunk into a deep sleep almost as soon as her head touched the lavender-scented pillow.

Morning came without sunlight, but was heralded by the appearance of Elsa, the cook, bearing a cup of milky hot tea, soon followed by Aunt Mabel, wrapped in a pale blue, ruffled morning robe, who sat on the edge of Kitty's bed, eager to hear the details of the evening before. Kitty had to place the cup down on the bedside table for fear of spilling it, so full of the joy of the evening before that she fairly bounced in her bed.

"Oh, Aunt Mabel, did you see how finely he was dressed? That suit, the tie, that crisp white shirt?" Kitty clasped her hands in front of her as if she were imploring her aunt to answer and praying that the answer would be the one she sought.

"Yes, he appeared to be a fine gentleman," her aunt said, smiling. "Even though he brought you home rather late."

"Really, though, I'm not a child. And half past ten is not that late at all, at all. My brothers come in much later than that any old night of the week." Kitty's attempt at a pout was overcome by the smile that persisted in pulling up the corners of her mouth.

"Yes, child, 'tis true. But you're a young lady—or at least your parents and I have done all in our powers to help you become one—and young ladies follow much stricter rules than your wild Irish brothers."

"Oh, Aunt Mabel, he had such fine manners. And he knew just what to order, wine we had, so sweet, like the sugar water we give to Sean. And Viennese meat—wiener-whatever, so tender and delicate—it wasn't like eating meat at all. And pastry—great billows of it—I thought to myself, it's in heaven I am, and we're nibbling at the edges of the clouds for afters."

Aunt Mabel smiled and patted the edge of the bed. "Up and out with you, child, it's back to earth you must be coming. You can continue to tell me about your grand night on the town over breakfast. Elsa has been cooking bacon and eggs for her darling Kitty. Can't you just smell them, dragging us by our noses into her kitchen?"

❧

Kitty emerged into the kitchen fifteen minutes later, her hair drawn up into a relaxed version of the pompadour she had worn the night before, dressed in a creamy white shirtwaist and her black bombazine skirt, enlivened by a red tartan belt around her narrow waist. She felt taller and more adult from the waist up, but her feet itched to dance.

"Ah, miss," said her Uncle Patrick, leaning back in his chair. "Don't you just look as fresh as dawn itself, despite your gallivanting about the town for all hours." He winked at his wife across the table.

"Uncle Patrick, don't be so silly," Kitty said, taking her place where the lacey tablemat had been set. "Hardly gallivanting, I was. It was a nice dinner with a fine gentleman of my acquaintance. A friend from long-ago schooldays."

"And what, may I ask, were the fine gentleman's intentions?" Uncle Patrick asked. "A question I might have taken up with the young gentleman himself, had he not scampered down the street like a scared rabbit."

"Don't you think it's a bit early to be asking about intentions?" Aunt Mabel asked as she raised her teacup to her lips. "And after all, you're not Kitty's father."

"I'm her father's brother, I am, and that's close enough for me. And I have seen a lot of fine gentlemen in this town who, once you get a little closer, aren't quite as fine as they make themselves out to be. It does no harm to be a little careful in a city like Chicago. We get all kinds here, you know, coming in from all sorts of places."

"It's all right, Uncle Patrick, I understand," said Kitty, patting her uncle's ham-like hand that made the teacup grasped in it look like a thimble. "There are all sorts of men in this city who it would be dangerous to get close to. I know that. But remember, he attended Lake View High School with me, so I've known Henry Thomas quite a long time."

"And his family lives just over on Kennesaw Terrace," Mabel added. "They're practically neighbors. It's a very good address."

"And he's going to be an architect and build great buildings and make Chicago an even greater city," said Kitty, a note of pride edging into her voice.

"Is he now, going to build buildings?" asked Patrick. "Well, we'll see them when we see them. And as for now, my darling Kitty, let's just see that he brings you home on time. If you can't trust a man in the small things, you surely can't trust him in the big things."

"Yes, Uncle Patrick," Kitty said, looking down demurely, but hardly able to contain the bubbling feeling she felt when she realized that even Uncle Patrick assumed that she would be seeing more of this worldly-wise beau, Henry Thomas.

TEN

T hank you, Madame Nettlehorst. You have given me a great deal to think about. Yes, I have your sister's address. I will let you know how I am doing." Kitty gently shut the door and slowly walked down the stairs to the street door, clutching the sheaf of music to her bosom and taking long, slow breaths so as not to cry. Madame Nettlehorst, her music and voice teacher ever since she was a wee young girl in her first year at Lake View High School, was retiring. She was going to move away from Chicago, move to Madison, Wisconsin where her younger sister taught at the university. Kitty felt as if the breath had been sucked out of her, the news had come as such a surprise.

The sunshine after a week of gray days did nothing to lighten her spirits as she walked down Clarendon Avenue to the streetcar. The bushes getting ready to bloom reminded her of nothing but brittle dead sticks rammed into the dry ground. For how many years had she been walking down this same street with music in her heart and mind to play and sing with Madame? Let's see, if she were twenty-one, nearly twenty-two, why that was seven, nearly eight years. And Madame had seemed an old woman even from the beginning, with her many chins caked in rice powder much whiter than her skin and uneven splotches of rouge on either cheek. Long necklaces rattled over her large bosom, and her voice, even on the high notes, leapt and trilled like the birds of spring. Life without Madame Nettlehorst, that was difficult to imagine. No milky tea and stale cakes after the lesson. No more "You must listen to this, my dear," and then she would play the most elaborate musical pieces on the grand piano as if she were just improvising, and it would be the latest work of some German composer sent to her from friends in Berlin or Munich.

But, far worse than the prospect of life without Madame Nettlehorst, was the prospect of life without music lessons at all. When Kitty had asked whom Madame would recommend for her to continue her voice lessons with, Madame looked at her kindly for a moment without saying a word. Then she turned to the piano and played a difficult section of the Mahler piece she had just introduced to Kitty. And then she spoke, words that Kitty would long remember as the most cruel, and the most kind, she had ever heard.

"Katerina, *mein liebe*. You have a very pretty voice. But it is a voice for the home, for the church perhaps. It is not the voice for the opera, or for the stage. To tell you otherwise would be to do you the greatest disservice. I believe I have taken you as far as you can go. I do not believe you can go any further. I am sorry, *mein liebchen*, but that is the truth." Madame folded her hands in her lap and looked sternly at Kitty.

Kitty bit her tongue to keep back all the words she wanted to say. All the hopes and dreams of who she would be, and what she could become, danced through her head. She had heard that the way to keep yourself from crying was to look upwards, so the tears would not spill out, and she had looked up at the ceiling with its drapery of cobwebs, not at Madame.

"Thank you, Madame. I appreciate your honesty. You have given me so much . . . ," and here her voice cracked, and Madame reached over and patted her hand.

"There, there, *mein liebe*. We have much for which to be grateful. All the many years we have spent together, all the music we have sung and played and heard . . . " The tears began to run down through the maze of wrinkles on Madame's cheeks. "Perhaps it is better if you go now, Katerina. We shall remain friends, you and I, isn't that true?"

As Kitty walked slowly down the pavement, her own tears dripped from her face. If she wasn't a music student, nor a musician, nor a singer, who was she to be? She had a high school education, strong arms and legs and a strong back, a pretty face—or so people had told her—surely there must be dozens of jobs she could take on. At this moment, though, she couldn't think of one.

As the streetcar rumbled along the cobblestones of Clark Street, Kitty gazed out the window at the storefronts that lined the busy shopping street. Late at night, she had heard, this was where the ladies of the night strolled, waiting to be picked up by men who would pay to have their way with them. While she could hardly imagine such a thing, her brothers had on occasion pointed out such women.

"I had rather see you dead than dishonored in that way," her brother Daniel had once told her, after they had watched a woman younger than herself walk off arm in arm with a man who had just approached her on the street. Kitty had been admiring the woman's dress and was startled to hear the vehemence in her brother's tone. And, although she pressed him with questions about the woman and the man they had seen, he refused to tell her more. In fact, he had seemed embarrassed that the subject had even come up between them.

It wasn't that Kitty had never heard anything about sex. She and her female friends at high school had whispered about what men and women were said to do in the dark, and had commented wisely on the fates of their classmates who suddenly disappeared from school before a term was over. Her mother had spoken to her about how a man and a woman would be blessed by the holy sacrament of matrimony, and from that the good Lord would share his children with them. But none of it added it up to what might be happening to a man and a woman in a dark alley at night. She only knew that it was best that she stay away from such occasions of sin.

Usually, on Monday afternoons after her music lesson, Kitty would go to the church basement to practice on the piano there. There didn't seem to be much reason to do that today. But if she went home, her mother, who reserved Mondays for laundering, might ask too many questions. Or might even expect her to help. Of course she could get off the car downtown and visit her aunt in her millinery salon at Marshall Field's. But Aunt Mabel didn't like to be disturbed while she was working, especially now at the turn of the season when things were so busy. And she might have too many questions as well. Including the question Kitty most feared, "Have you heard from that nice young Henry Thomas chap?" The answer was always no, and Kitty didn't like to think about him any more. After all, it was March already, and that meant he had left for Europe without getting in touch with her.

Kitty considered her options—where to go when she was expected to be elsewhere? Aha, what about her sister Margaret's house? Now extremely pregnant with her second child, Margaret rarely left her home. And she would be happy to have company. And, best of all, Margaret was so full of herself that she rarely asked how you were doing. Instead she was happy to have an audience to regale with details about her many aches and pains and the slights and oversights that she, martyr-like, was forced to endure.

"Oh, Margaret. You're huge!" Kitty said when her sister came to the door to let her in. Margaret had swollen up like a balloon, her usually sharp features lost in her puffy face.

"Yes, and now tell me something I don't know," Margaret said, motioning for Kitty to come in. "And close the door tightly behind you, mind you. I don't want our Sean to go wandering down the street."

Sean looked up from the blocks of wood he was playing with by the fireplace when he heard his mother speak his name. He smiled when he saw his aunt enter the room. "Auntie Kitty, Auntie Kitty," he said, bouncing up and down in his joy.

"Now Sean, let your aunt at least take off her bonnet before you go jumping all over her," his mother said. "And I suppose, Kitty, you'll be wanting a cup of tea," she said, sighing as if the effort would be more than she could manage.

"That would be nice, yes," said Kitty. "Can I help you with the tea?"

"No, no," said Margaret as she trudged heavily into the kitchen. "I am not so feeble yet that I need help making a simple pot of tea. Not in my own home yet at all."

Kitty cleared away a pile of clothing from the sofa and sat down, familiar with Margaret's utter disregard for housekeeping. She found the inside air difficult to breathe after the cold outdoors. It was a presence in itself, dry and dark and noxious, like the bowels of a furnace but containing as many flavors as a witch's brew, onions and old clothes, cabbage and coal gas, sewage and sweat. Kitty longed to rush to a window and open it to let fresh air in, but she knew her sister feared drafts, believing that they would bring in illness.

When Margaret returned, carrying a tray with two cups and a cracked teapot, she proved true to Kitty's preconception. Oh, how difficult it was to be pregnant. Oh, how she tossed and turned at night, sleep was impossible. Oh, how her husband and son were no help . . . The list went on as Kitty sipped her tea, content to be distracted by a litany of woes not her own. Sean was immersed in his own building-block play, jabbering in different voices for playmates only he could see. The room was warm and the late afternoon sun illuminated the dirty windows. Dust motes shimmered in the dregs of sunlight. Margaret's voice droned on and on, stultifying Kitty until she had to struggle to keep her eyelids up.

"And what is this about you, Miss Kitty, and Mr. Brian Kelleher, walking out together now? And your taking him away from Miss Bridie O'Toole, herself with all them freckles, poor soul."

Kitty sat upright. "Brian's a good friend of Daniel's," she said. "He comes to the house from time to time."

"That's not all that I've heard," said Margaret. "I've heard that Brian's truly sweet on you, he is, and he's dropped that Bridie O'Toole completely."

"Brian sweet on me?" Kitty was flabbergasted. "Now how would you know that?"

"Oh, it's the talk of the neighborhood, isn't it, dearie. Brian so sweet on you, and you, the Protestant princess, you hardly give him the time of day."

"What is this all about, the Protestant princess?" Kitty said, slamming her cup down onto the tray. "I never heard of such a thing. Don't I spend every single Sunday morning singing my lungs out in the choir loft at St. Pat's? And working with Father Egan to plan the feast day celebrations at Christmas and Easter and Pentecost? And people are calling me a Protestant?" Kitty stood up and shook out her dress, preparing to head for the door.

"There, there, dearie, don't get your Irish up. I'm just telling you what people have been saying about you for years, you'd think they'd get tired of it. It doesn't mean that it's true. It's just what people might have thought, might have thought that you thought. That perhaps you thought you were better than the rest of us because you left the Patch to go to that Protestant school."

Margaret's usually angular face looked as mild as milk due to the swelling of her pregnancy, but Kitty knew that she thrived on controversy, and that she enjoyed getting a rise out of her younger sister.

"And didn't I graduate from that so-called Protestant school years ago? Are you saying that no one has anything else to talk about after all these years?"

"Well, it doesn't seem to bother Brian that you went to that school," said Margaret in a conciliatory voice.

Kitty sat back down on the sofa. "It's difficult to know what it is that Brian thinks," she said. "He doesn't talk much."

"Oh, now, isn't that the way with them, these shy Irish boys," Margaret said, pouring Kitty another cup of tea. "But 'tis said that silent waters run deep. And I believe you've got a deep one there . . ."

Kitty searched her mind for any indication of unplumbed depths on the part of Brian Kelleher. She had been seeing him regularly, she admitted to herself, ever since that party at the new year, not just when he'd come over to visit Daniel. He had escorted her to a few parties in the neighborhood and was very polite and thoughtful, helping her into and out of her coat, walking on the outside of the sidewalk like a gentleman. She wracked her brain for something to say to him because he always seemed to be waiting for her to speak. Brian was a bit of a burden in that way, although he was an excellent dancer and loved to dance, especially when he had a few pints in him. But he never did have much to say, unless Kitty asked him direct questions about his family or his job. He'd had a steady job for years now, working for his father and uncle's lumber and construction company. A few weeks before, when he escorted her to a Young Hibernians' dance that was being held in a bar downtown, he had pointed out a few buildings he had worked on.

"So what's wrong with Brian?" Margaret asked. "He's a good man, he goes to church, he's got steady work. You could do worse."

"Brian's a fine man, Margaret, I haven't said he wasn't," Kitty said. "All that I'm saying to you is that he doesn't talk much."

"And all that I'm saying to you, sister, dear, is that it's your future you should be thinking about. You don't find a good man like Brian Kelleher hanging out on every street corner. And you know you're not getting any younger, Miss Kitty." Margaret leaned back in the armchair, her hands clasping her mound of a stomach, nodding her head. "A nice, quiet, hardworking man like Brian—those types make good husbands. Steady, don't you know, that's what you want."

Kitty looked at her sister and imagined herself in her place. Hugely pregnant, with one child already hanging off the apron, wearing a faded and unflattering housedress with the buttonholes so stretched out by her burgeoning figure that you could almost see her underwear. Sitting in the stifling, dirty, and cluttered parlor of a house that shook every time a van rumbled past. Margaret's husband, at least, had some ambition, ambition that might someday take them out of this crowded, smoke-filled neighborhood—if Margaret would ever consent to leave. But Brian Kelleher—she just couldn't imagine him doing anything but working for his father and going out to the saloons and parties with the boys from the Cabbage Patch. She was about to explain this to Margaret when the sound of the church bells rang through the house.

"Six o'clock it is, Kitty, and our Kevin will be home soon for his supper. I'd best start boiling the potatoes, and you'd best get along home, I should think. Our mother will be wondering just where you are." Using her elbows, Margaret pried herself out of the armchair and, muttering, "Ah, me aching back, me aching back," saw Kitty to the door.

"Good-bye, Sean, come over and see me and Gramma soon," she called out as she left the house, happy to be breathing the relatively fresh air once again. Home now for dinner. Now, the question was, should she discuss with her parents Madame Nettlehorst's pronouncement on her future or, better put, her lack of one?

Kitty returned home to find her mother, looking exhausted, sitting at the kitchen table, sipping at a cup of tea.

"There you are, Kitty. I was beginning to wonder. Aren't you usually home by the six o'clock bells? Well, anyway, I was hoping you'd be helping to put the supper on the table. The potatoes are boiling and there's the joint left over from yesterday's dinner. I'm just thinking you can fry up some hash."

Washdays were wearing on her mother more and more, Kitty could see. Her father's and the boys' heavy clothes, caked with mud from their construction jobs, all the household linens. These were heavy loads to wash in a tub of water heated over the fireplace, then rinsed and wrung through a wringer. At least on this mild day she was able to pin things up to dry outdoors. Usually when Kitty would arrive home on dark Monday afternoons, she'd find laundry lines strung across the kitchen. Was this what her mother had wanted out of her life? Kitty wondered as she pulled an apron over her head and began chopping the potatoes. Is this all that she had to look forward to?

"Set some aside for the boys," Mrs. Coakley said. "They're working out near Lockport these days, and they won't be coming in 'til late. Your Dad will be in presently, though."

Kitty set the table for three and filled the kettle for the evening tea. Then she sat down at the table across from her mother.

"Mama," she said. "I've got something to tell you."

A look of wild horror crossed over her mother's face. "What is it, child?" she whispered, as if in fear.

"It's Madame Nettlehorst," Kitty said. "She's moving to Madison, Wisconsin, to be with her sister."

Helen Coakley made a quick sign of the cross. "Thanks be to Jesus, Mary and Joseph. You'll be getting a new music teacher, then? Someone closer to home?"

"Well, that's just it," Kitty said. "Madame Nettlehorst says . . ."

Just then, Michael Coakley walked in through the door. "And what is it that the lovely Madame Nettlehorst is saying to my own dear Kitty? Could it be that she's to replace the great Nellie Melba on the Auditorium stage?" Michael Coakley was fond of comparing his daughter's talent to the most famous opera singer of the day.

"No, Da, that's not what she said at all," Kitty said, once again staring upward. "She doesn't believe that I have any future in music."

Mr. Coakley scanned his daughter's face and then reached over to pat her on the shoulder. "There, there, our Kitty. It's all right. We wouldn't have wanted you to go on stage and leave home. I can't imagine what we'd do without you here."

Helen Coakley looked over at Kitty, who was brushing tears from her eyes with the back of her hand. "Not to worry. It's time you gave up all that singing stuff anyway, and found yourself a good man and settled down like your sister Margaret."

With this, Kitty flung her head down on the table and sobbed deeply.

"There, there," said her mother. "You'll find someone soon who will change your mind entirely. You're still very young, Kitty, you have plenty of time."

Kitty looked up, her eyes red and swollen. "But maybe I don't want to settle down. Maybe I want something more than what Margaret has."

"Don't be daft, girl," Michael Coakley said, pacing across the kitchen floor in his heavy boots. "There's nothing better in life that what Margaret—and look, your own mother—are doing. Marriage and having babies and keeping a good home for your husband and family. It's all that the good Lord has intended a woman to do, it is."

"We never should have sent you to that Protestant school," said Kitty's mother. "What were we thinking of when we sent you there? Why wasn't St. Patrick's school good enough for you, the way it was for your brothers and sister? It's that aunt of yours, it is. She's been putting ideas into your head all these years. Living above her station and she one of those good-for-nothing Kennelleys from Belfast. Living on her own. A dried-up old maid when she married Patrick, she was. And where are the children that your Uncle Patrick would have loved? No, there was no having children for that selfish woman. So she tries to take mine."

"Ach, Helen, that's water under the bridge now, it is, isn't it," said Michael Coakley. "We've got our daughter here with us now, and here she is to stay. At least until I escort her up the aisle at St. Patrick's and give her over to a decent young man."

Kitty sat up straight at the table and folded her hands in front of her. She knew that she would get nowhere discussing this with her mother and father—it was clear the sort of life they expected her to live. Her only hope, as she saw it, would be to talk to her Aunt Mabel, much as her mother despised her. Her aunt, she knew, had a broader picture of a woman's place in what was soon to be the twentieth century. Her aunt even thought that women should be allowed to vote, just like men! She promised herself that at the earliest possible time, even tomorrow if she could get away without telling anyone where she was going, she would visit her Aunt Mabel and talk with her about what she could do to plan a future life that wasn't just like Margaret's. Or her mother's.

ELEVEN

itty adjusted her straw boater as she entered into the opulence of Marshall Field's grand emporium through the door on State Street which was held open by a smiling livery-clad doorman. She inhaled the enticing scent of a thousand perfumes that transported her into a larger world than the muddy and windy one outside. In this cosmos of French perfumes and Chinese silks and Persian rugs and Austrian crystal, anything could happen. She could be anyone—a princess, a queen, a debutante, an opera diva, an heiress—but even as a poor American-born Irish girl from Chicago's West side, she had every right to stroll these marble floors that she had explored since she was a child. Her long skirt sweeping the floor, she kept her head high and her boater tipped forward at the most up-to-date angle as she turned down one aisle and then the next on her way to her aunt's millinery salon, tucked away near the back of the enormous floor. She nodded to the gentlemen floorwalkers, dressed so properly in their morning coats, and watched out of the corners of her eyes the oh-so-obvious tourists who oohed and aahed over the fittings and the merchandise, unlike anything that had ever been seen back home in Muncie or Waterloo.

Kitty was a woman on a mission and she took no time herself to linger over the glass cases of jewelry and watches. She reached the millinery alcove that was now a garden bower befitting the season and using many of the same pink and violet flowers that blossomed on this spring's elegant hats. Flowers like the tiny bouquet of violets, wrapped in a pink and purple moiré ribbon, pinned to the brim of her own hat, an early Easter gift from her aunt. Aunt Mabel was now showing a bonnet to a large, well-dressed woman, but she smiled and nodded her pompadoured head to Kitty, indicating that she would soon be finished with her customer.

Kitty read the signal and turned to explore the garden of millinery that surrounded her. The variety of objects, colors and materials that stylish women would wear on their heads! Clouds of tulle. The feathers of an aviary of birds, dyed to improbable shades of pink and lilac and green. Shining, sword-like pins to anchor these creations firmly to one's head against the greedy Chicago wind. What a fairyland—yes, there even appeared a gossamer fairy attached to a puffy meringue of a hat, brandishing a tiny wand of golden wire. What fun it could be to work each day surrounded by these delightful, impractical hats. Kitty glanced over to her aunt and recognized a familiar expression that said on the outside, "How lovely you look in that hat!" but kept her true thoughts to herself. The customer seemed pleased with her purchase and fumbled in her expensive leather handbag to pay the ridiculous price, not just for the small amount of straw and silk Kitty's aunt was carefully placing into the hatbox, but for the cachet of the distinctive green and gold hatbox itself, as well as the tender ministrations of Madame Mabel, the most fashionable milliner in Chicago.

Having escorted the effusive customer to the door of the salon, Aunt Mabel approached her niece. "Whew," she said, shrugging her shoulders as if delivered of a heavy burden. "That was quite a trial. Let me make sure that Caroline is available to tend the shop, and I'll take us both off for a cup of tea." Ordinary shop girls were not allowed to step away from their posts and mingle with the customers, Kitty knew, but her aunt was not a shop girl, but an owner/proprietor, and therefore not subject to the strict discipline that ruled the store.

Kitty loved walking through the store at the side of her tall, elegant aunt, noticing every deferential smile and nod she rated from those working inside the store. She saw too, the open sizing-up she received from the store's patrons, who stopped in their tracks when they noticed the imperiousness of her gait and her glance, and then checked out the fashionable dress she wore. Aunt Mabel carried herself like royalty in this, her kingdom. Kitty wondered if she herself could follow in her aunt's footsteps and hold sway over customers and store people alike. Or would she prefer, instead, to stay at home and create a happy atmosphere for a husband and children? What a pity it was that a woman couldn't do both. But Aunt Mabel was unusual, a married woman with a job and a working husband. Of course, she had no children, but most married women stayed at home. At least those who could afford to.

As they sat down at the tiny tea table in the third-floor café, she asked her aunt, "Do you ever regret coming out to work each day?"

Her aunt laughed. "Today, I do," she said, motioning for the waitress to come and take their order. "But that's not how I usually feel. It has been a difficult day. But most mornings, I delight in closing the door behind me and riding the car downtown. There's so much more happening out here each day than there would be at home. I let Elsa take care of that."

Kitty thought of her own mother and how beaten down she had looked on Monday night after spending the day doing the washing. This morning her mother had told her that she actually looked forward to Tuesdays when, with the washing completed, all she had to do was iron. Kitty knew that she wanted more out of her life than that. To bring her aunt up to date, she launched into her tale of Madame Nettlehorst and the snuffing out of her dream to be an opera singer, stressing that she had feared all along that her parents would never allow her to go on stage and travel around the country. "So," she concluded, "here I am. All grown up and I don't know what to do with my life. I was hoping you could help me."

Her aunt took her time in answering, stopping first to pour from the china teapot the waitress set in front of them, and then adding milk and sugar to her own tea. Then she spoke. "Kitty, it's really your decision, not mine. I know what your music has meant to you. And I would hate to see you leave it behind altogether. You have spent so much time with it. And, truly, you do have talent. But I see the wisdom in your parent's wishes that you not go on stage. It can be a harsh and cruel life. And I'm sure that Madame Nettlehorst realized that, too."

"But what can I do? Sit around home and wait until someone asks me to marry him? That hardly seems like a life."

"Oh no, there's so much more to life than that," Aunt Mabel said. "Let's see. What could you do?" She placed her chin in her hand and looked out across the bustling floor of the department store.

"But what about working here?" Kitty asked, following her gaze. "You seem to enjoy it. And it would get me out of the house and I could meet all sorts of interesting people here."

"All that is true," Aunt Mabel said, as she lifted the cup to sip her tea. "But it isn't a life I would wish on you, Kitty. The hours are long. The pay is low. And the rules are strict. I feel sorry for the girls I see. Take Caroline, for instance. She has very little time for fun. At the end of the day, when she goes home to the boarding house, she says she has little time or energy to do anything but wash out her things to prepare herself for the next day. I think you need to do more with your talents than stand behind a store counter all day, waiting on silly ladies with too much time and too much money."

Kitty sighed. In her heart of hearts, she knew that she'd soon be bored waiting on other people, even in a setting as rich and glamorous as this store. And she'd want to spend her money on all the finery that surrounded her. "The problem is, what else is there? I don't have a university degree, so I can't teach. Oh, perhaps I could teach music, I suppose. But where? We don't even have a piano at home."

"Do you think you would like to teach school?" Aunt Mabel asked. "Maybe teaching little children? I think I see a woman I know who heads a program to teach young women to tend to the little ones. She's coming our way."

Just then, a neatly dressed older woman stopped by their tea table and smiled broadly at Kitty's aunt.

"Madame Mabel, I want you to know that the hat you made for me was a grand success," she said, cupping the back of the floral bouquet perched on her head with one hand, her elbow in the air, a gesture that appeared at odds with her prim demeanor. "Your hat—my hat, I suppose is more correctly put—gave me the courage to go right up to the office of the Commissioner of Education and ask—no, I shall say demand—demand that the Chicago Kindergarten College get better funding for the kindergartner training program in September. Can you imagine—he agreed right away. And I'm sure my success was due to your beautiful hat."

Mabel smiled and turned to her niece. "Mrs. Campbell is a customer of mine who teaches the art and science of kindergartening. That's how you say it, isn't it, Mrs. Campbell?"

"Yes, kindergarten. A garden for little children. Very popular in certain places. Of course, the American program started right here in Chicago."

Kitty was intrigued. She hadn't heard about the kindergarten program before. "A garden of children," she repeated. "Outdoors in the country?" she asked.

"No, no," said Mrs. Campbell, hooking a chair with her umbrella and plopping herself down on it. "Not outdoors, but in a school. Of course, we do encourage the little kiddies to play outdoors. It puts such roses in their cheeks." Mrs. Campbell's high color suggested that she too spent her time outdoors.

"Well, what makes this garden of children any different from the schoolroom?" Kitty asked, seeing that this woman was so full of her topic and her plans that she would welcome questions from a stranger.

"We teach young children through playing with them," Mrs. Campbell said, raising a finger in the air to catch a waitress's eye. "We use certain special toys like blocks and balls. And music, lots of singing and dancing. So lively. It's all the grand design of a German educator, Herr Froebel. Quite the thing in Europe and all along the East Coast. The daughters of some of the wealthiest men in the Midwest come to Chicago to become kindergartners."

Kitty caught the woman's enthusiasm. If it were something that heiresses were doing, why couldn't she? And if it were available right here in Chicago, she wouldn't even need an heiress's money. She thought of her nephew Sean, playing with his blocks in front of the fireplace at Margaret's place. Wouldn't it be fun to sing and play all day with little ones like Sean, rather than dealing with capricious and crabby adults? She envisioned herself in front of a room full of smiling children, playing the piano and singing. She could do that. She'd like to do that. "I would like to hear more about your course of study," she said to Mrs. Campbell. "In fact, I believe I would like to sign up right now for the course at the Chicago Kindergarten College. May I?"

Kitty turned to her Aunt Mabel. "Perhaps this is a sign from God," she said. "Perhaps this will be what God has put me here on earth to do. And I'm sure such a plan certainly would please my mother and father. Wouldn't they see it as good preparation for having my own little ones?"

Her aunt pursed her lips before she spoke. "I'd certainly rather see you becoming a kindergartner than working in a shop," she said hesitantly, as if thinking it over as she spoke. "And teachers are professional women, who hold a high place in the community. I've had many teachers as customers, and they tend to be lovely people.

Mrs. Campbell smiled and nodded and sipped her tea.

So it was that, on her way home from downtown, Kitty found herself lost in dreams of classrooms full of joyous, singing children. She knew this was unlike her, to make a decision so quickly about something so important, but she had always had her dream of a life of music before, and she had felt adrift without a destination for her future. Besides, she knew this was the right direction to go in. Mrs. Campbell had told her that as a graduate of a Chicago public high school, she could attend classes at the Chicago Kindergarten College for almost nothing at all other than the carfare it took to get to the south Loop, where the school was located. It wasn't until Kitty saw the familiar façade of her parish church, she realized she had missed her stop, so lost in thought she had been. I'll take a moment and visit Father Egan, she thought. And discuss with him this kindergartner business. Mrs. Campbell had told her she would have to have a letter from a priest or a minister to apply, so it seemed a good idea to talk with him first.

The dour housekeeper who answered the door grudgingly showed her in to Father Egan's study. "Now don't be taking up all his time chatting, missy," she said. "The good Father has more important things to do today than natter away with the likes of you."

Father Egan was more welcoming. "Miss Kitty Coakley!" he said. "And aren't you as pleasant to see as a rainbow after the rain. To what do I owe the honor of this visit? Don't tell me you've chosen a lucky man and you want me to officiate at a wedding? How could you ever narrow down your choices to just one man?"

Kitty smiled. Everyone said that Father Egan must have kissed the Blarney Stone, he was such a flatterer. Still, she hoped that he saw her as more than just a silly young woman. She trusted his judgment and, over the years, had counted on him for advice. She knew that if she presented an idea to her parents saying that Father Egan had suggested or supported it, they would be convinced it was the best thing for her. It was Father Egan's support of her attending Lake View High School years ago that had swayed her parents into letting her go. He hadn't worried about her losing her faith, not at all. He knew that the public school had the best facilities for her to learn more about music. He was proud of his parish schools, there was no denying that, but he also knew their limitations. He was delighted to hear about this possibility opening up for her.

"Yes, yes, I've heard about these kindergartners. Young ladies they are, usually of good families. And what a fine vocation it is—as the twig is bent, so grows the tree! Teach children early and they are yours for life," he said seriously. "I'm afraid though, Kitty, we won't be able to find a place for you to teach here, once you have trained to become a kindergartner. Without the good sisters here, we wouldn't be able to afford our school. If we had to pay for schoolteachers, we couldn't have a school. Many good Catholic girls become teachers in the Chicago public schools, though."

"Oh Father, I'm not looking for a job," Kitty said, her cheeks ablaze in the warmth of the study. "No, I'm just hoping that you will think it a good idea. One that my parents will go along with. You know they think the world of you."

"And I of them, Kitty. And I of them. They are good people and they want the best for you. I know that. Would you want me to be talking to them about this new plan you've got, this kindergartner thing? I could do that, you know."

"Thank you, Father. I'll let you know about that. I expect that if I tell them that you approve of it, they will approve. If I have any trouble with them, though, I'll come back to you about it."

Kitty fairly skipped the few short blocks home from the rectory. If Father Egan thought it was a good idea, her parents would as well. And this way, she didn't have to mention Aunt Mabel's support of the idea. Father Egan's ideas were much more readily acceptable at home than Aunt Mabel's ideas, she had noticed over the years.

Before turning down her street, Kitty stopped to watch a tough little neighbor boy putting up his fists against another, bigger boy who had challenged him in some way, and she sighed. Life in this neighborhood was far different from the life she had envisioned downtown at Marshall Field's. People here had more children than possessions. And if any one should scrape together more of anything they needed, they would most likely share it with other members of their families, or even others in need. The church made sure that the poor who were always with them were taken care of, with food and coal or wood, with cast-off furniture and clothing. No one went hungry in St. Patrick's parish, but no one was sporting fur coats and French perfumes either.

She wondered what kind of world her future life as a kindergartner might open up for her, hoping that it would be a larger and more interesting world than the one she had been brought up in. She knew she had been lucky, luckier even than her sister Margaret, who had come first in the growing family, when work hadn't been as stable for their father and the number of mouths to feed had increased just about every year. And both her parents had left Ireland after the horrible potato famine, when the people there had died by the hundreds with grass stains around their mouths because that was the only possible thing to eat. She shuddered at the memory of some of the famine horror stories she had heard. She had been so lucky all her life, never going hungry, never being in a household where there was fear about paying the rent or purchasing groceries. She was an American born in Chicago, that exciting and growing metropolis. She felt that she was standing on the threshold of a new and promising life, an opportunity where she could put to use her time and talents to create an even better world in this land of opportunities. Now, if only her parents would agree. But how could they deny her this new future? Especially as Father Egan had already given his blessing.

TWELVE

P ah!" The Frenchman's expression of disgust was so vehement that drops of spittle flew from his mouth onto the sleeve of Henry's wool jacket. "You have given me a picture of a machine, not a building. Where is the art of your design? Where is the spirit? Where is the soul?"

Henry sat up straight, wordless and enraged, staring at his carefully drawn architectural design, each line perfectly straight, each corner etched with an upright at exactly a ninety degree angle, each dimension meticulously marked in his precise, angular hand. His professors back home at the university would have told him, "Well done," and clapped him heartily on the shoulder. Yet this Frenchman, whose noxious perfume barely covered the unpleasant smell of human sweat dried into wool, this Frenchman dressed in such tight pants that his manhood was clearly outlined, this Frenchman whose range of emotion seemed to be limited to a sneer, this Frenchman had actually spat upon him and his work. Henry rubbed his eyes with the back of his hand, trying to avoid rubbing into them the shadows of charcoal that remained on his hands no matter how often he washed them. He had stayed up past midnight last night in his cold and dank room at the pension in order to capture the precision of his thoughts with the accuracy of the lines he drew. His eyes still smarted from the gas residue that permeated the air of his small room, five flights up, but called the *quatrième étage*, in the seventeenth-century building on the rue du Bac.

He admired Paris, its gentle symmetry and wide boulevards imposed upon it by the Baron Haussmann less than a half-century before, soothing him as he walked along the streets between the pension and l'Ecole, watching the green leaves spring out on the branches of the trees. There were at least as many people on the pavements here in Paris as there were in Chicago, but the pulse of the city was so different. In Chicago, he had more a sense of energy, of people who had places to go, people to see, deals to strike and money to make. Here in Paris, the attitude was so much more relaxed. The men and women strolled, they were languid, they took their time to look in the big glass *vitrines* of the shops, to chat, to call out to friends or acquaintances rolling by in the showy horse-drawn broughams or the occasional fume-belching horseless carriages. Maybe it was because it was spring in Paris, with gentle winds and green leaves and flowers appearing—a season remarkable in Chicago mainly for the mud and the abrupt, daily, or even hourly, changes between harsh, bitter winds, blazing sunshine and torrential rains. The people here didn't dress for the weather, as they did back home in Chicago, swathing themselves in layers to protect them from every extreme fluctuation the heavens might bring. No, here in Paris, they dressed for fashion, with the women draped in fine fabrics and sheltered by tiny parasols that would never last in a Chicago rainstorm, and the men wearing high-heeled shoes that would render them immobile in the sucking Chicago mud. Mincing, pretty-boy shoes like those worn by M. Coriot, who had actually spat upon him and his drawing.

Henry looked upon the rendering he had stretched out on the wooden desk before him and smiled. It was an elegant solution to an architectural problem, filling an irregular lot with a structure that, even at six stories, would let in air and light and yet not dominate the setting. And M. Coriot spat upon it because it had no soul. Henry got up from the wooden stool and stretched his arms and shoulders. Bending over a drawing board for hours at a time made him wish to be out on a tennis court hitting white balls into a clear blue sky. He walked down the aisle of students hunched over their own renderings, looking over their shoulders to see what their hands and eyes and imaginations had created. Fanciful things, for the most part—Turkish mosques, Spanish castles, French chateaux. Impossible to build. Ridiculous to place in the context of the setting. Buildings that called attention to themselves like a gold front tooth. He stood still in his tracks, listening to hear M. Coriot praising the work of a fellow student from the university, Joshua Evans, a fairly flamboyant man from St. Louis. Henry could see that the drawing was beautiful, for Evans had a delicate, ornamental hand, and had used colored pencils to great effect. But he could also see that there was no way that fanciful building could ever be constructed, that its massive upper levels would smash the puny foundation below. But who was he to say, Henry thought as he grabbed his hat from the rack and descended the narrow staircase to the freedom of the streets below. Evans's drawing was like the French people he had seen and met, they might look good from afar, but the closer he got, the less substance they seemed to have and they became almost offensive when you really saw what they were, more style than substance. Henry walked along, his hands in his pockets, his head down, over to the wide walks of the *jardin*, where he could sit on a bench and admire what he saw from a distance that kept him safe from a harsher reality.

Springtime in Paris, he thought, as he sat upon the park bench and watched the children rolling their hoops and laughing. A man should be grateful for the opportunity to be here and experience the learning and creations of centuries. But it was just so slow. Even the preparations for the grand exhibition that was opening that spring seemed more about discussions, theories, a lining up of friend and enemy nations, than about action. Henry contrasted that with the excitement and activity of the great 1893 World's Columbian Exposition. In all of Chicago there had been no more exciting event than the immense world's fair that put the city on center stage. But here in Paris, if one brought up the subject of *l'Exposition*, one just received a puzzled glance.

And Henry didn't agree with the way the Parisians regarded the beautiful Tour Eiffel. He recognized it as an engineering accomplishment, similar to the construction of the world's first Ferris wheel for the Columbian Exposition. Yet the commonly held judgment of the Eiffel

94

Tower was that it was an excrescence on Paris's beautiful cityscape, a steel monstrosity.

Henry loved to stroll across the bridge at dusk and view the Eiffel Tower as the lights went on and it lit up the sky as a beacon to the new century to come, when the human race would stand tall in, and against, the sky. He had climbed to the top, too, on one of his first days in Paris, and, amid those immense steel girders, had admired the construction as well as the view of the city stretched out beneath him. He would do that again, he thought, before his university group left Paris for Rome, and he would remember to bring his camera to capture the birds-eye view of this ancient and eternal city.

Henry pulled a pipe out of his coat pocket and clumsily tamped down the tobacco he shook into it from a waxed paper bag. His parents would be appalled at his pipe-smoking, but he embraced it. While back home, it might seem the badge of a bumpkin from the country, here it was seen as more continental, a sign of sophistication. Funny, he thought, as he inhaled deeply to get the pipe going, how one thing can mean something in one place and something else in another. He liked the smell, if not the taste, of the tobacco, fruity and warm, and appreciated even more than that, how it gave him something to do with his hands and mouth while he was thinking. Especially when he was thinking in English and then trying to communicate his thoughts by translating them into French to speak to the natives. "Frogs," his friend Milton called them, the French. Milton claimed that they not only ate frogs but they looked liked them, with their skinny legs and big heads.

Milton had certainly taken to Paris—the expatriate Paris of Americans—in a big way. Through family connections he had been invited to parties at the American embassy and had met the daughter of some wealthy American railroad czar or something and seemed to be head-over-heels in love with her. Milton hardly showed up at l'École any more. He seemed to think that he could do more for his future by pursuing this young woman than he could by pursuing his studies. Perhaps that was true. Henry let his eyes drift over to two women who were walking past him, down toward the river. The hats they were wearing reminded him of birdcages and he laughed to himself at how they would fare in a stiff gust of Chicago wind. He found his mind wandering to thoughts of his winter outing with the fair Miss Katherine Coakley, whose brilliant red lips and apple red cheeks were the result of that cold Chicago wind, not the thick application of *maquillage*, like these two young women. The thought of Miss Coakley made him feel a bit guilty. He had, after all, meant to arrange to see her before his departure from Chicago at the end of January. But the week before his rail trip to New York, and thence the sailing, had been consumed by his mother's demands for shopping and visiting every relative he had ever known or not known, as in the case of some cousins in Woodstock.

"Do you think I'll never return from Europe?" he had asked his mother on the train ride back to the city from McHenry County. "Is that why you persist in showing me off to all these people?"

His mother closed her eyes and sat back in her seat. "One never knows. There are wars and anarchists everywhere these days."

Not that Henry, ensconced in his Paris pension, was aware of such things. But he was lonely, he admitted to himself, and with Milton, his one close friend from home, otherwise engaged, it was difficult not to feel a bit homesick. Perhaps he would write a letter to Miss Kitty Coakley, yes, that's what he would do. Not because he missed her exactly, no, that wasn't quite it because, even though they had attended the same school, they weren't really close. No, he missed her attentiveness, that's what it was, how she really did seem to listen when he told her, over the Wiener schnitzel at Henrici's, about his plans for the future, his plans for Chicago. She actually seemed to believe that he could accomplish what he set out to accomplish. Or at least she didn't laugh at him, or, he shuddered at the thought of it, spit at him. He wondered if he had remembered to pack the address directory he had kept from his Lake View High School days.

Smoking his pipe, musing about how to write a letter describing Paris in such a way as to make it sound inferior to Chicago in order to impress a certain young Chicago lady, Henry sat back on the park bench, more relaxed, he realized, than he had been in the past week as he had worked on the architectural drawing. His eye caught an anomalous sight in the distance, a man running. Parisian men didn't run, they sauntered. He watched steadily as the figure grew closer and larger, idly thinking thoughts about perspective, when he realized the man was his friend Milton Sprague. And he was running from the direction not of l'Ecole, but of their pension. "I say, old man, I've got something for you," said Milton, huffing and puffing as he reached Henry on the wrought iron bench. "It's a telegram." He handed the flimsy paper to Henry.

A telegram—that can only bring bad news, thought Henry, although later he wondered how he had come to that conclusion, having never received a telegram before in his life. Perhaps it was the expression on Milton's face as he struggled to regain his breath after his exertion, perhaps it was the chill that ran down his spine as he read the words that would change the progress of his life.

Sister gravely ill. Return home immediately. Father.

"Eleanor?" asked Milton, stupidly, Henry thought, as if he had any other sister.

"Eleanor," he said, removing the pipe from his mouth and scratching the side of his face with the stem. "I have no idea what it could be. She seemed perfectly fine when I left. And none of their letters have said . . ." A picture of Eleanor came to his mind as she looked when the family waved him off at Central Station in Chicago that January day. She towered over their tiny mother, looking like a creature from a different species, a giraffe next to a . . . he floundered, trying to think of an animal to compare her to that would capture his picture of his mother. Not a seal, exactly, although wrapped in that big fur coat she looked like the sea creatures they loved to watch at the zoo in Lincoln Park. No, with that hat of flowers and feathers, more birdlike, more showy. He looked down at the paper in his hand and read it again: *Return home immediately.*

"So what are you going to do?"

Henry's head jerked up. He had actually forgotten that Milton was standing there, so transported he had been to the scene at the station, the tears on his mother's face, the proud yet envious smile on his sister's face, his father's firm handshake with the one hundred dollar bill tucked inside.

"What am I going to do? It doesn't appear that I have a choice, does it?" Henry looked up at Milton, standing silhouetted in sunlight so bright that he had to blink his eyes several times to keep them from tearing up. Eleanor. What could he do to save her?

"Actually, old man, you do have a choice here. No matter what your father says. It will take you weeks to get home—and by that time . . ." Milton's voice dropped off.

"And by that time, the situation will have resolved itself. Is that what you mean?" Henry asked, feeling a clench of anger in his voice.

"Well, yes. Nothing on your sister, not at all, old man. She's a jolly girl. But, but . . . what can you do? You're not a doctor or anything. And in the meantime, we'll be pulling up stakes here in just a week or two, and it's off to Italy. Do you intend to miss Italy—after all the prints we've seen, and the lectures we've heard, and, and the ruins that are there? Italy!" Milton's voice crept up until his last iteration of the place name came out in a squeak.

Henry remembered that Milton's heiress and her mother were scheduled to spend the summer in a villa outside Florence, and that Milton had plans for long visits there while they were supposed to be sketching Roman villas.

"Italy. What's Italy compared to my only sister, you fool?" Henry stood up and brushed the dust of Paris from his trousers. "Come along, now. I'll need your sweet-talking self to help me get passage back home. I've got to get a steamship ticket immediately. What's sailing today? Or tomorrow? Shake a leg, Milton, I can't waste a minute. Forget this continent. I'm going home to Chicago." Henry grabbed his friend's sleeve and pulled him along. "Let's get moving here."

It wasn't until Henry was actually aboard ship, watching the busy port of Cherbourg recede in the distance, that he allowed himself to think what his ready acceptance of his father's command meant to his own future. He wouldn't be completing the coursework in France and then the travels in Italy and Greece that he needed to complete his degree and graduate. He hadn't taken the time to speak to the resident professor from the university to set up any alternatives, had only left him a terse note about the family situation that had occasioned his sudden leave-taking. And, while he had wired his parents that he would be sailing on the *Kaiser Wilhelm*, originating at Bremerhaven and arriving in New York on May 8, there hadn't been any time to await the receipt of a letter that would explain his sister's illness or update him on her progress. He looked out at the sea-filled horizon ahead of him. All that he could see was water. Of me, it can be said that I am really and truly at sea. I should write that down, he thought, reaching into his coat pocket for a pen. Perhaps now is the time to begin keeping a journal.

But Henry found that the seven long days of the voyage hardly lent themselves to sitting quietly and writing, so filled were they with activities and young people returning home for the summer from their studies, their seasons, and their grand tours. As an unattached young man, he was welcomed by many mothers who wanted their debutante daughters to refocus their ambitions onto American men after Europeans had been examined and found wanting. And Henry, filled with the exhilaration of being released from the demands of his studies, found that he could enjoy himself.

"I swear, I've danced this week more than I danced my whole university career," he told one young lady, a Miss Van Eckert from Rhinebeck, New York.

"You poor boy," she said. "I hope we haven't worn you out." She grabbed his hand and led him back onto the dance floor.

It was a different world aboard the *Kaiser Wilhelm*, more German than French, where Henry felt more relaxed in the correct, almost military postures of his well-dressed German acquaintances than he had with the French. It seemed more like home than he had felt in Paris. The music was more likely to be Strauss for dancing, Beethoven for listening, than the more insubstantial Debussy and Chopin that were being played everywhere in Paris. The food was more substantial too, and more familiar. He could better understand the German people than the French—after all, hadn't his family visited the ancestral homeland three summers before, the summer between his graduation and his matriculation at the university? And the Germans aboard ship were courteous and correct, speaking precisely in English to him and becoming even friendlier when he responded in the German he had learned in his youth. Unlike the French, who would sneer at his accent when he tried to speak their language. The Germans and the French had a history of conflicts, he thought, so it was not surprising that there was no love lost between the two nations. Henry was pleased that fate had given him this opportunity to sail home on a German ship rather than a French one. He had had all he wanted of the French, of that he was most sure. He took the gloved hand of the lovely Miss Van Eckert from Rhinebeck and twirled her around to the heady strains of the *Blue Danube*, the popular waltz by Johann Strauss.

Waking early the next morning, his head aching from the wine and smoke of the night before, Henry lay upon the stateroom bed, his hands beneath his head and stared out the porthole. We'll be landing tomorrow, he thought, and then what? Assuming all was well, should he return to school in Champaign, and resume his studies and somehow still graduate in June? Or should he forget the studies altogether and take up the job he was promised at D. H. Burnham and

Company? Would they take him without a degree? Or perhaps he should look for a job in New York, considering his newfound shipboard friends. Perhaps the party could continue if he chose to live and work in New York.

He must have fallen back to sleep in that position, because when the steward came, bringing fresh towels, Henry jerked awake, muttering a mild curse at the ache in his head and upper arms. He returned briefly to thoughts of his future as he washed up and shaved, thinking darkly that it didn't do to plan ahead, his actions would depend upon what he found at home and what his parents would expect of him. As he packed up his belongings, he resolved that he would build the arguments he needed for the path he planned to take, whatever that would be. New York held its charms, as did Chicago. And why complete his studies, when opportunity, no doubt, awaited him and his skills in any of the burgeoning cities of North America?

THIRTEEN

M ud, mud, mud. If there was anything that Kitty hated it was the slimy mud that oozed up from Chicago's wet and dirty streets after a heavy rain, a foul-smelling stew of manure and garbage and who knew what else. It sucked up around the soles of her boots, weighed down the hem of her skirt, and even splattered her stockings. As awful as squishing through the fresh mud was brushing off dried mud with the horrible stench of its origins from the street and sewers. She sat in the drafty entryway into their cottage, an apron covering her dress and a scarf wrapped around her hair to protect it from the dirt and dust. She held her breath and attacked her boots once more with her brush in her attempt to remove the gobs of dried mud with their leaves and sticks and whatever else that held them together like bricks. She wasn't going to be embarrassed going to church with mud lines on her boots showing how deeply her foot had sunk into the mud the day before. It felt good to hit the boot hard with the brush, as if she were hitting … no, not her father, nor her mother … but their hard-headed Irish stubborn belief that more education wasn't good for a girl, not their daughter.

Once she had Father Egan's support, she thought that convincing her parents would be a piece of cake. So she had waltzed into the parlor the evening before—having done all the washing up and even folded her apron in front of the fire—to tell them about her decision to become a kindergartner. The room was dark except for the reflected light from the fire, they hadn't yet lit the gaslights. So her parents seemed to be two actors on a stage, waiting to say their lines. Her mother was sitting on the sofa in front of the fire, her father standing, with an elbow on the mantel, softly talking about God knows what, when she came in. She probably should have noticed the solemn expressions on their faces and her mother's pallor, but she was sparkling with the idea that her future would be something other than housework.

"I've made a decision," she announced, pleased that none of her brothers were around to make fun of her confident air. There was nothing they loved so much as to take someone down a peg who was struggling to rise above his or her station.

"So, this decision, Kitty, has it anything to do with us?" Her father's expression remained serious.

"Not really," she said. "It has to do with me, and what I want to do with my life."

"And what could that possibly be?" asked her mother, her tired face taking on a glimmer of interest. "I daresay it's someone we know?" She looked almost smug, then, as if she were aware of something that Kitty hadn't said.

"It isn't what you're thinking about, Ma," Katie said, recognizing her mother's implication. "It's about a job. Or at least, the schooling to get a job."

"Schooling, haven't you had enough of that?" said her father, slapping his hand down on the mantel. "Haven't you been in school your whole life?"

"This is a different type of schooling. It's to become a kindergartner, a teacher of little children."

"A kindergartner? Sounds like some foreign thing. You don't have it in your head to go off to some foreign land and be someone else, do you? You're exactly where you're supposed to be, Kitty Coakley, where God put you and watches over you." Her father's face, flushed already from the heat of the fire, grew even redder.

"You're not leaving home, Kitty, are you?" her mother asked faintly. "You know I depend upon having you here to help."

"And she'll be needing you more and more," Kitty's father said angrily. "You know . . ."

Mrs. Coakley held her hand up to stop him. "Shush," she said gently.

"Now don't go jumping ahead of me with your thinking," Kitty said, trying to remain calm. "Just hear me out. Father Egan thought this was a grand idea."

"Just remember I'm your father here, not some soft-handed priest," her father muttered.

"Yes, Da, you know I would never do anything without your permission. It's just that this is a new program, right here in Chicago, and I met the woman who is going to teach it, Mrs. Campbell, she's one of Aunt Mabel's customers."

"Ah, Mabel, is it? Her with her ideas of women working and even getting the vote. You'd best stop listening to that anarchist if you want to stay under this roof," her mother said bitterly, pounding on the sofa cushion next to her.

Kitty was taken aback by what her mother said. She knew her mother wasn't fond of her sister-in-law, but she rarely expressed it aloud, her dislike usually simmered beneath her words like a kettle about to boil. And she had no idea where her mother had gotten the word "anarchist," or even if she knew what it meant. Usually when someone attacked her aunt, Kitty would fight back, but she didn't want any argument about her new plan.

"Well, this wasn't Aunt Mabel's idea—not at all," Kitty said, keeping her voice soft. "You see, we were just having a cup of tea, when this woman came by, a woman that she knew because she had sold her some hats, that's all, and the woman came from Wisconsin to head up this program in Chicago, she got the okay from the Chicago Board of Education, and it's going to start in the fall, here in Chicago, and, and . . . and I said that I'd sign up for her classes." Kitty stood tall and lifted her chin as she said this. She had made a decision and she was going to go through with it, no matter what her parents said.

"Now you listen to me, young lady," her father began, but her mother shushed him.

"Just wait a minute, Michael, let's hear the girl out. She hasn't said yet exactly what it is she plans to do."

Kitty took a deep breath and started off as calmly as she could. "The Chicago schools offer a program to train young women, decent young women from good families, to be kindergartners. Kindergartens are classes of young children who will sing and learn and grow up to be good Americans," she said, holding back in her mind that it was a German program originally. Her parents believed that all the evil in the world came from across the ocean, and this was something they just didn't need to know. "And kindergartners are the teachers that help them learn and grow. Like gardeners in a garden, a garden of children." She tried to read their faces to see how they were reacting. Her father had moved from the fireplace to sit down next to her mother on the couch, and his face seemed to be cooling off.

Kitty felt her whole body tense, as if she were ready to fight. She had never been one to give up easily. Even when she was little, and her brothers had tried to pin her to the ground, she would struggle and lash out with her fists and her feet, screeching like a banshee her mother used to say, until whichever brother it was would back off and walk away, afraid not just that the inequity of the attack would bring down parental wrath, but that little Kitty herself might do him some bodily harm. "So what do you think?" she whispered.

Her mother sighed, and her father looked into the fire. "I don't suppose we can stop you," he said, keeping his eyes on the flames. "You always end up doing whatever it is you want anyway. But don't think just because you're going to school you can stop helping your mother here. She's getting older, you know—aren't we all—and all the washing and the ironing and all, well, that's taking its toll on her. She needs your help, and you being a good girl, I know you're going to keep living here, and helping her, helping me really, because it's my job to take care of the family."

"Of course, of course," Kitty said, practically jumping with joy. "I'll not be going anywhere, I'll be right here, with you. Yes, I'll go off to classes, and perhaps I'll have to spend some time away—I'll sleep here every night and I'll be here every day to help out—I won't go letting you and mother down. It's not like me." Kitty knew that she would promise anything to get their permission to follow this path. She wondered if they could ever understand just what this new plan meant to her—an open door, a way out, an escape route. A promise that her future would not consist only of soiled nappies, and muddy boots, the cooking of vast pots of stew and the laundering of work clothes stiff with mud and God knows what else. It would be a step up into a professional world, a cleaner world, where there were ladies and gentlemen, not just laborers and launderers.

She attacked her boots once more with the brush, bringing the energy of all her dreams for the future into each swipe. Maybe it wouldn't be easy, but she hadn't expected her life to be easy. She was a Chicagoan, born and bred, and Chicagoans didn't back down. She thought about the story she had heard as a child, a story told to every schoolchild in Chicago, about the man who wasn't going to let the newly settled city of Chicago sink down into the mud. What was his name? Ah yes, it was George Pullman, but before he made his millions on the railroad cars, back some fifty years or so ago, when Chicago was just a rough and rowdy Western town. He had just come to Chicago, and he was staying at the hotel downtown, what was its name? The Tremont House, that's it, at Lake and Clark. He found everyone talking about how the hotel was sinking into the bottomless swamp on which the city had been built. No one could figure out how they could pull the hotel out of the mud, because it was solidly made of brick. And Mr. Pullman said he could do it. He got a thousand men or more and set up hundreds of jackscrews in the basement of the hotel. When he gave the signal, each man gave the jackscrews a half turn. Inch by inch, so gently that no one in the hotel could feel or hear anything, the building rose up from the mud. It was one of the great Chicago stories, an example of why the settlement on the muddy shore of Lake

Michigan grew so quickly into the major metropolis it had become. Because people of vision came there, and they refused to give up. She gave her boot one last lash of the brush, and thought, and I'm one of them.

Her father appeared above her and asked, "Are you ready to leave for Mass now?" He was pulling on his overcoat. It was the end of April, which should have been the beginning of spring, but Chicagoans learned not to trust the calendar when it came to predicting the weather.

"Almost, Da. Just need to take off my apron and put on a nicer headscarf." Kitty raced into her room to change.

It wasn't until they were halfway down the block that Kitty noticed that her mother hadn't come out of the cottage behind her father. "Where is she?" she asked, pulling the scarf from across her mouth, where the wind had whipped it in a savage thrust.

"Your mother? Ah, she's feeling a bit under the weather this morning. And isn't this some weather that we're under." He had smashed his hat down on the top of his head with his hand, in order to keep it from flying away.

As they walked the few blocks to the church, the heavy wind pushing them from behind, Kitty felt guilty that she hadn't been aware that her mother wasn't feeling well. It wasn't like her mother at all to miss Mass. She must be truly ill. She felt her skirt dragging in the fresh mud and, as she walked, she could feel the mud spatter upward, begriming her stockings beneath her skirt. Staying clean in Chicago demanded constant effort.

They joined the throng of parishioners climbing the steps into the church. This early Mass attracted mostly the older folks, people Kitty's age were more likely to sleep in after a wild Saturday night. She glimpsed Brian ahead with his father, and waved to him. The Kellehers had always attended this Mass and usually sat in the same pew with the

Coakleys. Brian hadn't used to attend this early Mass with his father, for, like Kitty's brothers, he slept in on a Sunday morning. But when his mother had fallen ill last winter, and so quickly passed away, he began accompanying his father.

Mr. Coakley led Kitty to the pew and then stepped back to let her go in first, sitting next to Mr. Kelleher. Kitty smiled at him, and then, throwing her hair back over her shoulders, knelt to say a prayer for her mother. She loved the rituals of the Mass, the warm glow of the candles, the tickle of incense in her nose, the familiar music, even the elegant satins and silks of the priest's vestments. She felt safe and supported, listening and responding to the Latin prayers, moving to the intricate choreography of standing and kneeling, bowing and genuflecting. But all the beauty of it receded into the background of her mind as she pondered what could be wrong with her mother. Her guilt intensified as she realized that she had been too busy thinking about her own self and her plans to notice how her mother was doing. Yes, she had seemed pale last night, when they were talking about Kitty's plans to become a kindergartner, but who wasn't pale after a long Chicago winter?

She tried not to have her attention diverted by Brian, sitting on the other side of his father, but her awareness of him penetrated through her guilt about her mother. He was wearing his heavy, dark green jacket, she had noticed, and she thought she even could smell his woody, sawdust smell from where she sat. The familiar sounds and rhythms of the Mass lulled her into a fugue state, where she alternated between her concern for her mother and her interest in what Brian might be thinking about her. As the last "*Ite missa est*" with its answer of "Amen" from the parishioners echoed in the emptying church, she jumped up from the pew and hurried down the aisle behind her father's long-legged lope. Brian would catch up, she knew, the Coakleys and Kellehers usually walked home together after Mass.

"He's such a good boy," Kitty's mother would say whenever she saw Brian walking alongside his father. His youth, energy, and good looks contrasted strongly with his father's depressed face and stooped body. She

108

thought Mr. Kelleher looked like a turtle compressing itself to escape back into its shell.

Brian did catch up to Kitty just as she and her father made the turn up Adams, and Kitty's father fell back to walk with Mr. Kelleher. "So your mother's ill, I hear," Brian said, a worried look on his face. "She hardly ever misses Mass on Sunday, does she?"

Kitty looked up into his face and saw his genuine concern. She adjusted her smile to his mood, and said, "I know. I was praying for her through the whole Mass, wasn't I? I only hope that God in His mercy will see fit to bring her back to good health."

Brian nodded, and they trudged together in silence, as if burdened together by this worry. The sharp wind in their faces made it difficult to look ahead, and they both had their faces down toward the pavement, such as it was. The harsh winter had cracked the paving stones in places, and it was difficult to maneuver through the obstacle course the pavement had become.

Kitty thought about sharing with Brian her exciting plans for the future, of becoming a kindergartner and cultivating a garden of children, but she hesitated, knowing that anything she told Brian would soon reach the ears of one or another of her brothers. She wasn't ready to release the idea to their scrutiny and most likely their jeering, it was too fragile a thought yet, like a flower still emerging from the mud. She'd wait until it was a stronger and healthier plant before she would share it with anyone who might trample her dreams.

They reached the intersection where she would turn right, and he turn left, and stopped. Brian leaned down over her and brushed her cheek with his lips. "I hope your mother gets to feeling much better," he whispered in her ear. "I know how much you care for her." And then his father caught up to him, and the two of them turned south, while Kitty's father came next to her and they headed north.

Kitty felt her eyes prickling with tears, not because of his soft kiss, but his concern about her mother. She had almost forgotten again that her mother was sick, so closely was she hugging the idea of her new future to her chest. She realized that her mother's health could easily play a bigger part in her future than any plans she might make, and she hurried to keep up with her father's long-legged gait toward home.

FOURTEEN

F inally, when it seemed as if winter would go on forever, the season changed and summer came upon Chicago like an unexpected kiss. All around, the world became green, the trees arching over the streets, turning them into cool, green tunnels. Wildflowers bloomed everywhere, lining the streets, circling the houses, sprouting out of the cracks between the paving stones. The smells of the street were diminished, even the odor of road apples the horses left behind seemed less pungent in the bouquet of scents that awaited Kitty as she stepped outdoors. She stood on the stoop and breathed in deeply. Feeling the warmth on her skin and smelling the greenery made her feel more energetic than ever, as if her hibernation had come to an end, and she needed to make up for the months spent dozing.

With her mother's health still of concern, and her sister's pregnancy burgeoning, Kitty became the domestic resource for the two households. Her moments of breathing the fresh, clean air were limited to those spent pinning laundry to the clothesline and carrying meals down the street to Margaret's house. Three-year old Sean became her constant companion, tugging at her skirt and slowing her steps as she carried the hot containers of food or wet mounds of linens. She would stand patiently at first, wiping her forehead with her forearm, as he asked question after question about the neighborhood and the vehicles that rattled down its cobbled streets.

"That's a milk cart," she'd say. "That man delivers the milk to the people who live around here."

"Why?" he'd ask, his blue eyes looking up at her as if she knew the answer to every question in the world.

"Well, to make sure the children drink their milk to make them grow up big and strong."

"Why?" He teetered on the edge of the road, watching the cart go by as if he were about to dash after it.

"Well, Sean, we all want to grow up big and strong."

"Why?"

She grabbed his collar to keep him back from the road and wondered why small children asked so many questions. Did all children ask questions constantly? Would she have to deal with the same persistence as a kindergartner, multiplied by a dozen or so? Yes but, she rationalized to herself, she wouldn't have to be cooking and washing up at the same time. The children would be different, and they wouldn't be her relations. And, she'd be able to leave them behind when she left school.

When she could turn her undivided attention to Sean, she enjoyed teaching him games like throwing a ball into a basket, and singing the songs she had been taught as a child. All the attention she poured upon the child, however, just made him cling to her all the more, and she wondered some days if she'd ever get to live her own life again. While her mother and her sister slept most of the day, she never knew when they might wake and ask for a cool drink or a back rub. And they didn't encourage any conversation that didn't have to do with themselves.

Fortunately, Brian came over most days before dinner, even when her brothers weren't around. Although Brian's habit of silence had once bothered her, she found the silence and his presence comforting. They didn't need to talk, she thought. Probably, she knew what he would say. He'd go off to the lumberyard with his father each morning, deal with customers who would want two-by-fours and such, and come back home to dinner again with his father. His wasn't a very exciting life either.

So she was surprised the day he offered to take her to a beer garden on the North Side that Saturday evening.

"Won't you come with me?" he asked, looking not at her but at Sean, running around in circles in the open land behind the cottage. "A fella told me that they have a great band at this Bismarck Gardens, up there in the German neighborhood. And they know a little bit about beer there too."

Kitty remembered her classmates talking about the Bismarck Gardens, at Halsted, Broadway and Grace, not that far from Lake View High School. It was a very German place, where families gathered to sing and dance and perhaps drink a stein or two. Brian's mention of the German neighborhood gave her a twinge, because she hadn't thought about Henry Thomas in weeks, what with not hearing from him at all since the note she had received from him after their dinner at Henrici's. He was most likely still in Europe, she thought, and even less likely to be run into at the Bismarck Gardens. It was a loud and rowdy place, she had heard, not a likely place for him. "Yes, I'd love to go," she said. "And we can dance away our troubles." She too looked at Sean, and sighed. It was time for him to take a nap, but she hadn't the energy for the tussle it would take to get him inside the cottage. She smiled up at Brian, "I'll look forward to it."

Brian smiled in return, and raised his hand in salute. "I'd best go now," he said, "Father will be wanting his supper." And he sauntered down the street as if he hadn't a care in the world.

Kitty sighed. Between his aging father and the growing competition they were getting from bigger lumberyards, Brian had a lot on his shoulders. They both deserved a night out, dancing. She felt her toes tapping already as she picked up the dirty little boy from the puddle made from the washing water she had thrown out that morning and escorted him into the indoor gloom to take his nap before dinner.

It had been a hot day, and Kitty and Brian appreciated the coolness of the lake breeze when they stepped off the electric car on Halsted, at the corner where the Bismarck Gardens lit up the sky. Brian was all slicked up, as her brothers would say, in a black suit, white shirt, and a green tie that she recognized as one of his father's. Kitty herself had on her white dress that had been new for Easter, with a pretty pink ribbon for a belt to make it more summery. Her hair was pinned up in a way she felt made her look more sophisticated, and atop the pompadour, she wore a pink curve of a hat, secured well with hair pins so it wouldn't take flight while she danced. The band blared loudly, the tuba especially strong, as they walked among the crowded tables to find a seat beneath the trees. The strong beat made Kitty want to head for the dance floor immediately, but Brian was intent upon finding a table and ordering a first round to "wet his whistle," as he said.

Kitty looked around at the faces of the crowd, wondering if she would run into anyone she knew under the electric lights hanging from the trees. Usually, when she and Brian would enter a saloon in the neighborhood, they would be greeted by many of their friends and neighbors. This was different, entering an unfamiliar part of the city. She thought she recognized some of girls she'd gone to high school with, but it was difficult to tell, as many of the women were wearing big hats that shaded their faces. She smiled left and right, as if she knew everyone, and sat down at the wire table where Brian had pulled out a chair for her. "Do you see anyone you know?" she asked him, patting her pompadour to make sure it had held up.

"Not a one," he said. "Makes you realize what a big city Chicago is, don't it?"

Kitty looked at the people seated at the tables around her. There must have been hundreds of them, smiling, laughing, singing along with the music. It was a wonder—as many people at least who'd fill St. Pat's at a Christmas or Easter Mass—and she didn't know one of them. It was thrilling, that's what it was, to think that the beer garden was full of people she might possibly know one day. Beer garden, kinder garden—the Germans seemed to love their gardens, didn't they? She amused herself trying to guess which of the patrons were Germans and which Irish, deciding that the Germans were the plumper ones, more likely to be sitting with families, while the Irish had the thinner faces, and were more likely to be in crowds of young men than families. Then she found exceptions to her rules and gave up trying to classify and just settled in to enjoy the music. Brian returned with a dripping stein of beer for himself and a frosty glass of lemonade for her. "They said a waitress would come around soon," he said, plopping himself down next to Kitty. "But I got us something for the wait."

Looking over the edge of her glass at Brian, Kitty thought about how good-looking he was. His work at the lumberyard had built up his shoulders and tanned his face, and he looked healthy and strong. She noticed the white stripe on his forehead that showed he had his hair cut for the occasion. Perhaps her sister Margaret was right, and she wouldn't find a better man than Brian. He was in no hurry to settle down, what with the lumberyard and his father as his responsibilities. Perhaps that was good, she needed time herself to try out being a kindergartner, and there was plenty of time ahead of them.

Brian finished his pint, and wiped his mouth with his sleeve. "Time to dance," he said, knocking his chair over as he got up from the table. He set it upright, and then stretched out his hand to her to bring her to the open-air dance floor.

The band was loud and brassy, the crowd was lively, and Kitty and Brian danced to one song after another. They waltzed serenely to the *Blue Danube* and other Strauss waltzes, and do-si-doed in an elaborate country dance. With dozens of other couples, they galumphed around the floor to the *Beer Barrel Polka*. Finally, breathless and laughing, they returned to their table for another round of cold drinks, while a much-heralded exotic dancer performed on the stage. It was cooler under the trees than it had been on the dance floor.

Kitty had been curious, as well as a bit worried, about this Miss Evan Burrows Fontaine, who was advertised as a decorative, interpretive classic dancer. She wondered if she was like the exotic dancers who performed on the Midway at the Columbian Exposition. Not that she was old enough at the time to have seen the dancers, although she remembered her older brothers hooting and hollering about them. She found the fully dressed dancer's bare feet and seductive poses more amusing than erotic and thought the music that accompanied her was rather shrill. Brian, however, couldn't keep his eyes off the dancer, except to order another stein of beer from the dirndl-clad waitress.

"What did you think of her?" she asked Brian as the dancer left the stage, a cloud of scarves wafting around her body.

"Who? The lady who was dancing?" he replied, turning back to the table and Kitty.

"Yes, her. Did you like her?" Kitty was curious about the effect the woman had on Brian.

"She was pretty, but not as pretty as you." He gulped his drink. "And she was a pretty good dancer. But you're a better dancer, Kitty. And prettier. But I didn't think what she was doing was . . . proper, you know. I don't think your mother would approve if you danced like that." He sat up straighter in his chair and ran his hand through his sweaty hair, making it stick up like a farm boy's. "Probably not your dad, either."

"I wasn't planning on dancing like that," Kitty said sharply. "Egyptian dancing, that's what she called it. Didn't look like Egyptian to me, not that I've seen such a thing."

The band had started up again. "You're a much better dancer, Kitty," Brian said, finishing his beer, and standing up to escort her back to the dance floor.

They danced for another hour, until the band started up with *Good Night, Ladies,* and returned to their seats for what Brian called "just one more beer." He ordered two for himself, as well as a lemonade for Kitty when the German waitress came by for the last call. The band had left the stage, and the lights were dimming. Most of the others had gone, and Kitty could hear the wind whistling through the trees. She shivered. The night air was getting cold.

"Time to go?" she said to Brian, who had removed his jacket, unknotted his tie, and rolled up the sleeves of his once-white shirt and slumped back in his seat.

"Time to go," he repeated, and started to get up with an effort.

Busboys had cleared all the tables around them, and were waiting in the shadows to finish theirs. Kitty reached out her hand to Brian and tugged him from his seat. "Come on, Brian, and don't forget your jacket. The cars don't run all night."

Brian nodded and stumbled with her to the gate. Broadway was dark, except where the cones of light fell from the gas lamps, and nearly deserted. Kitty could hear murmurs from the beer garden as workers finished up, but little else. The corner of the city that had seemed so lively just an hour before, now seemed as quiet as a prairie. She shivered again in the cold night air, and wished she had brought a wrap with her.

Brian leaned against the wall, and said to her, "Come over here, I'll keep you warm." He reached out a strong arm and pulled her toward him until they were facing each other. Brian's face had changed with the drink, she noticed, and his arms drew her closer. Kitty tried to move away from his beery breath, she felt trapped. But any time she'd draw back, Brian would move closer in, clutching her tighter. She could feel the hard bulge at his midsection that she thought at first must be his belt buckle, but then she realized what it was as he moved one hand up from her waist and fumbled with the buttons on her dress.

"Brian, no!" she said and pulled away from him, her face blazing with shame. Out here in the open, on a public street, what would her mother say?

The streetcar pulled into sight, and Kitty fixed her clothing and tried to calm her racing heart. She climbed aboard without waiting for Brian, who shuffled on behind her and threw a few coins into the fare box before sitting down next to her.

Brian slept on the way home, but Kitty remained alert. As they rode into downtown, she saw more people on the street, men mostly, and many of them staggering. She shivered again, although it was warmer on the streetcar. The dark seemed more ominous than it had under the trees in the beer garden. Yes, this was a big city, and anything could happen. She knew Brian was drunk, but having him next to her was some protection. She hoped that any more protection than he provided wouldn't be needed and that she wouldn't need protection from him. She felt uneasy until Brian had walked her as if in a trance to her front door, and raised his hand in farewell. He was asleep on his feet, she thought. I wonder if he'll remember what he was trying to do to me. She stepped out of her dancing shoes and into her soft, comfortable slippers. Ahh, that feels good, she thought, and tiptoed toward her bedroom, hoping not to wake up her family.

Fifteen

I t wasn't until the *Kaiser Wilhelm* landed in New York that Henry allowed himself to think about what lay ahead for him. He had had no communication aboard ship with his family, and he expected that there would be a message awaiting him when they docked. What he hadn't expected was his Uncle Herman Thomas, a bulky, bearded man in a black coat and tie and bowler, patiently waiting for him just outside the customs shed. Uncle Herman never spoke much, but Henry could read from the expression on his face that the news he had to bring wasn't good news.

"Uncle Herman, tell me," Henry implored, still feeling slightly off-balance on solid ground. "What is the news of Eleanor?"

Herman looked at him sadly. "She's gone," he said. "We buried her at Graceland last Saturday. Next to Oma. We had hoped that she could hold out until you returned, but that sickness . . ." He pulled a black-bordered handkerchief from his pocket and loudly blew his nose into it.

"But what was the sickness?" Henry asked. He wished the jostling crowd around them would disappear, he wished they were home in the parlor at Kennesaw Terrace, without the terrible distance of the train ride before them.

Herman mopped his eyes with the handkerchief and returned it to his pocket. "It was cholera, that's what Dr. Geiger said. She went so quickly, Sonny, that I don't believe she knew what took her."

Cholera. It was a common death sentence in Chicago even before it had become a city, with nearly annual epidemics taking hundreds of lives. And cholera was one of the many diseases that were said to be water borne. His father's magnificent project, the reversal of the flow of the Chicago River, had been designed to put an end to such diseases. But it didn't save Eleanor.

Henry slept in the comfortable seat on the train, bolstered by the reassuring bulk of Uncle Herman, as it steamed overnight through the industrial wastelands of New Jersey and then the green open fields of Pennsylvania, Ohio and Indiana. When he awoke, the sun was rising over Lake Michigan, and they were riding north along the lakeshore to the city center. Henry rubbed his eyes. He had slept deeply and he knew that he had dreamed, dreams of himself and Eleanor playing in the sand of that same lakeshore, but in his reentry into the conscious world, those dreams evaporated away.

As the train pulled into the new Grand Central Station at Wells and Harrison, Uncle Herman said, "No one will be meeting us. We'll take a cab to your house."

Henry was relieved that he would have time on the long cab ride home to the North Side to compose his thoughts. He dreaded going home to a house that didn't contain Eleanor, which had never been the case before. He didn't know what to say to his father, or worse yet, his mother. He knew that grown men didn't cry, yet try as hard as he might, he couldn't stop that prickly feeling in the back of his throat or the welling fullness behind his eyes.

When they left the train, walking down the platform and emerging in the great hall of the station that had been built ten years before, Henry was overcome with the sensation of energy that came from the hustle and bustle of the place. He could see the faces of many nations, of every hue. Mixed in amongst the crowd were hearty boys in blue, large-boned policemen, usually with beefy Irish faces, scanning the crowds and smacking their own gloved palms with their wooden clubs. Stalls set up around the edges of the great hall offered everything from coffee and sandwiches to flowers and newspapers, the cries of their vendors mixing in with the general din of the scene. Henry took in a deep breath of the bouquet of strong odors, trains and people and food, and smiled. I'm home, he thought, I'm actually home.

119

Outside the station, the sun burned brightly on the fine May morning. As the carriage patiently crept through the throngs of pedestrians, bicyclists, vans and carriages of all sorts, Henry looked eagerly around at all the signs of growth and vitality that marked his native city. Before he had left for France, he had read that the population of Chicago had grown from fewer than thirty thousand inhabitants in 1850 to more than one million by 1900. From his window seat in the carriage, it appeared that they had all descended upon the city at once.

As they turned off Lake Shore Drive and onto Kennesaw Terrace, Henry felt the pangs of anxiety clutch his stomach. What could he possibly say to his parents? The carriage stopped by the curb in front of the house and Henry could see the black mourning wreath on the front door, alerting the neighbors to a recent death in the family. The door swung open, and out strode his father, attired in a familiar business suit, but with a wide black armband enclosing his sleeve above the elbow. Even from a distance, Henry could see how uncharacteristically drawn his father's face looked, how even his usually bright white mane of hair looked tired and flattened. Close behind him came his mother, dressed completely in black, a color she rarely wore because she claimed it made her look "so washed out." Washed out and wrung out, thought Henry, in those few moments that it took him to ascend the steps and embrace her. His mother looked as if she'd aged ten years or more in the three short months he had been away from home.

"Oh Mother," Henry said, his arms around her. "I'm so sorry, I'm so sorry." The tears that he had blinked back for so long now came to his eyes.

His mother broke away from his embrace and wiped the tears from her own eyes with the back of her hand. "She tried, you know. Eleanor tried to hold out until you came home. She wanted to see you again, she said, to say good-bye. But the cholera was stronger than she was. The cholera took our Eleanor away."

Henry Senior had gone down the path to join Uncle Herman in wresting the suitcases from the carriage. Henry welcomed the interruption of his father and uncle with the suitcases and grabbed the heaviest from his father's hand, preferring action to standing there still not knowing what to say to his mother. Thus, they all entered the house, and Henry and his uncle struggled with the heavy suitcases up the stairs to his room.

"I'll have Maggie prepare some lunch for you, Henry," his mother called softly up the stairs. "We can all sit in the dining room, and you can tell us about Paris."

Before he came downstairs to join them, Henry opened his smallest case to get his brush and comb in order to tidy up his hair and mustache. Digging through the case, he came upon a bundle wrapped in one of his softest cashmere sweaters. He unwrapped it to find the fine Limoges china version of the Eiffel Tower that he had bought for his sister just after he arrived in Paris and climbed to the top of the strong and graceful structure. He had intended to give her the china knickknack and tell her all about the tower and the climb and the view. He would compare it to when he had ridden to the top of the Ferris Wheel at the Columbian Exposition and waved to her, a mere speck on the ground, while looking out at the broad landscape of Chicago spread below.

As he placed the china statue on his bureau, he wondered if Eleanor was now in a place far above the clouds, watching him on earth where he would appear as a tiny speck below. He despised those Sunday school descriptions of heaven and the afterlife, but at times like these, he had to admit they were reassuring. He had never lived a life without his older sister before, so he would like to think that somehow she would still remain a part of his life on earth.

෯

When Henry entered the dining room Maggie was placing a plate full of sandwiches made of fragrant, home-baked rye bread at his habitual place at the table. She too wore black, and the starched white apron that covered her ample bulk also was trimmed with a black ribbon border.

"So sorry for your loss, Master Henry," she said as she passed him on her way back into the kitchen. Her red-rimmed eyes clearly showed Henry that the loss of Eleanor was Maggie's loss as well. He would have liked to acknowledge her sentiments, but he couldn't bring the words from his throat into the air. The dining room had for him the unreal feel of a stage setting—his parents seated in their normal seats, his father at the head of the lace-covered table, his mother at his right. His own place at his father's left. The only jarring note was Uncle Herman in Eleanor's place, looking tired and rumpled after his all-night train ride. No one spoke, and his mother sighed wearily as her teaspoon clinked against the side of the delicate china cup when she stirred her coffee. His father stared into his own cup as if some secret message might be contained in its inky depths. A sense of exhaustion pervaded the room, emotional as well as physical.

Henry cleared his throat to prepare to speak and all faces turned to him expectantly. "I'm so sorry," he stammered, repeating the words he had said to his mother on the doorstep. "So sorry. I don't know what else to say. I wish I had been here. I wish I could have seen Eleanor. I wish . . ."

His mother lifted her tired eyes to his. "That's all right, Sonny. We know. But you're here now, and here you will stay." She managed a weak smile and resumed stirring her coffee. For a few more moments the only sound in the room was the rhythmic clinking of silver against china. Henry stared at the sandwiches set before him, wondering if the lump in his throat would ever go away, if he would ever be able to swallow again.

Finally, his father broke the silence. "Well, I must be off," he said in a voice that sounded almost normal. He placed his big hands on either side of the lace placemat and lifted himself into a standing position. "No rest for the wicked, I'm afraid. They're expecting me at the office this afternoon." He came around the side of the table and clapped Henry on the shoulder. "Good to have you home, son, safe and sound. Perhaps we'll be able to go out for a ride in the next day or two. I'd like to show you the progress we've been making down near the Ogden Slip." And he left the room.

His burst of energy seemed to dispel the gloomy pall that had settled over the table. Uncle Herman pulled his turnip of a watch out of his coat pocket, consulted it, and said, "I'd best be on my way, as well. Duty calls." And he too left the room, leaving Henry alone with his mother.

Anna Thomas shaded her eyes with one hand, as if the light in the room were too bright, and once again stirred her untouched coffee until Henry wanted to take the spoon from her hand and say, "Talk. Don't stir. I'm here, even if Eleanor is not." But he kept his peace, and devoted his attention to the thick ham and cheese sandwich before him.

His mother spoke. "Henry, I feel one of my sick headaches coming on. Do you suppose . . .?" She let her sentence trail off.

Henry recognized his mother's need to retreat from the situation. "That's quite all right, Mother," he said. "Why don't you go and have a little lie-down? The rest will do you good."

"Thank you, dear," Anna Thomas said to her son as she too left the room. "We'll see you again at supper."

Henry sat for a moment before his empty plate. He hadn't realized how hungry he had been. Nor how satisfying Maggie's solid slabs of meat and bread would be. He stretched his arms and shoulders. From the pool of sunlight that sneaked into the room despite the heavy velvet portieres, he could see that outside it was a fine spring day. Perhaps he could go out for a walk, maybe down to the beach to give notice to Lake Michigan that he, the wanderer, had returned to its shore. On his way upstairs to fetch his jacket, though, he noticed a silver tray on the sideboard in the hall, heaped high with envelopes, many adorned with black edges. He recognized them as sympathy notes, familiar to him from when his grandmother died, not so very long before. He knew he would be expected to help his mother answer them eventually. He was torn. He ached to go outside and breathe the fresh air of the lakeshore. But he knew it was his duty to read the notes so that he could acknowledge the senders who had been so kind to take the time to write them. He sat down on the stairs to think. It didn't take long. The loss of his sister was so unreal to him that he knew he had to do something to feel it, like biting down on an ailing tooth to experience the pain. He got up, picked up the tray, and brought it with him into the parlor. Perhaps taking the time to read these letters would bring her back to him for a short while and help assuage the guilt he felt for not being there when she needed him.

It was a painful afternoon for Henry. Many people had written their reminiscences of Eleanor as a kind person, a thoughtful person, a helping person. He learned about how she had shared her own lunches with a friend throughout her years of high school, because that friend had no money to buy her own lunch. A friend from art school wrote how Eleanor, "Ellie," she called her, helped her conquer her fear of the spinning potter's wheel, even as the clay of Eleanor's own creation was drying out on the table behind them. A distant cousin out near Palatine wrote how grateful she and her daughters were when Eleanor would send them her cast-off—and "hardly worn"—clothing to share with them. Henry found himself wiping away the tears as he sat and read these touching sentiments in the quiet house. Eleanor. His Nora. What he would give if she would suddenly appear at the parlor door, and say, "Anyone for tennis?" or "How about a ride along the beach?" Or even, "Sonny, if you're so bright, why can't you . . ." and any one of a number of complaints about his behavior would emerge from her smiling mouth. Henry buried his head in his hands, beyond tears. Eleanor, his sister, his friend. And most of all, his ally against their loving parents, who always knew what was best for both of them, whether they believed it or not.

As Henry washed up and changed for dinner, he braced himself for a repetition of the silent lunch he had endured. His parents seemed so deeply into their sorrow—his mother wallowing in it, his father denying it—that he felt the burden of dealing with them heavy on his own shoulders. Should he prattle on about the joys and disappointments of Paris? Or try to draw them out about what they had undergone during Eleanor's last days? Or relate to them the touching stories he had read in that pile of sympathy notes? He wasn't sure that he could put up with the family tradition of silence during the meal. Not now. Not when there was so much to say.

When Henry entered the dining room, his parents were already seated and Maggie was serving the soup. His mother smiled gently at him, his father started immediately on his soup. As Henry sipped from his own bowl, searching in his mind for something neutral to say to break the tension in the room, he was startled to hear his father speak out.

"So Henry, now that you're home, I'm hoping you will have some time to join me down at the locks. There's never been a feat of engineering like this in the history of the world. You'll learn more down there in a week than you would learn in a year at the university."

The no-nonsense tone in his father's voice alerted Henry to his desire to go forward, rather than to look back. There was nothing his father could do about Eleanor's illness and death, but there was an arena in which he had power, and that was his work. Little matter that his wife was weak with sorrow and loss, his philosophy was that of his German forebears—whatever didn't destroy you entirely, made you stronger. In a way, Henry admired this quality in his father, this strength of mind, this firmness of purpose. But he also wished that somewhere in that strength there was a place that could accommodate the anguish it was apparent his mother was experiencing.

His father spoke more about the accomplishments of the Metropolitan Sanitary District, and Henry found himself drawn into a discussion about it, asking questions about how the river's reversal was changing life in Chicago, and the logistics of the engineering that would maintain it. His father warmed to his interest and, uncharacteristically, pushed aside his half-eaten sauerbraten and demonstrated what was being done, using the silverware on the tablecloth as well as the salt cellars and even the candelabra. Henry could see out of the corner of his eye that even his mother's interest was piqued by this discussion and that she seemed to emerge a bit from her previous gloom. Maggie, when she came in to pour the coffee, bit back a smile at the construction of tableware that Henry Senior had concocted. She and Mrs. Thomas exchanged a look that seemed to say the boys are back with their toys once again.

Henry Junior sat back in his chair and gulped his coffee. How much more interesting was his father's description of what was actually happening down at the Chicago River than M. Coriot's fantasy castles in the airless Paris studio. He marveled at the accomplishment of the plan—thousands of men spending years and years digging a canal that would enable visionaries such as his father to take control of a natural phenomenon and make it do their bidding. Taking what had become a choked and fetid sewer that endangered the lives of the growing number of people who had chosen to make Chicago their home—and returning it to its natural state as a free-flowing stream. Why, it truly could be, should be, considered one of the wonders of the modern world, as the newspapers had been crowing for years. And his father had been an important part of that miracle. It made Henry feel proud to think that his father had made a contribution to an undertaking that would likely make Chicago a city recognized throughout the world for its imagination and ingenuity.

Henry's reverie was interrupted by his father's words.

"And so, Henry, I hope you'll be joining us soon. I've spoken to the men at the office—you know many of them—and they are willing to take you on. You can start on Monday, if you'd like."

Henry gave a quick look at his mother, who was smiling, and then at his father, who was beaming. He felt like an animal caught in a hidden trap. What about his own plans, to complete his university training, to work at D. H. Burnham and Company and become an architect, perhaps to move to New York? His father hadn't asked him what he wanted for himself, but had assumed, as usual, that this opportunity he had created would be the best thing for Henry. What about his own dreams? He thought of the animals he'd seen that would gnaw at their own entrapped foot to escape, only to perish from loss of blood further down the trail. No, he mustn't see this as a trap. It was a bona fide opportunity. Here he was being given the chance to participate in the management of one of the wonders of the modern world. A university degree couldn't guarantee that—why not take advantage of this unmatchable opportunity and see where it would take him? But that was his father's dream, not his own. He knew his future was with the Burnham Company for he'd been working toward that throughout his university life.

He smiled at his parents and explained his plans. He would return to the university downstate and find out what he must do to complete his coursework and gain his diploma. After that, he would take up his promised job at the Burnham Company. He wouldn't be leaving home, but would stay with them while he worked at Burnham's. That much he could assure them. After all they had been through in the past few weeks, he would help them forget the past and look forward to the future, his future as a Chicago architect. With that in mind, he could stand one more year or so of living under their roof—and their control—couldn't he?

SIXTEEN

Kitty sat on the bench behind the cottage, hidden in the cool shade of a towering maple tree, enjoying the late afternoon sunshine. Because the wind blew heavily from the northwest, it erased the noxious stockyard odors usually emanating from just a few miles south. On the days when the south wind came up, Kitty stayed indoors, otherwise she'd have to hold her nose to prevent the smell of rotting flesh from settling in her throat.

Brian dozed in the grass before her, exhausted from his lumberyard work in the heat of the day. Ever since she had chastised him for his drunken behavior after their evening at the beer garden, he had followed her around like a guilty puppy, begging her forgiveness for his transgression. He seemed always to be underfoot.

"None of the boys have been around much at all lately," Kitty told Brian, who had begun to stir. "Seems I haven't seen Daniel in weeks."

Brian sat up, his arm over his eyes, pushing back his sun-lightened hair. "Aye, I hadn't been seeing him much myself," he said. "Not since he got that involved with the Clan na Gael guards."

"Clan na Gael? Don't tell me he got himself all mixed up with them idiots who think they can free Ireland all by themselves?"

"Ah, they're not like that at all," Brian said, standing and unfolding like a carpenter's rule. He stretched his arms out straight from his shoulders. "I think it's just an excuse to go boozing with the boys. Nothing for you to worry about."

"I'm not worried about Daniel, he can take care of himself," she said, lifting her feet in the air to look at her old black shoes, so cracked over the toes they looked gray and with their soles separating from the uppers. She wondered if her father would stand her the price of a new pair for when she started school next week. Not that she had needed them any sooner. She had been spending so much time at home, taking care of her mother and Margaret and the new baby, that she hadn't been able to work for wages for a while. She'd definitely have to have decent shoes before she could go off to a new school.

"How's the new baby coming along then?"

Margaret's baby, born just two months earlier, had been a joyous light in the midst of the drudgery of the summer. Baby Helena, named after Mrs. Coakley, had emerged screaming and healthy early one July morning. Kevin, Margaret's husband, had run over to the Coakley cottage before dawn and roused Mr. Coakley, who woke Kitty to tell her to get over to Margaret's house fast. Once Mr. Coakley had pulled on his brown work pants, a rough shirt and his boots, he ran to fetch the midwife. Mrs. Coakley heard the commotion, and, after her husband and daughter left, quietly made her way down the street to the O'Connors' cottage. Thus when Mr. Coakley arrived with the midwife, they found Mrs. Coakley at her older daughter's side, waiting to be the first to hold the baby when it arrived, while Kitty was in the kitchen, boiling water.

"Ah, she's a beauty, Baby Helena, she is," Kitty said, brightening at the thought of the tiny pink and white child. "And the joy of it is, she seems to be the very medicine that's curing whatever ailed my mother. Mama is up early, and over at Margaret's every day now, isn't she, fussing over the little darling. I think Margaret's getting a wee bit jealous of the grandmother, she's holding the baby so much."

"And your mother's up to it?" asked Brian.

"Yes, and seems to be getting better every day, thanks to the grace of God and the joy of Helena," Kitty said. What she didn't tell Brian was that her mother's illness was the result of a miscarriage she had suffered last spring. She hadn't known about it herself, until Margaret spoke out one day, saying how silly it would have been for her and her mother to be having a baby at the same time. Margaret didn't hold back, telling her all about the cramping pain and the flowing blood of their mother's miscarriage, details which Kitty would have been embarrassed to hear from their father. Her mother shouldn't have been thinking about having another baby at her age, Margaret had said, but you know, men are like that. Kitty didn't know that's what men were like, and, when she thought about it, she preferred not to know. She wasn't even sure how old a woman had to be to stop having babies. She'd think about those things when she had to, no sooner.

"Now with your mother up and about, and Margaret on her feet, what are you going to be doing with yourself?" Brian asked, chewing on a sprig of grass he pulled out of the high weeds. "Are you thinking about looking for a job?"

"Thinking about it," Kitty said. "But more than that, I'm thinking about going back to school to learn a new trade." She might as well let Brian in on her plans to be a kindergartner, not that it would change her life all that much. She'd talked it over with her parents, and, in the flush of good feelings about the new baby and Mrs. Coakley's recovery, they had agreed, with the stipulation that Kitty must continue to live at home and to help out with the household chores.

"A new trade? What, a cobbler or a blacksmith?" Brian laughed.

"Maybe trade's the wrong word. It's actually more of a profession. I'm going back to school to become a kindergartner." Kitty stood up straight and tried to look as mature and self-assured as a teacher, although she felt like more a kindergarten student herself, dwarfed as she was by Brian's great height.

"What kind of gardener?"

"A kindergartner. It's a new way of taking care of little children, teaching them things, like art and music. It's like a garden of children," Kitty said primly, picking at the twigs and dust on her skirt. She threw a challenging stare at Brian, daring him to laugh at her again.

Brian stared back at Kitty, with a look on his face as if he were holding back from what he would like to say. "Surrounded by kids every day? Are you some sort of a fool? Wouldn't they be like to drive you mad?" he said, shaking his head.

"And so what are your great plans for your own brilliant future, Mr. Brian Kelleher?" Kitty threw back at him.

Brian shrugged his shoulders and said, "Don't know, don't much care. Whatever happens, happens." He looked up as the Angelus bells resounded through the neighborhood. "Time to get dinner for the old man. I must be off." He raised his hand in farewell and ambled off in the direction of home, bits of grass sticking to his worn trousers.

Kitty kicked the nearest rock, hurting her toes and further splitting the seam of her shoe. Brian could be so infuriating. What he said was a good way to stay exactly where you were, she thought, and that's exactly where she didn't want to stay, looking at the back of the Coakley cottage as it sagged on its foundation, closely hemmed in on both sides by the neighbors' ramshackle wooden cottages. Especially when she was doing housework, she would daydream about a bigger house, finer belongings, household help in the kitchen and the parlor. She didn't want to be doing laundry and cooking dinner every night of the week. The world was a wonderful place and she wanted to see more of it before settling down again to housework. Maybe starting school as a kindergartner wasn't an obvious way to see the world, but it was a step out of the humdrum life she was living.

Once she had her parents' permission to attend the Chicago Kindergarten College to study kindergartening, Kitty had written to Mrs. Campbell and asked her how to enroll. She received a warm letter in reply, in which Mrs. Campbell accepted her into the program and invited her to the school to visit with her and view the facilities.

Kitty prepared carefully for her journey to the college. The night before, she'd trimmed the fashionable boater hat her aunt had given her for Easter with a new red ribbon, and had mapped out the trek on the map given out by the office of the transit system. It was a direct route on the streetcar, first heading east from home and then changing cars in the Loop for a short trip to Van Buren Street. That morning, she packed her black canvas bag with a book to read and some bread and cheese wrapped in a handkerchief. Her father scoffed at her as she made her preparations in the kitchen.

"So, are you going to the very ends of the earth, my girl, or are you just going downtown for the day?" he said, folding his newspaper and pushing back the wooden chair from the kitchen table.

"Shouldn't I be prepared for whatever might come my way?" she said, stabbing a long hatpin through the crown of her hat. She'd heard of women who used their hatpins for protection and she never traveled without one.

"That's my girl," her father said, picking up the newspaper once again.

Kitty fairly ran to the corner and just made it onto the streetcar that ran east on Adams. She opened her book, *Trilby*, it was, the story of a young girl unable to sing and Svengali, the magician who made her into a star. Her aunt had given her the romantic novel, saying it was all the rage on Chicago's Gold Coast. She could feel the eyes of others, particularly young men, as she held up her book practically to her nose, but today she wasn't interested in making eye contact with anyone else.

The State Street stop came just as she was finishing a chapter, and so she reluctantly placed her bookmark, tucked the book away in her bag and departed the car. As she threaded her way through the crowd to the middle of the street where the State Street car boarded, Kitty looked around her. Tall buildings that reminded her of mountains, even though she'd only seen mountains in picture books. Every kind of vehicle clogging the street—from pushcarts to fancy coaches to heavily loaded drays to bicycles, horses, oxen, stray dogs, throngs of people going this way and that—the energy of the city surged through her body like an electric current. Despite the grit in the air, the dirt under her feet, the heat, the smells and the noise, was there anything as thrilling as Chicago? She closed her eyes and breathed in the complex bouquet of city smells, people and horses, manure and garbage, lake breezes and smokestack fumes, and thought how fortunate she was to have been born here, at this time, to have the city in her blood.

She opened her eyes, and the very first person she saw was Henry Thomas, standing on the east side of State Street, waiting for the traffic to clear so he could cross. He had a serious look on his face, his brow furrowed under the rim of his fedora, his mouth pursed beneath his bushy mustache, seemingly oblivious to the people jostling around him. A black armband blended into the shoulder of his gray suit like a dark shadow, except for its regular lines. Who had died? Not his father, that would have made the papers. Certainly not his mother, she hoped, making a quick sign of the cross. She had a great fear of mothers dying, and had said many a prayer for her own that summer.

Before Henry was able to cross, the streetcar Kitty was waiting for pulled up in the middle of the street, clanging loudly and obscuring her view of him. Should she let the car pass without boarding it, in hopes of greeting him? She'd arrive late for Mrs. Campbell if she did that. Only two people waited to board the car, and if she didn't hurry, she'd miss it.

She dashed for the streetcar and jumped on just as the conductor rang the bell. As the car lurched ahead she fell onto the wicker bench that ran the length of the car. Realigning her hat on her head, she twisted her body to look out the grimy window, hoping to catch another glimpse of Henry. Perhaps he had seen her and stood watching her depart, wondering where she might be heading. But he had disappeared into the inevitable crowd on State Street. Wasn't it almost a miracle that, in this crowded city of almost two million people, their steps had crossed on that particular corner, on that particular day? Surely that must mean something. She slowly pulled out her book from her black bag and resumed reading it, although she found herself reading each sentence several times in order to understand it, so occupied was her mind with thoughts of Henry and what had happened to him since she had last seen him. Why hadn't he written to her? Didn't he say he was going to travel in Europe all summer? Did she want to speak to him? Didn't he look much older than the last time she had seen him, that night—was it only last January?—when he took her to dinner at Henrici's? Kitty awoke from her reverie just before the conductor started up again at Van Buren, and hopped off the car before it began to pull away from the stop.

She had never before seen the Chicago Kindergarten College, but the massive red brick castle resembled her own high school, where she had met Henry years ago. School hadn't started and no students or teachers were milling around, yet she fancied that she could smell the same sweat and chalk dust aroma that had permeated the halls of Lake View High School. Mrs. Campbell, hatless and dressed in a brown dress with white collar and cuffs, stood on the pavement beside the tall black wrought-iron gate to welcome her, beaming like a fairy godmother.

"Kitty Coakley . . . and you don't have to tell me where you got that beautiful hat." Mrs. Campbell tucked Kitty's arm under her own and practically dragged her into the building, showing how pleased she was to see her.

Kitty hardly had a chance to speak as Mrs. Campbell pulled her into a first floor classroom and pointed out the equipment uniquely suited for the care and training of kindergartners and their charges—a battered upright piano, stacks of wooden blocks, balls and sticks, miniature chairs and tables. "These are the Froebel gifts," she said reverently, gesturing toward the natural wood blocks and sticks as if they were golden treasures of the past. "The children play with them to discover the world around them and to try out their own abilities."

Kitty wasn't impressed. The gifts didn't look any different from the wooden blocks Sean played with, except they weren't as colorful.

"And just look here," Mrs. Campbell said, opening a side door with a flourish. "The children's very own playground and garden."

Kitty looked out at the yard, equipped with more of the miniature tables and benches, as well as string fences marking off garden rows, everything adjusted to the smaller scale of little ones. How nice it would be to go outside everyday, rather than be cooped up indoors in an office or a shop. She remembered her own school days, staring out a window on a day like today, squirming in a desk bolted to the floor like an animal in a cage. The rowdy boys in her class, treated like animals, acted like them too.

"Everything but the students," she said, turning to Mrs. Campbell.

"Oh, don't worry, we'll have the students beginning next week," Mrs. Campbell assured her. "Students like you who want to become kindergartners. Including you, we have twelve young ladies so far. And I've been speaking to Miss Addams, over at the Hull House on Halsted—such a gracious lady, Miss Addams—and she's assured me that they can give us twenty to twenty-five youngsters, four, five and six years old, to attend our classes. They have their own kindergarten over at Hull House, she said. To be sure, it sounded more like a nursery than a true, Froebel-based kindergarten. But they have little ones to spare." Mrs. Campbell clasped her hands and looked at the ceiling as if thanking the Lord for her good fortune.

Behind Mrs. Campbell's back, Kitty wrinkled her nose. The Hull House was a settlement house for the poorest of the poor, recent immigrants without jobs, who often didn't speak English. She imagined that their children would be dirty, diseased and defiant, not the sort of children she'd prefer to spend her days with. She brushed off her skirt just thinking about what she might come into contact with in the classroom. Still, once she had her certificate, she wouldn't have to continue to teach the poor. Better schools in more fashionable parts of the city would need kindergartners too.

She asked Mrs. Campbell about the other students, and her answer cheered Kitty. For her fellow students would be young ladies from very nice families, from all over the city. Mrs. Campbell hoped that Kitty would make quite a few good friends among her classmates. Thinking about the opportunity to make new friends excited Kitty and she found herself wishing that her classes would begin sooner than next week.

Finally, the first day of school dawned, and Kitty could hardly contain her excitement. She rose before the sun was up to fix her hair in her favorite and most intricate pompadour. She'd set out her clothes the night before, a green tartan dress that brought out her blue eyes, and the new side-buttoned boots she had bought with the money her father had given her. She brushed imaginary dust from them before she appeared in the kitchen doorway. "How do I look?" she asked her parents, who sat at the kitchen table, eating oatmeal and drinking tea.

"Like a beautiful Miss Coakley, the teacher all her students will fall in love with," said her father, giving her a wink and a nod.

"Like a proper young lady who will remember how she was taught to behave," her mother said primly, only the tone of her voice indicating how proud she was of her daughter. "You'll show those young ladies that a girl from St. Patrick's is a girl who can go anywhere and know how to behave herself."

"I'm off, then," Kitty said, collecting her books and the lunch she had made the night before. She could hardly breathe, she was that excited.

"God go with you," her father called out as she left the cottage.

"And with you, too," she said, walking down the street to the streetcar stop. "And with you, too."

That first morning, two young women brought in the twenty tiny kindergartners from Hull House. Each of the children held the hand of another, all of them staring wide-eyed and wary at the grownups circling around them.

"Now remember to behave yourselves," said one of their chaperones, a slight woman who wore a simple black dress without ornament. "And use your handkerchiefs if you sneeze," she said, pulling an embroidered one from her own pocket and wiping a slug's trail of mucus running from the nose of a tiny girl with big brown eyes and ringlets.

Kitty shuddered. Wiping runny noses wasn't the sort of work she had envisioned for herself.

One of the little girls, in a much-patched cotton dress that left her collarbones showing, burst into tears and threw herself onto the skirt of the second Hull House woman as she started to leave the room. "No, no, no," she screamed.

"I wonder what she thinks we're going to do with her here," whispered the tall blonde woman standing next to Kitty, whose expensively tailored dark blue brocade dress Kitty had noticed as soon as she entered the room. "Is she expecting torture, poor little thing?"

The Hull House woman quieted down the crying child and left quickly, closing the door firmly behind her. Mrs. Campbell then flew into the center of the classroom, fluttering her arms and clucking like the mother hen she was, and managed to seat the children at the miniature tables, four to a table with two student teachers at each. Kitty and the tall blonde held back, and Mrs. Campbell addressed them. "And you two can, can—let's see, Katherine, why don't you play the piano and Cecilia . . . Cecilia can turn the pages for you."

Kitty was relieved to take her place at the battered upright piano with her back to what she couldn't help calling in her mind "the urchins," and pleased to have Cecilia standing next to her. Cecilia didn't know the children's songs that Kitty played easily by sight, and turned pages whenever Kitty told her to, but she kept up a whispered monologue about the children.

"Oh, look, that little boy has got his finger up his nose, looks like he's prospecting for silver. And now the crying one's getting ready for another aria, she's about to sing. Yes, that's right, little Tonio, your sleeve is so much handier than a handkerchief. Oh, and would you look at that little one, she's pulling up her skirt to show us her underclothes, but she's forgotten to put them on."

Kitty could hardly see the music, she was giggling so hard that her eyes were running with tears. But she persisted with the lively music, and, encouraged by the efforts of the student teachers as well as Mrs. Campbell, the children left their tiny chairs and began to march around the room. One little girl, however, remained seated, her head down on the table, her dark brown hair curtaining her face, fast asleep.

"She looks like she's sleeping it off," whispered Cecilia.

"She is," Mrs. Campbell, close enough to the piano to overhear Cecilia's cynical remark, said softly. "As it happens, her mother sent her off to school after a breakfast of a slab of bread soaked in wine, I suppose to soften it. The poor little thing, I'll have to have a talk with the mother when she comes to pick up her daughter."

Kitty shook her head, while Cecilia's hands flew to her mouth. They had much more to learn about their students than they had imagined.

The morning session ended with the students lining up to receive their own thick, wine-free slice of bread, and marching out the door to *Stars and Stripes Forever* that Kitty banged out loudly on the piano, delighted not to care whether she hit the wrong keys.

Cecilia relaxed her shoulders and heaved a great sigh of relief. "Well, we've finally met our kindergarteners. We've seen what we have to work with. By the way," she said, stretching out her hand, "I'm Cecilia Carter, please call me Ceecee, everyone does."

Kitty held out her own hand. "I'm Katherine Coakley, but most everyone calls me Kitty."

"My pleasure," said Ceecee, dipping into a bow.

"The pleasure is all mine," said Kitty, laughing.

The afternoon session was much too quiet by comparison, and Kitty found herself staring out the window, envying the little ones who left at noon. Mrs. Campbell spoke first, extolling the Froebel gifts as the children's tools to use to understand the world around them. And to play with these gifts was the children's work. Kitty found Mrs. Campbell's tone and gestures almost operatic, and amused herself imagining her in the robes of a great diva, singing out her Froebelian ideas. She could see Ceecee hunched over her desk, two rows ahead of her, industriously taking notes.

Mrs. Campbell then introduced the other teachers—Miss Gunnarson, a blue-eyed, blonde-haired woman in a middy blouse who looked like she would rather be swinging a tennis racket, and Mr. Meyer, a plump, older man who spoke with a heavy German accent and claimed to have studied with Herr Froebel himself. They outlined what they would cover in the weeks ahead and assigned readings for the next day's classes.

When the classes finally ended and she had picked up her books, Kitty caught up with Ceecee, standing at the same trolley stop where she caught the car herself. She noticed Ceecee's hat, which must have cost approximately what a kindergarten teacher would make in a week, once she was employed. "Are you going to the north?" she asked.

"Yes, and beyond," Ceecee replied grimacing. "I'll be spending hours on these cars."

"Me, too," Kitty replied. "Where do you live?"

"Far, far away," Ceecee said. "Up to Adams, and then I transfer to a car going west to Ashland. I live just off Union Park."

"Actually, that's not far from me. I live on Adams, just west of Desplaines." Union Park was a very fashionable area, just south and west of Kitty. "What parish are you?"

"What parish? What does that mean? We've attended the Congregational Church in Union Park all my life."

Kitty was embarrassed. She should have known that Chicago was a city of parishes only to the Catholics who lived there. The others, the non-Catholics, would have no clue what that was all about. But to a Chicago Catholic, the parish you lived in would tell a great deal about you. Where your parents had come from, sometimes how long you and your family had been in Chicago, often how wealthy you were, and where your loyalties lay. It was a useful shorthand to get to know someone, but that someone had to be Catholic for it to apply. She was about to tell Ceecee that she was from St. Patrick's, but she realized that it would have no meaning for her.

"So what do you think of the program so far?" Ceecee asked, once the streetcar arrived and they had arranged themselves next to one another.

Kitty thought for a moment before she spoke. Should she reveal what she really thought, or just say nice things? Ceecee had made her laugh so much, making fun of the children, so she obviously wasn't the sort of person who would only say the polite, right things and not disclose what she was really thinking. It should be safe to be honest with her.

"To tell you the truth," Kitty said, "I don't really want to touch those dirty little children with their noses running and no handkerchief but the back of their sleeve. But I guess we'll get used to them. And while all this Froebelian wisdom seems a little much at first, well, what else is there?"

"I know just what you mean," Ceecee said. "I had to fight so hard with my parents for them to allow me to sign up for this program. Did you see the demonstration school they had, years and years ago, at the Chicago Fair? That impressed me—the children got to act like children and not just little adults."

Kitty searched her mind for a memory of a Froebel demonstration at the World's Fair, but could only come up with memories of the glowing electric lights of the beautiful White City, the thrilling Ferris Wheel, and the bumpy camel ride. But she nodded her head and acted as if she knew what Ceecee was talking about.

"It took forever for me to convince my parents that this would be a worthy occupation for me. Seven years, I guess it was," Ceecee said. "At first I thought I had to go to Germany to learn all about this Froebel method, because there wasn't anything here in Chicago. Of course my parents wouldn't say yes to that. But finally I found out about Mrs. Campbell and her program, it was in the *Tribune* this summer, and my parents finally broke down and let me come. I had to promise all sorts of things, of course, but I did get my way." She smiled. "I usually do."

"My parents weren't very happy about my enrolling either. They wanted me just to stay at home and take care of them, waiting until I got married or became a dry old maid." Kitty grimaced.

"I know. I'll have to be so careful about what I tell mine. I'll have to pretend that everything is just hunky-dory, you know, or they'll get worried and pull me out of the program." Ceecee stretched her arms and yawned. "I suppose I'll get used to getting up so early and traveling all this way down here. It's a long ride home."

But the ride seemed much shorter to Kitty in Ceecee's company than it had on her own. The two chattered about their classes and their teachers, and didn't stop talking until it was time to transfer to the West Side car.

After Kitty left Ceecee on the streetcar going west, she walked home to the strains of the Sousa march still throbbing in her head. She felt wrapped up in her happiness about a new friend and the new direction her life seemed to be moving in. This is what she had wanted, she thought. A bigger world, more opportunities to become the person she wanted to be.

When she arrived on her street, she saw her mother sitting on the front stoop, shelling peas and talking to a neighbor. She was glad that Ceecee hadn't come this way with her, being sure that in Union Park no one sat outside and did kitchen work.

Mrs. O'Flaherty nodded at Kitty as she walked up to the cottage, and waved a farewell. Supper had to be put on the table at the O'Flaherty home as well.

Kitty sat down next to her mother and took the peas out of her hand. "I'll take care of these, you've had your hands full today, I'm sure, what with Margaret and Baby Helena and little Sean."

"Sean's that much bigger these days," Mrs. Coakley said, brushing the pea strings off her apron. "He's always asking about his Aunt Kitty, isn't he?"

Kitty knew that was her mother's way of telling her not to think that because she was going to school she could neglect her own family. "And Baby Helena?"

"Ah, what a beauty she is. And so smart. Can't she just tell me apart from her mother already. And isn't it her grandmother that she wants to sing to her, not her mother? And won't I miss her when they move?"

"Move? What's that you say? Margaret and her Kevin moving?"

"Oh, you haven't heard about that? Sure, it's probably not until spring, but Margaret says they're going to start looking for a bigger house, probably out west in Austin or even Oak Park. I don't know what I'll do when they go. I suppose I'll just have to go with them."

Kitty stared at her mother, dumbfounded. This was the first she had heard of her sister's plans. Certainly, she'd been hearing Margaret complain for years about the neighborhood going downhill, old cottages being torn down to build warehouses and factories. The area's closeness to the river and to the railroad made it a good location for industry. Fewer people were moving into the area, and St. Patrick's parish was getting smaller—she could tell by the number of people in the pews at Sunday Mass. But move out of the neighborhood? They had always lived here. It was fine for her to have new plans for her life, she just never thought her parents would.

"So you think you'd move, too? We'd move?"

"Oh, don't you go worrying your head about it. You know your father, he'll stay here until they carry him out feet first. We haven't talked about it at all, at all."

Her mother went back into the cottage, mumbling about the potatoes. Kitty remained on the front stoop, her hands automatically shelling the peas, while her mind raced with the possibility of moving out of Chicago and into the suburbs. She knew there was public transportation out there, many people in Austin, and even Oak Park, commuted into the Loop to work, but it would be a shock to leave the street on which she was born, to leave St. Patrick's. Yet she should be getting used to the idea of change, for it was all around her. This new direction for her life, becoming a kindergartner, and a new friend, Cecilia—no, Ceecee—Carter. She was obviously from a family with money, but certainly had a mind of her own. And to think that Ceccee had wanted to be a kindergartner for seven years. While it was almost just a whim for her. Ceecee must have seen something to it to pursue the dream for that long. Maybe she could learn something more about the Froebel way through Ceecee, and find the flowers in what so far seemed a garden of weeds. She shouldn't really have any fear of leaving things behind when there were much more interesting possibilities ahead of her.

SEVENTEEN

Henry rarely left the Burnham and Company offices for lunch, but today he had an important errand to run. Stepping out the Rookery door onto LaSalle Street, he sniffed the air. The September day smelled of fall, with a cool crispness to the smoky air that reminded him of biting into a fresh apple. He turned the corner onto Adams, hands in his pockets, coat open, his fedora tilted back on his head, contemplating the growth of the building he was working on. The plans had filled his drawing board and his mind for weeks now, calculations of stress, weight, and area cartwheeling through his brain even as he slept. And this morning the order had come through—the building crew could begin to clear the land and dig the foundations. And soon the structure would go up in Pittsburgh, a city he had never even seen, growing from the blueprints he had helped to create.

As Henry returned to the day's reality in order to cross the busy, muddy intersection of State and Adams, he caught sight ahead of him of a woman alighting from the electric tram that had stopped on the north side of Adams. Holding the door open with one hand, she leaped onto the curb with the grace of a ballerina, combined with the wariness of a seasoned urbanite, avoiding the filthy mud, despite the large carryall she balanced on her arm. Something about her appealed to Henry and he slowed his step so that he could follow her through the crowds on the east side of State Street. She maneuvered through the crush of people as if completing the rituals of a country dance, and Henry found himself quickening his pace so as not to lose her in the crowd.

It was her halo of dark hair that convinced him. Yes, it was, it must be Miss Kitty Coakley he was following, and she appeared to be headed toward his destination as well, to the Marshall Field's emporium designed in 1892 by Burnham and Root.

Henry walked even faster so that he arrived at the door just a second before she did. "Miss Katherine Coakley, I believe," he said, opening the door with one hand, while doffing his fedora with the other.

Kitty looked up at him from beneath her eyelashes. "Why, Mr. Thomas, how good to see you. It has been a long time, hasn't it?"

"Too long, Miss Coakley, too long," he answered. He saw her dark eyes flicker for a moment on the black armband he wore on his dark suit, and then return to his face.

"Perhaps you remember my aunt, Mrs. Patrick Coakley," Kitty said, and raised her hand to indicate her Aunt Mabel, standing regally just inside the door.

"Mrs. Coakley, of course," Henry said and reached out his hand to shake her leather-gloved one.

"Mr. Thomas, is it? How nice to see you." Her aunt's face was unreadable, but her tone suggested that it might have been even nicer if she didn't see him.

"My aunt and I are going to have tea together at the Palmer House," Kitty said. "I would invite you to join us, but . . ."

Henry caught out of the corner of his eye the tightening of her aunt's lips and the smallest shake of her head. "Ladies, it has been my pleasure to see you," he said, bowing slightly. "But I must complete this errand in the brief time allotted me from my duties at Burnham and Company. I would like to catch up with you, however, Miss Coakley. With your kind permission, may I call on you, perhaps some time next week? I shall send you a card to specify the day."

"I shall look forward to your card," said Kitty, a smile tweaking the sides of her mouth as she followed her aunt, who had pushed past the incoming shoppers to exit to the street.

The vision of Kitty Coakley's face filled Henry's mind as he walked up the stairs to the candy department on the second floor of Marshall Field's. He had forgotten how captivating her dimples were, like ripples in heavy cream, how deep her blue eyes, and how appealing the curly tendrils of her dark hair that framed her ivory face. He was pleased that, for once, when taken by surprise, he had thought quickly enough on his feet to say what, in the past, he might have fumbled and failed to say. And then he would have beaten himself up for days afterward at the missed opportunity. Perhaps the experience of being questioned about the work he was doing, at any time and any place, by any member of the vast Burnham staff, had trained him to engage his mind so quickly when he opened his mouth to speak.

He wondered if her aunt's obvious coldness resulted from his not writing to Kitty during his trip to Europe earlier that year or whether she just didn't like him. He had been afraid that if he had apologized to Kitty just then, he might have spilled a torrent of words, telling her of his early return from Europe because of the heartbreak of his sister's death. Or the intensity of the first few months of working at his dream job at the Burnham Company. He shook his head, hoping that there would be time for that. He would write her a note that afternoon, as soon as he got back to his office, and invite her out. Perhaps to the symphony, she would enjoy that.

He went about his errand with a happy heart, lingering over the selection of each chocolate to make up the ribbon-wrapped box he would present to his hostess, Mrs. Daniel H. Burnham, when he attended her Sunday afternoon party at the end of the week. He had heard about these parties—held at the Evanston estate of "Uncle Dan," as the younger designers and engineers called the head of the firm—but he hadn't yet attended one. He knew that sometimes his fellows would bring along wives and sweethearts. Perhaps some day, I'll be bringing Miss Katherine Coakley, he thought, and decided he'd pick out a box of chocolates for her as well. He would keep it at work until he saw her. That way, his mother wouldn't have the chance to comment on it at home.

By the time Sunday rolled around, the weather had taken on the worst of its fall character, gray and nasty, occasionally spitting a blast of cold rain. Henry didn't let the gray day dull his spirits, though. He had put on a bright red tie to go with his charcoal gray suit, and pulled on his gabardine raincoat. "Don't hold supper for me, Mother," he said as the two of them stood by the front door waiting for his friend Dick Connell to pick him up and take him to the Burnhams'. "I'm sure there will be plenty to eat."

"Enjoy yourself, Henry," Mrs. Thomas said, straightening his tie. "Make sure you make a good impression. And don't forget the chocolates for Mrs. Burnham." She handed him the box.

Had his mother shrunk or was it that he had grown since Eleanor's death and his return from Paris? She seemed frailer, paler, as if she too might slip away. Or was her pallor just the inevitable result of the five months of mourning she had endured after her daughter's death?

Henry ran down the path with the box of chocolates beneath his coat as Dick Connell pulled up to the curb in his automobile, which announced its presence with loud smoking pops, like fireworks exploding inside garbage cans. Although the car was a sedan with a hard roof and a windscreen, Dick handed him a pair of goggles, shouting to be heard over the engine's noise. "You'd better put these on—sometimes stones fly up from the road and come in through the sides."

Henry dutifully donned the goggles, fitting them over his eyes and feeling as though he had become a large insect, and sat back in the seat. He had only ridden in an automobile once or twice before, and he was interested to watch how Dick manipulated the gear shift and trod on the pedals and turned the steering wheel all at the same time. He didn't understand how stones could fly up from a roadway that looked like a river of mud, but he was willing to learn about this new world of automobile travel. He and Dick had begun at the Burnham office the same July day, and were learning the ropes together, exchanging notes over the lunches they brought from home and in the evenings when they'd walk up to the train station together. Dick lived not far from Henry, in Ravenswood, close to Rosehill cemetery. His father owned a garage, so Dick had access to an automobile despite the low wages they both were paid. Conversation was nearly impossible in the car, due to both the noise of the engine and the wind that whistled in through the ill-fitting windows, so Henry was able to sit back and watch the city recede as they traveled north to Evanston. They drove up Green Bay Road, which had been an Indian trail like all the streets that deviated from the grid lines of the city. And then past Indian Boundary Line in Rogers Park, the imaginary line set by the Treaty of Chicago after the Blackhawk War to keep the Indians away from the growing village. Beyond the line were more farms, with stands of large trees, their autumn colors dimmed against the pale gray of the sky.

Dick concentrated on his driving, peering out through his goggles at the road in front of them, swerving around stalled wagons and slow-moving horse carriages. Fortunately, traffic was sparse on this gloomy Sunday. Dick had once told Henry that he had driven an automobile at the speed of thirty miles an hour, which Henry found difficult to imagine. But today, the car lurched along much more slowly, so that at times, young boys ran past them laughing and shouting things they couldn't hear over the combustion of the engine. Slow but steady was their pace, without any of the stalling or tire changes that so often marred automobile rides. Not that these would have delayed them much—Dick bragged that he could change a tire in less than a minute, and that engines rarely stalled for long under his experienced hand. So it was that they arrived early at the Burnham estate, when pale sunshine still illuminated the day, and pulled the car into the driveway that circled through the rolling front lawn. The house resembled many of the other large mansions they had seen along Sheridan Road—a large, gray-stuccoed Queen Anne, with turrets and several levels of roof. Nothing about it suggested that it was the home of one of the nation's foremost architects.

"What shall we do? It'd be rude to appear early," Henry said, consulting the watch he pulled from inside his raincoat.

"Well, it's no day to go out for a walk along the lake," Dick said, removing his goggles and rubbing his eyes. "I say we just go in. What the ho! It can't hurt to look eager."

As they walked up the drive to the large gray house, a lace curtain twitched at a front window, and the young men could see a woman waving to them. This was as much of an invitation as they needed to climb the broad steps and ring the doorbell. A white-aproned maid answered the door, and took their coats and hats. The woman from the window appeared in the doorway of the parlor.

"Welcome, gentlemen," she said. "How nice of you to join us this afternoon. I'm Mrs. Burnham. Mr. Burnham will be joining us in just a moment."

Henry introduced himself and handed her the box of chocolates, saying, "In gratitude for your hospitality, Mrs. Burnham." She thanked him and handed the box to the maid.

Margaret Burnham was the daughter of John Sherman, one of the richest men in Chicago, and she dressed and carried herself as though she was well aware of what she was worth. Her tiny diamond earrings and the gold watch pinned to her black brocade dress, as well as her quiet, self-assured manner, suggested that she had no wish to intimidate. Nevertheless, Henry immediately feared he would knock something over and embarrass himself.

The parlor was dark and cozy, despite the misty windows that looked out over wet green and brown lawns to the edge of the raging gray lake. The wide windows were swathed in burgundy velvet, with thick, twisted gold braid fringe. A vast stone fireplace, big enough to stand in if there hadn't been a forest of logs ablaze in its center, threw a blanket of warmth throughout the room. Marble statues of classical antiquity mounted on pillars guarded the corners of the room. Henry and Dick were the first to arrive. The long table covered with a lace tablecloth and studded with plates of cakes, cookies, and other pastries stood untouched.

"Please go ahead and help yourselves to something to eat, gentlemen," said Mrs. Burnham. "I know that young men your age are perpetually hungry. Bridget will be bringing in the tea shortly. Or perhaps you would prefer coffee?"

Henry and Dick assured her that tea would be just fine and stepped over to the table to make their selection of sweets. Henry was balancing a loaded plate and trying to decide what would be the best seat, where he could watch the interactions without being too much a part of them, when Daniel Burnham entered the room. And when Daniel Burnham entered a room, he filled the room.

Burnham was taller than Henry, well over six feet, and stood very straight, lord and master of all he surveyed. Henry especially noted how well he was dressed, his pin-striped wool suit impeccably draped on his large commanding body, the trouser cuffs breaking over his highly polished boots at exactly the right place. His face drew Henry's immediate attention, framed by dark brown hair curling over his broad forehead, a thick handlebar mustache of reddish brown obscuring his upper lip and highlighting his strong dimpled jaw. Daniel Hudson Burnham radiated robust health and power, and his presence drew all eyes.

Mr. Burnham rarely appeared in the Rookery Building offices of D. H. Burnham and Co.mpany or at least that had been Henry's experience in the two short months he had been employed. He was most often traveling by train to the money and power centers of the East Coast—New York, Boston, Washington, and apparently Pittsburgh, where the construction project that Henry was working on was located. Mr. Burnham took charge of the business side of the firm, gaining the large commissions that kept the home corps of designers and engineers hard at work. Well known for masterminding the creation of the White City as head of construction for the 1893 Columbian Exposition, Daniel Burnham was more an engineer than an architect. He was said to take greater pride in his problem-solving skills than in any artistic ones. Henry admired these problem-solving skills over artistry because he felt that that was his own strength as well.

Burnham's first step took him to his wife, whose hand he clasped. He thanked her for greeting his guests—"my colleagues," he said with a sweeping gesture that included everyone in the room, by that time a good twenty-five to thirty men, with just five or six women whom they had brought along.

Henry watched as Burnham mingled with the guests, recognizing the principals of the firm—Ernest Graham, the general manager; Peirce Anderson, who headed the design department; Edward Probst, who headed the department of working plans where Henry worked; and H. J. White, who ran the superintendence department. He then made the rounds of the junior men, shaking hands, asking questions, favoring each man with the direct light of his deep blue eyes. He stopped before Dick, who rose from his seat when Burnham approached.

"I say, old man," Burnham said, clapping Dick on the shoulder, "Was that your Duryea Motor Trap I spied from my window? The one making all that racket?"

"Yes, sir," Dick said. "My father's automobile, actually. He lets me drive it sometimes."

"Well done, well done," Burnham said. "We'll have to chat about your auto some day, won't we. I haven't yet purchased a horseless carriage myself, but I can see it's the transportation of the future, isn't it?" And he looked over at Henry, who had also stood up when he reached their out-of-the-way corner, as if asking him to comment.

"Yes, sir, it certainly will be the transportation of the future," Henry said, with all the confidence he could muster.

"So we'll have to begin building our cities to accommodate them, won't we?" Burnham said, clapping Henry's shoulder as he moved past him to the next clump of guests.

Henry sat down, grateful to have the chair's stability to support his shaking knees. He pulled his handkerchief from his pocket to wipe the perspiration from his brow. He and Dick exchanged relieved glances; they had acquitted themselves competently in the force field created by the great man.

"It is something to think about, isn't it?" Henry said to Dick. "How will we build cities if more and more automobiles will be sharing the space with people?"

"I don't think it's something to worry about, sport," Dick said before he bit into a tiny custard tart. "Only a few people will be able to afford them, don't you know. The auto will be a rich man's toy."

Despite Dick's brush-off of the idea, the question continued to intrigue Henry until the party decamped to the music room across the hallway, where chairs had been set up for the guests to enjoy the music of a string quartet made up of members of the Chicago Symphony Orchestra. Burnham was the vice president of the Board of Directors of the orchestra, and it was he who introduced the musicians to his guests and announced the names of the Beethoven pieces they were to play.

Henry approached one of the few empty chairs in the room, next to one of the few women, a young blonde woman in a light blue wool suit. "Is this seat taken?" he asked.

"No, please, sit," said the woman. "The music is about to start."

Although the woman sat quietly during the music, her eyes closed as though she were watching an inner drama, Henry was very much aware of her presence. He could smell just a touch of a floral perfume and saw, out of the corner of his eye, a lock of her dark blonde hair fall loose from her elaborate chignon. She hardly seemed to breathe and, in fact, appeared to be asleep. Yet, when the musicians took their violins from their shoulders and the listeners clapped politely, her eyelids popped open and she added her applause to theirs.

"Wasn't that just too beautiful?" she sighed, turning to Henry.

Her question knocked him out of his deep reverie, and it took him a moment to nod his head.

"We haven't met. I'm Cecilia Carter," she said, holding out her hand. "I haven't seen you here before. Mr. Anderson, my uncle, or at least I call him that, brings me along to these parties regularly. To meet and greet, he says."

The young woman's easy, open manner reassured Henry, and he shook her hand and introduced himself as one of the newest hires in the Burnham office.

She looked at him thoughtfully and began to ask him questions about his duties, showing that she was well informed about what went on in the architectural office. He was just about to ask her how she spent her time when the music started up, and he once again became lost in the musical web Beethoven wove. When the concert ended, he turned to her to continue their conversation, but she was leaving, with a wave and a smile, on the arm of the distinguished Mr. Anderson.

Henry sat back in his chair, still wrapped in the warmth of the music and the room, and watched as his host reached for his wife's hand and clasped his small son, introduced as Daniel Junior, who sat on his knee. Mrs. Burnham had explained earlier that the four older children were away at school in the East. Prestige, wealth, a loving family, and a beautiful wife, perhaps like the very charming Miss Carter. Or perhaps even the lovely Miss Coakley. Henry wondered if he too could aspire to these rewards for his hard work. There were probably very few men in Chicago, even in the world, who could compare to Daniel Burnham. Could he ever reach the heights Burnham had scaled? How important to his career had been the marriage to the wealthy, well-connected woman? Or could he have accomplished all he had through his own talents and hard work? Henry didn't know the answers to these questions—how could anyone know? But the one thing he was sure of was that he had something that Daniel Burnham himself had not had at his age—and that was the example of Daniel Burnham himself to serve as a beacon of light to lead him forward through his career.

EIGHTEEN

On Saturday morning, Kitty brought her nephew Sean down to the Chicago River to look at the boats, one of his favorite pastimes. The autumn sunshine glowed through the trembling auburn and orange leaves, their last gasp of beauty before the dark days of winter. They sat on the bank near one of the shipping piers and watched barges being loaded and boats of every description sailing by the large grain elevators just beyond Wolf Point. The oil and tar of the boats as well as the smoke of burning leaves on the shore permeated the air with the romance of the open seas. A slight breeze jangled the rigging of the sailing boats, creating its own music.

Kitty began singing one of the kindergarten songs they taught at school, and Sean picked up on it. The song encouraged him to act out the words, and she stood next to him while they mimicked planting the seeds, hoeing the garden, and harvesting the crops. A steam whistle and the shouts and waves of sailors sailing by embarrassed her, so she sat back down again in the grass and encouraged Sean to go on. While she didn't have the actual "gifts" of balls and sticks to teach Sean the Froebel way, she could at least pass on some of the music.

After taking him through the song four times—"Again, Aunt Kitty, again," he'd beg—she convinced him to sit next to her in the grass and watch the boats. Sean knew that his Coakley uncles were working on the ore boats up in Lake Superior, and he tried to convince her that he saw them on the boats in the Chicago River.

"I see Uncle Mickey? I see Uncle Pat? I see Uncle John? I see Uncle Billy? I see Uncle Danny?"

"No, Sean, your uncles are on different boats now, not on the river, but on a big, cold lake up north."

"I see Uncle Brian?"

"No, Sean, remember I told you? Uncle Brian's off on a trip with his father, on another big river, the biggest river in all of America, the Mississippi River. They went to New Orleans on a railroad train." Brian and his father had taken a trip down to New Orleans, exploring some connections with lumberyards in the South. He had been gone for more than a week, and Kitty missed him. Without her brothers around, she and her parents rattled around the house, always needing to know what the others were doing. Brian at least made a diversion, and would often take her away from the house. "Remember, Sean, what the train says?"

"Choo, choo, choo, says the train," Sean sang delightedly. "We see trains today?"

"No, not today, little one. We have to get back to the cottage and get you some lunch. Your gramma will be wondering where we are." Kitty grabbed his hand and they ran laughing up the bank of the river, and back to the Coakley cottage. Sean took every opportunity to scuff his feet in the dried leaves piled up in the gutters. Kitty remembered when she was small, she used to do the same, finding satisfaction in their crunching noise and the smoky smell.

Their sojourn outdoors in the fresh autumn air made Kitty more aware of the stifling air inside the cottage. It was a different smoky smell indoors, greasier and more cloying. Ever since her mother had suggested that they were considering moving out, Kitty became more aware of the dinginess of her surroundings. Especially without her brothers home, the cottage was like the discarded shell of some animal, worn out, cracked and dirty, something to be tossed away. She noticed how the windows fit so poorly in their frames and were layered with grit. The once pristine curtains were falling down in places and had become gray with the ever-present Chicago smog indoors and out. Even the floorboards were uneven, a constant reminder that the city was built on a swamp, and the structure was slowly settling back into it. Everything indoors was covered with the fine layer of soot inescapable in the city. She began to think more positively about moving out of the heart of the city. In Austin, the streets would be less crowded and the air not so dirty. She'd heard there was an elevated train connection to Austin and Oak Park just beyond it. Perhaps her long commute to school could be shortened. Of course, by the time—and if—they moved, she would nearly be finished with her course and would be looking for a school to hire her as a kindergarten teacher. Imagine, a teacher! She could see herself, buttoned up into a fine wool suit, a modest hat on her head, wearing shiny black boots and carrying a leather schoolbag. The very image of knowledge and respectability.

⊷

Thinking about moving made her anxious about what she might leave behind. The proximity to the Loop would be one thing, especially as that proximity also meant access to her Aunt Mabel. She hadn't seen her aunt since she started the program—today might be a good time to go visit her downtown at Marshall Field's.

As they cleared up the lunch dishes and cut up the leftover meat for the evening's stew, Kitty told her mother she was going to spend the afternoon downtown, making it sound as if it were something she had to do for school, rather than just a whim to pop in on Aunt Mabel. Her mother looked around the cottage, and couldn't find anything necessary for her to do that afternoon, so she grudgingly said, "Be off with you then, I'll expect you back by the Angelus bells. And won't you pick up some potatoes on the way home?" Kitty left the cottage, feeling like a bird freed from its cage.

⊷

The streets downtown were more crowded on a Saturday afternoon than any weekday, filled with people enjoying the golden fall day and, like squirrels, stocking up for their winter hibernation. Kitty made her way down the packed streets, dipping and turning one way and then another to pass the dawdling window shoppers, caught up in a rhythm she thought of as the city dance. She quickly arrived at the Marshall Field's store, and just as quickly made her way through the hordes of shoppers to her aunt's millinery boutique. Her aunt had a customer in the small shop, with another one waiting, and she told Kitty to come back in half an hour to see if she were free. Her assistant would be back by then, and she would be able to take Kitty to tea.

What a treat, Kitty thought—a half hour to linger among the showcases of the department store, looking at goods far more expensive than she could ever afford. She could pretend she was a princess, or a queen even, pointing out this and that and that other thing that her minions would pay for and carry home to her glamorous suite in the Palmer House or some other fine hostelry. Where should she begin?

Kitty wandered through the majestic first floor, anchored by huge Greek columns as tall as trees, supporting floor after floor above them. She passed through the inner atrium, overhung by the glittering Tiffany ceiling, a mosaic of deep jewel colors and gold. The electric lights throughout the store made the goods themselves glow as if everything were made of gold, not just the jewelry that sparkled within the glass cases. She lingered over such a vitrine, filled with pearls of impossible sizes, dreaming about what it would be like to wear such shimmering objects around her neck. She sighed, feeling both happy and sad. Happy to share in the beauty of such jewels; sad, because she knew that she would never afford them, certainly not on a kindergarten teacher's wages.

She returned to the millinery shop, where her aunt was just pulling on her black kid gloves and giving directions to Caroline, who would tend the store in her absence. A hat in the latest, multi-feathered style adorned her head, a fine advertisement for the wares she sold. "Let's go then, Kitty. How about tea at the Palmer House? It's a fine day for such a treat."

Kitty laughed inwardly. Of course, the Palmer House, that's where a princess would go for tea. The Palmer House was another State Street stalwart, a Chicago landmark from before the Chicago Fire of 1871. The original hotel had burned down in that blaze, but Potter Palmer had rebuilt it, bigger and better, on the same site, and the new building had won an international reputation for its elegant trappings and tender care of the elite.

❦

As they started south down State Street, their progress slowed by the crowds, Kitty's aunt stopped suddenly, causing an old man in a long overcoat to step on her heels. Apologizing, he moved on. Aunt Mabel stepped to the curb and held up her hand to stop a horse cab. She then turned to Kitty and said, "I want to show you something." She pushed Kitty into the cab that had appeared immediately, stopping to tell the cabbie something in a voice so low that Kitty couldn't make out what she was saying. The cab took off, heading even farther south on State.

"Where are you taking me?" Kitty asked. It was unusual for her aunt to act this spontaneously, she was normally a very deliberate woman with careful plans and itineraries.

"Don't worry," Aunt Mabel said. "You'll see it when we get there."

After passing the great skyscrapers at the south end of the Loop, the cab continued through narrowing streets, containing at least the same number of people as in the Loop, but much shabbier and lacking the high spirits and sense of purpose of the Loop shoppers. Kitty identified the area as the place that she had always heard referred to as the slums, an area she had been taught to avoid. This is probably where the Hull House children live, she thought.

"But why are we coming down here?" she cried. "We could be robbed, or worse." She had heard stories of women being drugged in this type of place and taken into white slavery.

"You have nothing to worry about," Aunt Mabel said. "I know where I'm going." And just then, the cab turned a corner and pulled up in front of an old tenement building from which, if it had ever been painted, the paint had peeled away so long before that the wood had a porous look, like a sponge. The cab driver pounded on the side of the cab to indicate that they had arrived at their destination. Aunt Mabel

157

descended from the cab and pulled from her black reticule a few bills, pressing them onto the driver so that he would wait for them.

Kitty climbed out of the cab and stood on the wooden sidewalk, or what there was of it, sunk deeply into the mud. She breathed in the dead cow smell of the stockyards as well as a closer, more cloying smell of unwashed clothes and bodies. She wondered if her aunt's reticule held smelling salts, because she thought she might pass out from the smell. But before she had a chance to ask, her aunt had picked up her skirt and made her way to the front door of the tenement.

"I want you to meet someone," she said. She knocked sharply on the door, which was opened by a small, barefoot girl, whose feet looked almost as if she wore high boots, the mud on them was so thick. Her dress had been made out of a flour sack. "Is your mother home?" Aunt Mabel asked the girl.

"Maaah," the girl bellowed, looking at Mabel as if she had flown in on a cloud. Then again, louder, "Maah."

"Hold yer horses, hold yer horses, Jenny, I'm coming." And an old woman appeared, holding her back as if in pain. The old woman stared at Mabel as if there were something about her that seemed familiar, then scratched her head.

"You don't remember me, Adelaide?" Mabel asked quietly.

"Now I've got it," the old woman said. "I know that voice. It's Mabel, Mabel, isn't it? Mabel, ah dang, what was it then? An Irish name, Mabel Kenn-something. Mabel Kennelley, that's it." The woman wiped her hand off on her apron and held it out to the visitor. "And who's this with you, it's not your daughter is it? There's a surprise."

Aunt Mabel turned to Kitty. "No, this is my niece, Katherine Coakley. My brother-in-law's daughter. Part of the family I married into. Remember the policeman who walked the beat on Halsted? Patrick Coakley? He's now my husband, I'm Mrs. Patrick Coakley."

"Well, isn't that nice. And this is my Jenny," Adelaide said, giving her daughter a nudge. "You waited a long time to be a married lady, you did, Mabel, but you sure look good. Marriage agrees with you." Adelaide stood up straighter in the doorway, smiling at Mabel and Kitty.

"I'm showing my niece around the old neighborhood, and I wanted her to meet you," Aunt Mabel said. "We'll be on our way."

"I'm sure pleased you stopped by, Mabel, you looking so good. And happy to meet you, miss. I'd invite you in for a cup of tea, but the stove has been on the fritz, hasn't it now, Jenny?" Adelaide said, nudging her daughter who continued to stand in the doorway, staring at Kitty and her aunt.

"Yes, Ma," Jenny said.

A group of boys playing stickball in the street stopped their game, and stood watching as the two well-dressed women walked past them. Kitty noticed them, and whispered to her aunt, "I hope they're not plotting on how to rob us."

"Don't be ridiculous," Aunt Mabel said. "I lived down here for years and no one ever bothered me."

"I'd bet you weren't dressed as well then as you are now."

"Kitty, don't worry. No one is going to harm us down here." And she indicated that they would turn the corner and walk down another wooden sidewalk on a street with a grocery story and corner saloon. "I just wanted you to meet Adelaide. Adelaide and I worked together, many long years ago, at the milliners where I learned my trade. *Hats by Mr. Richlieu*, it was, not that there ever was a Mr. Richlieu. We sewed hats together for hours on end, chatting to keep the boredom away. We got to know everything there was about each other. Not that I had that much to tell, I had grown up just down the street from here, over there, near that firehouse," Mabel said, pointing across the street. The tenement she indicated had evidently once been dark green, and an advertisement painted on its side said "Buy Brown Label. Tobacco with Taste" in sun-bleached colors.

Kitty's stomach ached as she took in the broken-down building, garbage strewn over its front yard, the two small and very dirty children watching them from the front stoop, watching them as if they were the prey that would be their dinner tonight. All she wanted was to get out of there. "I don't understand this, Aunt Mabel. Why did you bring me here today?"

"As I said, I wanted you to meet Adelaide," Mabel said, motioning for the cab to pick them up. "Adelaide grew up around here too, she's the same age I am, a friend of mine from school. But she ran off to marry a wealthy man, a man who would keep her in the style she wanted to become accustomed to. And they were happy for a few years. Long enough for her to have three children. But he took to the bottle, started gambling on the riverboats, and it didn't take long for him to lose the fortune he once had. If he ever did have it."

"And they moved down here?"

"Not exactly. They were living in a nice hotel downtown, I forget which one. He went off to work, Adelaide stayed in with the babies. It isn't so easy to take care of children in a downtown hotel."

"And then what happened?"

"Her husband went away—he said he was going to New York on a business trip, but he never came back. Adelaide stayed in the hotel for a few days, but they were soon after her to pay the bill. She didn't have any money—her husband hadn't left her any. And there she was, with three little ones, no money, and these people threatening to throw her and her children out on the street."

"So, what did she do?"

"Eventually, she came back to the old neighborhood, this neighborhood, where we had grown up, and she got a job at Mr. Richlieu's. But there were a couple of years before that she never accounted for. At least not to me."

"Do you think she was a . . . lady of the night?" Kitty asked, searching for the least offensive euphemism she could think of.

Aunt Mabel barked out a short laugh, one without humor. "A lady of the night? Is that what you call them? Your Uncle Patrick has a long list of synonyms for the word you're searching for. Do I think she was a prostitute? Is that what you're saying? I don't have any hard evidence, as your uncle might say, but I just know she never showed a bit of interest in men at any time after she came back. And she used to be a pretty, flirtatious girl, one that many young men were interested in, back when we were young."

The cab drew up beside them, and Kitty and her aunt got in, after telling the driver to take them back to Marshall Field's.

"But Aunt Mabel, do you really think that I would do something like your friend Adelaide? Throw myself after an untrustworthy young man and, in doing so, ruin my life?" Kitty lifted her eyebrows.

160

"I certainly would hope and pray that you wouldn't do something like Adelaide did, yes. I wouldn't wish her life on any young woman."

"Do you really think someone like Henry Thomas would do something like that, that he would seduce and abandon me?"

"My concern is not with this Henry Thomas, I know nothing about him. The person I'm concerned about is you, Kitty. You love expensive things. You seem to be interested, as far as I can tell, in a man just because he appears to be able to provide you with luxuries. I just don't want you to be seduced by appearances, as poor Adelaide was. I want to see you make something of your own life, to be able to support yourself, if need be. To make something of yourself, whether or not a man is involved." Aunt Mabel leaned back on the seat of the cab and closed her eyes, as if exhausted.

Kitty opened her mouth to protest to her aunt that she wasn't like that at all. She was, after all, enrolled in a teaching course and intended to get her certificate, and then to teach, at least for a year or two. She knew being a teacher would never bring her the riches she dreamed of, but she would be able to support herself if she had to. Teaching was a respected profession; and she would never have to be ashamed of herself. But she could see that her aunt wasn't in a receptive mood, that she was worn out from the visit to her old neighborhood and her old friend. She had been planning to tell her aunt about her classes and her new friend, and the dirty little children they were learning to teach. But there would come a time for that. Meanwhile, perhaps it would be best that her aunt believed she was responsible for her ambition to be a teacher.

Kitty pondered the mixed messages her aunt seemed to have given her as she selected potatoes at the greengrocers that afternoon. She picked up a large potato, the kind she preferred, as peeling it took no longer than peeling a small potato but delivered much more to serve, and addressed it aloud. "What does Aunt Mabel expect me to do—join a convent?" she asked the potato before throwing it into her bag. She picked up another and, wagging her finger as she spoke, asked it, "Just because she was a spinster until she was thirty doesn't mean I have to be. And how can she say not to encourage such a fine man as Henry Thomas? Just look at him. And won't I be accepting any invitation he sends me, well, almost any one?" She scrutinized the potato and threw it back into the bin, rejecting it for the green tinge that appeared beneath its skin. She pulled out another, larger potato and once again spoke aloud, "And would you believe that Brian Kelleher has not even written me, not in the weeks and weeks he's been away in New Orleans. Not even a picture postcard!"

"May I help you, madam?" asked the storekeeper, who had scurried over to her side of the shop, wringing his hands. "Are you finding what you need?" He kept a safe distance from her, wary of a woman who appeared to be carrying on a conversation with root vegetables.

Kitty held out the bulbous potato that she clutched in her hand and gestured at the shopkeeper with it. "Yes, sir, I am finding what I need as it comes to potatoes. But the question I have, sir, and this is not a question I'd expect you to answer, is whether I am finding what I need as it comes to the life I intend to live." And she marched out of the store without even paying for the potatoes, leaving behind a flabbergasted storekeeper who could only think that something about his potatoes had upset her.

Kitty stomped along for almost two blocks before she realized that she had forgotten to pay for the potatoes. She would stop in on Monday morning on her way to school and give the man the money. It would do her no good to have to avoid the shop in the future. He had the best produce in the area and good prices, too, when she remembered to pay. The incident made her laugh at herself, and she amused herself for the rest of the walk thinking about how she could embellish the story about her conversations with potatoes. How her parents would laugh at such a story! Perhaps it wouldn't be a good idea to share with them the actual topics of her harangue—it was bad enough to be caught addressing potatoes with her problems, but it would be better not to specify those problems.

NINETEEN

The note from Henry Thomas arrived, addressed to Miss Katherine Coakley in care of Mr. and Mrs. Patrick Coakley, at their Magnolia Avenue address. Aunt Mabel handed it to her, unopened, when Kitty stopped by Marshall Field's to visit her after her classes on Wednesday. "If the lad knows what's good for him, there had better be an apology in this," she said, her face grim.

Kitty ripped open the envelope and quickly scanned the note. She smiled. "Yes, there is . . . an apology." She didn't tell her aunt that Henry's apology was for posting the note to her at her aunt and uncle's address because he didn't have her home address.

"So are you going to see him?" Her aunt's curiosity was stronger than her stern manner.

"Yes, yes, yes. He's asked me to a concert, the Chicago Symphony concert, next Sunday. At the Auditorium Theater, no less." Kitty twirled around, clutching the letter to her chest. "The Chicago Symphony."

"And just where is the young man going to be picking you up? Must I supply a cover story for you once again?" Had Kitty looked up at her aunt's face, she would have seen that her no-nonsense tone didn't match the twinkle in her eye.

"No, Aunt Mabel. I don't think that will be necessary. He offers to pick me up at home, if I give him the address. But I just might make other arrangements." Kitty's mind was racing. She'd prefer that Henry not visit her home just yet. She tried to convince herself that it wasn't because she was ashamed of it, but she knew that's what it was. There must be a way to meet Henry without involving her parents. She wished Ceecee had stopped with her at Marshall Field's and hadn't taken the streetcar home. Ceecee was good at doing exactly what she wanted and explaining it in the most convincing way.

"Well, let me know if there's anything I can do to help," Aunt Mabel said to Kitty, as a customer approached her, demanding her attention.

"I will, Aunt Mabel, I will," Kitty said, walking slowly away from the shop, her mind swimming with possible strategies. "Thank you for delivering my letter." She wished they were on the telephone at home, she could call Ceecee, as the Carters had a telephone. But a telephone was a luxury that her father did not see as necessary. She would have to wait until tomorrow to confer with Ceecee on this important matter.

Ceecee wasn't on the same streetcar the next morning, so Kitty wasn't able to get her advice until lunchtime, when the two of them sat at one of the small, children's tables under the trees where they brought their lunches. A cold wind was blowing, bringing down the last remaining leaves, but they preferred the privacy over the warmer, yet more crowded lunchroom. Ceecee had met Henry at a party, she had told Kitty, and she was curious about what Kitty saw in him. She understood, though, why Kitty might not want to bring Henry home to meet her parents just yet.

"After all," Ceecee said, "You don't want to get them excited about him—or against him—right away. At least not until you decide if he's worth it. Why upset them unnecessarily? It's just kinder to put off their meeting him until you're more sure about him."

"More sure about him?"

"Yes, whether you want to make the effort for him. Men take a great deal of effort, you know."

Kitty envied Ceecee's self-confident manner. She had many suitors, Ceecee had confided, and it took a great deal of work to make sure that none of them were aware of the others. "Although it might be fun to pit the dudes against each other," she had said. As if she were speaking about dog fights. It wasn't an attitude Kitty fully shared, but Ceecee did make it sound exciting. She decided she'd reply to Henry's letter from home that night, after she and Ceecee were able to spend the whole streetcar ride home discussing what strategy to use in her response.

"My dear Mr. Thomas," Kitty wrote, sitting on her bed with one of her schoolbooks propped against her bent knees to use as a writing desk. Her bedroom was the only place in the small cottage where she could find the privacy to write her letter. Without her brothers home, her parents had only her to watch over, and they did, as if she were the last baby bird left in the nest. "Thank you for the invitation to hear the Chicago Symphony perform," she wrote. "It will be my pleasure to accompany you on Sunday."

All right, that was the easy part. Now she had to make sure that he wouldn't insist on picking her up at home. She and Ceecee agreed that it was best to meet him there, and avoid any confrontations with her family. "As it happens . . ." She stopped and sucked on the end of the pen. "I will be in the neighborhood of the Auditorium Theater on Sunday . . ." She paused again, wondering if she should make up a reason for being there or just skip over it. Least said, soonest mended, she thought, and continued, ". . . and I will meet you there at half past two." Did she need to say anything more? Best to keep it short. "I look forward to seeing you on Sunday." There, that should be enough. Now, did she put her address on the envelope? Her home address? Or her aunt's? She looked into the mirror sitting on her dresser. Did she look like someone who lived on West Adams Street? Or did she look higher class, perhaps? Like someone who lived on Lake Shore Drive. Or Magnolia Avenue. She sighed. She could use the West Adams address if she wanted to receive an answer that wouldn't come through Aunt Mabel's hands. But her parents would be sure to comment if she received a missive from him at home. Best not to put any address.

Kitty jumped off the bed and fluffed out her skirt. She'd post the letter from the Loop on her way to school in the morning. She still had chapters to read in the schoolbook that had done duty as her desk. Perhaps a cup of tea would help focus her mind. She tiptoed into the quiet, dark kitchen. It was late, and her parents had gone to bed long before. But there would be hot water in the kettle.

It was raining, the cold, sleety rain that gets into your bones and makes you feel old, Kitty thought as she raced down Michigan Avenue to the Auditorium Theater. The streetcar had been slow and filled with wet, angry people. She meant to leave plenty of time to meet Henry, but on Sunday, the cars didn't run as frequently as they did during the week. She stopped on Michigan before the elegant arches only to find that this was the Auditorium Hotel. A friendly doorman directed her to the Auditorium Theater around the corner on Congress Street. She turned the corner, ran down the colonnade almost all the way back to Wabash, and there was Henry, leaning on a furled black umbrella. She took a deep breath, so she wouldn't look hurried, and sauntered up to him.

"I do hope I'm not late," she said, looking up at him.

"Not late at all," he said, offering her his arm. "Come, let's go in."

Kitty took his arm as they walked through the golden doors into the theater. The marble floor of the lobby glittered with the reflection of the elaborate chandeliers. Despite the size of the crowd, it was quiet and orderly. Most of the men wore suits, like Henry's, although possibly not as well tailored. Kitty was pleased that she had chosen the dark dress she wore, as the women were dressed well, in somber tones, if not in black.

"Egad," Henry said. "It's my Auntie Lou." Kitty saw a short, persistent woman dressed in black pushing through the crowd toward them.

"Aunt Louise, what a pleasant surprise," he said as she reached them. She stood there with glowing eyes and a big smile, staring at Kitty. He hesitated, and then stammered, "Aunt Louise. May I present my friend, Miss Katherine Coakley. Kitty, this is my aunt, Miss Louise Thomas. No relation, of course to today's conductor, Maestro Theodore Thomas."

Kitty had never been introduced to any of Henry's family back in their high school days, although she could recall seeing Henry's parents at their graduation, when Henry had been valedictorian. This little woman resembled Mr. Thomas, and Henry, for that matter, in many ways—the pale white skin, clear light blue eyes, angular face, thin pale lips, erect stature. Her light brown hair was pulled back from her face with a black band, making her look like a schoolgirl dressed in grownup clothes. Thin as she was, her face was youthful and inquisitive. She smiled as if at a secret joke, and said, "I'm very pleased to meet you, Miss Coakley, is it?"

Kitty bobbed a little curtsey and said, "And I am pleased to meet you, Miss Thomas." She wondered what that smile might mean on Henry's aunt's face. Did she think it was amusing that Henry had invited her to the concert?

As Henry was trying to explain to Kitty that he hadn't known his aunt would be here, a heavyset man broke through the press of the crowd, panting slightly like a hunting dog trying to keep up with his prey. His forehead gleamed with perspiration, and he pulled out a giant white handkerchief from his pocket and wiped it. "Henry, my boy, good to see you. Your parents never told me you'd be here today."

Henry went through the introduction of his Uncle Herman to Kitty, explaining that his aunt and his uncle were his father's sister and brother. Kitty didn't see how that mattered, but it seemed important to Henry to emphasize that they weren't married to each other, even though their surnames were the same. Miss Thomas explained that Henry's parents had given them their tickets to that afternoon's concert, when they realized that another engagement would prevent them from attending. Henry nodded to show that he knew his parents wouldn't be there, but he seemed somewhat astonished to see his aunt and uncle.

The four of them stood there in silence after the introductions, until Henry, looking up at the high vaulted ceiling, said, "Do you know this building is the largest in Chicago, possibly the world? And the tower was the tallest spot in Chicago when it was built ten years ago."

"Why yes, dear. I remember when they were building it—traffic was tied up in every direction," his aunt said. "Now, Miss Coakley, did you say you were related to the Hiram Coakleys of Astor Street? They're faithful customers of mine."

"No, ma'am," Kitty said. "The Michael Coakleys of West Adams Street. St. Patrick's parish." As soon as the last three words came out of her mouth, Kitty regretted them. Since the parish name meant nothing to non-Catholics, why did she persist in identifying herself in that way?

Miss Thomas pursed her lips.

Henry, who had been standing with his head bent back, admiring the ceiling, broke in. "Mr. Adler solved a number of engineering problems when he built this building," he said. "Not to mention creating its perfect acoustics. Would you like to hear about them?" Kitty could see that he was completely caught up in his admiration for the architecture of the building, rather than his aunt's interest in her.

"And just what it is you do?" asked Miss Thomas. "On West Adams Street."

Before Kitty had a chance to answer, an usher walked through the throng, tapping a small gong, and Mr. and Miss Thomas left to take their seats. As they walked up the stairs to the second balcony, Kitty forgot her nervousness about Henry's family, so enraptured was she with the majesty of the setting. The arched ceiling was made of gold, with tiny lights embedded in it. Kitty felt as if she were entering heaven.

Henry seemed to take a personal pride in pointing out the architectural details that made it unique, as if he himself had been the architect. "This is the largest auditorium in America," he said. "Bigger even than New York's opera house. In the summer, it's air-cooled and even now, heated, through the concealed ducts in the arches. More than four thousand people can be seated in here," he said, as they found their own seats toward the middle of the third row.

"Now is it your aunt or your uncle who lives with your grandfather?" Kitty asked, arranging her cloak over the back of her seat.

"Shh," Henry whispered, staring ahead, "The music is about to begin."

"Beethoven," Kitty said, opening the program. "Henry, I adore Beethoven."

Maestro Theodore Thomas had already picked up his baton, and Henry lifted his finger to his lips. Kitty continued, "Did I ever tell you about when Madame Nettlehorst was working with me on Beethoven's *Ode to Joy*, and . . ."

"Be quiet," Henry said directly into Kitty's ear. "The orchestra is playing." A man in front of them whipped an angry glare over his shoulder. Kitty stared down in her lap, feeling like a pet that had just been reprimanded. At all the concerts she had attended before, people always talked in a whisper when the band was playing. It seemed unnatural to sit in such an enormous group of people and not hear a sound but the music. How did the musicians know that their audience appreciated them?

When Maestro Thomas put down his baton to signal the piece was over, Kitty waited to applaud until Henry began. "Such wonderful music," Kitty said. "And did you notice the violinist over there, not the first violin, but the, let's see, the fourth one back from him? Doesn't he just look like your Uncle Herman, was it? In fact, I thought . . ."

The maestro tapped his baton for silence, and Henry held up his hand. "We'll talk at the interval," he whispered quickly. Kitty pouted, didn't he want to hear what she was thinking? He seemed to be interested only in the music and not in her.

Kitty recognized the next piece by Bach, and beat the time with her hand on the armrest, as Madame Nettlehorst had done when Kitty played it. This action enraged the glaring man in front of them, who stared back at her as if his gaze could make her disappear. Henry put

169

his hand over hers, and she looked up at him and smiled. She could feel the warmth of his hand atop hers as he gripped her hand tightly.

The first thing Kitty said when they headed to the balcony lobby for intermission was, "Thank you for inviting me today. I've never been to a symphony concert before. Not a real symphony, that is."

"You mean Madame Nettlehorst never brought you here?"

"No, a music teacher's income couldn't cover such luxuries," she said. "Nor mine." She had wondered whether she should tell him this—would he think poorly of her?—but at least it would make him realize how much his invitation had meant to her. Ceecee had pointed out that was a good thing to do, to let a man know you appreciated what he did for you.

Henry leaned over to whisper into her ear, "You are the loveliest woman here at the concert." Kitty glowed—she did feel beautiful in this gorgeous setting, the heavenly music still in her head. Henry left her to get them wine and she looked over the railing at the people on the main floor. She wondered if any of them were looking up at her and admiring her too, wondering who she was. The music had lifted her up into another sphere of beauty and light.

Henry returned with the wine in slender glasses, and again regaled her with descriptions of the building and how Louis Sullivan and Dankmar Adler had solved a myriad of engineering problems to erect this structure. Kitty remained in her bubble of beauty, hardly registering what he was talking about. She sipped the sweet wine, wondering if she already was drunk on the richness of her experience.

Kitty's otherworldly mood continued through the second half of the concert, Bach in his most melodious themes and variations, and she could hardly believe it when Maestro Thomas put down his baton for the final time. The previously passive audience sprang to life, jumping up in their seats and pounding their hands together, shouting "Bravo! Bravo!" Henry seemed livelier than she had ever seen him, and they chatted in their seats while the others made their way out of the auditorium.

"Well, how did you like it?" Henry asked.

"It was beautiful, Henry, beautiful. I felt as if I were in the most beautiful church in the world, or in God's heaven. Heavenly, that's what it was, heavenly," Kitty whispered.

Henry looked as pleased as if he had been playing the music himself. "Would you care to join me in a light supper at the café?" he asked.

"I'd love to, but I must get home, my parents are waiting for me." Kitty and Ceecee had planned this out beforehand. If he asked her out to eat, she should say she had to get home. Missing a meal might cause her parents to be suspicious of where she had been. It was best to keep their meeting short, Ceecee said, leave him wanting more.

"Then allow me to escort you home," Henry said, standing and offering his hand to help her out of the seat. "It gets dark early these days, and I believe it might still be raining."

Kitty was tempted to say yes. After spending the afternoon in heaven, it would spoil her mood to go home by herself. In the plan she and Ceecee had cooked up, she was to take the streetcar home alone. They hadn't dealt with the fact that she might actually *want* to be escorted home. "Let's see what the weather is like," she said. "If it's raining, we may not be able to get a cab."

The crowd had thinned and they reached the outside door quickly. Looking out through the colonnade arch, they could see how dark and wet and bleak Congress Street looked. And empty, except for a line of carriages for hire waiting quietly along the curb, stretching nearly to Michigan Avenue.

TWENTY

A nd where shall I direct the driver?" Henry asked, sitting forward on his seat in the carriage. Kitty hesitated. While she would prefer to go to the better address where her aunt and uncle lived, she knew that she had to return home that afternoon. And she knew that her parents would be home—where else would they be on a Sunday afternoon during a heavy rainstorm? She could think of no way to avoid introducing Henry to them. And them to Henry. Perhaps it was time to do so. Certainly, if she wanted to see Henry again. She gave Henry her address on West Adams Street.

In the darkness of the cab, Kitty began to worry about what Henry might think when he saw where she lived. If he knew that she had set her sights above her origins, she thought, he might not judge her harshly. So she told him about her ambition to become a kindergarten teacher. She described the "urchins," as she and Ceecee called them, and impressed upon him how her fellow students represented some of the best families of the city.

Henry was supportive of her dreams and praised her for seeking out the training. He then confided his own ambitions. He told her how his grand tour of Europe had been curtailed by the death of his sister Eleanor in April, how he had cut off his studies and remained in Chicago after the funeral, first to work with his father on Chicago's Sanitary District, and then, how he had managed to secure a position with the architectural firm headed by the Chicagoan he most admired, Daniel Hudson Burnham. "You'll remember Mr. Burnham," Henry said fervently. "He's the man who brought about the White City at the World's Fair."

172

"Of course," Kitty murmured, nodding in the darkness. "Daniel Burnham." She thought she might have heard his name before.

"So now I'm working every day in the office of D. H. Burnham and Company, in the Rookery Building, you know, at LaSalle and Adams. I help draw the blueprints builders use to create the buildings. It's a grand stepping stone to where I want to go, to designing the buildings themselves."

Kitty was impressed that Henry was actually on the way to achieving his goal, to build tall buildings. And she did recall the Rookery, that tall, reddish building, looking like an immense Moorish castle set down on a corner in the city's financial district. Didn't she pass it on the streetcar twice a day on her way to and from school? It was on that corner where she had seen Henry, weeks ago, crossing the street as if in a dream. Maybe he had been in a dream of designing his own buildings. She pressed him to tell her more about his job, more about Mr. Daniel Burnham. She had never heard him speak so long and so animatedly about any subject.

Henry was still describing the plans he was working on for a building in Pittsburgh when the carriage came to a stop in front of Kitty's home. It was still raining, and the cottage looked woebegone in the dark mist, with wet leaves plastered on the stones that served as a pavement up to the door. "You needn't come in," she said to Henry as he stood in the rain to help her out of the carriage.

"I'll see you to the door," he said, crooking his arm for her.

Kitty looked up to see a face at the front window. Oh dear, was it her brother Mickey? When did he get home? And if Mickey were home, that meant most likely Pat and John and Billy would be too. Oh, why hadn't they stayed up in Superior for one more day? Why hadn't she taken the streetcar home?

Henry had begun to thank her for accompanying him to the symphony, when Mickey threw open the front door. Kitty turned her head to say something to her brother just as Henry bent down to kiss her. His kiss landed on the edge of her cloak, which Kitty had pulled up over her head because of the rain.

Mickey said in a stern voice, "About time you got home, Miss Coakley!"

A look of surprise appeared on Henry's face at the sight of the disheveled brother in the doorway, only one suspender buckled, unkempt whiskers on his chin, smelling of smoke and unwashed clothes. He stepped back, then took Kitty's hand and bowed over it. "A pleasant good evening, Miss Coakley," he stammered, and he fled back to the safety of the cab.

Kitty stood on the front porch, hands on her hips and glared at her brother. "Michael James Coakley, how dare you?" Kitty said, stamping her foot on the wooden porch. "How often is it that I have a friend over, and here you go and scare him away." Tears were brimming in her eyes.

"Calm down, Kitty, calm down. You don't want that sissy anyway. Why would you even look at someone like him when there's men like Brian Kelleher who would love to be putting his arms around you?"

"Mickey, I could kill you. If Brian Kelleher wants to hear from me, well, he just better let me hear from him. Sometimes I think it's just you and Daniel have made up Brian's being interested in me. I hear more about it from you than I ever do from Brian."

"Brian's just, just . . . Brian just doesn't say much. But that doesn't mean he isn't thinking, he's thinking a great deal about you. I know that to be true."

"How could you possibly ever know that, Michael Coakley? Brian's been away for nearly a month, and he is sure not one for writing. And it's not as if you're a one for reading."

"I hear things. I hear things around the neighborhood. Brian has friends he keeps in touch with one way or another. If you ever stayed in the neighborhood yourself, Miss Kitty Coakley, perhaps you'd be hearing those things too."

Their father was standing with his back to the fireplace, smoking his pipe and watching the discussion between brother and sister as if watching a prize fight to decide which fighter to put his money on. He smiled at them and finally said, "Enough, enough. Michael Coakley,

Junior, can't you see you're upsetting your sister? Keep this up and we'll have no one to put our dinner on the table."

"Oh, you men," Kitty said, throwing her cloak at a hook in the hallway. She stamped her foot once again, and turned on her heel to enter the kitchen. She grabbed her gingham apron off the hook and pulled it over the head. She pulled a boiled potato out of the pot with a fork, put it into a bowl, and began to mash it as if it represented the head of an enemy. Might as well put my anger to work, she thought, starting on a second potato. An angry woman's mashed potatoes have no lumps.

Soon she got into the rhythm of the task, and her mind cooled down until she was casting back on her afternoon spent with Henry Thomas, and how well he had looked, and how well-dressed, despite the weather, and how interesting his conversation about his job and his dreams. And he had said he'd like to see her again. These pleasant thoughts filled her brain, pushing out the negative thoughts occasioned by her brother's taunting, and slowed her rhythm as she mashed the potatoes and poured in milk, adding some lumps of butter and a few pinches of salt, and then covered the pan and put it on the stove to stay warm. By the time she pulled the aromatic roast out of the oven, she had regained her cheery manner, and was singing to herself the chorale from the Bach piece.

Her father poked his head into the kitchen. "Aha, Kitty darling. And weren't you ever the one not to hold on to your anger. That's an excellent good virtue to have, my dear. Especially in dealing with Irish men."

By the time Kitty was able to join her family at the table, the boys were regaling their parents with tales of their exploits on the lumber schooners of Lake Superior. Kitty slid into her chair and focused on the food in front of her. She could feel her mother's eyes on her from across the table, but she stubbornly refused to raise hers to meet them.

When the boys paused to shovel their food into their mouths and the table was quiet, Mrs. Coakley cleared her throat. "And so, Kitty, what do you have to say for yourself? And who was that young man escorting yourself home today?"

The faces of everyone at the table were turned toward her. She didn't want the attention, she would have preferred to eat quietly and ignore the others, but she knew she had to speak up for herself. "That was Henry Thomas. He's a friend of mine, he is. I knew him at Lake View High School. He's now an architect, designing buildings. He works for the great Daniel Burnham. I suppose you know who he is?" She stared defiantly at her parents and her brothers.

"He's the one who built the White City," Pat said, looking up from his plate momentarily. "So what?"

"So why didn't you bring him into the parlor to meet us?" her father asked. "You're not ashamed of us, are you?" He had a smile on his face as if he were joking, but Kitty knew he was serious.

"I would have brought him into the parlor if my dear brother Mickey here hadn't chased him away," Kitty said.

"Oh, as if someone afraid of me would be able to handle you," Mickey jeered. "You're far the fiercer one, I should say."

"Be quiet, Mickey," Mr. Coakley said. "I won't have you making fun of your little sister. So where did you find this Henry Thomas, Kitty? And how was it he was bringing you home?"

"I ran into him at a symphony concert this afternoon," Kitty said. "And because it was raining so badly, he said he would give me a ride home. He's a very nice man." All that was the truth, just a little bit stretched out.

"Do you plan on seeing this very nice man again?" her father asked.

"I don't know. Perhaps."

"Well, if you do, make sure you bring him inside to meet us," Mr. Coakley said. "I don't like the idea of your spending time with someone I haven't met yet."

The boys muttered things under their breath and nudged one another. Kitty pretended to ignore them, but knew the sorts of things they were saying. Anyone better dressed or more successful than themselves was subject to their ridicule. She'd heard it all before.

After dinner, her father and brothers melted away, off to their own considerations, and Kitty and her mother cleared the table. "I'll clean up the kitchen, Mama," Kitty said, seeing how worn out her mother looked. "You go in and relax. I'll bring you a cup of tea." She was just as happy working by herself anyway, without any intrusive questions. She liked being left alone with her thoughts, especially when she created a fantasy for herself that this was her own home and her own kitchen, and it was her husband, not her father, sitting in the living room, reading the newspaper. She didn't identify this man in her fantasy, he was just "the husband." And she, "the wife," bustled around the kitchen, putting things where she could find them, rearranging the contents of cabinets, straightening linens and curtains until they were just so. She knew that she should spend some time going over her lessons for the next day, but she felt content, for that evening anyway, to be just a housewife.

It wasn't until she put her head down on her pillow much later that evening that she allowed herself the luxury of thinking about the concert and about Henry, poring over everything he said and did and wondering what he thought of her and how she had appeared to him. She didn't like him shushing her during the concert, although he had done it quietly. She did like that he fit in so well at the symphony and was comfortable and entranced with the music. She wished they had a longer time to talk, and that she could have told him more about her life, her schooling and her plans for the future. The pleasant memories of her time with Henry at the symphony concert filled her thoughts, and before she knew it, she was fast asleep.

Kitty was surprised, when she awoke, that she had slept through the night without stirring, as full as her mind had been when she went to sleep. It was still dark when she heard her father's footsteps creeping down the stairs, trying not to wake the rest of the family. She pulled on her dressing gown and followed him into the kitchen.

"Where's Mama?" she asked.

"I'm letting her have a bit of a lie-in this morning. She seemed tired," he said, putting on the kettle. "I'll bring her up a cup of tea when it's ready."

Kitty went back into her room and dressed carefully for her day at school. Now that she knew where Henry worked, there was every chance that she might run into him in the Loop. She wondered if he'd write her again and set up another date. If he posted a note this morning, there was every chance she might even get it this afternoon.

Why was it that without Ceecee the school day passed so slowly? Kitty had been so eager to share the details of her date with Henry that she forgot that Ceecee had said that she wouldn't be there on Monday. Apparently, her parents thought it more important for her to entertain her aunt and uncle from New York than to attend classes. The children, having been cooped up because of the rainy Sunday, were full of energy on Monday morning. And the afternoon of lectures seemed much too confining when the sunshine outside teased her through the window. She was certain that the large clock on the schoolroom wall had stopped ticking. When the final bell rang, Kitty gathered up her books and flew out of the room. Racing to the streetcar stop, she jumped on the back of the departing car, causing the motorman to pull her in by the hand and say, "Whoa, take it easy, young lady."

Kitty contemplated not transferring to another car when she reached the Loop and walking the mile or so home. It was such a beautiful fall day, and she knew there wouldn't be that many more of them. And who knew, she might run into Henry Thomas. She hopped off the car at State and Adams and headed west, the sun in her face, carefully checking the faces in the crowd especially as she passed the Rookery at LaSalle. It was mid-afternoon, and the streets weren't as crowded as they would be at the end of the day. No Henry appeared, but the energy of the Loop, the rushing people, horsecars and bicycles, carriages and pushcarts, invigorated her further. She loved the bustle of the city, and almost bounced as she strode toward the river, St. Patrick's and beyond.

Because she had caught the earlier car, Kitty arrived home about the same time she would have if she had transferred streetcars. She would have preferred to sit on the front stoop and continue to admire the day, but Monday was her mother's washday and she welcomed Kitty's help in pinning up the wet laundry. So she wasn't surprised as she came up the block to see her mother, a shawl over her shoulders, standing on the front porch and waving to her to hurry up.

"Come, Kitty, come. I've got a grand surprise for you!" her mother said.

It's probably the note from Henry, Kitty thought, smiling to herself, and quickening her pace.

"Our Kitty," her mother said excitedly. "Would you have a look at who's sitting here? Sipping tea in our very parlor."

Wiping her feet on the front mat, Kitty stepped inside the little house. And there was Brian Kelleher, sitting in front of the fire on the sofa, blowing across a cup of tea to cool it. His tan face looked rosy in the stifling heat created by the laundry tubs.

"Why, Brian, this is a surprise," Kitty said, fluffing out her hair where it had been crushed by her scarf. She sat down next to him on the sofa and reached across the small table to pour herself a cup of tea.

"Oh, Kitty, isn't it grand to see Brian again?" her mother gushed. "I've invited him to join us for supper, too. I hope that's all right with you."

"Of course, Mama," Kitty said, looking over at her mother, still wrapped in her shawl in front of the blazing fire, looking tiny and frail. Brian's presence had cheered her up, she could see from the animated expression on her face and the twinkle in her eye. There was nothing her mother loved more than an audience, and Kitty knew that with no one else in the house during the day, her mother was lonely. But wouldn't cooking a big supper and entertaining Brian destroy her own plan for the evening of finishing the laundry and catching up with her schoolwork? There weren't enough hours in the day for all she had to do, much less what she wanted to do. And it was good to see Brian again. Even dressed in his faded corduroy trousers, his big dirty boots dripping dark puddles into the rag rug in front of the fireplace, the bandana tied around his neck like that of someone who would shovel coal or drive a delivery cart. She mentally compared his appearance with that of Henry Thomas yesterday. Brian seemed to fit better in this room than Henry would have, she thought. But wouldn't it have been funny if Brian had appeared here yesterday, instead of today? That would be a story to share with Ceecee.

TWENTY-ONE

S o, Brian, how was New Orleans?" Kitty asked, savoring the rich taste of the tea, inhaling the spicy tang of the cinnamon her mother always added to the teapot.

"Good," Brian said, dropping his stare from Kitty's face to the depths of his teacup. "We managed to get a good price on a great deal of lumber."

"Brian's been telling me all about how him and his dad rode the railroad down to the Gulf of Mexico, Kitty," said Kitty's mother, more animated than Kitty had seen her for a while. Mrs. Coakley threw her arms around herself and shivered, despite the fire in the fireplace. "And would you believe that it's summer down there when it's winter up here? Down there in Louisiana, they don't even have to throw on a jacket or a scarf, when all of us are shivering and wearing everything we own."

Kitty smiled, for it was unusual these days for her mother to express much of a thought or an opinion. "So is that true, Brian, not even a coat or a scarf?"

Brian carefully placed his cup and saucer down on the table and wiped his upper lip with the napkin from his lap. Kitty noticed that her mother had given him one of the good Irish linen napkins usually kept for holiday dinners.

"'Tis true, Miss Kitty. And wouldn't you know, there are flowers everywhere? All winter, flowers growing in everyone's gardens. Even in January."

Kitty closed her eyes and thought about flowers growing up through the snow, their rich colors—red, purple, bright yellow—like fireworks exploding against a blanket of white. Although there wouldn't be snow if the flowers were growing. But winter in Chicago meant snow and dark, gloomy days. It was difficult to imagine a world without snow, difficult even to imagine walking on a clear pavement rather than through the dirty, wet and nasty slush that turned every Chicago street and pathway into an obstacle course of puddles. She opened her eyes to see Brian's gaze fixed firmly on her face.

"We're thinking of moving down there, down to New Orleans, me and my pa," Brian said. His eyes didn't move from her face.

Kitty closed her eyes again and sipped her tea. Brian couldn't have said what he just said. Moving? Why, the Kellehers had always lived in St. Pat's. "So when is it that you'll be moving?" she asked, gently putting down her cup on the tray.

Brian was biting his lower lip so hard that Kitty was afraid a jet of blood might spurt out from it, like water from a hose.

"I don't rightly know," he said, running his hand through his sandy hair. "Soon. But perhaps not too soon. But anyways . . . ," and here he managed a slight smile, a grin actually, that reminded Kitty of the little boy without his front teeth that Brian had been when he and Daniel started walking to school together in the first grade. " . . . Anyways, we'll be spending most of the summers here in Chicago. It's awful hot in New Orleans that time of year, and my pa says that Chicago will be growing more than New Orleans, and you'll be needing our lumber here more than they need it down there."

Kitty hadn't been aware that she'd been holding her breath until she let it out in one big woosh that caused the gaslight on the table next to her to flicker. She hadn't realized, until she saw him sitting there, across from her mother, that she had missed his restful presence in the few weeks he'd been gone. And then to hear that he was moving away. That sounded so final. But to know that she would see him from time to time, that he would return like the flowers returned, or like the red-breasted robins she loved to see, harbingers of the fine weather that prevailed in the summertime. That she could deal with.

"I was just saying to your mother, Kitty, that perhaps when she's feeling better, her and you can get on a train and come down to New Orleans some day," Brian said.

Kitty looked over at her mother, who was smiling and nodding. Poor dear, she hadn't much to look forward to, cooped up in this cottage, alone most of the day. Perhaps the prospect of a journey to someplace like New Orleans—a place that sounded so exotic, so French, and so unlike muddy old Chicago—perhaps that would encourage her to get better. As for herself, Kitty thought, patting her hair, New Orleans had always seemed like a fashionable place, like Europe almost, where ladies and gentlemen dressed in the latest fashions and attended dramatic presentations and balls and, oh, all sorts of exciting events you didn't find in Chicago. She looked over at Brian—his nose was running slightly in the warmth of the room and he'd wipe it with the back of his hand the way her brothers always did—Brian didn't look like her picture of a gentleman from New Orleans. But people could change, couldn't they? And who knew what effect New Orleans might have on an Irish hooligan from St. Pat's?

"I'll just be cleaning up these tea things and putting together supper for us," Kitty said, standing and shaking out her skirt. "No, that's all right, Brian, I can handle this. Why don't you just sit here and tell Mama more about that great metropolis of New Orleans. Get her all ready for our visit, don't you know, perhaps after Christmas when I have some time off from my classes." And she carried the teapot and cups into the kitchen, hoping that she could manage to pull down all the diapers and underwear that hung from the lines in front of the kitchen fireplace before Brian poked his head in and offered to help her with supper.

Kitty was grateful when her father came in and immediately took over Brian's attention. She could overhear him from the kitchen, asking Brian about his father and the business, and freeing up her mother to join her in the kitchen. While Mrs. Coakley wasn't up to standing and cooking, she was able to sit at the small table in the kitchen and fold the laundry while Kitty rattled around with the pots and pans.

When they finally all sat down around the dining room table, it was Mr. Coakley who said the blessing while they all bowed their heads. They all made the sign of the cross, and Mr. Coakley smiled and said, "We've all thanked the Lord, now let's thank our Kitty for what she's spread before us."

Kitty looked across the table at Brian—elbows on the table, hunched over his plate as if afraid someone would take it away, his knife gripped in one hand, fork in the other—he reminded her of her brothers. Her stomach tightened, for she still missed her brother Daniel, and actually all of her brothers when they were away on the boats. She never missed their laundry, though, so much in evidence now that they were home. When they headed out that morning, en route to look for jobs for the winter, they left mountains of unwashed clothes behind.

Brian caught her gaze and said, with his mouth full, "Good grub, Kitty."

Mrs. Coakley beamed. "Brian here's been telling me about the lumber business he and his daddy have got going for themselves. Looks like they'll be pulling in scads of money some day."

"Eventually," said Brian, reaching across the table to spear a potato with his fork. "'Twill take a few years, my pa says, to get the business off the ground."

"But you'll be coming home to Chicago for the summer months during that time, won't you?" Mr. Coakley said.

"'Pears so," said Brian, concentrating on the food in front of him.

Mr. Coakley turned to Kitty. "This could be a real smart operation of the Kellehers," he said. "Both Chicago and New Orleans are growing cities. And growing cities need lots of lumber." He nodded his head and watched Brian eat.

Kitty said, "Did Brian tell you that Mama and I might take the train down to New Orleans after Christmas for a visit? I've always wanted to go there."

Mr. Coakley patted his wife's hand. The strain of having company had begun to show on her face, and she looked exhausted. "I think your mama will have to get a little stronger before you start making plans. It's about time for me to tuck her up in bed for the night. Kitty, you'll see Brian out, won't you?"

Brian looked up from his plate, surprised that he was being dismissed.

Kitty said, "Oh, Brian, you don't have to leave just yet. There's apple pie left over from Sunday's dinner if you'll have a piece."

Putting food into Brian's mouth didn't mean that conversation would be flowing out of it, Kitty thought when she showed him to the door a short time later. Brian would answer questions, but would rarely offer information. "So when will we be seeing you again, Brian Kelleher?" she asked as she watched him bundle up against the wind that had been rattling the windows in the house all evening.

"I don't know, Miss Kitty. My pa and me, we'll be going back to New Orleans on Friday."

"So we won't even be seeing you in church this Sunday?"

"Guess not. Anyways, thanks for dinner." And he waved his hand as he set off in the darkness.

Kitty pushed the door shut and shuddered. Brian. Like one of her brothers, he was. Living from day to day, taking it all in his stride. No plans of his own, no great ambitions. Just doing what his father told him. And he didn't even kiss her goodbye. She went back into the kitchen and put her apron back on again. Dishes and laundry. Laundry and dishes. There must be a better life than this, she thought, grimly scraping the little that was left in a pan into the garbage.

Ceecee was back at school the next day, and Kitty couldn't wait to tell her about her two young men, Henry and Brian. Her opportunity came at noon, when the two of them were sorting songbooks in the empty practicum classroom.

"Tell me, Kitty, did Henry kiss you?"

"I suppose you could call it a kiss," Kitty said, giggling at the memory. "It was so comical, you see. He was so proper in opening the cab door and escorting me out of the cab and to my front door. And so earnest in telling me what a lovely evening he had and what a pleasure it was to accompany me to the concert."

"That's something," said Ceecee. "And . . .?"

"Just when he was bending down—he's very tall, you know, at least as tall as my father—my brother Mickey appeared at the front door. I turned my head to see who it was, and Henry landed the kiss on the edge of my cloak, which I had pulled up over my head. Because of the rain."

"Could you tell whether the kiss was directed at your cheek or your lips?" Ceecee always wanted the exact details and would keep asking questions until she got all the information.

Kitty blushed and shook her head, her hand over her mouth to stop her laughter. "No, I couldn't tell. All I could see was the look of surprise on his face, his lips pursed to kiss, his eyes wide."

"Then what did he do?"

"He just took my hand—I had my good leather gloves on, of course—and bowed over it, and said, 'A pleasant good evening, Miss Coakley.' And left straightaway in the cab."

"What did you say to Mickey?" An only child, Ceecee was fascinated with Kitty's family, especially her many brothers.

"I just glared at him, that imp. I swear he did it on purpose. 'Your toff,' he calls him. 'So did your toff give you a nice dinner?' says he. 'At one of those places where the sign on the kitchen door says, 'No Irish Need Apply?''"

"Are there really places like that in Chicago, Kitty?" Ceecee asked. Ceecee's Chicago was a small place where everyone attended the same Congregational Church as well as the same schools, dancing schools, and parties.

"Yes, of course. My brothers go up against it all the time. But I don't suppose Henry Thomas would."

"So do you think you'll see him again?"

"I don't know," Kitty said. "Sometimes I'm not sure that I want to."

"This is new. I thought he was the paragon of perfection to you. What happened? Is it Brian? Or is that Henry failed to kiss you?"

"Not that so much as, do you know, he shushed me during the concert several times. Made me feel as though I was ignorant, and me having studied music for so many years."

"You're a fine musician, Kitty Coakley, and don't let anyone tell you otherwise!" Ceecee, who would cheerfully admit that she couldn't carry a tune in a bucket, much admired Kitty's musical skills. "But you weren't actually speaking when the musicians were playing, were you?"

"Of course not. I was whispering. The musicians couldn't possibly have heard me."

"I see, that's it. Henry Thomas is German, now isn't he?"

"He was born here in Chicago, but I believe his grandparents did come here from Germany, yes."

"That's it. Fraulein used to tell me that the Germans treat music, especially the symphony, like a religion. They would consider it sinful to talk during the playing, just like it'd be a sin for you to speak while the priest is preaching. Henry was just trying to keep you from committing a sin, that's all." Ceecee more often referred to her "Fraulein," the governess who had been with her throughout her childhood, than to her mother, who, according to Ceecee, was rarely to be found at home.

Kitty was silent. While they were talking they had sorted all the songbooks and put them away on the marked shelves of the great wooden press that took up most of the classroom's back wall. How could something be a sin for one person, and not for another? A sin to talk while the musicians were playing? She'd never heard of such a thing. It was a small thing, but thinking about it made her feel strange. How could a person you thought you knew, a person with whom you had attended the same school even—how could that person be living his life by different rules than you were? And how could you not even know about it? And were there other rules of which she was equally unaware? Maybe not even just Henry Thomas, but other people, people like Ceecee even, obeyed other unwritten rules no one had ever mentioned to her. She had grown up being carefully taught the rules of right and wrong. But no one had ever explained to her that you could be different and also be right. How could she have missed that? She would have to think about this.

Ceecee was not slowed by Kitty's silence. "Now that we've finished the classroom, let's take a stroll in the park. The weather's clearing, and I do believe we might get a glimpse of the sun!"

The two young women, one tiny, one tall, strode out into the pale sunshine. "Winter's on its way," Kitty said. "It will be November soon, all dark and dreary."

"After November is December, and in December, we get our winter break. Four whole weeks with no school and no studies and, best of all, no students." The demands of drawing out language and music from these small children were particularly heavy when the poverty of their homes had given them few English language skills and still fewer reasons to burst into song.

"We're sailing to France on December 28, and from there we go by train to Geneva," Ceecee said, kicking a rock that threatened great damage to the toes of her delicate lace-front boots. "I so wish you could come with us, Kitty. It will be so boring without anyone to talk to."

Kitty's heart had soared when Ceecee first brought up the possibility of Kitty's joining her family for the voyage. "You wouldn't have to pay for a thing," she promised. To sail to Europe, even to take the train to New York for the sailing! Kitty had never left the city of Chicago. But she knew without asking them that her parents would never allow her to go. Not just because they didn't know the Carters, or even Ceecee. But both her parents had told her that after the holidays it might be possible to travel to New Orleans and visit the Kellehers.

Kitty knew that she couldn't disappoint them by making other plans. And as much as she yearned to see the sights and sounds and shops of the great capitals of Europe, she knew that she would welcome the sunshine and flowers of the South. Especially in January. And, perhaps, she had to admit to herself, she would welcome the opportunity to see Brian Kelleher once again.

TWENTY-TWO

H enry and his parents had been staying close to home, continuing their mourning for Eleanor, but a benefit for the Art Institute of Chicago drew them out one fine late October evening. Mrs. Potter Palmer, the leading light of Chicago society, was sponsoring the event, and invitations were treasured, not just because they opened the door to a benefit for a worthy cause, but because the event was held in the Palmer castle, on the reclaimed sand dunes along the lake north of the Chicago River. Ever since Eleanor began her studies at the Art Institute, the Thomas family had contributed to it. After her death, they continued to contribute in her memory. Attending the gala had been an additional inducement, for, although they had seen the castle every time they drove on Lake Shore Drive—which Potter Palmer had urged the city to build after he decided to move to the once-forsaken spot—none of them had ever entered it.

"How could we ever get in the place?" Henry asked as they approached the mansion. "They have no doorknobs." This fact about the house had emerged when it was under construction back in the 1880s—it was a fact that had puzzled the ten-year-old Henry at the time and had stuck in his mind ever since as a salient feature of the house.

"The Palmers don't need doorknobs on the outside," Mrs. Thomas responded in her smoothing-everything-over voice. "They have staff to open the doors from the inside."

"But what if the staff were busy?" Henry asked, more to lead his mother on than to explore the living habits of the extremely rich.

"Don't worry, Henry, they have enough staff to take care of everyone they choose to see," added his father, as their carriage approached the looming towers of the Palmer mansion.

The structure reminded Henry of some of the buildings his classmates at l'École des Beaux-Arts would sketch—impossible-to-construct habitats more appropriate to the pages of fairy tales than real-life constructions set down on the lakeshore of practical Chicago. Minarets, turrets, and towers sprang out of it at every level. Although the monstrosity looked more like a fiendish castle that might overhang the banks of the Rhine River in Germany, it wore the heavy robe of soot and smoke that characterized every Chicago building. Mr. Palmer could move the Gold Coast of Chicago away from Prairie Avenue on the south side, but he couldn't escape the emissions of the "dark satanic mills" that helped generate the incomes of his fellows at the Union League Club and elsewhere.

However Henry might criticize the mansion, he had to admit it was impressive to be helped out of their carriage by a liveried servant and escorted up the stairs to the open door by another, and greeted at that door by a third in the military-like livery of the household. He threw a curious look at the door as he passed, but was unable to confirm the absence of doorknobs, and wondered if it would be an appropriate question to ask when he was presented to Mrs. Palmer. He noticed his mother stretching herself up to stand as tall and as straight as she could as they approached the receiving line where Mr. and Mrs. Palmer stood, and decided that "company manners" were the order of the day and he was better off not mentioning doorknobs.

After passing through the receiving line that stretched the length of the wood-panelled foyer of the house, they were ushered in small groups to one of the two elevators, the only elevators in a private house in Chicago, although they were omnipresent in the bigger buildings downtown like the Palmer House. That hotel, owned and operated by Mr. Potter Palmer, generated only a small part of the real estate fortune that enabled the family to live like the crowned heads of Europe. The elevator whisked them up to the picture gallery at the top of the house, a seventy-five foot long room so full of artworks that they hung three or four deep on most of the walls. The Palmers collected the rather avant-garde French Impressionists—their collection was said to contain more than thirty Monet paintings as well as works by the better-known artists such as Pissarro, Corot and Sisley.

Tonight's entertainment was promised to be *tableaux vivantes*, living pictures copying famous works of art owned by the Art Institute, and peopled by some of the lovelier young women of the social circles that orbited around the Palmers.

The Thomases seated themselves at one of the small gilt tables surrounding the dance floor where one of the *tableaux vivantes* was posed. To Henry's amazement, the artist's subject, a young woman standing motionless in a wooden doorway looking out into the distance, came to life and approached their table.

"Mr. Thomas, I thought I recognized you as you came in," said the young woman holding out her hand to Henry.

Henry was surprised to see that the lovely young woman from the open doorway of the Rembrandt painting was the same woman he had met in the parlor of Daniel Burnham's house a few weeks before. Like the painting's original, her blonde hair was drawn severely back from her face, and her drab olive dress was enlivened only by a string of red beads and the glimpse of her chemise around the neckline. What was her name?

"It's Cecilia Carter," the woman said, smiling as if she had read his mind. "We met at . . ."

"Yes, at the Burnham party," Henry said, quickly finishing her sentence to let her know he hadn't forgotten her. He shook her outstretched hand. "You attended with your uncle, Mr. Anderson."

"Very good, Mr. Thomas, very good. Your memory will stand you in good stead when you're a famous architect like Mr. Burnham himself," she said, looking up at him and batting her long eyelashes.

"What makes you think I'll be a famous architect?" Henry said, touching his mustache as if to make sure it remained in the same place it had been when he left his house.

Cecilia giggled slyly. "Doesn't everyone who works for Mr. Burnham dream to someday become a famous architect himself? Chicago is full of such men, but those who actually work for Mr. Burnham seem to have the light burning much brighter in their eyes."

Henry was flattered that such a beautiful young woman would not only remember him, but would single him out in this gathering of well-born and well-connected Chicagoans. "Would you care to join us, Miss Carter?" Henry asked, gesturing toward the gilt table where his mother sat. His father stood nearby, talking to someone dressed in white tie and tails, and trying to make himself heard over the hubbub of the crowd and the orchestra tuning up. "I'm afraid I can't ask you to dance, Miss Carter, as my family remains in mourning for my sister, who left us last spring."

"I am so sorry, Mr. Thomas, I believe I heard about your sister. I used to see her at the Sunday sketching club that I—very briefly— attended. I was devastated to hear of her death at such a young age. So talented." She waved her hand at the table. "Do give my condolences to your mother and father. I'm afraid I can't sit just yet, Mrs. Palmer wants us to reenact the tableau in another parlor for yet another group of donors. A woman's work is never done." And she fluttered off in a cloud of French perfume, a blonde butterfly in the garden of black and white.

Henry watched her make her way through the maze of gilt tables, waving her hand at this dinner-jacketed gentleman and the next, the phrase "social graces" coming to his mind. Social graces, that was what this woman had in great amounts. Too bad his sister hadn't taken to society in the seemingly effortless way Miss Cecelia Carter did. He turned to look at his mother, smartly dressed in a black lace gown, a black cashmere shawl over her shoulders. She looked exhausted, poor dear, it must be difficult for her to take in all the people and talk when she had hardly left the house in months. Perhaps he should take her home. If his father wanted to stay, he could come back for him later. He hated to admit that the smoke and noise were giving him a headache. And he'd really rather be at home, reading a book or tinkering with one of the machines his Uncle Herman had given him. Maybe he lacked the social graces as much as his sister had.

Although his mother would have liked to stay and watch the *jeunesse dorée*—the golden youth as described in the romantic French novels she enjoyed reading—it was Henry Thomas Senior who insisted they make an early departure. Henry followed along, picking up the hats and coats they had surrendered at the door, holding out his mother's fur coat for her to slip over her shoulders while one of the many butlers held out his and his father's tall silk hats. Henry looked furtively for an outside doorknob as they left the house, but there was no hint of one in the deep darkness of the evening.

On the ride home, in the quiet interior of the carriage, Henry's mother asked him about the young woman he had been speaking to, who she was and how he knew her.

"I don't really know her, I met her just once, at the party at Daniel Burnham's house," Henry explained. "She just happened to be there with her uncle, Peirce Anderson, who just happens to be my boss."

"You must have made quite an impression on Miss Carter, for her to remember you all this time," Mrs. Thomas said, with some satisfaction. "She probably met several young men at that party."

"Perhaps she did," Henry said, trying to think quickly of a subject that would distract his mother from prying more deeply into his personal life. "What did you think of all those French paintings on the walls, the Palmers' collection of Impressionist art?" he asked as if he really wanted her opinion. "You know in Paris, those painters are considered to be scientists, not artists, dissecting light as if it were a dead specimen, throwing those gaudy colors on canvases without seeming to care what their subjects look like."

"Do you think you will see Miss Carter again?" his mother asked, undeterred. "Perhaps you could invite her to dinner one night. I'm sure she would be delighted to join us."

Henry could see the direction of his mother's thoughts. She was constantly suggesting that he get to know better the type of young woman she would like to see him marrying and starting a family with.

Although he would never in his life consider her to be a social climber, the young women his mother thought suitable were always from the upper echelons of society. He was her only son, after all, wouldn't any young woman be honored to meet a young man of his brilliance and good looks? Henry wasn't so sure. He knew he preferred someone of his own choice, someone like the lovely Miss Kitty Coakley, who made him feel important and accomplished, rather than a woman like Miss Cecilia Carter, in whose company he felt awkward and tongue-tied. The very social Miss Carter had made him feel like one among many, the last one chosen.

᪥

Henry brought the square envelope to his nose as if by smelling it he could capture the scent of its sender. But it smelled instead of the pocket of the heavy wool suit where he had kept it since it arrived the morning before. A warm, musty smell, if smells could be said to be warm. He looked again at the rounded copperplate return address: Miss Katherine Coakley, 1017 West Adams Street, Chicago. West Adams Street, just a few blocks from his office downtown. Across the river, of course. Very few people lived inside the Loop. He walked quickly to his bedroom window, pulled back the heavy curtains and looked out. A cold, drippy, sleeting snow fell, not the kind of weather that would make a long walk, or even a long drive, enjoyable.

He pounded down the stairs and called to his mother, lying encased in a fuzzy afghan on the parlor sofa. "Mother," he called. "I'm going out to the office for a bit. I should be home for dinner." And pulling his coat out of the hall closet, he plunged out the front door into the gloom of the November afternoon—before his mother could lift herself on her elbow, a finger marking her place in her novel, and ask, "Henry, the office? On a Sunday?" Or at least that's what he imagined she'd say as he raced down the street to Sheridan Road, where the tram occasionally ran on Sundays. He hadn't told her a lie, he was going to the Burnham office. He just wasn't going to stay there for long, just a minute or two to pick up the Marshall Field's chocolates he had stashed there a week or so ago. And from the office on LaSalle Street, it was just a few long blocks to West Adams Street, where a certain Miss Katherine Coakley lived, the Miss Coakley of the note inviting him to tea, the Miss Coakley for whom the chocolates had been especially chosen. Not that he had been sure which ones she would prefer when he chose them. But the chocolates he'd selected were beautiful, and so was she.

Fortune favored the bold, and the tram was pulling up to the corner just as Henry reached it. He bounced aboard, tossed a coin at the driver, and found a seat in the back, covered with a thin layer of ice from the open window beside it, a seat no one else had wanted. Except for the piercing wind that blew in through the open window and bit into Henry's face, the car was warm and cozy, permeated by the sharp yet somehow pleasing smell of wet wool. Henry put a newspaper beneath him, so the melting glaze did not dampen his suit, and if he just bent forward a bit, he could avoid the window's sharp arrows of cold. He put his face in his gloved hands and thought about the invitation. He had first written her, as he had told her he would, written to her at the aunt's address as that was the only one he had. She had responded promptly, in the next post, with an invitation to visit her and her family that Sunday afternoon. He knew she had at least one brother, for he'd been startled by him when he returned Kitty home from the symphony concert. But, hadn't she mentioned several on that occasion, years ago it seemed now, when he had escorted her to dinner at Henrici's? He wondered if the brother or brothers would be home. But they were all older, hadn't she said? Perhaps they were off on their own, married with their own families by now. He had always wished he had an older brother, someone to lead the way, to serve as an example. An older sister wasn't the same, although Eleanor had been his closest companion in childhood. Then, and even as young adults, she had helped focus their parents' attention away from him. But now she was gone. A sharp pang of loss passed through him. He tried not to think of Eleanor, how the two of them had been a unit.

He had been able to talk to her about things he couldn't talk about to his male friends, or certainly to their mother. Eleanor, although she had made fun of him in every way imaginable, the way big sisters did, still would take him seriously, would understand that he grew and changed every day, with new ideas, new plans, new directions. His mother still thought of him as her little boy.

Closer now to the downtown area, the tram lurched forward and then stopped more frequently. Henry wiped a circle in the frost on the closed window in front of him. The wind still howled along the lakefront, and the few people on foot looked as if they were rigid statues, bundled in blankets for a safe delivery. The car turned onto LaSalle, and Henry made his way to the exit. The sleet seemed to have stopped and he thought he could proceed much faster on foot.

Once he jumped off onto the curb, he realized his mistake. A thin, sheet of ice, as clear as glass, covered the pavement, crackling with his every step. His feet threatened to slide out from under him. He had to grab onto the tram stop sign to keep from landing on the sidewalk. He'd never get to the office like this. He looked at the street, but it promised even worse obstacles—great dunes of dark snow, with coal dust and horse manure mixed in. What he'd smell like after stomping through that! The sidewalk was the better option, despite its danger. After treading lightly for a while, grasping at posts and pillars, he soon found that if he slid his feet along as if he were skating, he had a better chance of remaining upright than if he minced along step by step. He put his hands in his coat pockets and pretended he was skating along Salt Creek, up in Palatine, as he and Eleanor had done as children, while visiting their cousins. There were few other pedestrians out in the sleety Sunday weather, and he made good progress, arriving at the Rookery in just a few minutes, his face on fire from his exertion in the cold air. His ears, which his hat didn't cover, burned when he entered the heat of the building. He bounded up the stairs to the Burnham offices, foregoing the elevator because it was too slow.

The doors were unlocked when he reached the sixth floor. When he opened the door to his department, he found some lights on, but it certainly wasn't the beehive of activity it was during the work week. A few green-eyeshaded heads rose up from their drafting tables, but no one greeted him. For some of his colleagues, the work they did was their religious observance on a Sunday, he mused, and they did not wish to be disturbed from their worship of the great god of architecture. He removed his hat, but not his coat, when he reached his table, and reached into the cubbyhole provided for his personal items. There it was, in the back, the beribboned box of candy. He would have to carry it beneath his coat to protect it from the elements.

Without calling out a goodbye to the workers, he raced back down the stairs and out into the street, skidding a bit until he regained his gliding rhythm. A cold sun made the winter sky look like a cataract in an old man's eye, thickly opaque, obstructing rather than illuminating. Henry stopped on the cold metal bridge to look down the ribbon of river, a frozen road where no boats could sail. Its surface was rough and dirty like the snow in the streets, in a city where coal dust filled the air more regularly than the snow.

Across the river, the going was much more difficult, with the wind blowing directly into his face, and the absence of sidewalks, or at least ones that were cleared. Henry was forced to walk down the middle of the street, his head bent against the biting wind, in the ruts made by the wheels of trucks and carriages. He hoped that he wouldn't be run down by a horse or a carriage, but there was little traffic to challenge his use of the roadway.

He trudged through the gray, knee-deep snow, despairing how his trousers would look, hardly aware of the neighborhood until he stopped at a tavern on the corner of Adams and Halsted. "O'Brien's", the sign said. It resembled every other Irish tavern—and there were many—in Chicago, with darkened windows, and the smell of stale beer filling the air. Taverns and saloons weren't supposed to be open on Sundays, Henry thought as he sniffed the air and watched an old man stumble through the front door, hardly dressed warmly enough for a spring day, much less the nasty onset of winter. Two blocks more and that's where the Coakley residence would be.

He tried brushing off his coat and trousers, but the thick wool soaked up whatever the elements dealt out, making the clothes heavier and stiffer than ever. He removed his hat and smoothed down his hair, gaining a layer of ice in the process, and used his fingers to comb the icicles out of his mustache. Why did anyone live in Chicago, with weather like this? He sighed, and slogged on, happy that his destination was just a block or so on, at the same time wishing that he had more time to prepare himself.

The little house was clearly marked "1017," so it had to be the one. Just as Henry raised his gloved hand to knock on the wooden door, it opened, and Katherine—Kitty—stood smiling at the door.

"Welcome," she said. "I'm ever so glad you could make it, what with this nasty weather."

Henry smiled. She was so lovely. He would have traveled to Timbuktu, wherever that was, to see that smiling face. She held the door open for him to enter the tiny entryway.

"I'll just hang your hat and coat in the kitchen," she said. "They'll dry better in the warmth from the stove."

He gave over his hat and coat and scuffed his feet on the mat in the hall. The indoor heat started melting the ice in his hair and mustache, and he tried to wipe them without calling attention to how wet they were. He entered the living room and saw two people he assumed were Kitty's parents—her father standing in front of the fire in his shirtsleeves and suspenders, her mother seated next to the fireplace, wrapped in a wool blanket, despite the warmth of the room.

"How do you do, sir," he said to Mr. Coakley, stretching out his hand. "I'm Henry Thomas. I attended Lake View High School with your daughter, Katherine."

Mr. Coakley took Henry's hand in a firm grip. "Pleased to meet you, son. Any friend of Kitty's is welcome here. This is my wife, Helen Coakley."

Henry bent over the woman in the blanket and took her hand. "My pleasure, ma'am." The tiny hand felt cold to his touch, and he couldn't make out the words she muttered.

"Oh, Henry," Kitty said as she brought a tray with a steaming teapot and cups in the room. "I was going to introduce you to my mother and my father." Her face was red with the warmth of the room and the heat of her exertions, but she looked like a rose atop, not exactly a dung-heap, but a rose in a setting that contrasted with her beauty, he thought.

Kitty placed the tray on the little table in front of the sofa, and patted a cushion to have him sit down. "I can't believe you came out in weather like this, just to visit," she said. "It looks miserable out there."

"If we Chicagoans never came out of our homes unless the weather was good," Henry said, "we'd never go anywhere at all." He caught Mr. Coakley's grin as he bent over to take the cup Kitty handed him.

"That's right, boy. Chicago isn't for the faint of heart."

Henry couldn't keep his eyes off Kitty as she bent to her task of filling the teacups. She concentrated on the flow of the tea into the cups, careful not to drip even one drop on the saucer that she had carefully wiped with a linen cloth before beginning to pour, biting the edge of her lip. Her eyes were veiled by her long lashes and for a moment Henry wished he were a painter, because the sight of her white skin, red cheeks, dark hair, and intensely blue wool dress made a picture that should be kept. Her dark hair was not pinned up, as it had been the last two times he had seen her, but billowed in a full halo around her face, making her look younger and more vulnerable.

"So, Henry, what line of work are you in?" asked Mr. Coakley, sipping from the tiny teacup.

Henry cleared his throat and brushed his mustache with a finger. It took a moment for him to return to everyday reality. "Architecture, sir. I work in the office of Daniel H. Burnham."

"An architect, eh? That's quite a job in this city."

"Yes sir."

The room remained quiet except for the crackling of the fire. Henry couldn't think of anything to say. He didn't want to talk, he just wanted to drink in the joy of watching Kitty as she poured the tea.

Finally, it was Kitty who broke the silence. "I have a brother named Daniel, actually. He just left to seek his fortune in the Pacific Northwest."

"Just got out of town in time," Mr. Coakley muttered under his breath.

"Daniel was always one to seek adventure," said Kitty.

"How many brothers do you have?" Henry asked. "I believe you've mentioned several."

"Five boys in the family, with Katherine and her older sister the engine and the caboose," said Mr. Coakley. "Katherine's still the baby."

Kitty fluffed up the skirt of her dress and smiled, her dimple coming into play. "Remember I'm no longer a baby, Da. I'm twenty-two years old, I am. An age when most of my friends are out of the house and on their own."

"You'll always be my baby, darling, no matter how old you are."

"Da. Please. Have some more tea, won't you. And Henry, does your cup need topping off?"

Henry nodded, if only to have her cross the room to fill his cup with more tea than he actually wanted. He liked to watch her movement, how she put her whole body into the simple gesture of pouring tea so that the gesture was transformed into a precise step in a complex dance. He sighed.

"Mama, I'll have to heat up more water to make you some fresh tea," Kitty said. And, with that, she left the parlor to return to the kitchen.

The sun must have just set. The brightness that had illuminated the room disappeared, and he could see the fraying plaid fabric of the sofa, barely covered by a wool blanket, and the worn spots in the rug, especially in front of the fireplace, where it also was marked by the burn marks of embers. He noticed, too, the plaster statue of a woman with her hands outstretched on the mantel, and the wooden crucifix on the wall above the chair where Kitty's mother was sitting. That must be a rosary twisted around her fingers, he thought, what he had earlier taken to be some sort of jewelry. He had never seen a rosary before, but had heard his grandfather complain of "those Papists, with their strings of beads," in his frequent rants against the immigrants lately come to Chicago.

Hearing the pounding of boots upon the staircase, he looked up, and saw a sleepy face peering over the railing.

"Hello, there. And who might you be?" asked the rumpled red-headed man, coming farther down the staircase.

"John, is that you?" asked Michael Coakley. "And weren't you supposed to be up and out early today, helping Uncle Patrick with his woodworking?"

"Saw him last night," the man said, poking around the tea tray. "In O'Brien's. Said what with the snow and all, he wasn't about to bring the lumber into the house. Said it could wait until spring. And who did you say you were?" John asked, grabbing a slice of cake and stuffing it into his mouth.

"I'm Henry Thomas, a school friend of Katherine's. And I take it you are her brother?"

John nodded, his mouth still full. His tousled head of red hair and freckles reminded Henry of someone he couldn't quite recall. Maybe it was Kitty's uncle he was thinking of.

Kitty reentered the parlor, balancing a teapot in one hand and a plate of sliced bread in the other. "Johnny," she said. "Whatever are you doing, eating all the cake when we have a guest and all? If you'd gotten up at a decent hour, you'd have had some proper food in you."

John's smile was slow and broad. "And didn't I have to come down to meet your latest beau?" he asked. "And won't Brian Kelleher be interested in hearing about this dandy from your Protestant school?"

"John Martin Coakley, that's enough!" said Mr. Coakley. "If you can't be civil to our guest, you can just leave the house."

Kitty turned to Henry and, putting her hand on his arm, said, "Don't listen to a word my brother says. He's always one for fun and games."

"That's right," John said. "Just trying to liven up a Sunday afternoon." He grabbed a slice of bread from the plate Kitty brought in, and turned to retreat back up the stairs.

Henry looked at his watch. His mother had drummed into him and his sister that personal visits, especially the first one, should last just fifteen minutes, or at most no more than thirty. He had already spent twenty minutes with the Coakleys and it was about time to take his leave. He looked over at Mrs. Coakley, who hadn't said a word the entire time he was there. She looked as if she had fallen into a trance or was at least asleep. "I must be going," he said, standing and offering his hand to her. "I promised my own mother that I'd be home for dinner." When she paid no attention to his proffered hand, he turned and faced Mr. Coakley. "I'm off, sir. It was a pleasure to make your acquaintance."

Kitty stood, and wailed, "Oh Henry, I was hoping you'd stay for supper. We have a lovely roast of beef." She looked straight at him and the blue of her eyes was so intense Henry found it difficult to answer her. More than anything, he wanted to stay, to be with her, but manners are manners, he said to himself, and he wanted to make a good impression not just with Kitty, but with her family.

"I must go," he said, breaking the lock her eyes had on his own. "It's a long way home." And in two strides, he reached the entryway on his way out.

"Oh, your coat and hat. They're still in the kitchen," Kitty said, and flew back to retrieve them.

"They're pleasantly warm," he said, taking them from her hands. "Thank you for that, and for your hospitality. I shall write you soon.

"Yes, oh yes. I mean, you're welcome. It was a pleasure to have you," she said, brushing the hair back from her face. "Have a safe journey home." And she closed the door as he stepped out.

Henry started down the now dark and deserted street. The cold air felt good on his face—it had been too warm in the room and his own scent of wet wool had made him uneasy. Short and sweet, the visit had been. Well, at least short. But that was proper. And sweet, well, it was sweet to see her again. He didn't feel that he had won over her parents, her mother had paid no attention to him at all, and her father, well, he was just one of those genial Irishmen you found almost everywhere in Chicago. And the brother? Henry could feel an underlying menace to John, but he couldn't imagine why. Oh well, he had gotten that over with, meeting the family. Perhaps the next time, the two of them could just go out together, without any family chaperones. He wondered what his mother would think of Kitty. And his father.

He spied a horsecab meandering down Halsted and hailed, happy to be getting out of the freezing cold. As he jumped into the back of the cab, he felt something jab against his thigh. He reached into his pocket and pulled out the box of candy he had so lovingly picked out with Kitty Coakley in mind. He hit his forehead with this hand. "Drat," he said aloud.

"What was that, sir? Where are you headed?" asked the cabbie over his shoulder."

"Oh, er, Kennesaw Terrace, please. Just off Clarendon, north of Addison," Henry said. He had forgotten to give Kitty the chocolates. What an idiot he was. What she must think of him, coming empty-headed! She would never want to see him again, he was such a clod. And he pondered his inadequacies throughout the winter evening's ride home.

TWENTY-THREE

W hat is it about Monday mornings?" Kitty asked, taking her seat at the piano as Ceecee came over to turn the pages of her music. "The weather is bad and the children are worse." She gestured to the throng of children running and jumping and pulling pigtails and knocking books from the bookcase as they entered the classroom.

"What makes you such a crosspatch this morning?" Ceecee replied, bending over to pick up the music sheets she'd knocked to the floor in her haste to turn the pages. "Does it have anything to do with Henry Thomas? What happened, did he never show up at your house last week as he'd promised?"

"He stopped by, yes, but it was possibly the shortest visit imaginable," Kitty said. "If I had blinked my eyes, I'd have missed him."

"How long did he stay?" Ceecee whispered, for Mrs. Campbell was calling the rowdy class to order.

"Half an hour at most," Kitty said, looking over at Mrs. Campbell for the cue to begin playing.

"That's actually a little long for a first visit," Ceecee said. "It's not really proper to stay much more than fifteen minutes. Let's talk about it more over lunch. Meanwhile, cheer up, you have nothing to worry about."

Kitty launched into a lively tune and the children marched around the classroom, trying to make as much noise as they could. Facing the piano, Kitty couldn't see their faces, but she could tell from their singing that this exercise was drawing on their seemingly limitless levels of energy. How clever Mrs. Campbell was to channel their energy at the beginning of the day, rather than let it flow into mischief and destruction.

By lunchtime, Kitty was in a much more cheerful state herself. Although the nasty weather had persisted through the morning, the children had settled down to quiet play with the blocks and art supplies they had been taught to use.

"The children who are leaving now seem a different group than the naughty ones who arrived this morning," Kitty observed to Ceecee as they opened their lunch bags. "Quieter, happier, much more pleasant than those little monsters who came in the door."

"That's the beauty of the Froebel program," Ceecee said. "It really does bring out the positives in the children. At home they are punished and treated like little scoundrels just for being children. We show them how to behave, and let them teach themselves through the things they do. We don't expect them to be miniature adults, always in control of themselves."

"You wouldn't know that these children come from the poorest of the poor," Kitty said. "Their clothes are old and patched, and their shoes cracked and thin, but they have taken to the manners they see us display here in the classroom."

"Children learn by example. They are such mimics, actually," Ceecee said. "I saw little Maria, once, the one with such darling ringlets, imitate Mrs. Campbell perfectly. The same arm gestures, the voice— yet I don't even know if she knew what she was doing."

Kitty laughed. "I suppose that's how manners and propriety get spread around. We are just mimicking others. Speaking of which, you said that it was proper for Henry to stay just a short time?"

"Oh, yes," Ceecee said. "Even a half an hour is stretching it a bit. On a first visit, you should just stay fifteen or twenty minutes. Otherwise, you're acting a bit familiar with people you hardly know."

Ceecee's information seemed to belong to a different place and time. Sure, if you were just going next door or down the street, fifteen minutes was fine. But out on the prairies, where it could take days of hard traveling to get from house to house, it seemed ridiculous to stay for just a few minutes. Chicago certainly wasn't the prairies anymore, but to travel some distance in dangerous weather just to stop by for a few minutes seemed like pushing polite manners a bit too far.

"I'm just worried that he didn't get a very good picture of my family," Kitty said. "Maybe if he'd stayed longer, stayed for dinner maybe, we would look better. I was cooking a beautiful roast beef for dinner."

"A proper young man would never presume to invite himself to dinner the first time he visited a young lady," Ceecee said, pursing up her mouth as if she were a dried-up old woman. "It just isn't done. And why do you think your family didn't come off so well?"

"Where do I start? My father fairly grilled Henry with questions about his prospects. My brother Johnny came in and acted so rude, I was embarrassed. And my mother, she hardly said a word. And she was praying the rosary the whole time, as if he was some heathen she had to protect herself and her family from."

Ceecee tried to keep a straight face as Kitty listed her family's grievances. "All in just a half hour? It sounds like a lot was going on. But don't worry about it, Kitty. If it doesn't work out with Henry, I'll introduce you to someone else. I know plenty of young men who wouldn't be put off by your family. Men who would be delighted to meet a young lady in training to become a kindergartner. Just think of what wonderful mothers we'll make. What does Mr. Thomas have to say about your professional training?"

"He seemed interested when I told him about it. But I didn't get the impression that it made a big difference to him," Kitty said. "He's so full of his own plans for the future, designing big buildings, that my efforts to become a teacher seem unimportant next to his."

"Don't you ever believe that, Miss Katherine Coakley," Ceecee said, her hands on her hips. "Just remember, it's the hand that rocks the cradle that rules the world."

"You're beginning to sound like one of those suffragettes," Kitty laughed.

"Well, what's wrong with that?" Ceecee snapped back. "There's nothing a woman can't do, if she puts her mind to it."

"Okay, okay, now you're sounding like my Aunt Mabel. Maybe you're right. But if we don't put our minds to getting to this afternoon's lecture, we're not going to accomplish anything." Kitty got up from the table, and brushed the crumbs off her dress.

The afternoon lecture on the training of reason in children did not engage Kitty's attention, and she spent much of the time daydreaming. Daydreaming about herself, dressed in beautiful clothes, visiting grand houses, one after another, just ten or fifteen minutes at a time. Until the lecturer told the story of drawing a picture of a horse for a child and, when she was unable to complete the drawing because the paper was too small, the child burst into tears. The idea the lecturer conveyed with that incident was that the sense of incompleteness the child received from the partial drawing was akin to the sense of dissatisfaction we feel on dark and dreary days, when we have no clear idea of the future and the good that lies ahead. So true, Kitty thought, as she wrote in her notebook the words "child's instinctive desire: understanding continuity/progress." She found great wisdom in these teachings, a comforting understanding of her own thoughts and desires. She recognized how she herself needed to be making progress, to move ahead, rather than to accept the way the world was. She recalled the motto of a new woman's magazine she had seen: "Moving forward, but not too fast."

Even before Kitty opened the door to her home that afternoon, she could hear the uproar within. She knew Sean had been spending the day with his grandmother, but it couldn't have just been one child making all that noise. When she entered, she saw the source of the uproar. Apparently, Mickey and Bill were home and had convinced their mother that they could be responsible for Sean. Her brothers had turned the parlor into a war zone, holing up in a fort they had made from the sofa, and they must have encouraged Sean to throw his blocks at them, and in turn, they had thrown pillows back at him. An exhausted Sean was now prostrate on the floor, screaming and pounding his fists on the threadbare carpet. When Kitty appeared in the doorway, Bill said, "We tried to make him take a nap, Kitty, honestly we did. But he didn't want to stop. We didn't hurt him, not at all. He just started crying all on his own."

"What do you expect? You've certainly overtired him. Why don't you two just clean up this mess and disappear for a while. I'll quiet him down."

But Sean didn't want to be quieted down. When he saw his uncles righting the sofa and putting the pillows back, he tried to help them. "Sean big boy," he said. And when Mickey and Bill were pulling on their jackets, he resumed his crying. "Sean go with boys, Sean go with boys."

Kitty lifted him onto her lap, although he kept pulling away from her, struggling to join Mickey and Bill, even after they left. "Come on, Sean, come on. Let the big boys go, it's time for you to rest." She ran her hand over his tousled blond hair.

"Sean no rest, Sean no rest. Sean big boy," he cried, and he hit Kitty in the face with his small fist.

Her eyes tearing, Kitty's first impulse was to swat him back, but she took a breath and thought for a minute. She heard the gentle voice of Mrs. Campbell in her ear telling her that all she would be teaching him was that the proper response to violence was violence. Remember you are the adult and he is the child, she recalled. The child looks to you for ways to comport himself. She bit her tongue to keep from reproaching him and started to rock him slowly back and forth. It wasn't easy, because Sean wouldn't give up his idea to follow the big boys and he struggled to get loose of her grip. It took a while for Kitty to calm him down enough to keep him on her lap, because for a little guy he was a fierce fighter. But she sang gently under her breath until she at least felt the tension leave his body. "Do you want to learn a new song?" she whispered in his ear.

"No," he said, turning his head. "No song." He put his hands over his ears and remained in his huddled position on her lap.

Kitty continued to gently rock him, humming the song. When she could feel his body relax again, she said, "Now Sean, I'll teach you a new song. Give me your hand."

With his head still turned away from her, he stretched one hand behind him, the other still over one ear.

Kitty held his hand and, taking his fingers one by one, she sang,

This is the gramma, good and near,
This is the mama, loving and dear,
This is the papa, with hearty cheer
This is our Sean, stout and tall,
This is the baby, the pet of all.
Behold the good family, great and small!

Sean turned to look at his hand, with all the fingers clasped in Kitty's grasp. "The good fammy," he said, raising up his other hand. "My fammy." He snuggled up to Kitty and placed the thumb from his other hand in his mouth. "My fammy," he said as he continued to look at his outstretched hand.

"Now it's time to put the family to sleep," Kitty whispered. "Here, let's take them one by one.

Go to sleep, little thumb, that's one,
Go to sleep, pointing finger, two,
Go to sleep, middle finger, three,
Go to sleep, ring finger, four,
Go to sleep, little finger, five.
Let's take them and tuck them snugly all in bed, sound asleep.
And let nothing disturb them.

And by the time she had touched each of his fingers, Sean, his thumb still in his mouth, was sound asleep on her lap. Kitty sat there for a few minutes, making sure that he was truly asleep, and then carefully placed him on the couch by himself, so she could step away.

"That was very nice, Kitty," her father whispered from the doorway where he had been watching silently. "You'll make a lovely mother yourself some day."

Kitty smiled and went into the kitchen, pulling her apron off the hook so that she could begin dinner. The peace she had created in Sean remained with her, and she approached her evening chores with a quiet contentment.

TWENTY-FOUR

T he next Sunday Henry was again on his way to the house of a young woman, and he couldn't help but contrast the two occasions. Unlike the Sunday before, he traveled in the family carriage through the city. Also unlike the Sunday before, he was going with his parents' full knowledge and, indeed, encouragement. For when the invitation for the open house arrived from Cecilia Carter, his mother had plucked it out of the mail and examined the heavy cream-colored stationery with the engraved return address before handing it to him and asking him if it were from the young woman he had introduced her to at the Palmers' party.

"If you'll wait a second, I'll tell you," said Henry, staring at the envelope before opening it. His name and address had been written in a flamboyant peacock blue ink that was all the rage with the people he knew from the university. He had received many invitations addressed in that ink during his college years, but they had become much rarer since he returned to Chicago. The return address was Union Park, where many of the best families lived, including Carter Harrison, Jr., the current mayor. Cecilia Carter, he read, and an image of the young lady came into his head, dressed not in the simple dress of the Rembrandt portrait she had enacted at the Potter Palmer party, but in the pale blue walking suit she had appeared in at the Burnham party where he first encountered her. Then she had been accompanied by his supervisor at the architectural firm, Peirce Anderson. Her sort-of uncle, she had said. Which meant that this invitation was not just for a social afternoon as much as it was a command performance. Or at least that's how it seemed to him, which meant he didn't look forward to it as much as his parents seemed to.

That Sunday afternoon, Henry wasn't able to leave the house without his mother's scrutiny. Twice she sent him back upstairs, the first time to change his tie, the second to change his shoes. He felt like a child, all dressed up for his dancing classes, where the best social connections were made, as his mother put it at the time. His mother's interference made him feel more confident, though. Because he would never confess his nervousness to her, he fooled himself by pretending to be relaxed and sure of himself. He straightened his tie as he exited through the front door, and took the reins of the carriage as if he drove out to Ashland Avenue every day. He, who passed the review of his superiors nearly every day, had no reason to fear a Sunday afternoon open house. Certainly not now that he had passed the even more intense review by his mother.

Henry relaxed and let the horses go at the even trot they preferred. The week had been unseasonably warm and what had been ice the week before had become thick, gluey mud. Other than the reduced pace the mud required, it was a pleasant ride through streets lined by leafless trees. From time to time he touched his hat with his whip in recognition of an acquaintance out for a Sunday afternoon drive. He arrived at the big graystone house facing Union Square later than planned, but he didn't regret a minute spent outdoors on what was probably one of the last of the year's sunny days.

He knocked on the heavy mahogany door of the house, and was permitted to enter by a stiff manservant who took his hat and asked his name so as to introduce him to the merry group of men and women in the parlor. A lively, almost familiar tune was playing on the gramophone—was it *Camptown Races*? Henry wondered. Apparently no one wished to be the first to dance, although there would have been room enough in the giant room with warm cherry paneling and thick Persian carpets, once the carpets had been rolled up. He accepted a glass of sweet white wine from a silver tray, and strolled around, looking for familiar faces. He nodded to a few young men he had known at the university, smiled at a young woman he thought he recognized as a friend of Eleanor's, either from the Art Institute or one of the committees she was always meeting with, and searched for his hostess. He thought he spied her surrounded three or four deep by men and made his way toward them, careful not to spill his wine as he slid between the wide skirts of several older women.

"Mr. Thomas," cried Cecilia, as she caught sight of Henry. "How good of you to come." She threaded through her admirers and made her way to Henry. "Please, let me introduce you to some friends of mine," she said, taking his elbow in a possessive manner and then putting her arm through his. "I'm sure you'll find you have lots in common with them."

Cecilia introduced him to "my dudes," four or five young men that she named so quickly that they came across as a blur. They all seemed to be about his own age, and the only career any of them mentioned was managing family investments on LaSalle Street. Compared to the men, the women seemed to be in short supply, other than a few older women dressed in black Henry thought must be friends of Cecilia's mother, as they clustered around her, speaking in whispers as if someone had died. After *Camptown Races* someone put on a recording of a Beethoven concerto. He could see Cecilia's father outdoors on the terrace, smoking a cigar with other men, all attired in black suits with stiff white shirt collars. He recognized Mayor Harrison with his dark, bushy handlebar mustache, and banker Lyman Gage, now President McKinley's Secretary of the Treasury, both friends or at least business acquaintances of his father, but he didn't feel like penetrating the cloud of smoke that surrounded them.

Cecilia left him with an older man to whom she introduced him as "the rising young architect from Daniel Burnham's office, where Uncle Peirce works," and danced off to greet a group of laughing newcomers who had just come in the door. The man, whose name he didn't catch, peppered him with questions about Burnham's role in the building of the Columbian Exposition. Henry had to explain that he had only recently joined the firm, in fact had been almost a child when the Exposition was going up, but that didn't stop the gentleman from launching into a long story about his own experience, supplying building materials for the fair. The man didn't have much of a story to tell, as he seemed to have run the business from a LaSalle Street office without ever visiting the site, but that didn't stop him from going on at great length about something or another. Henry turned off his mind and tried not to nod and smile for fear of encouraging the man, especially when he launched into details about the fair's ending with the terrible death of his neighbor, Mayor Carter Harrison, Senior, the father of the man happily puffing on a cigar out on the terrace. Henry reflected that he had become much more socially inept since his sister's death, and he couldn't remember how to disengage himself from a conversation he had no interest in. Perhaps he could find a cigar—not that he liked to smoke—but that would take him outside, away from this boring man and his boring story.

He was just about to look for the door to the terrace when, out of the corner of his eye, he glimpsed an almost familiar cloud of black hair bouncing on a woman who came only to Cecilia's shoulder. It couldn't be, could it? Kitty Coakley arm-in-arm with Cecilia Carter, just as he himself had been earlier? How would she know Cecilia? He couldn't imagine a scenario that would bring those two women together. Not at the same level of society, he ruefully thought. Unless perhaps Miss Coakley was going to sing . . . no, that couldn't be, music might be played but popular singers didn't perform at parties like this, not in mixed company. He shook his head as if he could erase the image of the woman he mistook for Kitty. He should be thinking of his hostess, not other young women. But he supposed that when someone thought about another as much as he had been thinking about Kitty lately it was bound to happen that he would imagine seeing her everywhere he went.

Perhaps he should join the men on the terrace and establish his right to be there by identifying his father to these pillars of the community. Or perhaps he should just leave, taking time on the carriage ride home to concoct some story for his mother about the beautiful women he had met. But he continued to stare at the young women, watching as Cecilia introduced her to her young dudes, who seemed to fall all over her with attention. Cecilia sent one of them off, presumably to get Miss Coakley a drink, as another one bent over her possibly to catch what she was saying. He couldn't hear her himself, but he could see her delicious dimple flashing and her dark curls bouncing off her shoulders as she nodded her head in response to something the young dude had said.

Henry couldn't stand to stay any longer. Even if the young woman was not Katherine Coakley, and it seemed nearly impossible that she could be, he couldn't deal with the writhing emotion he felt within him. How could he feel ignored by a person he most likely had never met? And if it were Kitty, he was sure that she couldn't have seen him in the crowd. He strode quickly to the doorway, retrieved his hat, and walked purposefully out the door, nearly blinded by the feeling he diagnosed as anger, if not jealousy. He realized the irrationality of his feelings, but couldn't stand being in the same room as these young men as they fawned over this woman who was, by all rights, his. He stopped before he reached his carriage, taking a deep breath and assessing the situation. He was not only irrational, he was being impolite. Not to thank the hostess and her mother for inviting him to the party—he doubted he had ever left a party like that in his life. The social graces had been drummed into him so thoroughly as a child that he never questioned the rules but obeyed them without thinking. What would his mother think?

Hang what Mother thinks! Henry loosened his tie as he sat himself in the carriage. No one came rushing out the Carter doorway, saying, "You can't leave without saying goodbye and thank you to the hostess." Probably no one even noticed his departure. He cracked the whip over the horses' heads, urging them north on Ashland Avenue. All he could think of was that he needed to get away from that house and those people.

He hadn't gone far before two thoughts became clear and pressing. First of all, he hadn't greeted Mr. Anderson, his boss, and would have to come up with an excuse the next time he saw him, probably the next day at the office. And secondly, where was he to go on a bright but cold November Sunday afternoon? He knew he couldn't return home so soon, his mother would question him thoroughly about the party and his short time there. He also couldn't go to his office. Peirce Anderson, knowing well what Henry was working on, would question why he would choose to spend time at the office rather than at his niece's party. He wished he had someone to talk to about his concerns. The only person he could think of to confide in was his sister Eleanor. And Eleanor was no longer on this earth.

The horses continued their trek north on Ashland as he struggled with his thoughts. He soon realized that he was nearing Lake View High School and didn't want to think about the school, for that was where he first had met Miss Katherine Coakley. And once she was on his mind, he knew he would think of nothing else. He directed the horses to go east to Clark Street. Before long, he saw the brick walls of Graceland Cemetery ahead. He could go there. He could visit Eleanor's grave, which wasn't of course the same as having Eleanor to talk to, but somehow he felt he would be nearer to her that way.

The path was muddy, but he knew just where to go once inside the cemetery. The Thomas family plot was on the north end, almost to the small lake and east, toward Lake Michigan. It was colder walking than it had been driving in the carriage, with a sharp wind from the east rustling the few remaining leaves on the trees, but Henry trudged on. He knew to walk toward the massive pyramid that was the Ryerson tomb, dreamed up by the architect Louis Sullivan. He admired Sullivan for his audacity in replicating a structure meant to commemorate Egyptian pharaohs to memorialize a Chicago lumber baron and his family. The Thomas plot lay behind the Ryerson one, just off the path to his right. No such edifice as a pyramid marked the graves of his family, just small stones with the names and dates of those members of the family who had died. Henry removed his hat and stood looking down at the very new stone marker that marked his sister's grave, just next to her grandmother who had died the year before. He didn't understand death. Was it just the end of everything or the entry into a totally new sort of existence as he had been taught in Sunday school?

Were his sister and grandmother watching over him as he stood in this chilly graveyard?

"Henry? Henry, is that you?"

Henry spun around. He saw no one else near him. The voice seemed to come from afar, but it was a familiar voice. Male, not female. He didn't believe in ghosts, but if he did, Graceland would be a likely place to find them.

"Henry," the voice quavered. "Over here."

Henry looked across the path behind him to the magnificence of the Pullman tomb that sat like a Greek temple on the other side, with an enormous Corinthian column that spoke to the wealth and power of the man entombed beneath. Heavily entombed, as he recalled. When George Pullman had died, not long after the Pullman strike in 1894, he had left instructions that he be buried in such a way that his body couldn't be exhumed by the angry workers who had fought against him and lost. His coffin was sunk in a concrete block bigger than a Pullman railroad car. And on top of that were buried railroad ties, with more concrete poured over them. No one or nothing could reach George Pullman's body—he had made sure of that. And atop the underground fortress of his grave he had requested to be built a lovely Greek courtyard, with stone benches for sitting and presumably discussing philosophy. And slowly rising from one of those benches was the man who had been calling out his name. His grandfather. Henry put his hat back on his head and went across the path to greet him.

His grandfather had settled back down in the stone bench, a newspaper beneath him to absorb the stone's cold and his two hands in front of him atop his cane. He was almost panting from the exertion of calling out to his grandson.

"Vati, what are you doing here? It's awfully cold for you to be sitting out." Henry sat down beside him and put his arm around his grandfather's shoulders.

His grandfather shrugged off Henry's arm. He had caught his breath, but it still was labored as he spoke. "I might ask . . . the same of you."

Henry sat back and pushed his fedora onto the back of his head. He looked out across the gently rolling hills of the cemetery punctuated by dark and empty trees and looming marble mausoleums. "I guess I'm here because I miss her. Eleanor. I was used to having her around. You know, to talk to. There's no one else. No one else who has known me. Known me forever. Who can tell me what I want, and want to do. Eleanor always could do that. Tell me what to do. Not what she wanted me to do, not that. Tell me what I want to do. She knew me, better than I know myself. And now there's no one."

His grandfather looked down at his gnarled hands atop his cane. Henry remembered how when he was little, he liked nothing more than to watch his grandfather peel an apple. His strong steady hands could pare an entire apple in one long skein of skin, a talent which Henry much admired and often tried, without success, to emulate. Now, those arthritic hands could hardly hold a knife, much less pare an apple. He wondered if his grandfather had fallen asleep, as he said nothing in response.

And then his grandfather spoke, raising his shaking fist to the sky. "*Gott*, you have taken away mine Augusta, and you won't take me to her. How you expect me to live without my heart, my *lieb*? I sit here and I pray, take me too, *Gott*. I am ready to go. But I stay here. Without my heart."

Henry fought back the tears from his eyes. He remembered his grandmother as a tiny, bent-over woman who rarely spoke, just stared right through him with her watery blue eyes. She hadn't been well for most of Henry's life, her legs swollen with some disease, so that she could hardly walk and never left their little apartment above the grocery store. But her brain had been sharp, and she did the accounting for the grocery store almost until the day she died. Aunt Louisa would tell stories about her, about how she came to Chicago as a baby and how her parents had traded with the Indians, right from that same little store a block from the river. Or at least the same location, the store had been built up, like the city that grew up around them. Oma had taught her daughter how to bake the best cookies in Chicago, and breads, and cakes and confections that would just melt in your mouth, Auntie Lou would tell him. He had difficulty reconciling his picture of Oma as a decrepit old woman with his grandfather's enormous grief at her loss. But he rationalized love was said to be that way, beyond logic, beyond understanding. He himself could understand his love for Eleanor, she was his sister, after all, and had been with him all his life. But he still had problems determining why he felt the way he did when he saw Kitty Coakley, for example. Yes, she was beautiful, but he knew many young women who were equally beautiful. She had a lovely singing voice, anyone would agree with that, but was that a reason to love someone? He knew that his parents, or at least his mother, wouldn't approve of her, because she was Catholic, and Irish. He didn't think Aunt Louisa approved of her completely, but she was not as forthcoming with her opinion as his mother was. Was that why his stomach still felt queasy after seeing her with other men—if it had been Kitty Coakley at that party. Did he see her as a rebellion from his mother's tastes? That just didn't sound like the way he operated. Eleanor would know. But Eleanor wasn't here to tell him. He looked around him, at his grieving grandfather, at the ornate Pullman tomb, at the growing cloudbanks covering the sky, and shook his head. Love and death—both too unfathomable for his brain.

"Come along, Vati. It's getting colder. I'd best get you home. Auntie Lou will be wondering where you are." He pulled his grandfather to his feet and got him to put his arm on his shoulder so he could support his weight as they walked down the rutted path to the carriage. His grandfather grunted as Henry pushed him up into the carriage and covered him with a woolen blanket. "You good boy," his grandfather said, patting him on the hand. "Mine Augusta say, you grow up good."

TWENTY-FIVE

Henry wrote a polite note, as he had been taught, thanking Kitty for letting him visit. He added to it an invitation to go ice-skating the following Saturday. It was a way of seeing her away from her family, he reasoned, and he'd also be able to show off his ability on the ice. He and Eleanor had skated every winter almost from the time they had begun to walk, and he enjoyed it still, even though he was grown. Yes, he thought, here was something at which he excelled, and did want to show off for her. He might not be able to stand up to one of her hulking brothers, but he knew he could skate. And there was the likelihood that some of his college friends might be home for their winter break and would make an appearance at the Lincoln Park lagoon skating rink—that way, he could show off the beautiful Miss Coakley.

Kitty replied with a short note, thanking him for the invitation and accepting with pleasure. She didn't have ice skates, so was pleased that he had indicated that they could rent them there. Good, he thought, looking forward to it through the short dark days of the week. Winter was so long in Chicago, but ice-skating was one way of making the most of it.

Henry picked up Kitty on Saturday evening—his parents had traveled to the symphony with friends, so his father had given him the use of their carriage. He was pleased to see that Kitty was ready and waiting at the front door when he arrived and, as soon as he brought the horses to a stop, she was running down the path, calling out goodbye to whoever was in the house. She wore a dark red cloak, long tweed skirt, and blue and white striped mittens. A blue knit hat—one that he was sure her fashion plate aunt wouldn't approve of—covered her hair and looked as if it would keep her ears warm. She obviously knew how to dress for a cold night on the ice. She hopped into the carriage before Henry could jump down and help her into it.

"Ooh," she said. "An open carriage. Will we be warm enough?"

"We should be," Henry said, arranging a plaid blanket over her lap. "The wind has changed, it's not blowing over the lake now, but across the prairies. So it's a good deal warmer near the lake, where we'll be, in Lincoln Park. And I daresay, with the clouds clearing away, we might be able to see a few stars." He clucked to the horses and turned the carriage north on Desplaines towards the park.

Despite the outside temperature, they were warm in the carriage, bundled up with blankets over their legs and feet. There was no traffic and the cold air seemed to amplify the regular clopping of the horses' hooves on the pavement. The occasional street lamp burned brightly but shed no more light than a match lit in the darkness. Henry concentrated on driving the horses, as they moved complacently and steadily through the snow-filled streets, their breath great clouds of steam in the cold air.

Finally Henry pulled the carriage into the shelter of a shuttered boathouse. He jumped down, hitched the horses to a fence, and threw blankets over their backs before he helped Kitty alight. Kitty shivered as Henry held out his gloved hand to her. "You're not cold, are you?" he asked.

Kitty shook her head and took his hand in her own mittened one. They could hear the happy sounds of people skating just beyond a grove of trees, where a ring of brighter lights glowed.

"Come on now, let's go skating. It will warm us up to be moving about," Henry said, anxious to get out on the ice and show his skill. Holding Kitty's hand, he led her through the trees and toward the glowing lights of the skating rink.

To get to the ice they had to pass through the warm and stuffy café, where red-faced skaters had doffed their hats and gloves and sat enjoying hot cocoa and coffee at small wire tables. Henry was glad he'd chosen not to wear his glasses, as they would have steamed up in an instant and he would have to stop and clean them. On a cold night, vision that wasn't too exact was preferable to steamed-up glasses.

They both rented skates. Henry hadn't had time to dig his old ones out of wherever his mother had stored them last year. Kitty confessed, as they approached the rental stand, that she had never skated before. Henry knelt to attach the skates to her boots, and walked her slowly along the terrace until she took her first cautious steps onto the ice. She stood still, unsure of herself on the single-bladed skates.

"Now, all you have to do is slide one foot, and then the other, on the ice and I'll guide you," Henry said, stretching out his arms to Kitty. "Take your time, you'll build up speed once you've built up your confidence."

Kitty slid her feet along the ice, one after another, still holding Henry's hands. "But that means you have to skate backwards!" she said.

"Don't worry, don't worry. It's not that difficult. But I expect you to watch out to make sure we aren't running into anyone else."

Henry watched Kitty's feet as she cautiously slid them across the ice. He could feel his fedora sliding to the back of his head, revealing his high forehead to the cold and sensed his breath turning into ice crystals that graced his mustache, but he kept his grip on Kitty's hands. "That's it, that's it," he said. "One skate after another. I say, you're a natural at this, Kitty."

Kitty beamed, returning Henry's grin with her own. And then, a small boy in a red cap skating much too fast came crashing into Henry, who landed on the ice, pulling Kitty down as well. "Pride goeth before a fall, I guess," Henry said, coming to his knees and wiping the ice from his coat before he hoisted Kitty up.

Her skates slid too far along the slippery ice and she went down, laughing. "This is the only time in my life that I've wished I wore a hoop skirt!"

Henry laughed, too, and pulled her up once again. "Let's just try a slow circle around the rink, side by side. You'll find you're even more stable when you're moving than when you're standing still."

Kitty took his hand, allowing him to pull her along to the far edge of the rink. They skated slowly in the shadows around the edges, where there were fewer skaters, Kitty sliding twice to keep up with each of Henry's long-legged steps. "That's good, that's good," he'd murmur each time she slid along. She was cautious, but he could tell she was determined to stay up by her firm grip on his hand. By the time they had made it almost halfway around the huge oval, he could feel her relax and move without consciously having to signal each step.

Over the sounds of skates grinding on the ice and the laughter and shouting of the other skaters, they could hear soft strains of music. "Listen," Henry said, holding up the hand that wasn't holding Kitty's. "I do believe it's Tchaikovsky."

"But where is it coming from?" she asked. "How can an orchestra play and skate at the same time?"

Henry tried not to show how amusing he found her naïve comment. "It's a gramophone," he said, pointing to the courtyard of the café. "It's playing the closing waltz from Tchaikovsky's *Nutcracker Suite*."

Hand in hand, they skated slowly across the center of the crowded rink to the fence outside the café where the gramophone stood, its metal plate revolving slowly. A large hornlike object that looked like an overgrown flower was attached to it and directed the music outward toward the ice.

"How wonderful!" Kitty said, admiring the machine. "Music without musicians. Why, you could listen almost anywhere."

"You mean you've never seen one of these before?" Henry asked. "Father bought Mother one last Christmas and we've been collecting the music plates for it all year." He looked over the crowd in the outdoor café. Were there any free seats by the ice? "Would you like a cup of cocoa? We could sit out here. I think I see a table over there by the parapet. Or if you'd prefer to sit inside, we could go in and look."

"Inside please," Kitty said, shivering as she removed her skates. So they entered the café, which smelled agreeably of wet wool and chocolate, and found a table being vacated by a boisterous group of rosy-cheeked skaters.

Henry watched Kitty as she threw off her cloak, pulled off her mittens, and rubbed her hands together to warm them up. She pulled off her knit hat and her hair cascaded out of it. How beautiful she looked, her red cheeks and white skin, her blue eyes glowing with the exercise, and her long dark hair framing it all.

Kitty looked up to catch him staring at her. "Why, what is it? Do I have dirt on my face?" she asked, rubbing her face with the back of her hand.

"No, no, you look fine," he said. "In fact, you look quite beautiful. Your cheeks are redder than roses."

"I expect they're just chapped," she said, rubbing them. "I shall have to put some rosewater and glycerin on them tonight."

Henry was embarrassed by how much he wanted just to sit there and stare at her. He jumped from the table and said, "The service seems somewhat slow here tonight. Suppose I go up to the bar and order our cocoas?" He needed a moment to compose himself. He had planned to ask Kitty something tonight, and he wanted to be in control of himself and the situation.

By the time Henry returned to the table, a harried waiter had plunked down two cups of cocoa in front of Kitty. "It's a busy night," Kitty said, looking up at him.

She seemed a bit tongue-tied herself, Henry thought, which made it easier for him to approach his request. "It certainly is," he said. "I saw a few of the fellows I knew down at the university on the ice. I daresay they've come home for Christmas already. We have a bang-up dinner at home on Christmas Eve. Do you suppose you could join us this year? My parents would very much like to meet you, you know." Henry wiped his dry forehead, expecting to find it sweating from the exertion of asking such an important question.

"Oh dear, I . . . I don't know. On Christmas Eve? I'm not sure if I can. You see, I'll be singing at Midnight Mass, I always do. I can't let Father Egan down."

She seemed genuinely concerned, which was good, Henry thought. Perhaps she could be convinced. "Midnight Mass? Why, that's at midnight, isn't it? I can have you back in time for that," Henry said. "We generally finish dinner and the singing by ten. Please say you'll come. It will be a difficult Christmas for us, what with Eleanor, you know."

"How sad," Kitty said, her expression clouding over as if she might cry. "The first Christmas after someone in your family has died. Perhaps if I explain to my parents. Oh, and Father Egan. I will try, though. I know it's important to you."

"Please, Kitty, please. It would mean so much," Henry said, reaching out to grasp her hand. They had held gloved hands on the skating rink, but this was his first touch of her bare hand. Despite the warmth of the café, her hand was cool and smooth. It felt kind and sympathetic.

"I will do my best," Kitty said, and she looked as determined as she had making her way across the ice.

Henry hadn't revealed to his parents that he intended to bring Kitty to dinner on Christmas Eve, he hadn't wanted to tip his hand before he knew if Kitty would accept the invitation. But he had thought ahead about the traditional celebration and worried that it might be too bleak with such recent memories of Eleanor. Kitty could not replace his older sister, but he knew that his parents, his mother in particular, would rise to the occasion to entertain a female friend of his. Kitty would provide a welcome diversion at the dinner, and it would be a strategic occasion for him to introduce her. Perhaps she could even sing for them.

Meanwhile, two young men had stopped to talk to Henry, and he introduced them to Kitty as his friends from the university, Robert Thompson and Milton Sprague, who was visiting him. They invited Kitty and Henry to join them on the ice to play Crack the Whip. Kitty declined, saying she had had enough skating for the evening. She turned to Henry and said, "You go ahead if you like, I'll be fine sitting here."

After offering to get Kitty another cocoa, to which she shook her head, Henry sprang up eagerly to follow his friends outdoors. His relief at having extended the invitation, even if it only had elicited a tentative response, filled him with an energy he could use on the ice. He had held back in squiring Kitty around the rink, but now he could show off his skating skill.

Out on the terrace overlooking the ice, the gramophone was playing a lively polka. The skaters had formed a line, one holding on around the waist of the skater in front of him, and they were skating rapidly around the rink. Henry and his friends joined the line at its end. The music blared and the line of skaters kept increasing its speed until, as the skaters made a turn, Henry and the others at the tail of the whip moved faster and faster. Milton kept turning his head and laughing at Henry, who was himself laughing and yelling. The whip cracked once on the far side of the pond, and was heading toward the terrace. The line made the turn almost in front of the terrace, and the last of the skaters whizzed over toward the trees that marked the edge of the rink. Someone ahead of him must have lost his grip, Henry thought, as he and Milton and Robert and a few others were thrown off the ice and toward the trees before they could gain control of their skates.

Henry found himself sprawled face down, his skidding path along the granular ice and snow broken by the trunk of a substantial tree. His first thought was that he was glad he didn't have his glasses on, as they would have been broken. His second thought was that he hoped Kitty hadn't seen him fall. He struggled to his knees to get up, but the ice beneath him made it difficult to get a grip and his head was still spinning from the blow. Then, he must have blacked out for a moment.

Henry awoke to find himself lying in the snow, his breath still knocked out of him by the force of his fall. Milton squatted next to him, talking to him in a quiet voice. He felt something, it might have been melted snow, running down the side of his face. And somehow, Kitty was standing next to him, looking down with a concerned look on her face.

"Oh, Miss Coakley, I'm glad you're here," said Milton. "This friend of ours has gone and smashed his head a bit. Not to worry, he is conscious and seems to have his wits about him. And that's just a shallow cut on his temple, head wounds bleed like the very devil. And he may have sprained his ankle a bit as well. I think it's best he sees a doctor, though."

"Don't be alarmed, Kitty," Henry said, rising up slightly on one arm. "It's no more than a scratch. I can still drive the carriage, and we'll take Milton and Robert home as well. Then after I drop you off at home, they will be with me to make sure I make it home. I'll be all right once I get these blasted skates off me." And he struggled to get up, one hand on the tree that had scraped his face. Milton jumped up to help him stand.

Henry winced as he placed his weight on his right leg. "Did I mention our friend Mr. Thompson is studying to become Dr. Thompson?" he asked. "He's all the doctor I'm going to need tonight, I'm sure."

The four of them were a tight fit in the small carriage but they were warm under the blankets. Although his vision seemed blurred it wasn't much worse than just not wearing his glasses, Henry thought. He took some pleasure in Kitty's hand tightly clutching his as he drove along, and her frequent queries as to how he was feeling. Milton and Robert were jammed in the tiny back seat, and they began telling silly jokes, making them all laugh. The ride in the cold darkness passed quickly, and they soon arrived at Kitty's cottage, where a light shone over the front stoop and clouds of smoke plumed out of the chimney. Kitty jumped out of the carriage on her own, thanking Henry and his two friends. Although she tried to stop Henry from jumping down and accompanying her to her front door, he gingerly extricated himself from the carriage and walked her up the icy path, his arm under her elbow to make sure she didn't fall. As they approached the cottage, Kitty put her finger to her lips for him to remain quiet and whispered, "Goodbye, thank you, take care of yourself." And she reached up to pull his shoulder and head down and gave him a kiss on the forehead, near a patch of dried blood.

Henry stood on the path, watching Kitty enter the little cottage. She turned and waved goodbye before she closed the door. Henry looked up into the darkness. The sky was polka-dotted with hundreds of bright pinpoints of light. He started back to the carriage with a light step, despite the pain in his right ankle, and returned to his friends. He was eager to hear their congratulatory remarks on his choice of ice-skating companion. Even though his head was throbbing like the very devil in the cold, and he wasn't sure if it was the crash or fatigue that made his eyesight even blurrier than before, he considered himself a lucky man. His injuries were slight, but he knew they would elicit his mother's care and concern. Thus making it that much easier to announce to her that he would be bringing to their Christmas dinner a young woman his parents had never met.

TWENTY-SIX

K itty received Henry's note promptly on Monday, assuring her that he sustained no permanent damage in the ice and snow on Saturday, and renewing his request that she join his family on Christmas Eve. The evening would start at five o'clock, he wrote, with services at their church, St. Paul's, and then dinner with his family and friends, and singing Christmas carols around their tree. He promised her that he would have her home in time to attend Midnight Mass with her family at St. Patrick's. His family was looking forward to meeting her, he repeated. Not as much as I am looking forward to meeting them, she thought.

It was with some trepidation that she broached the subject with her parents at dinner on Monday night. Her father laughed, saying, "So the boyo wants to show you off to his parents, does he? Well, why not? Sure, you're as good or better than any of them, aren't you?"

Her mother was not as easy-going. "St. Paul's, is it? There's no St. Paul's Catholic Church that I'm aware of on the north side. It must be that St. Paul's Lutheran Church, it is. And you as the good Catholic girl that I'm hoping you are, you'll not be going into a Protestant church on Christmas Eve or any night of the year."

"I knew it was a Lutheran church, but it's not as if I'd be receiving holy communion, is it?" Kitty said.

"You'd better not be receiving holy communion in any church other than a Catholic one," her mother said, waving her spoon in the air. "And if you even step foot in that church, you'll not be receiving the sacrament at St. Patrick's either, for it'll put the stain of sin on your soul to be attending services in that other church. And not to receive

229

the holy sacrament at Midnight Mass, now wouldn't that be a shame in front of all our neighbors?"

Kitty's father was no help, he just shook his head and tried not to laugh. They both knew that if there was anything sure to get a rise out of her mother, it would be the intent to commit a sin in front of the eyes of God and the neighbors. Especially the neighbors.

"Well, perhaps I could just go to the dinner, not to the church at all," Kitty suggested. "Henry could pick me up after he attends his services. There wouldn't be anything wrong with that, would there?"

Her mother stared into her soup, muttering about God and His angels, but didn't respond to Kitty.

Her father smiled and said, "Go ahead, Kitty. If you want to spend the evening with them Protestants, we won't be standing in your way."

Mrs. Coakley then raised her head and said, "But you'd just better be sure to be at St. Pat's in time for rehearsal before Mass, or Father Egan will never be speaking to me again."

Kitty thanked heaven for her father, who could see beyond the shadow of the church, as she went into her bedroom to write Henry a return note with the conditions of accepting his invitation.

❧

When Henry pulled up at the Thomas house, Kitty could see, even from outside, that they celebrated Christmas in a big way, despite Eleanor's death earlier that year. The massive front door was decorated with an enormous wreath of evergreen branches and a red ribbon bow. As Kitty removed her cloak in the vestibule, Henry asked her to wait there, he'd bring it upstairs before they went in. The front door opened behind her with a blast of cold air, admitting an old man and Henry's Aunt Louisa, whom Kitty recognized from the Auditorium Theater. She assumed the man was Henry's grandfather. Henry had told her that Louisa, his father's youngest sister, lived with her father and served as his housekeeper and companion. He and his sister had been especially fond of Auntie Lou, he had said, whose pocketbook had always held sweets for them when they were children. Louisa carefully held a plate of Christmas cookies, stars and trees and angels, colorfully decorated in bright sugar icing.

Henry, rushing down the front stairs, greeted them with "*Froehliche Weihnachten,*" and "Merry Christmas." He introduced Kitty to Mr. Thomas, "my Vati," he said, and motioned them to join the others in the parlor, where his mother's piano playing and the wreath of smoke from the gentlemen's cigars rose above the guests' heads.

Henry excused himself to attend to his grandfather, who was shuffling slowly along, gripping the backs of chairs. Kitty could see that Vati had once been a tall muscular man with strong arms and back. She remembered that Henry had told her that his grandfather had managed a market garden on the family lot on the Near North Side and later ran a grocery store on Illinois Street, not far from the river. Oma, his grandmother, had died the year before, Henry had said, and since then Vati seemed to shrink and become old.

Kitty found it a bit uncomfortable standing there with Louisa once Henry left. But she could see Louisa's eyes following her father's painful progress, and said, "It must be difficult to see your father suffer so."

"Yes," Louisa said. "But I fear he suffers in his mind as much as in his body. That must be why he retreats so much into the past nowadays. Sometimes I'm not even sure he knows where he is or what year it is."

"Well, at least he knows that you're here with him."

Louisa smiled at her and reached over and patted her hand. "You seem to be a nice girl, Katherine," she said. "Why don't you join me over there on the sofa and tell me about yourself? Henry has been keeping you something of a secret, you know. We know so little about you."

But before they had to chance to talk, Henry returned, crooking his arm for Kitty to join him, and brought her into the enormous parlor. She had never seen a room so festive, all strung up with holiday decorations. Great swags of evergreens stretched across the mantelpiece and continued onto the built-in bookcases with cunning stained glass doors on either side. A beautifully carved and painted wooden nativity scene sat on the sideboard nestled into a stage setting of fir branches with pine cones, and guarded by a plaster angel in golden robes of satin. She looked for the tree that Henry had promised, but couldn't find it. Everyone in the room looked up when Kitty entered, about half a dozen in all. Kitty felt so awkward and underdressed in her homemade Christmas dress that was no match for the tastefully tailored clothes the women wore. She could see that she was the youngest person there by far, except for Henry, so she reasoned that no one could expect her to be wearing their kind of clothes. She tried not to make comparisons, but it was difficult.

Henry brought her over to his mother, who sat at the beautiful Kimball grand piano playing what Kitty recognized as a Bach cantata, but no one was singing.

"Mother, this is Katherine Coakley, my friend from Lake View High School. Kitty, my mother, Mrs. Thomas," Henry said.

Mrs. Thomas sat on the piano stool looking like Mrs. Potter Palmer herself, Kitty thought, having seen pictures of the society leader in newspapers. She sat straight-backed and regal, her blonde head erect like a proper lady. Her dress was pewter satin, trimmed with black lace at the cuffs and neckline, not quite mourning yet not quite what one would choose for a jolly Christmas gathering either. The only jewelry she wore was a short necklace of small pearls, almost like a choker. Her deep blue eyes shone out from her pale, powdery skin, and when she stood up, Kitty was surprised to find that they were the same height.

"Good evening, Miss Coakley. We're so pleased you could join our little gathering tonight. Come, you must meet my husband," Mrs. Thomas said, taking her hand and escorting her to the corner of the room where Mr. Thomas was standing, talking to a man and woman seated on a low sofa. "Henry, I want you to meet Sonny's little friend," she said in a low voice that nevertheless sounded like a command.

Kitty looked over at Henry. "Sonny?" she whispered.

"Pay no attention to that," Henry said, looking flustered. "Father, this is Miss Katherine Coakley."

Mr. Coakley, a tall, well-dressed man with a head of thick, white hair, bowed his head. "So nice to meet you, Miss Coakley. How good of you to come tonight." The lights from the heavy crystal chandelier gleamed on his thick eyeglasses, so that she could hardly see his eyes.

Kitty panicked, wondering what to say to these elegant people after she had greeted them, wished them a Merry Christmas, and thanked them for inviting her to their home. She was relieved when Louisa came to her rescue, appearing from behind them and asking Henry if his friend might join her.

Louisa led Kitty to a golden-striped satin loveseat in front of the blazing fireplace and patted the cushion next to her. "Come, Katherine, tell me a little bit about yourself."

Kitty perched on the edge of the cushion and carefully arranged her skirt as she thought about what to say. "There isn't much to tell, really. I knew Henry at Lake View High School and since then, I've mainly been living at home with my family." She bit her lip before blurting the neighborhood as "St. Patrick's parish," as she usually did. "On the West Side. Oh, and this fall, I began a course to become a kindergartner. At the Chicago Kindergarten College."

"A kindergartner? Henry didn't tell me about that. Do tell me more."

Kitty wasn't sure if Louisa was just being polite or whether she truly was interested. "A kindergartner is one who teaches small children, they call it a garden of children, kindergarten."

Louisa tilted her head as if she were interested. "Please go on, I hadn't known you could learn to be a kindergartner here in Chicago."

"Oh yes, the Chicago Kindergarten College has been here for several years. They teach the Froebel method. Friedrich Froebel was a teacher in Germany, who . . ."

"Yes, yes, I saw a demonstration of Herr Froebel's teachings at the World's Fair. The children are encouraged to learn about the world on their own. They are given shapes and balls and art supplies, *nicht wahr*?"

Kitty could see that Louisa was so excited about what she was saying that she hadn't realized that she had dropped into speaking German. "Yes, the gifts . . . Froebel's gifts. We learn how to introduce the gifts to the children and to guide them in their explorations."

"I think that's so brilliant," Louisa said. "Simply brilliant. But I had no idea they were training people to actually teach kindergarten. I believe when I first heard about it, it was a method for mothers to use in teaching their own children. I tried to incorporate it into my dealings with Henry and Eleanor when they were young." She looked down into her lap when she mentioned her niece, so recently taken from them.

"Yes, the school offers lectures for mothers as well. But the training program is for women without families who want to enter the teaching profession, to teach kindergartens. More and more of the schools in Chicago are starting kindergartens. So there should be quite a few jobs available for us when we graduate." Now that she was taking about something she knew, Kitty found it easier to speak. She felt proud to say that she had a profession to look forward to—she felt more modern than those young women who were just waiting to become someone's wife.

Then she saw Henry standing in the open doorway to the dining room and motioning for her to join him. As Kitty stood up, Louisa caught her hand and said, "I would love to hear more about your studies, Katherine. Your program sounds so useful. I wish I had such an opportunity when I was your age."

Henry had entered the dining room and was helping his grandfather into his chair at the end of the lavish dining table. Kitty walked over to them, admiring the table and the wealth of good food on it. There was a great, golden roast turkey at one end and a fragrant ham scored and studded with cloves at the other. Between the meats were silver shells containing mashed potatoes, boiled carrots with what looked like dill, a nutty bread dressing and other dishes she couldn't identify. At each end of the table blazed a silver candelabra, from which six green bayberry candles sent out their evocative fragrance.

Above the table hung a crystal chandelier that must have been converted to electricity with garlands of evergreen and holly twined through it. It all smelled like a deep and beautiful forest, with a hint of the scents of the magnificent supper to come.

When Kitty reached the end of the table where Henry had seated his grandfather, she overheard him talking in a mixture of German and English, "If only your Oma could be here, *mein* Henry. How she loved Christmas. Yah, yah, *mein* Augusta *in himmel.* If *mein* Augusta could only be here," Vati said, as much to himself as Henry. Then he turned to Kitty and said, "You know, *mein* Augusta spoke with the Indians. This was but an Indian village when she arrived."

"How interesting," Kitty said, not knowing what else to say.

Henry said, "Yes, Vati," in a comforting voice and shook open his grandfather's damask napkin and placed it on his lap. "Oma conversed with the Indians."

Then Henry sat Kitty at her place. "As far as I'm concerned," he whispered in her ear, "the only Indians in Chicago are carved from wood and stand in front of cigar stores. My Chicago is the White City, a booming metropolis that will lead the world, not a muddy swamp populated by savages." He made sure she was comfortable and turned back again to his grandfather. "Eat, Vati," he said, patting his shoulder. "You must keep up your strength."

"For what, *gruss Gott?*" his grandfather said, staring at the brimming plate the white-gloved waiter had set before him. "To eat brings me no closer to *mein liebchen* Augusta."

Henry took his own seat between Kitty and his grandfather. At the head of the table, Henry's father tapped the crystal water glass before him. His deep voice boomed out, "First, we must thank our God," which, Kitty noticed, he pronounced "*Gott.*" "For this abundant feast, for the many blessings we enjoy, not the least of which is the love of our most beloved family." And all the other guests bowed their heads and recited the grace in German. Kitty started to raise her right hand to make a sign of the cross, but she quickly brought it back to her lap when she realized no one else was going to.

Kitty kept her head up and tried to orient herself to the others at the table, who Henry had introduced before they entered the dining room. At the head of the table, of course, was Henry's father, whose white mane of hair gave him an imperial look befitting Henry's nickname for him, Henry the First. Next, sat his mother, to his father's right, her hairdo an intricate wheaten maze with tiny pearls woven through. Then, next to his mother, was Henry's Uncle Herman Thomas, a paler and more unkempt copy of his father, and next to him was Aunt Louisa, her dark hair parted in the middle into two symmetrical semicircles. Next came Mr. Gerhardt Hemplemayer, their neighbor on Kennesaw Terrace, a widower whose meatpacking business had made him wealthy and kept him busy. Earlier, Henry told Kitty that he suspected that his mother had tried to match up Mr. Hemplemayer—whose bald head matched the color of the sliced ham on the table before him—with his beloved Auntie Lou, but the matchup did not take, no matter how hard and how often his mother pushed the two together. It must have been difficult to resist Mrs. Thomas's urgings, she looked like a woman one didn't say no to.

Then Vati, Henry, and herself. On her right, Kitty could see the profile of Henry's mother's older sister Aunt May, a widow dressed in black, and beyond her, Mr. and Mrs. Geist, Walter and Margaret, who had both grown up with Henry's father on the Near North Side. Henry had told her how the Geists had fled with the Thomases to the cold waters of Lake Michigan when the vicious flames of the 1871 fire jumped the river and ravaged their neighborhood.

"And now, a moment of silence," Mrs. Thomas added, while heads were still bowed. "For those who cannot be with us on this holy night, those who have departed from us to join God in his heaven . . ." She paused for a moment, still looking down at the white tablecloth, and then finished, her voice cracking just a bit, ". . . and for those who remain on this earth, separated from us by distance."

Kitty thought of her own family, and said a little prayer of thanksgiving for her parents, all her of brothers, her sister and her brother-in-law Kevin, little Sean and baby Helena, Aunt Mabel and

Uncle Patrick, and her other aunts and uncles scattered across Chicago and northern Illinois. Except perhaps for Aunt Mabel, how they would be in awe of this grand house and overflowing table, she thought, although she shuddered to imagine what her brothers would make of it. She thanked God for allowing her to be here to enjoy the food and the company, and added a little prayer of thanks for Henry's Aunt Louisa, who had made her feel like a person in her own right, not just someone Henry had brought to dinner.

Kitty had looked at the place setting with some nervousness when she first sat down, but she remembered Aunt Mabel's advice to start at the outside and work your way in. Before she picked up her soup spoon she looked across at Aunt Louisa to see which spoon she was using, just to make sure she didn't embarrass herself. Later, she wasn't able to remember what it was that compelled her to turn to Henry, just as her hand was stretched out to pick up her water goblet. She did not see the wine glass next to it, and knocked it over, spilling its contents into her bowl of lobster bisque. As a waiter quickly removed the glass and bowl, and brought replacements, Kitty looked up in anguish at her hostess, Mrs. Thomas, and caught the sneer that quickly passed over her lovely and serene face.

Henry had noticed it too, she saw, and he leaned over to her and patted her arm. "Don't worry," he whispered. "Happens all the time."

Henry had told her that she would hear his family's familiar stories of Christmases past, brought out at this time of year as regularly as the ornaments themselves—Christmas in Germany, in poverty, in the early years after immigration when these now-prosperous Americans had been greenhorns from the other side of the ocean. So Kitty was surprised to discover that no one at the table spoke when there were plates heaped with food in front of them. The silence that prevailed in the dining room was punctuated with only an occasional clink of a fork against fine china, a guttural "*gut*" deep in a throat, and the tinkle of the gold charms on Mrs. Geist's bracelet as she raised her crystal water goblet to her lips.

When they were finishing up the meat course, Kitty wasn't sure if it was by accident or on purpose that Henry's elbow brushed against his half-empty glass of red wine, which spilled onto the white tablecloth. The glass fell to the carpeted floor without a sound except the indrawn breath of those who sat around the table. Kitty was even more puzzled as he looked up to his parents at the end of the table and said, lightheartedly, "Mrs. Potter Palmer's soup tureen, I suppose?" No one said anything, as a waiter picked up the goblet and placed a white damask napkin over the spreading stain. Feeling that Henry's faux pas, or "fox paw," as her aunt would laughingly term it, outdid her own, she was able to relax herself and enjoy the rest of the meal without feeling uncomfortable about her own accident.

Two maids in white aprons appeared at the door of the kitchen, brandishing large platters bearing sugar-glazed pastries and a snowy coconut layer-cake. Waiters with white gloves came to clear the plates, without a sound. A maid placed her platter in front of Mrs. Thomas, who whispered in her ear, causing her to disappear into the kitchen and reappear almost immediately, balancing a huge silver tray with a shining silver coffee service. She placed it on the sideboard where cups and saucers were already set out, dropped a curtsey, and returned to the kitchen. Kitty's eyes followed the waitress, who could have been one of her fellow choir members at St. Patrick's for all she knew.

The silence continued with dessert, which everybody took to with pleasure and gravity. Kitty thought they looked as if they had been called together to test, rather than to enjoy, the rich pastries, so serious were their faces. As soon as someone cleaned his plate, a waiter removed it, without a sound. The waiters hardly seemed human, they moved so quietly and efficiently. Another waiter passed out cigars from a carved wooden box. The men pushed their chairs back from the table, accepted cigars and leaned in to receive a light, and then sat back and puffed contentedly, even Henry. Mrs. Thomas rose, tapped Louisa on the shoulder, and the two of them left the dining room together. Kitty was unsure of what she was expected to do, so she just sat there, breathing in the cigar smoke. She wondered what Henry would have done if she had taken a cigar herself. She would probably cough and cough and then get sick, she thought, so it would not be worth the uproar her behavior might cause.

Before long, the strains of the piano playing reached them. Kitty found the music was familiar enough—*Oh Come, All Ye Faithful*, or *Adeste Fideles,* as she'd call it at St. Pat's. No one broke into song, but got up from the table, some of them groaning at the weight of their stomachs, smiling as they entered the parlor.

Henry and Kitty sat close together on the striped satin sofa, while Mrs. Thomas and Louisa struck the beginning chords of *O Tannenbaum,* the German Christmas tree song. All turned to the closed doors that separated the back parlor from the front. Much to Kitty's delight, the doors slowly slid apart to reveal a fir tree, which must have been seven feet high, completely covered with golden apples, wax angels and shimmering crystal globes, illuminated by a hundred candles glowing in the darkness. Everyone uttered "Ah" and then applauded as Louisa and Mrs. Thomas finished the carol in German. Both, Kitty noticed, had tears running their faces as they sang. She remembered that Henry told her it had been Eleanor who sang with her mother on this occasion, and she thought that they were probably thinking about her. She turned to Henry to comment, but he held out his watch to show her that it was time for them to leave in order for her to make it on time to the rehearsal at St. Patrick's.

In the darkness on the ride home after the singing, Kitty told Henry that she had never seen such a beautiful Christmas tree. They never had a tree at home, even though the German custom was becoming popular in Chicago and the trees were often sold in shops and on street corners.

Henry said, "I can't imagine Christmas without a tree. You know, even though we always keep buckets of sand nearby as a precaution against fire, the candles have never set fire to our tree. Although I don't usually take notice of such superstitious nonsense, it does seem to be the magic of Christmas."

Henry didn't usually talk about such things, magic and all that, Kitty thought, but how could he not, with all that beauty in just one room? She snuggled a little closer to him in the cold of the carriage and thought about the evening. It had meant a lot to Henry that she would come to his family party, and even though she had been anxious after she had knocked over the wineglass, she felt that Henry's family had accepted her. She wondered why no one asked her to sing, but she didn't ask Henry about this. A few blocks before they arrived at St. Patrick's, he stopped the carriage beneath a streetlight and handed Kitty a little box. "Merry Christmas," he said, and kissed her on the cheek. She opened the box then and there and found a beautiful silver bracelet inside. She put it on immediately, said, "Thank you, Henry," and kissed him back, shamelessly in the semi-darkness beneath the streetlamp.

TWENTY-SEVEN

A unt Louisa and Uncle Herman were both dinner guests the following Sunday. Henry knew he shouldn't have been surprised, one or the other of them were often guests at the Thomas's dining table to even out the balance between men and women. But his mother had invited both of them that night as she and his father would be leaving soon for a European trip. The dinner was an occasion to say farewell, and to invite them to watch over their only son while they traveled to Germany for a two-month stay.

"There you are, Henry," his mother said when he entered the parlor where his parents, aunt and uncle had gathered for a drink before dinner. "That was quite a long walk you took."

"I was puzzling over a problem I've been working on, a construction problem," Henry said, telling the truth, but only partially. For most of his walk along the thawing lakefront, he had been thinking about Christmas Eve and the many charms of Miss Kitty Coakley. He had enjoyed his inner fantasies of teaching her the niceties of manners that would soon make her welcome at any house in the city. He helped himself to a slice of cheese, placed it on a cracker and popped it into his mouth.

"What kind of problem was that, son?" his father asked, turning away from the leaded glass window through which he was monitoring the activities of the street. He was dressed in his usual black suit and a wide black tie.

Henry held up a finger to indicate that he was still chewing, and then stopped to take a sip from the glass of sparkling white wine his mother handed him. The eyes of all the people in the room were focused upon him, as if he were going to deliver some great news.

241

"It isn't a big problem, just a question of how to allot the floor-space in the building I'm working on. Interesting, though, because it helps determine where to place the utility sections. Did you know that new buildings, at least ours, of course, are making no provision anymore for gas lighting? It's all electric, without question."

"And here we thought, not so long ago, that electricity was just a passing fad, certain to go out of popularity within just a year or two," said Aunt Louisa.

"Yes, times do change, don't they?" said Mrs. Thomas.

"And children grow up," said Uncle Herman. "I can remember, Henry, when you and I were conducting experiments with electricity in my cellar. Ach, the fun we had!"

"I seem to remember some fires you set, as well," said Mrs. Thomas, brushing crumbs from the skirt of her deep gray silk dress. "I do wish you'd reconsider coming with us to Berlin," she said, looking up at Henry who stood with his arm stretched across the mantelpiece, welcoming the warmth it gave to his entire body. It had been a long walk, accompanied only by winter's bitter chill.

"Mother, we've gone over this time and time again. I'm holding a job, a job I quite like, thank you very much, and I have a certain responsibility to continue in that job."

Mrs. Thomas glanced over at her husband. He cleared his throat and spoke.

"Henry, we understand about your job and, yes, the responsibility you might feel for it. But draftsmen are a dime a dozen, and how far are you going to get by spending all your hours at a drafting table? Just like any business, architecture is not only *what* you can do, but *who* you know. I cannot imagine that your Daniel Burnham made his way by drawing pictures every day. No, he was out there meeting people, building relationships, making sure he knew where the money and the power were."

Henry recognized this as a new tactic on his father's part. His parents' pleas for him to join them on their trip had formerly stressed how they didn't want to leave him behind, how they would miss him, how he deserved a respite from the past year, what with his sister's death and his having to drop his program at l'École des Beaux-Arts and all. They had suggested that he could just take a leave from his job, and that D. H. Burnham and Company would welcome him back after a two-month respite, a scenario he truly doubted.

"Think of all the people your father can introduce you to over there," said Aunt Louisa. The Thomas's trip was built around business as well as pleasure. The German government had heard of Chicago's success in reversing the flow of its river, and was interested in discussing the accomplishment with members of the team that had managed it. So, Mr. Thomas had accepted invitations to speak with high-ranking military and government ministers. There had even been talk that he might receive a decoration from the Kaiser himself. Both parents believed that Henry should accompany them. But Henry had been adamant, standing firm in his decision to remain here in his home, in his job, and in Chicago.

"Henry, Henry, it would mean so much to your father and mother if you would just go with them," Uncle Herman said, shaking his head. "Think of all that they have given to you. Don't you think it's time you did something for them?" Uncle Herman had never been comfortable with any disagreements in the family, even when Henry was a young boy.

"Yes, Henry," Aunt Louisa chimed in. "Why not share in your father's glory? It will make it all the more important to him, and it can't do you any harm, now can it? Think of the people you'll meet, important people in Berlin, people who make the decisions, not just those who cut the stones and drive the carts."

Henry looked out at the four of them from his vantage point standing by the fireplace. His mother, his father, his aunt, and his uncle were the people he had loved the most his entire life. The only one missing was his sister Eleanor, and she would have taken his side, he was sure. And of course Vati, although he wouldn't have participated in the disagreement. But here they all were, united in an attempt to turn him from what he wanted to do, in order to make him follow their will. His was a family that rarely argued, where one almost never raised one's voice. Yet he began to feel the gathering of volcanic forces within himself, forces that he feared would erupt into angry shouting and eventually the loss of control, something he would not allow himself. How could he control his anger and respond to the unanimity of these people who insisted they had only his best interests at heart?

The room remained silent, except for the crackle of the flames in the fireplace. When a log popped, Mrs. Thomas jumped, but no one said a word.

"I don't know why you've dragged out this question again," Henry said finally, as evenly as he could manage. "I thought we'd decided that I would stay here while you traveled. I'm a grown man, you know, and I have a job to do."

"No one is questioning your ability to take care of yourself," said his mother, who still packed the lunch the cook prepared for him each day, and who reserved the right to veto any piece of clothing he purchased for himself. "We think that perhaps you might meet some people more your . . . not class, exactly . . . let's just say you are more likely to meet people who might share your tastes while traveling than here at home."

"You're questioning my choice of friends?" Henry asked.

"Not all of them, Henry," his mother said. "You have made some lovely friends over the years. No, I'm just thinking about . . . let's see . . . that young man whose father runs the livery stable over in Ravenswood, for example."

"Dick Connell? Mother, that's not a livery stable, it's a garage, and Dick works with me at the Burnham Company. He's a fine man . . ."

"And what about that sweet Irish girl you brought at Christmas, a lovely girl, but do you really think she could handle the social obligations you'd face as one of Chicago's leading architects?" Mrs. Thomas stared at Henry with a stern look on her face. "Just look at Daniel Burnham's wife, dear, the daughter of John Sherman, one of the wealthiest men in Chicago. Don't you think she's added quite a bit to his success?"

Oh yes, here it was. This was what had reopened the question of his traveling with his parents. His family didn't think Kitty was good enough for him, and they thought they had better get him out of town, before he became more involved with her. "Irish girl? Irish girl?" Henry could feel the cauldron within him begin to bubble over. "Mother, that Irish girl, as you so quaintly call her, is a classmate of mine from Lake View High School, someone you must have met several times during my years there." He could feel his face going red and his collar growing tight.

"And really, dear," said his mother gently. "Mrs. Potter Palmer's soup tureen?"

"Mrs. Potter Palmer's soup tureen?" repeated his father. "What in tarnation are you talking about?"

"It's a well-known story," Aunt Louisa interjected, turning to Mr. Thomas. "I'm surprised that you, Henry, haven't heard it. As the story goes, Mrs. Potter Palmer was holding a very formal dinner. One of her guests, a most nervous type, I gather, was so intimidated by dining at her table that he knocked over his bowl of soup, spilling it all over her priceless Persian carpet. Mrs. Palmer seemed to ignore it completely at the time, but a few moments later, as one of the waiters was removing the giant tureen from which she had ladled the soup, she knocked it with her elbow, causing him to drop the whole thing, spilling even more of the soup, creating a much greater to-do."

"Now tell me," sputtered Mr. Thomas, "why would a great lady do something idiotic like that?"

"Can't you see, dear," Mrs. Thomas asked, looking up sweetly at her husband's face. "She did it to make her guest feel less clumsy, by appearing even clumsier herself. And don't you remember, that's what Sonny did Christmas Eve. He dropped his glass of wine to deflect any embarrassment from his friend Miss Coakley, who had spilled her wine before that."

"That's absolutely ridiculous," Mr. Thomas snorted. "I've never heard anything so ridiculous in my life." He turned away from the women and walked over to the window, shaking his head in disgust.

Mrs. Thomas and Aunt Louisa shared a glance that seemed to communicate that they didn't find Mrs. Palmer's behavior ridiculous at all.

Henry looked over at his father, who had pulled aside one of the drapes and was staring out the window. "Father, what do you have to say about this? Not the soup tureen, but my choice of friends. Do you think I'm wasting my time with the wrong sort of people?" Surely his father would understand that you couldn't always judge a person by their nationality or background.

"Henry, I must stand by your mother, soup tureen or not. I don't believe you've demonstrated the maturity of someone we can leave here on his own. She and I would worry about you the entire time we were gone. I think it will be to your benefit all around if you join us. You might not appreciate it now, but I'm sure you will once we've started. It's your place to come with us, my boy." Henry the First had spoken.

TWENTY-EIGHT

itty and her parents reached Grand Central Station in plenty of time to board their train to New Orleans. She hadn't expected such a throbbing mass of people, noise and smoke, having never traveled by train—this was her first trip out of Illinois. She gripped her mother's hand, and her mother held tightly to her father, creating a human chain that made it even more difficult for them to make their way from the Park Row entrance to the gate where they would find their train. Kitty hoped their chain wouldn't turn into a crack the whip and throw her off into the crowd of all those people.

Mr. Donley had driven them to the station in his wheeled cart, and she was freezing. Even though it was January, she thought that it would be warm in New Orleans and she could wear her lightweight coat to go with the hat Aunt Mabel had given her for the trip. She had found out when riding in the open cart that this was not a good idea. But she couldn't complain because her mother had told her not to wear that coat. Her father somehow managed to carry their two big bags beneath one shoulder, and she carried a small bag with books to read on the train, as well as a large shopping bag with provisions for the twenty-hour train journey. Somehow they boarded the train and crammed themselves into a coach that already seemed overfull.

"Now isn't this cozy?" her mother said as they huddled together on a long seat in the middle of the railway car. The cold and the excitement of the journey had brought more color into her face than Kitty had seen in a long while. And her Easter bonnet, retrimmed from last year's, framed her face in such a way that she almost looked beautiful. Kitty could see that her father appreciated her mother's rosy cheeks and high spirits, staring at her as he sat sprawled all over the seat, with his hat pushed to the back of his head, whistling a merry Irish tune like he owned the place. He looked younger than he had looked all year, what with one worry and another. He had told Kitty that this was the first time he and Mama had ever taken time off together, away from the family and their work.

As she sat at the window on the train, waiting for it to pull out of the station, Kitty could feel her fears about being on time and finding seats lift from her shoulders too. "This should be a lovely trip," she said, leaning over Da and patting her mother's hand. "It will do us all good to get away for a while."

Her mother smiled back and then pointed to the large bag Kitty had placed on the floor beside her. "Now take care that you don't misplace our food, Kitty. We don't want to arrive in New Orleans starving to death, like them poor immigrants coming from Ireland on the fever boats." Her mother's thoughts never traveled far from the stories she was told as a child about the famine in Ireland and the many deaths it caused. She had packed enough sandwiches in the bag for an ocean voyage. There was no way they would go hungry on the day and night they would spend on the train.

As they slowly entered New Orleans's Union Station, Kitty realized that hunger was almost the only discomfort they hadn't suffered on the train ride. Her light coat was now more soot-colored than anything else, and her straw hat, which she kept on her lap so as not to crush it against the seat back, looked as if it had suffered a snowfall of cinders. Her eyes were burning from the ashes as well as from fatigue—it had been impossible to sleep through the noise. It had been much too dark to read, and she was too excited to sleep, hurtling through space at thirty miles an hour. She'd loved watching the landscape change overnight from brown, muddy snow to bright green grass. Her white handkerchief had turned into a greasy rag as she had used it repeatedly to clean a fresh spot on the window so that they could see the buildings and the fields as the train whipped past. She had tried to keep her mind on the travel itself rather than daydream about Henry Thomas. After Christmas, she had quickly dashed off a thank-you note to him for the bracelet, reminding him that she'd be away until the end of January. She didn't give him the address in New Orleans, as she thought it might be awkward receiving letters from him while staying with the Kellehers. She decided that she might send him a postal card of the city if she could find one.

Kitty thought she might have nodded off for a few minutes during the night when it was completely dark outside the windows, but she was sure she hadn't slept, as her parents did, huddled together with Mama's shawl over the two of them, Da's gentle snore somehow a comfort in the dark and unfamiliar railroad car. As the forward movement of the train slowed, she stood up, stretching her aching arms and legs and trying to brush off the veil of soot and cinders as well as she could. Then the train stopped suddenly, jolting her and she grabbed Da's shoulder to steady herself.

His eyes flew open and his hands reached out to grab her. "Whoa, my girl. Watch yourself. We'll not have you flying out the window to be the first to step foot in New Orleans."

"I'm all right, Da," she said, trying to get away from him so she didn't end up sitting on his lap like a little child. "But look, we're here, we're here."

Her father looked down at Mama, curled in a ball next to him on the seat. "Would you look at your mother now, I swear she can sleep anywhere." And he gently shook her shoulder to rouse her. She uncurled, not even opening her eyes until she was upright. She suddenly seemed very old, white-faced and haggard, but when she opened her eyes she smiled, and Kitty let out her breath in relief. One of her biggest fears had been that the journey would make her mother's health worse, rather than help her improve.

As Kitty and her mother helped each other brush off and adjust their clothing as best they could—not being used to sleeping in their clothes—

her father gathered their luggage, and led the way through all the other passengers fighting to reach the door of the train.

"Here, let me clean some of that smut off your face," Kitty's mother said, spitting into her still-clean handkerchief and rubbing her face. Kitty tried to squirm out of her way, not liking to be spit-washed, but she grabbed her arm and persisted. "You don't want anyone thinking you've gone and got spotty, do you?" her mother asked.

Kitty couldn't wait to be free of the train. Free to move her arms and legs and to see the city outside and all of the people. She admitted to herself that she was even looking forward to seeing Brian Kelleher, even though she would never let on to her parents. He wasn't one to write, that was for sure, and she had wondered how he was doing. She wondered too if he'd notice how different she had become since going to school. And maybe a little different because Henry Thomas was paying attention to her. At least she hoped so. That she was different. She didn't wear the bracelet Henry had given her because she didn't want anyone to ask about it, especially in front of Brian. But she kept it with her in her bag so she wouldn't forget him.

The New Orleans station was so different from the one in Chicago. The people walked much more slowly, and their clothes were much more colorful, and lighter, too, because it was so much warmer. Even the air seemed different, heavier somehow, more liquid than airy. Kitty could hear music playing, and smell coffee and cinnamon, which, even though she'd eaten well on the train, made her stomach tell her she was hungry. Something about the atmosphere made her want to slow down and take time to look at and appreciate what was around her. It was so unlike the hurly-burly of Chicago, where she often found herself rushing, whether she wanted to or not, just to keep up with the crowd.

Her father piled up the suitcases and leaned against them. "Matt Kelleher wrote and said he'd be over to pick us up. I told him what time we would be coming in, and it looks like we're a bit early. I suspect all we have to do is wait a few minutes. Matt always keeps his promises—eventually."

Kitty looked up at the massive station clock. It was nearly nine o'clock, and they had left Chicago just after noon the day before. Amazing that in such a short time they could have traveled to a place so unlike home. It wasn't just the air, the smells, and the colorful flowers in the flowerboxes that circled the station's indoor cavern. Even the advertising signs seemed brighter, more varied. Kitty twirled around with her head back, looking up at the ceiling. When she righted herself, feeling dizzy, she looked over the crowd of people and saw Brian Kelleher making his way toward them. How could he look at the same time so familiar, and yet so different? she wondered. It was definitely the Brian who had grown up down the street, his shock of sandy hair, his blunt nose, broken in a fight in the schoolyard—Kitty could remember the blood running down his face and his chipped front tooth. But his hair was lighter, his face darker from the sun. And it was as if the sun shone in his eyes when he spied them standing there in the middle of the station.

Father had seen Brian, too, and he yelled out to him and waved. Soon Brian reached them, and Father clapped him on the back and shook his hand. "We made it," he said. "The three of us, we finally made it just as we said we would."

Brian removed his hat and looked down at Kitty. "Well, well, Miss Katherine Coakley," he said, crunching his hat in his hands. "Doesn't look like you've changed a bit." His smile was sunlight itself.

"Nor have you, Brian Kelleher," Kitty said, patting him on the arm, and, standing up on her tiptoes, planting a swift kiss on his cheek. "Nor have you."

Their days in New Orleans took on a rhythm just like home. In fact, it became very much like home, with Kitty and her mother shopping and cooking, her father going off with Mr. Kelleher every day to the lumberyard. Kitty had hoped that the Kelleher house would be like the pictures in the guidebook, dripping with vines and flowers, and with a wide balcony looking over the street. It actually looked more like their cottage at home, with small windows, and a small yard, tightly set in next to its neighbors. Mr. Kelleher called it a shotgun cottage, and showed them how all the doors inside opened one behind the other in a straight line. "So with all the doors open," he said, "you could fire a shotgun from the front door through the whole house, straight out the back door." Brian and Father laughed and Mama made the sign of the cross at that, for she hated guns. Mr. Kelleher told them the neighborhood was called the Irish Channel, and Kitty could see that almost everyone, even the children with dirty faces and clothes, looked just like their fellow parishioners at St. Pat's. And there was a saloon on every corner, just like at home.

Oh, there were differences. The house smelled more like just-cut lumber, because it was. The air was so much more humid than home that Kitty found herself slowing down without trying to. People seemed friendlier, too, probably because there weren't so many of them. Shopping for food became more of an adventure at the open-air markets, where farmers brought their fruits and vegetables in to sell. There were so many different kinds of fruits and vegetables that she had never seen, much less tasted.

One morning as she and her mother walked toward the market, Kitty heard music playing, and smelled coffee and cinnamon, scents she much preferred to the nasty stockyard aromas of home. They arrived at one of the squares near the piers, where the market stands were shaded under great faded umbrellas thick with dust. Kitty was fascinated by the melons and papayas piled in heaps, and the big stalks of yellow and green bananas hanging on hooks from the trees. If she were by herself she'd buy all of them, just to try them, but her mother raised her eyebrows and said, "You don't know where they've come from." Kitty noticed many more types of people than she saw at home, including black people of all shades from the color of light coffee to the deepest ebony of piano keys. She rarely saw a black person in Chicago, except for the porters on the train to New Orleans. She admired the women of all shapes and sizes wearing bright red, yellow, and orange dresses, and white kerchiefs on their heads like turbans. They were friendly, too, although she didn't always understand what they were saying.

That morning at the fruit stand, a large woman wearing a dress as vibrantly colored as a blazing fire had offered Kitty an unfamiliar fruit, the size of a small melon with the color and texture of a lemon and the round shape of an orange. When she brought it to her nose and sniffed, it smelled like the laundry tub on days when she and her mother bleached tablecloths and sheets. A good, clean smell, but not one that tempted her to bite into the strange fruit. The woman motioned her to tear back the skin before she bit into it, which she did easily, finding the skin thinner and more pliable than a lemon rind. Kitty took a big bite of the lemon-like interior and her head jerked back in surprise. Its juice spurted up into her eyes, and it tasted as tart as a lemon. She pulled out her handkerchief, wiping her watering eyes while she chewed on the sinewy pith of the fruit. She had a hard time choking down the mouthful, her mouth was puckering so, but she did, aware of the eyes of the fruit-monger, as well as her mother, upon her while she chewed.

"Not too bad," Kitty said to them, unwilling to admit that she didn't care for it. "It's probably an acquired taste." The fruit-monger nodded and smiled, pointing to the sign that read "Grapefruits, three for ten cents," and, speaking with her hands and a big smile, suggested that Kitty buy them.

"Not today," Kitty said, shaking her head and pointing to a heap of apples instead. She knew what to expect when she bit into an apple. Her mother paid for the apples, and as they walked through the dusty aisles of the market to pick up some chickens, Kitty wondered why the fruit was called grapefruit, when it looked and tasted nothing at all like grapes.

Kitty's favorite place in the market was the stand where they sold fish and seafood. Live creatures she'd never seen before, like blue and green crabs in baskets, still alive and waving their claws as if they were saying, "Come and get me and set me free." And shrimp and crayfish and spiny lobsters. But her mother said she wouldn't know how to cook them, and who knew where they had come from. Kitty was disappointed to leave the fish-mongers, with only a piece or two of whitefish like she'd buy at home, when there were all those new things to taste. She was sure that some way they could figure out how to cook them. What her mother did like, although she had never tasted them before, were pralines, a pecan and brown sugar candy. The Kellehers had given her some when they arrived, so she figured they couldn't be harmful. Every time Kitty and her mother went to the market, they each bought a praline to eat while they were shopping. Kitty loved them, too, but they didn't stop her from looking at other new things she'd like to try.

Her parents wouldn't let Kitty go off by herself, as she was used to doing in Chicago, and they didn't like to go where they didn't know where they were going, so the only times she got to see New Orleans were when Brian would take her out for a ride in the wagon. Usually that was in the evening, after he'd worked all day in the lumberyard, and come home to eat the dinner that she and her mother fixed. It would get dark early because it was still January, even though it was much warmer than in Chicago. So, for the first week, anyway, all she saw of New Orleans was the Irish Channel, as Brian didn't want to go into the old quarter of the city where he didn't know his way around. And they'd usually end up in a saloon where a fair number of the men greeted Brian as if they knew him well.

One night, Kitty persuaded Brian to drive along the Mississippi, which flowed along the edge of the Irish Channel. The river was much wider than the Chicago River and smelled much worse. They got out of the wagon at one point and climbed up onto the levee to look out over the dark water. They were near a wharf where workers were unloading giant stalks of green bananas from a ship onto the wagons that were lined up to transport them all over the city. Brian told her that the longshoremen had to be careful because sometimes they would find long black snakes that had wound themselves into the banana stalks to make the journey along with the fruit. Kitty shuddered and tried not to feel sick, what with the fear of those snakes and the smells that came in from the slaughterhouses and refineries that lined the riverbanks.

As the wagon rattled along the cobblestone-lined streets, Kitty asked Brian if they couldn't go into the old sections of the town, where the French and Spanish first settled, long before there even was a United States of America. She had read about these early settlers, and the wealth and culture that had flourished here for centuries. She wanted to see the fabulous buildings, and shops and restaurants, and people who gave the town its reputation as a place of gaiety and pleasure. Brian shook his head and said that such things were not for the likes of them. He'd heard tell of the goings-on downriver, in the old part of the city, where the people behaved in a scandalous way that would put a blush on the face of a priest. And because he wouldn't know where he was going in those places, they'd be attacked by thieves and scoundrels and have all their money taken and much worse. Stories were going around of young girls like Kitty disappearing forever, the victims of the white slave traders, who preyed upon the tourists. "The pirates don't always stay on their ships," Brian said. "New Orleans surely is a city of sin."

Kitty tried to convince him that he shouldn't believe everything he heard in those saloons, that people made up stories to defend their own behavior. Stories like that were commonplace in Chicago and yet she'd never seen anything like them. Chicago was a much bigger city, although not as old, and Kitty had lived her twenty-two years in safety. She knew how to protect herself and stay out of danger.

"But that's Chicago, and this is New Orleans," Brian insisted, as he gestured with his whole arm. "There are dangers out there, dangers that you've never even heard of, like voodoo and witches and strange supernatural happenings, unlike anything we've ever heard about in Chicago."

"They don't describe that sort of thing in the guidebooks," Kitty said.

"Nor would they. Because if they did, no one would ever come to New Orleans."

Kitty bit her tongue to keep from calling him a superstitious idiot—but she thought he was. To be afraid of things that you couldn't even see, things you just heard about while you were sitting on a barstool. She wished she had Aunt Mabel there, or Henry Thomas, someone who wasn't afraid of what he or she didn't know, someone whose world was wider than a tight little knot of people who looked and thought just like themselves. One of them would explore New Orleans with her, she was sure of that.

When they arrived back at Brian's house, his father and her parents were sitting on the front stoop, enjoying the fresh air and each other's company. Kitty thought Mr. Kelleher looked so much better than he had back in Chicago, stronger and healthier, with more of a will to go on living despite his wife's death. Her mother and father looked happier too. The hard winters in Chicago had taken their toll, but the warm breezes and change of pace seemed to agree with them. When they saw Kitty and Brian coming up the path, Kitty's mother stood up and stretched and said, "It's time for us to go to bed, my young Kitty. We've got the laundry to do tomorrow and with all these men, it's a big one. You'll be needing your sleep and so will I." Kitty shared a bed in the smaller bedroom with her mother, while the three men all shared another room.

"It's such a lovely night, Mama. Don't you want to stay out here and look at the stars?"

"So it's stargazing you and our Brian have been doing, is it? That's not what we called it when I was young," Mr. Kelleher said, winking.

Kitty was still angry with Brian for not being willing to venture beyond the neighborhood, so she just smiled and followed her mother indoors, not even giving him a look or a hug or a "good night."

Her mother fell asleep immediately, but Kitty couldn't. She tossed and turned and ground her teeth, trying to make her body relax, even though her mind would not. She thought about all the enticing pictures she had seen in the guidebooks and how they were at most just a few miles away. There was a French opera house, and a grand old cathedral, and restaurants with food as good as, or even better than, what was served in Paris—or so the book said. And there were people there who had been in Paris, and Rome, and Rio de Janeiro, dressed in beautiful clothing and buying precious jewelry and paintings and all sorts of things more glamorous even than what they sold at Marshall Field's. She thought about running away one day and taking the streetcar downtown, just like she would at home. The guidebook had a map and described places to see and where to eat, and where to go to watch the people. It didn't mention the white slave trade, but cautioned that it was best to be careful, that the river brought many people to the city, not all with the best intentions, and it was best to be chaperoned or escorted by someone who knew his way around. Kitty felt trapped, a prisoner of her own family and the treachery of the town. Tears slid down her face as she buried her head in the pillow.

TWENTY-NINE

O n the day before they were to leave, Kitty's father took pity on her. "Let's take the streetcar downtown, to see what this city is all about before we have to leave it," he suggested. Her mother looked worried and said she didn't want to go, making up some excuse about having to pack their bags. Kitty practically jumped up and down with excitement. She pulled out her guidebook and showed her father the maps and the places she really wanted to see. He laughed and tried gently to convince Mama to accompany them, but she wasn't having it. He shrugged his shoulders and asked if the map showed where to find the streetcar. Kitty assured him that she could navigate their way through the town. She was practically out the door before he told her to wait and finish breakfast and help Mama with the dishes before they left.

As they walked to St. Charles Street, the houses got bigger and more grand, with pillars and balconies and tended lawns and gardens, and were set much farther apart from each other. This was the Garden District where the New Orleans elite lived, the guidebook said, and Kitty could see why. The air was clearer just a few blocks away from the river, and the streets were quieter. Kitty realized that it was so close to the Irish Channel that she could have been taking walks here all along, if she had gotten over her fears and explored a bit on her own. They boarded the electric trolley car with several other people, nicely dressed and soft-spoken, and rode through the area of fine houses for about half an hour.

Kitty felt a little strange, traveling alone with her father. As the youngest of seven, she rarely spent any time with him by herself, and she actually felt a little shy. She knew she shouldn't have, he was as enthralled as she was by the changing view along the trolley route, pointing out the unusual houses and buildings, reading off the signs so they had a sense of where they were. As the streets became narrower, and more and more people were getting off the car, he suggested that they start walking and see what they could see. According to the map, they were getting close to Jackson Square, where the cathedral was, which Kitty particularly wanted to see. They jumped off the car and began walking in the direction of the cathedral, along a street that was so narrow that they could hardly fit two abreast on the sidewalk. The homes had intricate wrought iron balconies above the street, but were very closed up so they couldn't see inside at all. One street-level door was open, to allow a delivery wagon to enter, and Kitty peered inside and saw a flower-filled courtyard with a fountain and an arcade with doors opening into the house. It was a castle, she told her father, with the walls fortified to keep out the enemy, and inside a plush garden sheltered from the outside world. He laughed and pointed out the vines draped over the balcony. Perhaps the prince could climb up the vines and find the princess, he said.

Not too many people were walking along the narrow streets. In fact, the city seemed deserted until they reached Jackson Square, where the park was like a carnival, with vendors selling food from carts, and jugglers and acrobats, and someone playing drums, and even fortune tellers in front of the church.

They entered the cathedral, cool and dark after the bright sunshine outside. Kitty's eyes took a minute to adjust, but when they did, she gasped at the size and beauty of the interior. Too many tourists were walking around and whispering to make it feel like a church back home, but she walked up to a pew near the front, genuflected, and then knelt and said some prayers for her family, the Kellehers and even Henry Thomas and his family.

Her father came up behind her and whispered that he was getting hungry and he'd perish for a cool glass of water, so they left the cathedral and began to look for somewhere to have lunch. Many of the restaurants along the square had their menus posted, and they looked at the prices, and then at each other, and passed them on. The farther away they walked from the square the lower the prices seemed, so they continued down the narrower streets, passing shops displaying antiques and precious jewels, and all sorts of objects of art that Kitty wondered who would ever buy. They finally ended up at a street corner bar with an Irish name. It didn't have a regular printed menu, but a chalkboard with specials and prices listed, and her father took a look and nodded his head. As soon as they sat down, a waiter came over and asked them what they'd like. He wore a towel around his waist like an apron, and had a familiar-looking face with freckles and sandy hair. He spoke in that "dese and dose" accent that Kitty had heard in the bars on the Irish Channel, and she asked him if he lived there. He said he did, introducing himself as Tommy Reilly, and he and Kitty's father struck up a conversation about the Kellehers and the sawmill and the neighborhood. Kitty finally reminded them that she was hungry and would like to order and asked if he could recommend something.

"So have you tasted much of this New Orleans food?" he asked.

Kitty had to admit that she hadn't really, although she had tasted a grapefruit and didn't think much of it.

"I'm thinking you'd like our special today, shrimp Creole," he said, nodding his head as if he had made a diagnosis. "And you, sir," he turned to Kitty's father, "I supposed you'll be having a roast beef sandwich and a lager?"

"You can forget the lager," he said. "But the roast beef sandwich will fill the bill. And a big glass of your finest water."

"Took the pledge, did you?" the waiter said, and turned toward the kitchen to put in the orders.

"Well, it might not be the finest restaurant in New Orleans, but we wouldn't want to be spoiling you so you'd never be coming back home to Chicago," Kitty's father said.

"I don't think you have to worry about that," Kitty said, almost without thinking.

"Why, don't you like it here?" Father asked. "Now that you've seen the posher parts and all."

"I'm sure there's much more to the city than I've seen," Kitty said. "It's just that, this isn't Chicago. I don't feel as safe as I do in Chicago, because I don't know my way around, where I can go and where I can't. And I don't feel like myself here, because I'm not free to do as I please, I don't know anyone except the Kellehers, and I don't really have anything to do except housework. At home in Chicago, I know lots of people, I know my way around the city, and I have my schooling and soon I'll have a job, where I'll make a difference to people, at least to children. Those sorts of things are important to me." She surprised herself with how certain she was, she hadn't really thought it out beforehand, and it all came out so wholeheartedly that she could feel tears coming into her eyes. She was glad it was dark in the bar and that her father couldn't see that she was almost crying. She didn't want him to comfort her, she wanted him to listen.

Her father seemed surprised, too, about what Kitty had said about herself. It wasn't like them to talk about serious things, ideas that meant a lot to them. Kitty thought that was what happened in a big family, especially one like theirs with all those boys in it, everything she said could be made a mockery of by the others, so she learned not to say anything that was too important to her. She saw it as a form of self-protection, but realized that it often did make her feel alone and unknown in a group of people who were supposed to know her the best.

"I didn't know you were so unhappy here," he said slowly, as if giving himself time to think about it. "I thought you were enjoying yourself, spending time with Brian, and with your mother and me."

"Oh, I'm not unhappy," Kitty said, praying that the tears wouldn't spill out. "It's just that I like my own life back home and I don't want to change it just now."

"So I don't suppose we'll be losing you to Brian and New Orleans?" he said. "You're not going to become a southern belle and start waving the stars and bars and singing that you wish you were in Dixie?"

"Not a chance," Kitty said, and she was grateful to see that Tommy, the waiter, was coming toward the table loaded down with their food.

"Now the shrimp Creole's a bit hot," he said, "But if you want to cool down your mouth, just take a bite of the rice, that'll do it."

As she told her father, Kitty nearly changed her mind about becoming a southern belle when she tasted that shrimp Creole. It was hot and sweet and buttery-smooth, all at the same time. She thought she had eaten shrimp before, but had never tasted anything as fresh as that. She took a few bites, and then put her fork down, savoring the mixture of tastes in her mouth. Tommy had been hovering over the table, waiting to see how she liked it, and he asked if there was anything wrong. Kitty shook her head and said, smiling, "If I had known that the food here was as delicious as this, I'd have come to visit long ago."

"You'll not be staying on in New Orleans, then?" her father asked.

"No, if I ate food like this every day, I'd grow to be as big as one of those steamboats, and you'd have to float me up the Mississippi River to get me home." Kitty picked up her fork again to continue the ecstasy, her toes curling in her shoes as she ate.

Her father talked about how he was looking forward to going home, to being in his own house, to sleeping in his own bed with his own dear wife and not with those boyos and their smelly feet, and living his own life. "I guess us Coakleys just weren't born to travel," he said.

Kitty nodded and continued eating slowly, savoring each mouthful. She couldn't really see anything wrong with traveling, if she could always go home at the end—home to Chicago. Perhaps she could find the recipe for this dish and make it at home. Although getting the shrimp as fresh as this would be difficult, she couldn't just fish them out of Lake Michigan.

With that big lunch in her stomach, all Kitty wanted to do was find a sunny park bench and watch the world go by. Her father was amenable to that idea, too. They found one on the edge of a park near the levee, and witnessed a parade of people. They could pick out those who were tourists, the clothes they wore more drab than the entertainers and their faces paler and more lined, more like the people they'd see on the street in Chicago, all trying to look about the same, more American, no matter where they'd come from. In New Orleans it seemed that, except for the tourists, people were trying—not to be different so much as they weren't trying to be anything, they were being themselves. Sailors and priests, and nuns walking in twos, mixed in with the tourists. Kitty was surprised when she looked at the nuns' faces and saw that they were black, beautifully framed by their starched white wimples.

Kitty realized that she hadn't yet sent Henry a postal card—she hadn't seen any in the Irish Channel—and so she told her father she needed to pick up something in one of the shops. By this time, he was almost asleep in the sunshine, so he just nodded his head and said to go ahead, he'd wait for her there in the park.

She found a tourist shop where there were stacks of postal cards, and stood there looking through them, agonizing over finding one that would be appropriate to send to Henry. She quickly rejected the one with the beautiful drawings of the cathedral—too Catholic— and flipped through the ones depicting the parades and revelry of the upcoming Mardi Gras—certainly not descriptive of her stay in New Orleans. She couldn't find one of the Irish Channel, which was no surprise, so she finally settled on one of an enormous Mississippi steamboat. What to say?

She finally wrote, "We traveled here much faster by train than we would have by steamboat. Now that's progress! Hope to see you soon. Kitty." She would have liked to sign it, "With love from Kitty," but with a postal card she never knew who might read it. It was difficult to believe that she'd be back in Chicago the day after next, probably by the time Henry received this card. She marveled at the idea that it could be carried on the same train they would be traveling on.

Before they left the French Quarter they bought a box of those wonderful pralines to bring back to Margaret and her family. Kitty and her father joked that they'd have to hide them from Mama on the journey back.

When they arrived back at the Kellehers, they found Brian and Mr. Kelleher already home, helping Mama set the table for dinner. Kitty thought she'd never be able to eat again after that big lunch, but she found that the fragrance of the familiar lamb stew wafting from the kitchen had the power to restore her appetite. They were all aware that it was their last dinner together for a while, at least, and everyone was in a festive mood. Mr. Kelleher insisted that Kitty sing some of his favorite songs, and he pulled out his battered old tin whistle to accompany her. Brian ran over to a local saloon and brought back a bucket or two of beer, and soon they were all singing and laughing and Kitty's parents were dancing together in the front room of the cottage. Then Kitty's mother and father and Mr. Kelleher began exchanging stories of their early life back in Ireland and what it was like to come to America. Brian and Kitty listened for a while, even though she had heard all the stories many times, and she figured he probably had too. He stood up, just a bit tipsy, and came over to her and whispered, "Let's go for a walk," and Kitty followed him out the door.

It was a clear night, with only a bit of a wind, but it must have been blowing away from the river, because there were no noxious odors of tanneries or refineries in the air. Kitty thought about how wonderful it was to be walking about without a coat in January, and wondered how cold it would be when they got home. Brian was quiet, which wasn't unusual, especially when he had had a drink or two, and the only sound for a while was their footsteps on the cobblestones.

Brian took her by the hand and drew her over to a dark corner by the levee. She thought later that she should have known what he was about to say, but her mind was still taken up with the joyous singing of the evening. "Kitty," he said, staring at her in the darkness, "will you marry me? Not right away, Kitty, because I have to get this business moving, but soon. It took me being away from you to know that I don't want to live without you." And then he bent over and kissed her gently on the lips before she could say a word.

Kitty didn't know what to say. She felt for him the kind of love she felt for any one of her brothers. But she didn't think that was enough, it would never be enough. She didn't want to live his narrow, closed-in life, not in New Orleans, not even in Chicago. She had been there and she wanted to move on. She could have put him off with a joke about how it was the beer talking, but she wanted to take him as seriously as he took her. "Brian," she finally said after a long pause. "You are a wonderful man and someday you will make some woman happy. But I am not that woman and I never will be."

He dropped her hand and put his forearm over his eyes as if he were being blinded by a bright light. "Are you sure about that, Kitty? Maybe when you go back home you might change your mind?" He spoke in a whisper.

"I'm sure, Brian. I'm sorry, truly I am. But I'm sure."

"Then we'd best go back to the cottage."

They walked back in silence, their footsteps ringing on the cobblestones as they had on their way over to the levee. They both knew nothing would ever be the same between them again.

THIRTY

O n the train ride back to Chicago, Kitty found herself smiling at the thought of going back to school and seeing the children. Before she left for New Orleans, she had been tired of dealing with the little ones she called dirty little urchins, and had been bored sitting through hours of instruction. Now, she was eagerly awaiting her return to school, having found her life of domesticity far duller than life in the classroom. She also couldn't wait to see Ceecee and tell her about every step of the trip, especially Brian's proposal. And, of course, she was perishing to see Henry again, and follow up on the grand time they had at Christmas. In fact, she must still have been dreaming when she awoke on the train, because she fully expected Henry to meet her and take her home in his carriage.

But all that greeted Kitty and her parents was the reality of the cold, dark and crowded station, coated with years of soot and the stains of hundreds of travelers. When she returned to school on Monday, there was no Ceecee. She had forgotten that Ceecee's trip to Paris and Geneva would keep her out of school for at least another week. She also had neglected to remember just how energetic and annoying children could be when they'd had time enough to forget everything they had learned at school. And what a burden warm clothing, scarves, hats, gloves, and all were! She seemed to spend endless time searching for missing mittens, and then getting them on all of the little children, before she could bundle up herself. That evening when Margaret turned over the pile of mail that had accumulated for the Coakleys and there was absolutely nothing for her from Henry Thomas, she was downcast. How could he have forgotten her, when she had been thinking of him practically every moment of every day?

By Wednesday, it was as if she had never left Chicago at all. It was dark when she awakened, ate her porridge, and trudged through mud and old, sooty snow to the streetcar stop. The cold weather seemed to slow the cars, and the heaters inside were never right, either not working at all—so Kitty felt icicles forming at the end of her nose—or so hot that she wanted to remove all the warm clothes she had just put on. And when the sun did rise, it hardly mattered. The sky remained gray and seemed to press down upon her, like cold flatirons before Mama heated them on the stove.

Riding home on the streetcar that day, she decided to break her journey and stop at Marshall Field's to thaw out. She waltzed in as if she were Mrs. Marshall Field herself, and sought out her aunt. Although the millinery shop was busy with women in fur coats, it was Caroline standing behind the counter, not Aunt Mabel. Looking up, Caroline shook her head and, after excusing herself from a customer, told Kitty that her aunt was out sick with influenza and wasn't expected back until the next week. Caroline was obviously overwhelmed by handling all the customers herself, and sighed as if a week without Madame Mabel would seem like a year.

Kitty found it so unusual for her aunt to be ill, that she stood and thought about it for a while before she could move on. Should she visit her? She had no idea whether Aunt Mabel would welcome visitors, and it would be rather a long trek to find out if she didn't. She thought that maybe she should send her a note, offering to stop by and help out if she could receive guests. Kitty had learned enough about influenza, with so many children home from school because of it, to know that it was best if she didn't go near someone sick with it unless it was entirely necessary.

What to do with a free afternoon? She knew she didn't have enough time to go visit Aunt Mabel and get home for dinner, but she did have some time before she was expected at home, and if she didn't make use of it she would be expected to help out with housework. She thought about visiting the public library down the street, but she felt restless after sitting all afternoon and, now that she had her freedom of the city back, she didn't want to waste it. She would have liked to drop by the Burnham Company in the Rookery Building to say hello to Henry, but didn't think that would be considered proper. As she was on State Street already, she thought she could take a stroll northward and happen by the grocery store Henry's grandfather owned just north of the river. She wouldn't have to stop in if she didn't want to, but ever since the Thomas's party on Christmas Eve, she thought that some day she might just visit Henry's Aunt Louisa.

Crossing the State Street Bridge, where you were exposed to the full force of the winter winds blowing up the river, was like being gnawed by monsters with glass-sharp teeth. Kitty could hardly see ahead of her because the frigid air filled her eyes with tears. But once she'd made up her mind to walk north, she didn't want to back down. She reached Thomas Groceries, at the corner of Illinois Street, out of breath and frozen to the core, despite her cloak, two scarves, leather gloves, and boots. She stood outside the door a moment to summon the courage to enter. Would it look as if she were running after Henry? Did she care? Finally, the biting cold drove her through the door.

The store had a clean, sawdust smell that made Kitty think of Brian at first. The dozens of products were arranged so neatly, it looked like a picture of a grocery, rather than the real thing. The produce was arranged in its boxes as if it had been set up to be painted as a still life—the shiniest red apples cheek by jowl, bright green celery, potatoes and turnips lined up in rows and looking freshly scrubbed. Very different from the greengrocer where she usually shopped, where everything was jumbled from people picking them over all day. She recognized Aunt Louisa—Miss Thomas, she should call her—behind the counter, talking to a tall, uniformed man. She wore a large white apron that looked as if it had been wrapped twice around her slim frame and her hair was pinned up in a very business-like manner that went well with her plain, navy blue dress. The man wasn't a policeman, but probably someone's servant in dark gray livery. She gave him her full attention and didn't seem to notice Kitty entering. Only when she had ushered him to the door did she acknowledge Kitty's presence.

"It's the kindergartner, Miss Coakley," she said, smiling graciously as if Kitty had stepped into her home. "And what can we do for you today?"

"Oh, I was in your neighborhood, and I thought I would stop by and see how you were doing." Kitty tried to give the impression that she had just been out for a stroll and had come in to say hello. Which, except for the stroll part, was true. No one in their right mind would take a stroll on a frigid day like that.

"How nice. Are you coming from your classes?" Miss Thomas was only half-listening as she carefully penned something in a ledger she had pulled from behind the counter.

"Why yes, we are let out early on Wednesdays. We only have one instructor after lunch." Kitty pretended to inspect a box of potatoes.

"That's nice. I suppose you know Henry's out of town. He's traveling . . ." She broke off as the bell over the door jingled, and a well-dressed woman swathed in a luxurious mink coat swept in. "Mrs. Davis, you're early today. I haven't quite finished your order."

As Louisa scurried to the back of the shop, Kitty said loudly, "Goodbye, Miss Thomas, I really must be going." She smiled at the imperious customer and let herself out. She didn't want to interfere with Miss Thomas's livelihood, and she had heard the approach of a streetcar, so she thought it would be a good time to leave. She also had received the information she needed, that Henry was out of town, although she would have liked to learn where he was and when he was expected home.

Kitty made it to the streetcar stop just in time to hop on, and headed back south to where she could transfer to a western car to take her home. It was as warm as that woman's fine fur coat inside the car and she could feel her fingers and toes thawing out. She wondered if Henry had received the postal card she had sent, telling him she was looking forward to seeing him again. And she especially wondered when she would see him.

❧

No one was home when Kitty returned and she was surprised not to smell dinner being prepared. When she threw down her books on the table before she reached for her apron, she noticed an envelope propped up against the salt cellar at her place. The envelope was unfamiliar, but she recognized Henry's handwriting. Just as she grabbed it, the door flew open and in rushed Margaret on a cold gust of air, with only a raggedy shawl thrown over her shoulders to keep herself warm.

"It's Mama," she said, breathing hard. "When I came by this morning to drop off the children, I found her lying on the floor. She was breathing, but not able to get up or talk. I got a message to Da—thank the Lord for Uncle Patrick, he was able to find him—and by the time he got here the doctor was here as well. They took her to Mercy Hospital. Mama, who's never been in a hospital in her whole life. He said it might be influenza, or something else."

Margaret herself looked sick, with dark circles underneath her eyes, her hair a rat's nest, her dress showing the stains of today's breakfast, and maybe yesterday's as well. And Mama. She had seemed exhausted since they had come home from New Orleans, but Kitty had thought it just the strain of traveling. She looked into the kitchen and noticed the trail of flour on the floor, and a bowl covered with a dish cloth. She must have been making bread when she fell. Kitty wondered if she should finish the bread or go to the hospital. She asked her sister what they should do.

Margaret had caught her breath and was busy replacing the pins in her hair. "There's nothing to do until Da comes home. I told him I'd catch you and bring you to my house. So he could come there to tell us both what was happening and have dinner himself. It'll be better that way."

Was it that Margaret didn't think Kitty was capable of preparing dinner for their father or did she just want Kitty to come and look after her children? Kitty felt a flash of anger, but then told herself she should be more charitable to her sister. Margaret had her hands full with the two children, and she should be grateful that she handled all this with Mama while Kitty was at school. She looked at the letter in her hand and quickly shoved it into her pocket. A letter from Henry was not something she wanted to share with Margaret.

Margaret's house was its usual jumble of clothes and toys and dust and disarray. Kitty cleared a place on the sofa to sit and immediately Sean jumped into her lap, demanding a story. Margaret said, "If you're just going to sit there you might as well hold the baby," and placed baby Helena in her arms. Sean babbled on about Gamma taking a nap on the floor, but Kitty was able to divert him with her tale of pirates off the coast of Louisiana. Margaret's husband returned home and the whole story about Mama had to be told again, and then the children needed to be fed and put to bed. Later, as the three adults finally sat down for a quiet supper, the door opened slowly and Da trudged in.

One look at his face and Kitty thought the worst, but that was fortunately not the case. Mama was to be kept in the hospital overnight. The doctor thought it was most likely the influenza, but she did seem weak and he just wanted to take precautions. Da himself looked as if he were ill, but Kitty thought it might just be the strain and exhaustion. He turned to her and, as if trying to cheer himself up, said, "Guess that shows you what taking a vacation can do."

"Oh, Da, I'm sure she'll be fine," Kitty said, putting her hand on his arm. "I heard that Aunt Mabel has influenza as well, there must be quite a lot of it around these days."

"That's right, Patrick did say Mabel was down with it too," Da said wearily. "Now, let's eat up this fine meal that Margaret has prepared. We must keep up our strength for the days ahead."

Kevin said grace, adding a brief prayer for Mama at the end, and they all made the sign of the cross and turned their attention to the meat and potatoes on their plates. Kitty thought it felt strange to eat without Mama at the table, and tears came into her eyes. And then she remembered the letter in her pocket and felt better, knowing that she had something to look forward to.

Kitty and her father didn't get home until fairly late, as she stayed to help Margaret clean up the kitchen while her father and Kevin sat at the table talking over cups of tea. At home, she confronted her schoolbooks spread over the parlor table, and realized that she had at least an hour of reading to do before going to bed. She then looked in the kitchen and saw the mess that had to be cleaned up. She decided to save the letter until she had done her homework and cleaned the kitchen and could retreat alone to her bedroom.

When the house was quiet and the kitchen clean, she sat on the edge of her bed and dug into her pocket for Henry's letter. Nothing was there except a handkerchief with a fine scrim of dirt on it from wiping Sean's dirty little face. She leapt up from the bed and ran into the hallway where she had hung her cloak. No letter in either pocket. She traced her steps to the parlor table, and then to the kitchen. She tossed her books around, thinking that maybe she had stuffed the letter into one of them. She emptied out her book bag and shook it over the table. It wasn't there. Maybe it had fallen out of her pocket at Margaret's. She ran to the hall and grabbed her cloak, thinking she could run back to Margaret's and see if somehow she had left it there. As she started to unlock the door her father had locked, she realized how late it was and knew that no one would still be awake at Margaret's. She looked out the small window in the door at the path to the street. Complete darkness—she couldn't see a thing on the path or the street at all. She stood there panting, her heart beating as hard as if she had run down the street to Margaret's. A letter from Henry! And she had lost it. She looked down at the pile of muddy shoes in the hallway and saw her mother's beat-up leather house slippers, so threadbare that she couldn't imagine how they could stay on her feet. How selfish can I be, she chastised herself. Here Mama's suffering all alone in the hospital, and I'm worrying myself about a little letter, that I'm sure I'll be picking up in the morning from Margaret's. I must keep my mind on what's important in this life. And she turned on her heel, not even realizing that she held one of her mother's scruffy house slippers to her chest, and returned to her bedroom.

As she knelt beside her bed to say her prayers, Kitty implored the Lord Jesus to let her mother get better soon. And, in addition to her own family, she prayed for Henry and his family, and for Brian and Mr. Kelleher. "And please, dear Lord," she whispered, "please let Margaret have my letter. And, please, please, please, make certain she hasn't opened it and read it."

THIRTY-ONE

Henry hung out the window of the carriage, his eyes on the doorway of the school and the young women passing through it. He spied Kitty leaving the building by herself and waved frantically. But she was walking without her usual animation, her eyes looking down at the gray pavement, her book bag clutched tightly to her chest. Her head popped up when she heard her name being called. Kitty ran over to the curb and gazed up at Henry in the driver's seat as if he had just appeared out of nowhere.

"So, didn't you get my letter?" Henry asked anxiously. "I said I would pick you up today. It looks as if you are heading for the streetcar. Wouldn't you rather that I drive you home?" He reached out his hand to help her into the carriage, swiftly removing his hat from the seat before she could crush it. He balanced the gray fedora on a knob in the front of the carriage.

Kitty sat down and stared at him as if she couldn't believe what she was seeing. "Your hair's gotten longer," she blurted out, and reached out as if to touch it, but then held back. She gulped, composed herself, and then said, "How lovely to see you. It's been since Christmas, you know. And your letter, Henry, I've lost it, I don't know how. Before I even opened it."

Tears suddenly filled her eyes, and Henry bent over and patted her gloved hand. The letter, her mother's illness and hospitalization all poured out from her in one powerful stream like river water, and he told her to just take a breath, slow down, and tell him what had happened. This seemed to quiet Kitty and she slowed down and told him about the events of the night before. Henry sat back and watched Kitty make her confused and remorseful explanation about losing his letter. Although he would have liked to take her in his arms and kiss her, he patted her shoulder gently. Then, she brightened up, wiping her tears away, and told him that she had missed him and had thought about him and worn his bracelet while she was away.

"So, did anyone comment on the bracelet?" he asked, a small smile playing over his lips.

Kitty looked down at her lap. "Not exactly," she confessed. "You see . . . ." and she paused for a moment. "The people we were staying with were very old friends of the family, and they don't have very nice things themselves, so I didn't want to make them jealous or envious. But I am wearing it now, see?" And she pulled back the sleeve of her white shirtwaist blouse to show Henry her ivory wrist and the intricate chain of delicate silver flowers that graced it. "I must be careful at school because I don't want it to catch on anything and break."

Henry caught Kitty's hand in his and brought it to his lips and kissed it. "But if you haven't read my letter, you don't know about my news," he said, beaming. "My parents wanted me to accompany them on their trip to Germany for a few months, but I didn't want to leave the firm for that long. And when I spoke to my boss about possibly taking a leave for that amount of time, he said I was much too valuable, that they wanted me to spend some time on the actual building site, in Pittsburgh. He said they thought I showed some ability in directing the work of others, and that they were considering promoting me." Henry smiled broadly and his chest expanded.

Much to his surprise, Kitty threw her arms around him and kissed him on the cheek. "Henry, Henry, that's so wonderful. It's just what you've always hoped for."

"So, Miss Coakley, canoodling right in front of school? Perhaps you should consider someplace more private to express your emotions." Mrs. Campbell's tone belied her words, her round face was pink and she looked as if she could hardly keep from laughing.

"Mrs. Campbell, I didn't see you coming out of the building," Kitty said, her hand flying up to cover her mouth.

"Obviously," Mrs. Campbell said dryly. "And who is this gentleman? At least one hopes he is a gentleman?"

Henry jumped lightly from the carriage and clasped her hand in greeting. "You must be Mrs. Campbell, the famous directress of the kindergartners' program at the Chicago Kindergarten College. Katherine's told me so much about you, I feel as though I know you already," he said. "I'm Henry Thomas, an old friend of Katherine's."

"So I see," said Mrs. Campbell, with a bemused smile.

Kitty, embarrassed, introduced Henry further as a former classmate from Lake View High School. "And this is the first I've seen him since Christmas."

"It's a pleasure to meet you, Mr. Thomas," said Mrs. Campbell. "Carry on, but please, not in front of the school."

Kitty laughed nervously as they watched her continue on her way along Rush Street. "I suppose I should have been more discreet, acting like that right out in front of my school," she said.

"Didn't bother me," Henry said, climbing back into the carriage. "In fact, I quite enjoyed it. In my letter, I said that I hoped you would join me tonight for dinner."

"That would be lovely," Kitty said. "Except that I must stop at home and see how Mama is doing. She just got home from the hospital, you see, and depending on how she's feeling, I might have to stay with her." A worried look crossed Kitty's face like a dark cloud scudding across the sky.

"Understandable," Henry said, clucking to the horses as he took the reins. "We can dine together another night, if need be. Although, with my parents abroad, Cook only works two days a week. We'll have to plan around her schedule as well as our own, I suppose."

"You're staying at home without your parents?" Kitty asked.

"Yes, staying at home alone," Henry said, chuckling as he looked ahead, directing the horses through the afternoon's heavy traffic. "They took some persuading, let me tell you, to allow their only son to remain on his own. I had to convince them that I was a responsible adult whom they could trust. As it is, my Uncle Herman comes in from

Palatine to stay with me on weekends. All that free time, who knows what mischief I might get myself into."

On the ride to Kitty's home, Henry tried to keep her mind away from her worries by asking about what had happened in the schoolroom that day.

"It's St. Valentine's Day," she said, looking down shyly into her lap, her flashing dimple telling him that she had been thinking of him. "We always celebrate holidays in kindergarten, it helps to assimilate the children into our culture, you know."

Henry nodded and smiled to himself, encouraging her to go on.

"So we talked to the children about love and who they love—their parents, their families, each other—and how they show that love. Well, of course this led to many stories from the children about love, and Henry, it was so difficult to keep a straight face." Kitty sat back in the carriage laughing at the memory of it.

"Do tell, Kitty. I'm all ears," Henry said, relieved that Kitty wasn't dwelling on the sad facts of her mother's illness.

"Oh, there was this one little boy, he said that he showed his mother he loved her by eating the food she had prepared for him. And then this other little dear, dressed practically in rags, told me she showed she loved her mother by not eating the food and leaving it instead for her mother to eat, because she was always hungry. I thought I would cry. But then Maria piped up. She said that she showed her love by not saying bad words at the supper table. I said, 'That's a good thing, Maria.' But that only encouraged Maria to share with the class some of the bad words she wasn't to say at dinner. It took everything I had to quiet them down after that."

Henry laughed at Kitty's story, and asked "So what did you do to settle them down—or did you?"

"I put my sternest look on my face and quickly changed the subject— I've found that distracting them helps. That's when I brought St. Valentine's Day into the discussion, explaining that it is a special day when you show the people you love that you love them by giving them valentines, in memory of St. Valentine." Her face grew pink.

"St. Valentine? So you celebrate Valentine's Day as a saint's day?"

"Oh, yes," Kitty said seriously, "St. Valentine was a Christian martyr who was put in prison for helping others. He had always loved children, and when he was in prison, the children would send him notes and flowers by throwing them through the jail windows. The children loved that part."

Henry looked over at Kitty and smiled. He liked thinking of her surrounded by children, she would make such a wonderful mother. "Go on," he said to her, flapping the reins to make the horses go faster. He had been letting them walk at their own slow pace while he was listening to Kitty's stories.

"Well, on the day Valentine was executed, he sent a note to one of the children signed 'From your Valentine.' That's how the sending of valentines was started. And the color pink is associated with valentines because when St. Valentine was killed and buried, a pink almond tree near his grave burst into bloom." She sat back in the carriage, smiling at the image.

"Is that really what happened?" Henry asked. "I've never heard that story before."

"It is the true story," Kitty said firmly. "It's the one I was told when I was a child."

"How did the children like that?"

"They found the story interesting, but several of the boys wanted to know how he was executed, did they use a knife or a gun, and was there a lot of blood? And there also was some curiosity about the prison," Kitty said primly, then collapsed into peals of laughter, which Henry succumbed to as well.

Still laughing, they approached the Coakley cottage, where they could see Mr. Coakley standing out on the front porch without a coat on, smoking and talking to one of Kitty's brothers. Their laughter stopped abruptly, Henry because he thought he recognized the brother as John, the one who had threatened him when he had stopped in for a visit before Christmas. When Henry pulled the carriage up outside the house, Kitty jumped out, without saying another word, and ran to her father. "Is everything all right?" she asked worriedly. "Is Mama all right?"

"There you are, my girl, I was wondering what was taking you so long, getting home," her father said, carefully tamping out his cigarette on the porch railing. "Herself is not doing so well today," he said, his eyes squinting as if he were looking into the sunset. "But she's home now. And I'm sure that with you here, she'll be as right as rain."

Kitty ran back to the carriage. "My mother's not so well," she said, nearly out of breath when she reached Henry. "I'd better stay home with her tonight. Perhaps we can see one another soon, maybe later this week?"

"Don't worry about it at all," Henry said. "I shall drop you a note offering some alternatives. I hope everything goes well with your mother." He bent down as if to kiss Kitty, but, aware of John still glaring from the porch, he shook her hand instead, gently stroking it with his thumb as he let go. Kitty didn't linger, but pulled up her skirts to run back to the cottage. Henry drove off, feeling disappointed that his Valentine's Day dinner was not meant to be.

On the long ride back home, Henry thought about parents and how much they controlled their children's lives. It was probably worse for women, he thought, and for a moment he considered Eleanor lucky not to have to deal with those restrictions anymore. But did that mean his obligation to his parents was greater with Eleanor gone? No, it didn't work that way for a man, a man was supposed to be independent, and to find a job and find a wife and settle down. A woman didn't have as many choices. He flicked the reins on the horses' backs and turned down Randolph Street toward the lake. He thought about Kitty and her animation in telling the stories about the little children she taught. So few women he had met took on challenges like teaching the poor. Oh, they might subscribe to charities or visit settlement houses, or sit on boards of charitable institutions. But so few actually interacted with the poor, as if they might get their hands dirty or pick up some disease from them. But with Kitty, he always felt that she would be in the battle, fighting to make things right. She was unafraid. He admired her for that. And he also liked the fact that she listened to him talk about his dreams, and believed that he could accomplish them. That faith gave him strength.

THIRTY-TWO

As Kitty entered the house, her father called out, "Perhaps you could have a look in the kitchen, dear, and do something about supper. Me and John are somewhat useless there, you know."

"Oh, you men," Kitty said. She stamped her foot and turned on her heel to go into the kitchen. She pulled her apron off the hook and pulled it over the head. "Stupid hair," she said, and twisted her frothy halo into a knot on the back of her head. If they're going to treat me like a kitchen scrub, well then I'll just go and look like one, she thought, jabbing hair pins in wildly.

Her father poked his head into the kitchen, "I brought your mother upstairs, she's still feeling under the weather, you know, and I told her you'd be bringing her up some soup in a little while. I wonder if you can do that for her, my dear."

Kitty smiled and nodded her head as she poured out the potato water into the pail of slops. She felt a little guilty that she had thought so little about her mother all day. It was easy to ignore her family when her mind was fixed on other things. Things like Henry. But he was no excuse for not taking care of her mother, poor dear. "I'll bring it up right away, Da. There's some lovely warm broth right here. And I'll stay with her until she takes some, it'll do her good and build her strength. Supper won't be ready for another half an hour anyway."

"You're a good girl, Kitty. You've been very good to your mother while she's been ill."

Da's being too kind, saying I've been good to Mama, she thought, as she stepped carefully up the stairs, holding a bowl of the beef broth that had been warming on the stove. I hardly pay any attention to her anymore, what with my schooling and the cooking and the laundry and all I do around the house. I wish I could just spend my time talking to her and praying with her and making sure she's comfortable every minute of the day.

She stepped quietly into her mother's room, where only a sputtering candle shed any light. The curtains had been drawn, though there would not be much sunlight on a winter afternoon. Her mother barely made a lump in the bed, covered as she was by the white quilt and the woolen blanket she used as a shawl downstairs. Her eyes were closed, and Kitty was about to turn away and bring the soup back downstairs when her mother spoke softly.

"Kitty?" she said. "Is that you?"

"Yes, Mama. It's your Kitty."

"You're a good girl, Kitty. You work hard."

"Thank you, Mama. And I'm happy to help."

"Kitty, you should be having a family of your own soon. Don't wait until you're too old, like those brothers of yours. Look at your sister Margaret. See how happy she is?"

Kitty thought about how her sister Margaret did nothing but complain, but bit her tongue. "Yes, Mama."

"But Kitty, that man, that man you went to school with?"

"Henry Thomas?"

"That one . . . he's not Catholic, is he?"

"No, I don't think he is. I believe he's some sort of Protestant."

"Kitty, promise me, you won't be going around with no Protestant. They're the ones who let the Irish starve."

Kitty stared at her mother's fragile white face. She already looked like a corpse, lying in a coffin at her wake. She felt tears coming into her eyes. She couldn't imagine what it would be to have her mother pass away, to rest with God in heaven. Nor could she imagine what it would be like not to have her dream of being a grand lady married to a fine gentleman. The only Catholic men she knew were laborers like Brian, or her brothers, who got their hands and clothes dirty every day—whose idea of a night out was hanging around a saloon with their friends, not attending the symphony or even an opera. She couldn't imagine a Catholic who dressed as finely as Henry, or who treated her as nicely, or dreamed such ambitious dreams. She couldn't actually imagine her future without Henry any more than she could imagine a future without her mother.

"Mama?" Kitty said. She wanted to let her mother know that it wasn't Henry Thomas's kind of Protestants that let the people of Ireland starve. Most likely, his family came to America because of religious persecution themselves, if she remembered her history correctly. But her mother had fallen off to sleep, her gentle breathing hardly moving the blankets that covered her chest. Kitty would have liked to stretch out beside her, to hibernate with her, and not face the supper that had to be served, the dishes that had to be washed, the life that had to be decided upon and lived. She knew she didn't want to take on a life like her mother's, she was serious about that. But she felt engulfed by a wave of the deep love she felt for her mother.

By Friday, her mother was able to come downstairs and eat with the family. Kitty sent a note to Henry saying she would be free to join him for dinner on Saturday. His note, received the next day, looked as though it had been dashed off in a hurry, but said he would pick her up at seven o'clock on Saturday evening. They would eat out, he wrote, because Cook didn't come in on Saturdays when his parents were away.

Kitty anguished over whether to tell her parents, particularly her mother, that she was going out to dinner with Henry. After all, her mother did ask that she not see him. But she had never said she wouldn't, she decided, and sent a note back to Henry to please pick her up in front of St. Patrick's church. That way, she could say she was going out with a friend from St. Patrick's and her mother need never know.

It was cold and dark, standing out in front of the church and Kitty was afraid she might run into someone she knew, or worse yet, someone her parents knew, and she would have to explain why she was standing there. Her fear was realized when she saw Father Egan come walking around the corner of the church, whistling *The Wearing of the Green*. She couldn't help but laugh, he looked so comical with his mouth pursed up and his hand outstretched, conducting an imaginary band. He stopped suddenly, surprised to see her and a bit embarrassed to be caught amusing himself in such an undignified way.

"And what are you doing, my dear girl, out alone on a winter's night? I hope not you're waiting for the likes of me. I would have hurried through my dinner had I known, rather than lingering over a second piece of Mrs. Harris's wonderful apple pie." His round Irish face was filled with affection for Kitty, whom he had known since he baptized her, nearly twenty-three years before. "And how's your mother doing, she that has been so unwell?"

"Oh Father, no, it's not you I've been waiting for," Kitty said, nervously looking down the street to see if Henry were about to pull up in the carriage. "A friend is about to collect me here, we are going out to have dinner. Mama is doing well, much better than she had been, thank the Lord. I just didn't want to bother her by leaving in the middle of her supper. My father and Mickey are home with her tonight, they'll be tending to her."

"You've taken on a lot this year, now, haven't you?" Father Egan said kindly. "What with your schooling and your chores and your mother's illness. I should think it's a good thing you're able to go out and have some fun with a friend tonight. Tell me, is it anyone I know?" He fairly twinkled as he said this, knowing he'd get a tidbit that would entice the cronies he'd be seeing after the eight o'clock Mass the next morning. For a priest, he had a reputation for being a gossip.

Kitty was aware of his reputation, and had always hesitated before sharing any information with him that she didn't want to get back to her parents eventually. "Just a friend from school," she said, not bothering to specify which school. "We're going out to have some dinner."

"Isn't that nice, my dear," Father Egan said. "If you want to come in from the cold, you're welcome to join me in the rectory until your friend arrives." He smiled and began walking toward the yellow brick rectory at the side of the church.

"No thank you, Father," Kitty said, praying that he'd be out of sight when Henry pulled up in the carriage. Her prayers were answered when she heard the heavy wooden rectory door slam shut just before she heard the clip clop of the horses' hooves. She wouldn't put it past the good Father Egan to stand at the window and watch as she got into the carriage, so she jumped in as swiftly as she could. She laughed nervously as Henry kissed her with lips as cold as frozen meat, and then nestled herself into the warm woolen blanket he provided.

"I could see you speaking to someone as I turned the corner onto Desplaines," Henry said. "Was that your brother safeguarding you until I arrived?"

"No, it was just Father Egan, taking the air after his dinner," Kitty said, arranging the blanket so it fully covered her legs. "He was curious about who was going to pick me up, but I didn't tell him. He's the biggest gossip in the parish, he is."

"Are you afraid he might say something about your coming out with me tonight?" Henry asked, turning to search Kitty's face for the answer, as if he were concerned about what she might say. "You're not ashamed of me, are you? Meeting me on a street corner like this? I'd be happy to pick you up at home, you know, and let your parents know just who you are going out with. I hope you don't feel you have to keep it secret. Or, far worse, that you're ashamed of me for some reason."

"No, no, that's not it at all," Kitty said. How could she explain this? She certainly didn't want to hurt Henry's feelings, and she did want to tell him the truth, but she wasn't sure that she could achieve both. "It's just my mother," she said lamely. "She's still sick and I don't want to upset her in any way."

"The sight of me would upset your mother?" Henry asked, focusing his attention straight ahead at the backs of the horses rather than turning to look at Kitty. "Now, why would that be? Is there something about me that might upset your mother? What is it, pray tell?" he asked stiffly.

What had she started? Kitty knew she didn't want to bring up the fact that Henry's religion was not acceptable to her mother—it was a subject she and Henry had never spoken about, not even at Christmas, when he had dropped her off on this same corner, just before choir rehearsal for Midnight Mass. "Mama gets upset when people she doesn't know come to the house," she said. "She's so careful about her cleaning, that she always wants the house to be immaculate, so guests will think well of her. I didn't want her to worry about the housekeeping when she wasn't feeling so well." Even though what she said was true, Kitty felt guilty not mentioning her fear that Henry's religion would upset her mother. Why wasn't she able to talk about religion with Henry, she wondered. She supposed it was because such a discussion might suggest a closer relationship between them then they had as yet. She didn't want anything about her to turn Henry away from that relationship, she decided, and she just wasn't sure enough about herself to bring up any subject that might challenge it.

Henry seemed satisfied with her answer and began to describe the dining room at the club where they had a dinner reservation. He had lunched there with a fellow architect from Burnham and Company and thought so highly of it that he had applied for membership. Because his own father had, unbeknownst to him, been a member there himself for many years, he was admitted almost immediately. On Saturday nights the dining room was open to ladies, as long as they were accompanied by a member. "So what do you think, would you like to eat there?" he asked Kitty, who hadn't said anything since she stepped into the carriage.

"Oh, I'm sorry, Henry, I wasn't listening at all. I was so distracted thinking about my mother."

"Pardon me for not asking about her immediately. And just going on and on about dinner. How is she doing? She must be getting better if you're able to leave for the evening."

"Yes, she did seem a bit better today. But she . . . she said she didn't want me to see you anymore." There, it was out. Kitty felt as though she had just thrown a giant rock on the seat between her and Henry, a rock that she had been carrying between her own shoulders for nearly a week. She felt relieved not to carry it alone, but worried that the metaphorical rock would separate her from Henry.

"She said you weren't to see me anymore." Henry said, as he steered the horses over to the side of the street and pulled up on their reins to stop them.

The carriage sat in the darkness away from the gas street lamp, shadowed by the bare limbs of a giant elm tree, as dark and quiet as a country lane in a small village. Although a cold rain dripped off the near-bare branches, the smell that suggested spring would soon be coming filled the air. Kitty sat back in the darkness of the carriage and breathed deeply before Henry spoke.

"She said you weren't to see me anymore?" he repeated in a dull voice. "So did you come out with me tonight to tell me that you weren't going to see me again?" He stared straight ahead in the darkness, not turning his head to look at Kitty.

"She asked me not to see you, yes," Kitty said. "But I didn't say I wouldn't. I didn't say I would see you, either. I just sort of ignored her request. What else could I do?" She pulled a thin branch off the tree and began twisting it in her gloved hands.

Henry's shoulders relaxed, and he turned to Kitty. "You could have told her that you were going to see me again. You could have told her you were going to marry me and build your own family with me. You could have told her that."

Kitty dropped the twig and stared at Henry with her mouth wide open. What was he saying? "Tell my mother I was going to marry you? Why would I do that?"

Henry took her hand and spoke in a pleading tone, "Well, won't you, Kitty? Won't you marry me?"

All Kitty could think was how, not even a month ago, Brian had asked her the same question. Marry Henry? She wanted more than anything to say that she would happily marry him, but she thought of her mother's face as she lay in her bed, looking as if she were about to leave this world any second. How could she fly in the face of her mother's request, her near-deathbed wish, just to make Henry happy? Yet how could she not tell Henry she would marry him? He was the man she wanted, and he promised her the life she desired. How could she possibly tell him no? "Oh, my dearest dear," she said, tears coming to her eyes. "Of course I want to marry you. But I can't tell my mother that, just after she asked me not even to see you. Do you think we could wait, just a little while, so she has a chance to get used to the idea of you? I'm sure once she gets to know you as I do, she'll appreciate you as much as I do."

From the frown on Henry's face it was clear that this wasn't the answer he sought. He continued to hold her hand, but his face looked miserable. Kitty raised her other hand to Henry's face and stroked his cheek, the way she might caress a child who had just fallen and was about to burst into tears. "It will be all right, Henry. We will be all right. It's just that it's going to take some time." And she leaned over and kissed him gently on the lips.

Henry sat like a stone statue, not saying anything for what, to Kitty, seemed to be an hour. Finally he spoke, sounding like a child trying to justify his behavior. "We don't need their permission, you know. We are adults. We could just run off to Wisconsin or somewhere and get married in a day or two. People do it all the time."

"Henry, some people do it all the time, but we're not that kind of people. We love our families and they love us. You know we would want them to continue to be a part of our lives, how could we turn away from them at this time? I'd want them to share in our joy and happiness."

Henry's face brightened up when Kitty mentioned joy. "So, you do want to marry me?"

"Yes, Henry, I do want to marry you. But we just can't do it immediately. We need to think about people other than ourselves as well."

"Yes, but there comes a time in one's life when one has to break away from one's family and start making decisions for one's self," Henry said as if he were about to deliver a sermon. "To put away the things of the child, as scripture says."

Kitty smiled, thinking about the children in her classroom putting away their blocks and sticks before lining up to leave for the day. "Yes, but we can't put it all behind us. Not our family, our religion, our pasts. Like the poor in the scriptures, they are always with us."

"What if your parents refuse to allow you to marry me?" Henry asked angrily. "What then?"

"I'm not going to let that happen," Kitty said calmly, looking into his eyes. "We can make this work out, Henry, we have to. I don't know how, but I know that I'll do everything I can to make this work out for us. It just might take some time."

"How much time?" he asked testily. "Years and years? We'll be old and gray before your parents and mine will approve of our marriage."

"Don't tell me your parents are concerned about your marrying me," Kitty said. "You never told me anything about that." It was her turn to get angry.

"Don't you worry about that," Henry said. "I'm sure as they get to know you, they'll find that you will be a worthy wife for their only son." He picked up the reins and they drove off in silence, the hum of city traffic the only accompaniment to their thoughts.

At the club, where Henry was greeted by name, they chatted politely as if nothing had been said about their future together. Kitty rubbed the thick damask tablecloth between her fingers, feeling its heavy weight, the weight of wealth and luxury. The elegant French bone china, with delicate flower pictures painted on it in rose and green, the plates and cups bordered with gold, and the heavy silver cutlery that felt like tools in her hands. There were somber portraits on the paneled walls of men in dark suits with walrus mustaches and alarming muttonchop whiskers. A male bastion, to be sure, that made Kitty feel like a china doll, a precious toy to be brought out only when company came.

Henry launched into a technical description of the building he was working on in Pittsburgh and the progress being made toward its completion. It wasn't until they were served dessert—a chocolate cake with early hothouse strawberries drenched in cream nestled between its layers—that Henry reached for Kitty's hand and said, "We hardly look like a couple who has just gotten engaged. I have a ring for you, if you truly want to go through with this." He pulled out a small square box from his vest pocket. "This is for you, my love."

Dropping Henry's hand, Kitty opened the box, her eyes growing large as she pulled out an intricately woven golden ring, its whorls dotted with three tiny diamonds. The gold looked soft and timeworn. She immediately placed it on the ring finger of her left hand and held it up to the light. "Henry, it's just beautiful."

"It was Oma's . . . my grandmother's," Henry said. "Vati gave it to me after she died, saying that he hoped that when it was time for me to marry I would find a woman as strong and as lovely as she was. I've known that was you for a long time, but it took me a while to summon the courage to ask you to be my wife. I love you, Kitty, I have for a long time now. I want us to be together forever."

Kitty sat with her hand outstretched, displaying the ring before her. It was a minute or two before she could speak. When she did, the tears ran down her cheeks. "Henry, I do want us to be together, I do, I do. And we will, I know that in my heart of hearts. You'll just have to be patient with me, I don't want to run away from our lives and our families to get married. I want our families to be part of our lives. Especially wearing your grandmother's ring—I want us all to grow together, not grow apart."

Henry patted Kitty's hand. "It's not going to be easy, you know. I can sense that I'm hardly your brothers' cup of tea. And I'm not too sure about that policeman uncle of yours, either. Your mother may be easy to win over, compared to them," he laughed.

Kitty leaned back in her chair, thinking. What would her brothers say? She knew they would prefer her to marry Brian, as would her mother, even if she had to move down to New Orleans to do it. Her father might be easier to persuade, and Uncle Pat and Aunt Mabel. Perhaps she should speak to Aunt Mabel first, she was always one to encourage her to follow her own path. Aunt Mabel hadn't liked Henry when she first met him, though, and she wondered if Aunt Mabel would be able to change her opinion. It seemed there were uphill battles ahead of her, but she knew you could only achieve important victories if you worked for them. At least that's what they told the children in kindergarten. Kindergarten! She couldn't be employed to teach once she was married. She looked over at Henry's face as he ate his chocolate cake and a warmth filled her heart. Henry would be an important victory, she decided. He, and the future he could provide her, would be well worth the work she would have to do. He wouldn't give up easily either, so she knew that she could have a year or two of teaching before she settled down to be his wife and mother to the children they would have.

Henry looked across the table at her, a tiny bit of chocolate frosting caught in his mustache making him look like a mischievous child. "So you're willing to go ahead with this?" he asked.

Kitty leaned over and gently wiped away the chocolate. "Yes, Henry. I will. How could I possibly do anything else but?"

THIRTY-THREE

T he house was quiet when Henry dropped her off after dinner. She saw her father's coat in the hallway and gathered he was upstairs, asleep with her mother. John's boots weren't to be seen, so he must have gone out with his friends. Before she went to sleep, Kitty removed Oma's ring from her hand, ran a white silk ribbon through it and tied it around her neck. It would be best not to let others see it just yet, she wasn't ready for the questions it would raise. She fell asleep thinking of Henry and the big buildings he would build, for her and for all the people of Chicago.

The next morning, she could hear her father tip-toeing around the kitchen preparing tea for her mother, and she got up and joined him.

"Up so early, my lovely?" he said, pouring hot water into the teapot. "I hope I didn't wake you?"

"That's all right, I woke myself up earlier. Will you be going to Father Egan's eight o'clock Mass?"

"Yes, I'll be going, but we'll let your mother rest in bed this morning. I think she's doing much better."

"I'll be ready then to go with you," Kitty said, retreating into her room. She touched the small ring she wore around her neck, beneath her nightdress and thought, it's true, it wasn't a dream. I'm going to marry Henry.

The morning was cloudy, but warmer than it had been, the air smelling fresh washed from the rain the night before. Kitty breathed in deeply and thought about the new beginning of spring and how she was facing a new beginning in her own life as she and her father walked arm in arm, skirting the puddles that collected in the broken pavement on the familiar street. Father Egan stood at the church door, at the top of the steps, greeting parishioners as they entered the church. He waved a greeting to Kitty and her father, and then retreated inside to don his vestments for the Mass.

The church was quiet and attendance sparse this Sunday morning. "People must be sleeping off the night before," Michael Coakley whispered, looking around the cavernous semi-darkness of the church. They had gone to their usual seats, near the front on the Blessed Mother's side, and Kitty genuflected as she entered the pew, kneeling immediately to say a prayer for her mother's health and a longer prayer for Our Lady's intercession in convincing her parents—and Henry's— that they should marry. She supposed the Blessed Mother worked with Protestants as well, but she wasn't sure. She stood in the pew, proudly next to her tall father, as the procession walked up the aisle, the priest in his bright green vestments, the acolytes in their white robes that looked like nightdresses, carrying the cross and swinging the censer filled with smoking incense.

She repeated the familiar Latin responses automatically, and her thoughts drifted off to the time when she herself would be walking up the aisle, dressed in a cloud of white satin and lace, next to her father, who would give her away to the man who waited for her by the altar. She could imagine Henry at the end of the aisle, dressed so correctly in a gray cutaway, his tie perfectly straight between the lapels of the jacket, his hair smooth despite the top hat that rested on the front pew beside his parents. She could see his face as it had been at dinner the night before, faint lines of worry across his forehead, his eyes squinting a bit because he wouldn't wear his glasses in public, his mouth pursed beneath his mustache, until his eyes met hers and then breaking into that beaming smile that appeared only when he couldn't control his joy. She saw her sister walking slowly in front of her, in a red dress that fit correctly for a change, and was free of food stains and marks where the children had wiped their hands. Perhaps Sean could be the ring bearer, walking carefully so as not to tip the little pillow on which would be placed their wedding rings. She hoped this would take place in the near-enough future that there wouldn't be a question of baby

Helena being a bridesmaid herself. Where was her mother in the picture? Perhaps taking care of baby Helena, that's where she'd want to be. Her brothers as ushers, Daniel home for the wedding. A storybook wedding—probably they couldn't afford such a splash, but perhaps after she worked and saved for a year or two she could afford some of the trimmings.

As these images formed in her mind, Kitty stood and knelt and responded as an automaton, the familiar rhythms of the Mass a second nature to her. When Father Egan stepped up to the pulpit, she told herself that she should pay attention to what he said, but her mind wandered off to wedding cakes and bridal carriages, wondering if they could have the party afterward in the church hall. She heard the priest talking about Ash Wednesday and the coming of Lent and still her mind traveled to the celebrations of a wedding.

Father Egan stood once again at his place by the door after the Mass had ended, and Kitty and her father stopped and shook his hand. "So how is Helen doing, this morning?" he asked Mike Coakley. "Is herself feeling much better?"

"She's doing just fine, Father," he said heartily. "She'll be up and about before you know it. I expect her to be here, receiving the ashes come Wednesday."

"You're a good man, Mike Coakley," said the priest, patting him on the shoulder. "Tell her I'll be by later to give her the Eucharist. And you, little lady, you look none the worse for wear after your night out?"

Kitty smiled, she hoped mysteriously, and turned to descend the stairs before Father Egan began asking any questions. By the time she had her foot on the step below, Father Egan was heartily greeting another parishioner, and she was safe from further comment.

On the way home, as Kitty breathed in the clean fresh air of spring, her father went on about how he hoped her mother would soon be well and perhaps they could start looking for a new house, perhaps out in Austin where Margaret and Kevin were planning to move. A new house that wouldn't be as much work for her mother, and perhaps she could find a job teaching kindergarten out there, for that was where people were moving, not to the old neighborhoods like this. Sure, he was fond of Father Egan and St. Patrick's, but the parish wasn't what it used to be, people were moving out and the people moving in, now they just weren't the types of folks you wanted to know.

Her father hadn't used to talk like this, Kitty thought, he must have been listening to Margaret more, or worrying that it was this life that had made her mother sick. She hoped they would move to a smaller, newer house where there wouldn't be as much housework to do. That way, they wouldn't miss her as much when she left.

Her mother was sitting downstairs at the kitchen table, drinking tea, when Kitty and her father returned, and wanted to hear every detail about the Mass and who attended. Kitty busied herself making breakfast, feeling relieved that her father could fill in the details that she had missed when lost in her reverie. Her mother tired visibly as breakfast wore on, and Kitty said for her not to worry, but to go back to bed, she would clean up the kitchen and get the dinner started.

Once her father had helped her mother up the stairs to bed, and the kitchen things were put away, Kitty brought out her schoolbooks and set them on the table. She struggled for a while to follow the words on the pages, but she couldn't keep her mind away from the tiny weight of the ring that hung around her neck beneath her shirtwaist, and what Henry had said when it gave it to her. She jumped up from the table and went over to her father, sitting in his favorite chair, reading the newspaper.

"It's just too nice a day to stay inside," she said, pushing the newspaper away from his face. "I'm going to go up and visit Aunt Mabel, I've hardly seen her since she gotten over that awful flu. I'm sure she'll want to know how Mama is doing, too."

"Ah, it's a good girl you are, my Kitty. I'm sure Patrick will appreciate your keeping your aunt company for a while. He's hardly been able to leave the house himself, except to go to work. He'll be wanting some fresh air, I know that for sure."

Promising that she'd be back to fix supper, Kitty left the house, feeling released from servitude. She had always hated it when her brothers were away and she was alone with her parents—she wasn't used to being such a single focus of parental interest. It was good to be off and on her own. The day had warmed up and it seemed as if spring was trying to make an appearance. Kitty thought she could almost feel the roots reaching down in the ground and the buds swelling to burst, the tips of the tree branches ready to break out in leaves even on their muddy well-traveled street. It was still February and there was a lot of winter yet ahead, but it seemed that every year there would be a day like this, a promise of the spring to come. She could hardly keep herself from running and jumping as she walked down the street to the streetcar stop, but she knew the neighbors would whisper about her hoyden-like behavior if she acted that way. She tried to think prim, buttoned-up thoughts and slow her steps to a more maidenly pace, but inside she was dancing and turning cartwheels. Each struggling spear of green breaking through the hard packed earth seemed a reason for joy.

THIRTY-FOUR

K itty reached her aunt and uncle's townhouse still joyous, but knew that she had to control herself in their presence. They had met Henry and hadn't been wildly enthusiastic about him. It was true, he had brought her home late the night he picked her up at their house, but it hadn't been that late, and he had certainly done her no harm. Still, it was a good idea to appear more rational about him, that is, if she decided to speak to them about the engagement. She thought she might be better able to talk to her aunt than her uncle. Uncle Patrick was her father's brother and she had always thought that whatever she said to him went back directly to her father.

Aunt Mabel and Uncle Patrick, seated at the dining room table over coffee after their usual Sunday late morning breakfast, were pleased to see Kitty. Her aunt, dressed in a beautiful lace morning dress, still looked pale and worn, and her gestures were more languid than usual, but her eyes were lively and Kitty could tell that the appearance of a new face would give her energy. Her uncle thanked Kitty for her visit and, after asking her for news of her mother's health, asked her permission to leave the house for a bit. He hadn't been able to get away much in the past few weeks and he had things to do and people to see.

Aunt Mabel laughed and told him to be off with himself, she didn't need a chaperone to sit and talk with her niece. She put on a kettle to make tea for Kitty, who she knew didn't drink coffee, and announced that she was just what the doctor ordered, someone to talk to who wouldn't always be asking her if she felt well enough to be out of bed.

"Ah, Kitty, I haven't seen you for so long," she said, her thin face lighting up at the thought of a visit with her niece. "It must have been

Christmas-time, with you and your parents off to New Orleans the entire month of January. Tell me, how was the trip? Did you love New Orleans? Or tell me the real truth, now that it's just us girls. How was young Brian Kelleher?"

Kitty blushed and sipped her tea. "That was the strange part, Brian Kelleher. Here he hardly spoke to me the entire time I stayed in his house. And then, just before we were to come home to Chicago, he asked me to marry him. Have you ever heard anything like that at all?"

"He's a shy lad, he is, and he knows that you deserve someone better. Poor thing, I'm supposing you turned him down."

"Of course. Do you think I want to spend the rest of my life living in the Irish Channel in New Orleans, having babies? Not me. There's more to life than Brian Kelleher, I'll have you know that."

"I suspected that being a housewife wouldn't satisfy you, what with your kindergartner studies and all that. Being a teacher will be a much better life than you would have working at Marshall Field's, for instance."

"Yes, but look at all you have here," Kitty said, stretching her arm out and taking in all the beautiful fittings of the sunny room, the lace tablecloth and curtains, and the fine china, silver vases, and candlesticks in the mahogany china cabinet.

"Never believe that what you have is more important than who you are, my girl," Aunt Mabel said, looking around the room as if it was a cave, not an expensively equipped townhouse room. "My job has enabled me to live like this, yes, but more than anything money can buy, it's given me the confidence to live the way I choose. Not every woman considers herself free enough to do that."

"But you didn't have anyone telling you what to do, did you, Aunt Mabel?"

"That's what you think, Kitty. Everyone tells a woman what to do—her husband, her family, the Church, the people she meets doing her job. It takes a strong woman not to listen to that all," Mabel said, reaching over to pour herself some more coffee.

Kitty sighed. "That's where I am—where everyone's telling me what to do. At least, they will be once I tell them . . ." She traced a tiny circle in the sugar she had spilled on the highly polished table.

"What, pray tell, are you talking about?" her aunt asked. "Are you afraid that I'm going to tell you what to do?"

"All right. If you promise not to tell me what to do, I'll tell you what it is."

Aunt Mabel closed her mouth and mimed locking it and throwing the key over her shoulder.

Kitty laughed and said, "This is a secret now, I haven't told anyone else." Her aunt nodded, holding her breath and trying to keep a straight face. "Henry Thomas has asked me to marry him, and I told him I will. Maybe not right away, but soon." Kitty couldn't help but grin with pride at her announcement. It was quite an accomplishment, she felt, to become engaged to such a promising young man.

Aunt Mabel didn't seem to agree. She blew out her suppressed breath and said, "Henry Thomas? Oh, Kitty!"

"What's wrong with him, Aunt Mabel? He's a wonderful man, thoughtful and kind, and I've known him forever, really, and I think I love him."

"I suppose there's nothing wrong with the young man himself. He did bring you home late that one night, but he did you no harm. It's just, just . . . It's hard for me to define it, but I just don't think he's right for you."

"But . . ."

"No, let me go on. He's a Protestant, isn't he? How's that going to go down with your family? They're not going to accept someone into your family who's not of the Catholic faith."

"But they'll get used to the idea. It's not as if he's a heathen, after all."

"He might as well be. Take it from me. I was a Protestant when I married your uncle, and your mother holds that against me even now."

"You, a Protestant, Aunt Mabel? I never knew that. But you always receive holy communion when you attend Mass at St. Patrick's." Kitty stared at her aunt as if a new appendage had suddenly emerged, growing out of her forehead. She couldn't imagine there was something she didn't know about her aunt, as close a relationship as they had had for so many years.

"Well, I converted once I married your uncle. And I made your parents promise they'd never mention it again, especially in front of you children. But it's true. I was brought up orange, while the rest of you are green."

"I've never understood that orange and green stuff," Kitty said. "And besides, what does it have to do with my marrying Henry?"

"The Orangemen are the British who once were ruled by the Protestant Prince of Orange. And the green stands for Catholic Ireland, where they are still fighting to be free of British rule. And there's no love lost between the orange and the green."

"That's ridiculous," Kitty said, stamping her foot underneath the table. "Henry's not an Englishman, he's an American. And he's lived in this country all his life and so have his parents. It was his grandparents who came over here from another country, and it was Germany. And just because they are Protestants, that doesn't mean anything. We have freedom of religion here in America."

"That's true, Kitty, but it doesn't mean that the Catholics love the Protestants. Or vice versa. Take it from me, the papists make it difficult for their people to marry outside the Church. And the non-Catholics try to keep the Catholics down. There's no love lost between the two."

"What do you mean, marry outside the Church?" Kitty asked, imagining herself standing on the steps outside St. Patrick's in a white wedding dress, pounding on the door, begging to be let in.

"Well, don't imagine you'll be having a grand wedding, for one thing. If you marry a Protestant, as your Uncle Pat married me, it'll be in the rectory if it's allowed at all, with just a few members of the family present. If they'll come."

"If they'll come?"

"Ah yes, there are those, like your mother, for instance, who won't attend a wedding unless it's properly done at a Mass, inside the church."

"You don't think my mother would come to my own wedding?" Kitty asked, incredulous.

"She didn't come to mine," Aunt Mabel said, standing up to clear the cups off the table. "And she hardly spoke to me until I converted. And very rarely has since." She disappeared into the kitchen, carrying the tray of cups and spoons, sugar and creamer.

Kitty sat alone at the table, thinking about a wedding held in St. Patrick's rectory. The rooms were so small in there, how could she even fit her whole family, not to mention Henry's? And there would probably be no music, which would be so sad, as she had imagined Beethoven's *Ode to Joy* filling the church with sound. No bridesmaids, no ushers, no ring bearer. It would hardly seem like a wedding at all.

"So then, why did you do it? Marry Uncle Pat, that is."

Aunt Mabel stood framed by the doorway into the kitchen, a tight smile on her face. "I loved him. That was that. I thought I was marrying a man. I didn't realize I was marrying the whole family—and getting myself into a church that has lasted almost two thousand years. They made me sign a promise that we would raise any children in the Catholic Church."

"Oh, would they make a man do that, too?" Kitty couldn't imagine Henry promising something like that. Not that they had talked about such things.

"Yes, and he'll have to take instruction, too, in what it means to be marrying a Catholic. They call them 'mixed marriages,' they do, in the Catholic Church."

"A mixed marriage. That's what I'd have."

"A mixed marriage. But let me tell you, lass, every marriage is a mixed marriage. Even if you married your own brother—and there's plenty of rules against that—no one knows who it is they're marrying. Most people don't even know who they are themselves. Especially at your age." The color had returned to Aunt Mabel's face, and she looked more like the accomplished career woman who presided over Madame Mabel's in Marshall Field's.

Kitty looked out the window. All of a sudden, the room seemed stuffy and stifling to her and she knew she needed to get outside and take a walk. The sunshine called out to her to move outside and breathe fresh air.

"Oh, Aunt Mabel, this is so much to think about."

"It's better to think about it sooner than later, when it's too late," Aunt Mabel said sharply. Then, seeing that her niece was upset, she softened her tone. "Kitty, it's your life. Only you have to live it. Do what you need to do, to be the person you are."

"Thank you, Aunt Mabel," Kitty said, walking over to her and hugging her. People in her family were rarely physically affectionate, and she felt her aunt stiffen as she circled her arms around her.

But Aunt Mabel patted Kitty's shoulder and said, "You'll do fine, you will. But just go into things with your eyes wide open."

Kitty walked slowly down the steps of the townhouse, thinking about what her aunt had said. A mixed marriage, it sounded so second-rate, not pure, not authentic, but mixed. Then she thought of Henry—would he be getting a similar sermon from his family, from his mother or father or Aunt Louisa? His aunt hadn't looked that pleased to see her when she had stopped in at the grocery store. Kitty turned down Montrose Avenue and walked toward Sheridan Road, toward the lake. The unseasonably warm weather had brought people out from their winter-worn houses and apartments, filling the streets near the lakefront. She could see children rolling hoops and carrying kites to fly in Lincoln Park or along the beach. Freed from winter, like butterflies from their chrysalis, Chicagoans wanted to stretch their wings and fly. She turned on Sheridan Road, and saw even more people, families pushing prams and young men and women on bicycles heading toward the lakefront to enjoy the outdoors. She looked south, along the lakefront, and could see the grand towers that marked the downtown area. She had been taught to recognize the Monadnock Building on Dearborn, the Reliance Building on State, and of course, the Women's

Temple, just north of Marshall Field's. The group of tall buildings at a distance reminded her of a medieval city, a fortress that could be besieged, but not destroyed.

She could feel the ring hanging on the ribbon around her neck. Oma's ring, Henry had called it. Worn by the woman who had spoken to the Indians in a long-ago Chicago, a Chicago that no longer existed, burned away by the great Chicago Fire of 1871, torn down and rebuilt again and again in the years since. What was she like, the woman who had worn that ring? If she came to Chicago when the Indians were still here, she came to a swampy little village, hardly a town, one that no one had ever heard of, leaving the town in Germany where she had been born, meeting a man here from another German town she might never have seen, marrying him, creating a family, raising children in a culture far different from the one she had been raised in. And it went on and on. America was full of families like that, people who had come from other countries, fleeing from religious or political persecution, creating families, building towns, then buildings, then cities.

She looked up at the skyscrapers downtown, so far away in the distance they seemed misty and blue. The building would go on. The buildings her children would see standing here, on the rocks on the shore of Lake Michigan would be entirely different from the ones she viewed today, of that she was sure. As she walked along the lakefront, skirting the picnic blankets of the happy families, speaking their native languages as well as English, she could feel the little ring bouncing against her chest. This was what it meant to be an American, this was what it meant to be herself, to be a link in the chain that came from before, connecting it to an unimaginable future. To continue on, she must have faith, above all, faith in herself and the man she loved, faith in the future to come.

Acknowledgements

When someone asked me how long it took to research this book, I replied that I've been working on it all my life. I have always enjoyed reading about the history of Chicago and how, in less than a century, its inhabitants created a major metropolis from what was essentially a swamp. There are too many great books about Chicago to list them all here, but *The Encyclopedia of Chicago* (University of Chicago Press, 2004) should lead you to most, if not all, of them.

I want to thank my family for their support and inspiration. And my friends, from whom I stole lots of good stories. And Fred Shafer and his Novel Writing Group, who read, criticized, and helped me through the many years of writing and rewriting. And Fritz MacDonald and the Novel Writing Class at the University of Iowa Summer Writing Festival. And especially Rosalind Kaye and Anne Byrne McGivern, who read and critiqued the entire manuscript. And Emily Victorson, of Allium Press, who found, improved, and published this edition. And everyone else who believed in me and inspired me. I am grateful for all of you.

Reading Group Guide

Note: It is likely that the following reading guide will reveal, or at least allude to, key plot details. Therefore, if you haven't yet read this book you may wish to proceed with caution to avoid spoiling your later enjoyment.

1. As the novel begins, Kitty Coakley is twenty years old. How do you think a contemporary young woman of twenty differs from a twenty-year-old woman circa 1900? How did that era's perceptions of young women differ from today's?

2. Both Kitty and Henry have role models in their lives—Kitty's is her Aunt Mabel, Henry's is the architect Daniel Burnham. Do you think it is realistic of them to want what these people have? What part have role models played in your own life?

3. In Chapter 11, Kitty describes how she feels when she enters Marshall Field's department store. How does her experience compare with yours when you shop at a large and luxurious store?

4. Kitty's parents were immigrants to the United States, as were Henry's grandparents. Why do you think they left their native countries? Do you know why your ancestors immigrated to the United States? What, if anything, would convince you to leave your native land?

5. Religion plays a big role in the lives of these characters. Does this continue to be true in the lives of Americans? Is it true in your own life? In your parents' lives?

6. Kitty's dreams of becoming a singer are dashed by Madame Nettlehorst. What happens when a dream dies? Does Kitty's decision to become a kindergarten teacher fully replace her dream of becoming a singer?

7. Does what Kitty is learning at the Kindergarten College remind you of what you were taught in kindergarten? How, if at all, is it different? How do you think children were taught before the introduction of Froebel's ideas?

8. Who are some of the "real" people and events the author weaves into the lives of the fictional characters in this book? Were you aware of them before reading this book? Do these depictions change your ideas about them?

9. Three cities are described in this novel: Chicago, Paris, and New Orleans. Compare and contrast these three cities as they are experienced by the characters in the novel.

10. In Chapter 18, why does Aunt Mabel bring Kitty to visit her old friend Adelaide? What lesson do you think Kitty took away from this experience?

11. What do you think it is about Kitty that makes Henry fall in love with her? What is it about Henry that Kitty loves? Do you think Henry is a better marriage choice for Kitty than Brian Kelleher? Why?

12. In Chapter 23, Kitty recalls a motto for a women's magazine: "Moving forward, but not too fast." What do you think this means in the context of the era of the novel? Do you think that idea has relevance now?

13. What objections, if any, might Henry's parents have to him marrying Kitty? What about her parents—how would they feel about Kitty marrying Henry? Should Kitty grant her mother's wish about not seeing Henry? Why or why not?

LaVergne, TN USA
27 October 2010
202493LV00009B/64/P